Ornaments of Death

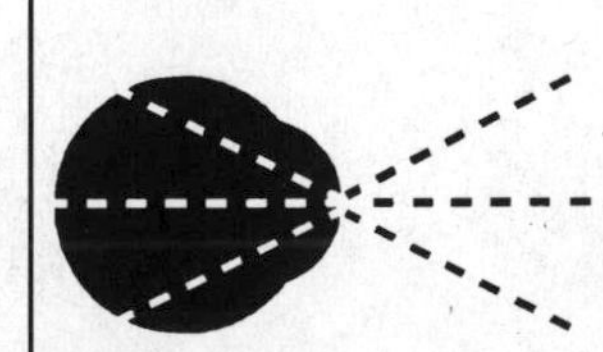

Ornaments of Death

Jane K. Cleland

THORNDIKE PRESS
A part of Gale, Cengage Learning

Farmington Hills, Mich • San Francisco • New York • Waterville, Maine
Meriden, Conn • Mason, Ohio • Chicago

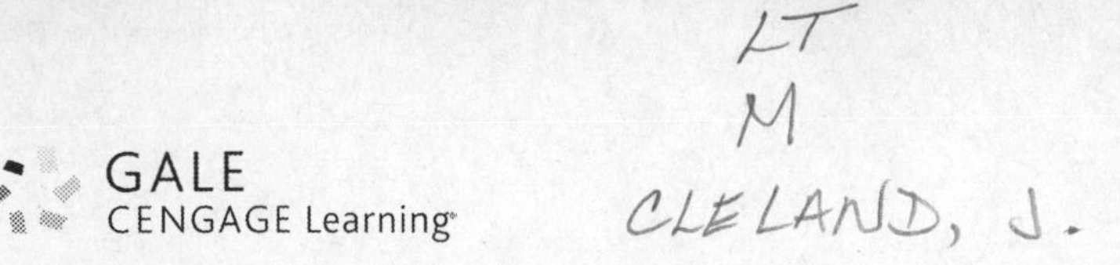

A Josie Prescott Antiques Mystery.
Thorndike Press, a part of Gale, Cengage Learning.

Thorndike Press® Large Print Mystery.
The text of this Large Print edition is unabridged.
Other aspects of the book may vary from the original edition.
Set in 16 pt. Plantin.

LIBRARY OF CONGRESS CATALOGING-IN-PUBLICATION DATA

Names: Cleland, Jane K., author.
Title: Ornaments of death / by Jane K. Cleland.
Description: Large print edition. | Waterville, Maine : Thorndike Press, 2016. | © 2015 | Series: Thorndike Press large print mystery | Series: A Josie Prescott antiques mystery
Identifiers: LCCN 2015047358| ISBN 9781410486813 (hardcover) | ISBN 1410486818 (hardcover)
Subjects: LCSH: Prescott, Josie (Fictitious character)—Fiction. | Antique dealers—New Hampshire—Fiction. | Murder—Investigation—Fiction. | Large type books. | GSAFD: Mystery fiction.
Classification: LCC PS3603.L4555 O76 2016 | DDC 813/.6—dc23
LC record available at http://lccn.loc.gov/2015047358

Published in 2016 by arrangement with St. Martin's Press, LLC

Printed in Mexico
1 2 3 4 5 6 7 20 19 18 17 16

This is for my literary agent,
Cristina Concepcion.
And of course, for Joe.

AUTHOR'S NOTE

This is a work of fiction. While there is a Seacoast Region in New Hampshire, there is no town called Rocky Point, and many other geographic liberties have been taken.

Chapter One

I did a slow 360.

When I'd asked Gretchen, Prescott's office manager, and Eric, our operations manager, to transform our antiques auction venue into a winter wonderland for tomorrow's holiday party, I'd envisioned a big Christmas tree, some pretty evergreen garlands draped here and there, and a few strings of twinkling lights hanging from the crown molding. I was utterly unprepared for the ethereal vision surrounding me.

I took a tentative step toward one of the billboard-sized photographs that hung from the picture railing on gold metal grommets. A series of them circled the room, covering every inch of wall space. Only the entryway, a nearby window, and the arched foyer that led to the restrooms were unadorned. Each photo aligned seamlessly with its neighbors like pieces of fabric in a well-made garment, creating an uninterrupted view of an idealized hardwood forest, the kind of snowy phantasma Robert Frost wrote about.

Starting about a foot from the walls, snow-tipped birch tree trunks stood in staggered rows. I blinked, half-believing that I was standing in a clearing in a forest. I approached one of the trees for a closer look and touched the peeling white and brown bark with the side of my finger.

"Get out of town!" I said. I looked at Gretchen, then Eric. "It's fabric."

"Aren't they gorgeous?" Gretchen asked, stroking the soft cotton.

"Astonishing. I was worried for a minute that you guys had cut down a forest."

Gretchen giggled. "Nope . . . all we did was cover plastic piping."

Eric pointed to the treetops. "The snow is cotton batting. We tossed in some clear sequins, too. That was Gretchen's idea."

I tilted my head back to view the ceiling, twenty feet above my head. Tiny white star-shaped Christmas lights dangled from a twined tree branch canopy, a celestial paradise. "It's exactly what you'd see looking up through trees on a clear winter's night. Really, guys. It's amazing."

I walked toward the back, where a fifteen-foot Douglas fir stood at the far corner of the room. Red and gold strips of skinny velvet rope and strings of red, blue, amber, and white lights twisted around and through the branches. My custom-designed holiday ornaments shone in the iridescent light. I leaned in close to inspect them.

I'd started the tradition of reproducing antique Christmas ornaments as gifts for staff and clients my first year in business. This year, I'd created two ornaments, one serving as my annual gift, the other designed to celebrate Prescott's tenth anniversary. Both were replicas. The Christmas gift featured a Victorian-era jolly Santa standing in front of a present-laden sleigh. *Happy Holidays from Prescott's Antiques* was inked in script along the top. The message on the other one, which featured the kind of ornate Chinese-inspired design favored by England's prince regent circa 1815, read *Prescott's Antiques: Ten Years of Honest Dealing.*

The intercom squawked to life. "Josie! Pick up, please."

I reached behind a panel for a wall-mounted phone.

"A man named Ian Bennington has stopped in," Cara, Prescott's grandmotherly receptionist, told me. "He was wondering if you had a moment to see him."

"I'll be there in a flash!" I said, a thrill of unfamiliar excitement tickling my insides.

Ian was here!

I cradled the receiver and turned toward Gretchen and Eric. They were watching me closely, their reactions consistent with their personalities. Gretchen was spirited and proud; Eric was anxious but hopeful.

"I need to go, but I don't want to. I wish I could stay here and admire every detail. You both did a fabulous job — it's more than I ever could have imagined. It's just perfect."

"Yay!" Gretchen said, clapping her hands, her emerald eyes sparkling like the sequins she'd scattered in the cotton snow.

"Thanks," Eric said, as shy and self-effacing as ever.

I took a long last look, noting the waist-high cocktail tables positioned here and there across the open space, the eight-foot-tall three-panel screens segregating the caterer's work area; the two bar stations standing opposite one another at either end of the room. The row of standing coatracks extended into the room from the entryway wall, serving as a kind of room divider/weather break. Near it was the sign-in table where temps would check off names and welcome guests, and where later the gift bags would be placed for people to take on their way out. The small stage where the band would play classical standards intermingled with holiday favorites was set up at the rear.

I thanked them again for their efforts, then beelined for the front. Hank, our company's Maine Coon cat, ran up to join me as I dashed across the warehouse.

"Hi, Hank. Are you having a good day, little boy?"

He mewed that he was.

I pushed open the heavy metal door that led to the front office. Hank followed me in, frisking alongside my legs.

Cara was on the phone giving directions to our weekly tag sale. My two antiques appraisers, Sasha and Fred, were at their desks, reading from their monitors. A tall man stood with his back to me, his hands in his pockets, gazing out the window.

"Ian?" I asked.

He looked over his shoulder and smiled. "Josie!"

His British accent was evident even from that one word. He walked toward me, his hand extended. We shook, and he pressed my right hand lightly with his left before releasing it.

"It's so good to meet you," I said. "Come up to my office — can I get you a coffee?"

"I'd love one, but I don't want to interfere with your schedule." His smile became rueful. "I drove here as a test, a dry run. This driving on the other side of the road is, might I say, distracting. And tomorrow, for the party, it will be dark."

"I can arrange rides for you."

"No, thanks. It's a matter of pride."

"If you change your mind, just let me know. I promise, no one will tease you." I pushed open the warehouse door and waited for him to approach. "This way."

"Are you certain you have the time?"

"You bet!" I turned to Cara, now off the phone, and asked her to bring a tray upstairs.

Ian glanced around as we walked toward the spiral staircase. There was a lot to see, from the orderly rows of shelves stocked with inventory to the workstations set up around the perimeter to Hank's private area, furnished with area rugs, cushy pillows, comfy baskets, and an elaborate climbing system made of wooden beams, platforms, and cylindrical pass-throughs, all covered with carpet, a kitty-condo, Gretchen called it.

Ian paused on the first step, his hand on the banister. "I'm impressed."

The 1885 building used to house a manufacturer of canvas products. When I'd bought it, I'd renovated it according to my business vision. The old shop floor was reconfigured as a warehouse and workroom. A huge side room, where in previous generations rows of office workers had labored, became the elegant auction venue. I'd kept the rustic feel of their old display room, expanding it into our tag sale area, and I'd upgraded the observation deck where managers had watched the men at work, transforming it into a cozy private office.

"Thanks. I updated the entire building when I opened the company."

"Is everything on those shelves for sale?"

"Yes," I said. "It's far easier to sell than buy, so we try to keep as much inventory on hand as we can." I reached down and patted his shoulder. "I can't tell you how glad I am to meet you, Ian."

"I feel the same."

I couldn't stop smiling. I'd heard from Ian for the first time only a month earlier when he e-mailed to tell me we were related, and I still couldn't believe it. In the dozen years since my dad had died, I'd been on my own. As the only child of only children, I'd never expected anything else, and over the years, I'd carved out a wonderful life for myself in my adopted home of Rocky Point, New Hampshire. My business was thriving, my relationship with Ty, my boyfriend, was flourishing, and I had solid friendships. Despite that, it was, to me, not the least bit surprising that I felt like clapping and kicking my heels together. For the first time in more than a decade, I had family.

I opened the door and waved him in ahead of me. He paused three paces in to look around. His eyes gravitated to the big window by my desk.

"What a super view," he said.

I followed his gaze, peering through the old maple tree, its limbs winter bare, normal for late autumn in New Hampshire, past the church spire, to the distant ocean. You couldn't hear or see the ocean, but the gulls that flew by proved it wasn't far, and even with the windows closed, you could smell it, a faint salty aroma, the scent of the sea.

"That's a million-dollar view," he said, "a power view."

"It's kind of funny to hear that here in New Hampshire. When I lived in New York City, that's what they always said about high-floor apartments or offices."

"Why did you leave New York?"

I knew that his question was merely polite chitchat, nothing more, but the answer was complex and intimate, too intimate to talk about with a stranger, family or not. That I'd been the whistle-blower in a price-fixing scandal, ostracized by my friends and colleagues, fired from my dream job, and vilified by the press was bad enough, but then my dad, my rock, died, and only two weeks later, my boyfriend at the time, Rick the Cretin, said I was getting to be a downer, his word, and split. Old news. I learned the hard way that when fielding hostile questions from the media, the best approach was to answer the question you wished they'd asked, and that's what I did now. Instead of telling him why I left New York, I told him why I chose New Hampshire.

"New Hampshire is a great place to do business. It has a deep core of American history — and antiques. And it's close to Boston. It was an ideal choice." I walked toward the seating area, a yellow brocade love seat and two matching Queen Anne wing chairs. "Have you always lived in Christmas Common?"

"All my life," he said.

He sank onto the love seat and leaned back against the cushions, closing his eyes for a moment. He raised and lowered his shoulders.

"Tough flight?" I asked, sitting across from him.

He opened his eyes. "Not especially. I think I'm getting old."

I knew from the genealogical chart Ian had e-mailed that he was forty-eight years old, but he didn't look it. His hair was solid brown, without a hint of gray. His face was unlined. He looked fit, too, like an athlete.

"You look way younger than I expected."

"Good genes, I guess."

Cara came in with a tray and placed it on the mahogany butler's table.

I thanked her and waited until the soft padding of her heels faded away before I asked, "Are we really truly related?"

Ian chuckled. "Questioning my research, are you?"

"Not exactly. It's just that I'm incredulous, gobsmacked, as you might say!"

He smiled. "You pronounced that very well."

"Thanks," I said, pouring coffee into Minton china cups. "It's not a matter of doubting your ability. It's the complexity of the project. Documents that are more than three hundred years old . . . well, they must be filled with errors and gaps."

Ian had reported that we were both distant relations of Arabella Churchill, a mistress of the seventeenth-century monarch King James II. Once their ten-year affair ended, Arabella married Charles Godfrey, the Master of the Jewel Office. By all accounts, the couple's forty-year marriage was happy. Their eldest daughter, Charlotte, had sixteen children. According to Ian, he and I were descendants of one of those sixteen, a daughter named Lucy.

I handed Ian a cup and pointed to the carefully arranged plate of cookies. "These are Cara's famous gingersnaps."

He took one from the silver platter and ate it in two bites. "Delicious," he said. "Actually, there aren't as many missing bits as you might expect. Royal records, including those involving royal mistresses, were meticulously kept and maintained in multiple places, making the process straightforward."

"I'm pretty excited," I said, "cuz."

"Me, too, cuz."

We smiled at one another for a moment.

"How is it you don't know anything about your heritage?" he asked.

"I know a little. My maternal grandmother, Deborah Austin, she of the Churchill line, was a war bride from London. She married my grandfather, Jed Prescott, an American, in 1945, when she was twenty-one. I think she was an only child, like my mom, and like me. They came back to Jed's home, just outside of Boston, in, I think, 1946. They both died before I was born." I lifted my hands, palms up. "You now know everything I do about my British ancestors."

He took another gingersnap. "I see evidence in front of my eyes that you, at least, are truly a descendant of Arabella. I think you look like her."

I grinned. "She was short?"

"She had intelligent eyes, a high forehead, and a determined chin. She was lovely — just like you."

I gazed into my coffee cup, embarrassed. "Thanks."

"You've seen the Sir Peter Lely portrait, haven't you?"

I opened a long-closed file cabinet in my mind. "Yes — if I'm remembering right. The woman in the painting is sitting at an angle, a three-quarters profile view. She's wearing a pale green dress, cut quite low. Her expression is more playful than distinguished."

"That's it. It's a beautiful piece. There is a miniature of her, too."

"By Lely?" I asked.

"No. By Samuel Cooper."

"You're kidding!" I exclaimed. Cooper was the finest miniature artist of his time. "His work is extraordinary. Is it on exhibit somewhere?"

One side of his mouth lifted, a cocky half-smile. "It came on the market a couple of years ago along with a match piece, and I bought them."

My eyes lit up. "A match piece?"

"King James II commissioned two paintings in 1670 as his Christmas gift to Arabella. One portrait is of Arabella. The other is of himself."

"Watercolor on vellum?"

"Yes, indeed."

"How big are they?"

Ian laughed. "The better question is how small are they. They're oval shaped and only one and three-eighths inches high. Like postage stamps."

"Where are they now?"

"I gave them to my daughter, Becca, as a housewarming gift."

"That's wonderful! And she's living here, right?"

"In Boston, yes, for the year."

"Which is why you're in Rocky Point, New Hampshire, this weekend! You're en route to Boston for a visit. If Becca would be willing to let me take a look at them, I'd sure love to get a gander."

"As it happens, I e-mailed her that she ought to ask you to appraise them. Given how hot the antique miniatures market is right now, I think she ought to update her insurance."

"That's smart, and of course, I'd love to do the appraisal" — I raised my hand like a traffic cop — "but do tell her that I'll understand completely if she decides to have a Boston-based company do it. There are plenty of excellent options closer to her than Prescott's."

"As it happens, a lot of her fieldwork is conducted right here in Rocky Point."

"How come?"

"Rocky Point is home to a lot of clams."

I laughed. "That's funny! I hope it works out."

We chatted for another few minutes in the way acquaintances do, about his flight from London and whether the oceanfront hotel I'd recommended was to his liking and how the December weather was less severe than he'd expected. When he'd finished his coffee and two more of Cara's addictive gingersnaps, he stood up.

"My bed awaits," he said, stretching. "I feel a long nap in my future . . . jet lag."

I walked him downstairs, and with a cheery wave, he left.

I scooped up Hank and cuddled him as I watched Ian get into his silver Taurus and drive out of the lot, turning right, toward the Atlantic, toward the Rocky Point Sea

View Hotel. I couldn't believe he was really here.

"Mr. Bennington seems very nice," Cara said. "A new client?"

I kissed Hank on the top of his furry head and told him he was a good boy as I lowered him to the floor.

"Nope," I said, grinning. "He's family."

Chapter Two

The party was in full swing. I was standing off to the side enjoying a quiet moment, watching the crowd. More than a hundred people milled about, chatting, laughing, drinking, and nibbling on hors d'oeuvres. Tuxedo-clad men carried sterling silver trays of cherry tomato caprese-salad on a toothpick; miniature crab cakes; red and green pepper–stuffed mushroom caps; bacon-wrapped asparagus spears; salmon mousse on pumpernickel bread cut into Christmas-tree and bell shapes; and cheeseburger sliders. The band was playing "The Christmas Song."

Through the window, I saw Starr, the pink-haired makeup gal on my TV show, *Josie's Antiques,* standing off to the side, smoking a cigarette, nodding as she listened to someone out of sight. She rubbed her upper arms and rocked from side to side, trying to stay warm.

My TV show's director-producer, Timothy, stood a few feet farther back, toward the trees that ringed the property. He was staring at his mobile phone as if he couldn't believe his eyes.

Ellis came into view. Ellis Hunter was Rocky Point's police chief and a good friend. Since he had begun dating Zoë, my best friend, landlady, and neighbor, I'd gotten to know him well. Ty and I had often gone out with them together as couples. Ellis stepped inside, saw me, and smiled and waved. He said something to the young woman staffing the reception table.

Zoë came alongside me and asked, "How are you holding up? Ready for your big moment?"

I was scheduled to say a few words at eight forty-five, and I wished it were over. I hated being in the limelight, which was odd, given that I was the face of Prescott's Antiques, often giving media interviews, and had just finished a full season of *Josie's Antiques.*

"As ready as I'll ever be."

"Divine party," Lia Jones, owner of my favorite day spa and a kayak buddy, said as she passed by.

Lia looked chic, as always. She used her spa's services, and it showed, from her curvy figure to her cascading auburn hair to her flawless complexion. She smiled and gave an airy wave as she darted away.

"Lia sounding upbeat," Zoë remarked. "What a concept."

"After the year she's had . . . ," I said, letting the half-expressed thought remain unspoken.

"After the year she gave herself, you should say. Her misery is a self-inflicted wound. Divorce sucks, but you don't have to drag it out."

"You're harsh."

Zoë shrugged. "Experienced."

"Your situation was different," I said. "No alimony was involved."

"True," she acknowledged. "My ex is still back in Oregon, too, whereas Lia's loser is here in town."

Ty and Ellis joined us, each carrying two glasses of Prescott's Punch, a holiday-themed martini I'd invented. A mixture of cranberry juice, ginger ale, and vodka, and garnished with a sprig of mint, it was sweet and tart and looked like Christmas.

"I love this martini, Josie," Zoë said, after tasting it. "I'm thinking you ought to start a side business as a mixologist."

Zoë, tall and model thin, was wearing her hair short this year. Ellis, over six feet and built like an athlete, was a perfect physical match to her, but their connection was more than physical. They fit emotionally, too, both wounded birds glad for a safe new nest. Zoë talked tough, but her divorce had drained her confidence. Ellis's wife's death had drained him as well. She had been a Broadway dancer, and like so many of them, she'd smoked. After she'd died a gruesome lung-cancer death, Ellis had retired from his job as a New York City homicide detective and taken the police chief job in Rocky Point, to see, he said, if Norman Rockwell had it right about small towns. The jagged red scar that ran next to his right eye was barely visible under the indirect incandescent lighting.

After we chatted for a moment, Ellis asked Zoë, "Can I steal you for a minute? There's someone I want you to meet."

After they left, Ty touched his glass to mine. "Here's to you, gorgeous."

I clinked my glass against his. "And to you, handsome." I sipped the martini, then asked Ty for the time. I never wore a watch because it always seemed to get in the way while I worked.

"Eight thirty. Why?"

"In fifteen minutes I have to say welcome and thank you and happy holidays."

"And you're dreading it."

"A little."

He leaned over and kissed the top of my head. "You'll do great." He nodded toward Ian, standing amid a clutch of thirty- and forty-something single women, Lia included. "Do you like Ian?"

"Yes," I said. "Knowing he made a fortune in software, I'd expected him to be, I don't know, reserved. Instead, he's friendly and funny." I sipped my drink. "What do you think of him?"

"He seems like a stand-up guy. I think you'll find you have a lot in common."

"Like what?" I asked.

"You're both research junkies."

"That's true. I hope I can match his record someday. He's learned more about his heritage in a year than most professionals could in a decade, and he said it was easy."

The music stopped abruptly, and I spun toward the band to see what was up. Timothy stood onstage, holding a microphone against his leg so it wouldn't pick up his voice. A drum roll sounded. Timothy walked to the riser's edge and surveyed the crowd, catching eyes, nodding at someone in back of me, smiling, waiting for quiet. He lifted the microphone to his mouth.

"Excuse me for interrupting everyone's

merry-merry. I'll only be a moment. I'm Timothy Brenin, and I work with Josie on her TV show, *Josie's Antiques.*" He looked at me and winked. "I've just gotten off the phone with New York — and for those of you who aren't familiar with TV lingo, that's a euphemism. 'New York' refers to the big-cheese powers that be who have the ability to green-light a project." Timothy paused, allowing anticipation to swell and swirl. He grinned, a big one. "The head of network programming just called to let me know that *Josie's Antiques* has been renewed."

Applause started in back of me and rippled forward until everyone was clapping, including Timothy, who tucked the microphone under his arm.

"Congrats!" someone called.

Someone else yelled, "Brava!"

I wondered if my amazement showed. I'd thought of the show as a lark and had been delighted that it had lasted a full season. Meeting Timothy's eyes, I put my hands together as if in prayer, chin high, and bowed my head, a silent tribute to the man behind the curtain.

He nodded, acknowledging my sentiment, and raised his eyes. After a moment, when the applause ebbed, he continued, "As many of you know, *Josie's Antiques* has been consistently reviewed as 'charming, informative, and entertaining,' What I've just been told is that *Josie's Antiques* finished the season at number one in its time slot among all cable reality shows." He looked directly at me. "Congratulations, Josie. You're number one."

The applause started again, louder now, and people surged toward me, patting my back, hugging me, sharing the joyous moment. Someone started a call of "Speech, speech!" and the mantra caught on, growing louder and more insistent.

I squeezed Ty's hand, walked to the stage, climbed up, and took the microphone from Timothy, hugging him briefly and kissing his cheek. He stepped down.

"In fifteen minutes," I said, "I was scheduled to make a few remarks." I smiled and paused for a moment, letting the goodwill from people I respected and admired flow into me. "I wanted to welcome you to Prescott's, thank you for coming, and wish you happy holidays. I planned to ask you to raise a glass and join me in a toast. I'll still do that in a moment, but first I want to thank Timothy." I lifted my glass in his direction and winked away unexpected tears. "Thank you." I raised my eyes and took in the room. "To the best director-producer in the world. To Timothy." I sipped my martini, sealing the toast.

"Hear, hear!" someone called from the back.

More applause rang out. Timothy clapped his hands along with everyone else.

"To the entire production team, many of whom are here tonight. Without them, *Josie's Antiques* wouldn't be a success. To the team!" More applause sounded as I raised my glass to the room. I took another sip of martini.

"And to us all," I said. "Here's to silver light in the dark of night." I took another sip, smiled, and ended with "Happy holidays, everyone."

I handed the microphone to the pianist, and as I approached the stairs, Ty appeared to help me down.

"Well done, Josie," he whispered in my ear. "Sweet, sincere, and short. The perfect speech."

I rested my head on his shoulder for a moment. I couldn't believe we'd been renewed.

The band started up again, playing "Jingle Bells" this time. I stopped trying to remember who hugged me and who shook my hand and who kissed my cheek. Everywhere I turned, people were smiling and clapping. After a while, the crowd quieted, and my staff came up. We did a private "Oh, my God! Can you believe it!" celebration before Gretchen had me pose for photos with Timothy and the crew.

I scanned the room, wanting to find Ian, when something outside caught my eye, a shimmering shadow crossing the outside spotlights that illuminated the entryway. A woman in a tan cloche hat pulled low and a dark brown coat, with the collar turned up high, stood in profile, her gloved hand covering all of her face except one eye. She peered into the room for three or four seconds before slipping away. A friend of a guest, I suspected, running late, wanting to see if he was here before she came in.

She didn't come in.

I didn't like it. Why would a woman peek in my company's window in the middle of a party, then disappear?

I dealt in high-end antiques, and any anomaly was worrying. The warehouse security system had been alarmed, so on the face of it, there was nothing to be concerned about. Still, with a room full of people, some of whom I'd met for the first time tonight, the risk of robbery, while small, was heightened. I slipped out through a side door by the restrooms and was hit by a blast of teeth-rattling cold.

"Yikes!" I exclaimed. White plumes of icy air encircled me when I spoke. "It's cold enough for ice cream."

My mom, the original I'll-make-lemonade-from-lemons gal, always used to say that when I'd complain about a particularly bitter cold snap. We tested her theory once and made ice cream outside, using a six-foot-high snowbank outside the kitchen door as our freezer. I smiled a little, remembering more than the yummy ice cream we'd succeeded in producing. Tonight, it was a wind-charged thirty, not incapacitating by New Hampshire standards, but about twenty degrees south of no-coat weather. I dashed around the corner, my heels click-clacking on the frozen pavement. No one was in sight. I ran to the middle of the parking lot, stopped, and listened for footsteps or a motor revving, for any sound of life. All I heard was winter quiet.

Pole-mounted lights lit up the entire lot. I did a slow survey but spotted no unexpected shadows or dark spots. I could see the small red dots indicating that the security cameras affixed to the light fixtures were on. Two men stepped outside, laughing. One thumbed on a lighter while the other leaned in so his cigarette could catch the flame. I took one last look around and headed back inside, calling a cheery hello to the men as I jogged past.

Inside, the shock of warmth was as paralyzing as the blast of cold had been, but in a good way. I smiled at the young woman working the reception table, a temp hired for the evening. She was setting out the goodie bags, aligning them in an attractive diagonal pattern.

Lia saw me and dashed over to give me a congratulatory hug, drawing me into the room, before flitting off toward the bar.

Gretchen came up. "I'm really, really excited the TV show's been renewed," she whispered.

"Don't tell anyone," I whispered back, "but me, too."

She giggled. "It'll be our secret."

"Here's another one. I want to organize a celebration luncheon for us all, just the key staff — me, you, Sasha, Fred, Eric, and Cara. Here in the dolled-up auction venue. Catered by the Blue Dolphin. Pick a day that's good for everyone. Get a temp in to cover the phones. Book Academy Brass. Don't tell a soul."

Her eyes lit up like stars. "Oh, Josie!"

"There she is!" Zoë called, talking to Ty, pointing at me. She waggled her fingers like a policeman directing traffic, telling me to come toward her.

I hugged Gretchen and zigzagged my way to reach Zoë and Ty, and just like that, I was swept back into the festivities.

Chapter Three

Midway through the party, Zoë said, "Ty and I want to know if you were as surprised your show was renewed as you looked."

"More."

"It's kismet," Zoë said.

"I thought it was hard work."

"Aren't they the same thing?"

"Now that you mention it . . ."

Ty brought me a drink, and we made our way to the stage where the band was playing "Blue Christmas." When they finished, we wove our way across the room, mingling, laughing, chatting, moving on.

Everywhere I looked, people seemed to be having a good time. Zoë rejoined me as Ty disappeared into the crowd, and we stood in companionable silence, our shoulders touching. Across the room, I noticed Ian and Lia, their eyes locked. Ian said something, and Lia threw back her head, laughing, her Titian hair falling in soft waves to her shoulders. I smiled with vicarious pleasure. Ian touched Lia's shoulder and nodded at something she said.

"Look," I whispered to Zoë, jerking my head in their direction.

"Good for her!" Zoë whispered back.

"I love her dress," I added.

Zoë tilted her head, considering Lia's outfit. Her forest green satin sheath was short, stopping three or maybe even four inches above her knees, and it fit her as if it had been stitched onto her. The long sleeves only served to emphasize the sexiness. She wore black stilettos and dangling diamond earrings. I thought she looked like a million bucks.

"It would look better on an eighteen-year-old," Zoë said.

"I think she looks fabulous."

"No question, she looks fantastic. That's not the issue. The issue is what she's trying to prove. She should dress her age."

"I think you're being unfair. All I see is a seriously attractive thirty-eight-year-old woman maximizing her assets." I glanced down at my own little black dress. The scalloped hem brushed the top of my knees. The scoop neck and three-quarter sleeves provided modest coverage. The heels on my sturdy black pumps were chunky and only two inches high. I wore a strand of pearls with matching stud earrings. I looked nice, in a conservative, appropriate way. It was my style, and I was okay with that, but secretly I wished I felt comfortable dressing like Lia — sexy and bold and glamorous. "I wish I looked that good."

"You do."

"You're just saying that because you love me."

"No, I'm not. You're beautiful, Josie, but you dress your age, not like a bimbette."

"Maybe I'll try dressing a little younger. Midthirties shouldn't mean dowdy."

"You don't look dowdy."

"Looking at Lia, I feel dowdy."

I told Zoë I'd see her later and headed off, taking a circuitous route toward Ian and Lia, greeting people as I walked, pausing to chat with various friends and clients.

"Hi, guys!" I said when I joined them.

"I'm glad you're here," Ian said, lowering his voice to a stage whisper, his eyes twinkling. "To impress Lia, I worked that we're distant relations to Winston Churchill into our conversation. Back me up, okay?"

"You got it," I replied, matching his tone, my eyes twinkling, too. I puffed out my chest. "Ian and I are related to Winston Churchill."

Lia giggled with delight.

"So is that a yes to dinner?" Ian asked her.

"Yes," she said, looking happier than I'd seen her in I couldn't recall how long. It was as if she'd shed her year of despair in an hour.

Ian looked at me. "Thanks, cuz." He puffed out his chest, mimicking me. "She said yes."

"Winston Churchill is a draw."

Lia laughed. "Ian knows I would have said yes no matter who he was related to."

"I take nothing for granted. Expect the best and plan, plan, plan, so you never see the worst. And this" — Ian spread his arms wide, changing the subject — "is definitely the best. What a magical party, Josie! The decor is remarkable. I wish Becca were here to enjoy it."

"You only have the one child?" Lia asked.

"Yes. She's in Boston for the year, working on a marine biology research project. And you? Any children?"

"None, I'm afraid."

"Maybe you will one day."

"Hmmm," Lia murmured. She sipped her drink, gazing at Ian over the glass rim, holding his eyes. "I bet you're a wonderful dad."

Ian shifted his attention to the band. The ensuing silence lengthened and grew increasingly awkward.

"Now that *Josie's Antiques* has been renewed," I said, jumping in, "maybe Becca will let me use those miniatures on air." I turned to Lia and explained about the pair of seventeenth-century watercolor paintings.

"I'll ask her," Ian said. "I should think she'd consider it an honor."

"Lia!" Madge Sweeny called, approaching us from the back.

Madge Sweeny was a much-admired client. She was smart and savvy and hadn't taken a wooden nickel in a year or eight. She was a dedicated collector of anything related to cocker spaniels, and a new member of our kayaking group. She joined our little cluster, and I introduced her to Ian.

"I'm so glad to see you," Madge said to Lia, leaning in for a butterfly kiss. "I want to organize a spa day event for my daughter-in-law's Christmas present."

"What a fun idea!" Lia said.

As the two women fell into a discussion of whether a seaweed treatment was a better option than a mud bath, Ian and I separated ourselves a bit.

"I worry about Becca being so alone," Ian said. He laughed and looked embarrassed. "That's me talking, not Becca. The truth is she's pretty introverted. I keep trying to get her more involved in the world, and she keeps telling me she's happy the way she is, that she's perfectly content keeping her own company." He held up his hand. "Don't get me wrong. She's a delightful young woman, very friendly. When you meet her, you won't have any sense that she might be feeling awkward. It's just that she prefers quieter gatherings to big parties."

"Is that why she skipped tonight?"

"No." He laughed again, this one self-deprecating. "She's in Nova Scotia, monitoring the hibernation habits of clams, if you can believe it. I won't see her myself until Monday."

"Yesterday when you said she was in Rocky Point because there were a lot of clams around, I thought you meant she liked eating them!"

"Hardly."

"She studies them," I said, understanding.

"Devotedly."

"There are worse things to be devoted to."

"A long, long list. Still, how a girl from Oxfordshire got interested in clams, well, that's a separate conversation."

"How did she?"

"I have no idea. One day, when she was about fifteen, she simply announced that she was going to research mollusks. In case you're worried that this aberration might be genetic, I can reassure you. Becca is the first person in our family to earn a PhD in mollusks. In fact, we have no history involving mollusks whatsoever."

I laughed. "That's hysterical, Ian."

"Perhaps she's a changeling. I simply can't explain it."

"There's no need. Our family's tent is large enough to include everyone of all persuasions, mollusk lovers included."

"What a relief!" he said, grinning.

"Speaking of your schedule, if you're not heading to Boston until Monday, how about dinner tomorrow? Or is that when you and Lia are going out?"

"That's right. Otherwise, you know I'd love it."

"How about brunch, then, just the two of us?"

He liked the idea, and we firmed up plans.

"There's a concert tomorrow evening at the Congregational church next door," I said. "Ty and I are going to hear Fred sing. You met him, right? One of my appraisers? It's a Christmas program, starting at eight. Maybe Lia would like to go, or you're more than welcome to join us on your own."

"Thank you, Josie. Probably the timing won't work, but I'll let you know."

Wes Smith, the reporter for Rocky Point's local paper, the *Seacoast Star,* approached us, along with his wife of a few months, Maggie. Wes was a buddy, hardworking, diligent, and reliable. Maggie was my banker, the assistant manager of Rocky Point Community Bank. She was cute as a bug, a pixie with curly brown hair and freckles.

"I heard about how you two are connected," Wes said, after I'd introduced them to Ian. "This will be an inspirational human interest piece. We might even be able to parlay it into national coverage. It's a pretty dramatic genealogical success story."

"I'm game," I said, thinking the publicity couldn't hurt my company or my TV show one bit.

"I don't know," Ian said. "I thought when I sold my company I was done with the media."

"It will be painless," Wes said. "Just a few questions."

"What do you say, Josie?" Ian asked me.

"I like the idea."

"For Josie, anything." He smiled, a weak one, his expression somewhere between resigned and longanimous. "E-mail me your questions and I'll do my best to get you answers quickly."

"Thanks!" Wes said. "I'll get your e-mail address from Josie."

We all chatted for another minute before we dispersed. Ian eased himself into a small group nearby. Ellis joined in, followed by Madge and Lia. Lia maneuvered herself next to Ian, but Ian seemed unaware of her presence. He was nodding, listening to something Ellis was saying. I couldn't tell if Ian was purposefully ignoring Lia or not.

I gave Maggie and Wes a little good-bye wave and moved aside, still watching Ian and Lia, trying to see if the dynamic between them had shifted as a result of Lia's comment about Ian being a good dad. Lia smiled at him and he smiled back, and watching the exchange, I smiled, too. My worry that she'd moved too fast for his comfort seemed off the mark. Sometimes it happens that way, I thought, a real romance that comes out of nowhere. For both their sakes, I hoped it would last a lifetime. Gretchen came up with the photographer, and she and I posed for him. Gretchen drew me away and staged additional photos: me with the staff; me with Timothy; me with Ty; me with Zoë, me with various clients and combinations of clients. I asked her to find Ian, and she said she would. Among Gretchen's many skills was ability to organize anything. The photographer assured me that he'd taken hundreds of candid shots, too. When Gretchen was satisfied, I made my way to the bar for another drink, and Lia sidled up next to me.

"So, what do you know about him?" Lia asked in an undertone.

"Ian? Not much. He's a widower who lives in Christmas Common, a hamlet located about half an hour outside Oxford, England."

"What a fabulous name for a village!"

"Isn't it?"

"What does he do?"

"He's retired. He designed some kind of software application for the trucking industry and sold it to a computer giant for a quarter of a billion dollars."

"*B* as in 'billion'?" she asked, incredulous.

I nodded. "So the newspaper report said. You'd never know it to meet him, though."

"I'll say. And I thought he was a catch before I knew he was a megamillionaire." Lia smiled provocatively, fanning herself with her hand. "As hot as it is around Ian, you'd think we were in Hawaii."

"You're a fast worker," I said, laughing.

Gretchen appeared out of nowhere to tell me that Timothy was leaving. I thanked her, excused myself to Lia, and hurried to the door to say good-bye.

"We'll talk," he said, squeezing my hand. "Time to begin planning the new season."

"I can't wait!"

Other people began to trickle out, and soon the trickle became a steady stream. I stood by the door, accepting thanks and congratulations and holiday good wishes, and then the party was over. I couldn't stop smiling. What a day — a newfound relative, a second season for my TV show, and a successful party. I was revved up like a turbine.

Later, as I sat in a green-tea-and-peppermint bubble bath, relaxing before bed, I thought again about the mystery woman I'd seen peering in my window.

A jealous wife, perhaps, wanting to see if her no-goodnik husband was at the party with another woman. It was possible, maybe even likely. I knew my clients personally, but I rarely knew them well, and I certainly didn't know the details of their personal lives. I tried to keep above the fray, avoiding asking questions that might prove embarrassing or gauche. When you deal in high-end antiques, you need to be discreet so wives won't learn what their husbands buy for other women and husbands won't learn what their wives buy for other men. Or how much things really cost. Or that one sibling was favored over another. She hadn't tried to rob the place and she hadn't made a scene, and in the final analysis, that was all I cared about.

Chapter Four

I took Ian to Ellie's, my top-choice restaurant for brunch. Ellie's was housed in a nineteenth-century chocolate factory, long since renovated into various upscale retail venues and professional offices. I got lucky and found a parking space directly in front of the restaurant, across from the village green. Evergreen garlands dotted with blue lights stretched across the street. Candy-cane-striped ribbons twirled up the lamp poles. A pinecone wreath adorned Ellie's front door. Inside, miniature Christmas trees bedecked with tiny red and gold velvet bows adorned every table.

I never looked at Ellie's menu since I always ordered the same thing — a crêpe filled with chicken and asparagus in a Mornay sauce. Ian ordered eggs Benedict.

"What's your favorite part about conducting research?" I asked after our coffees had arrived.

"The surprises. How about you?"

"Not being surprised! In my business, I try to confirm facts I've been given and hope are true, so when I'm surprised, that's rarely good news. What's the biggest surprise you've run into so far?"

"Finding you. What's your biggest disappointment?"

"An American-made maple table that I thought I could prove had been in a hotel frequented by members of the Continental Congress. I spent nearly a month researching it, including two trips to Pennsylvania to review documents in historical societies and museums."

"All this for one table?"

"It was a beauty, meticulously crafted with matched-grain wood and peg-and-dowel construction, lower than current tables, suggesting that it was made when people were shorter — perhaps in the eighteenth century. It was a little scratched, but no more than you would expect of a well-used object more than two hundred years old. Can you see where I'm heading with this?"

"A valuable piece."

"Worth a little research, that's what I told myself. Especially after I found a maker's mark tucked up under a side brace." The waitress came with our food. After I'd enjoyed a few bites of the creamy mixture I'd tried and failed to replicate, I continued. "To make a long story short, I was able to identify the mark as coming from a Philadelphia-based company that produced custom-designed furniture from 1752 to 1784. Their records indicated they sold a dozen tables that were described exactly like mine, down to the millimeter, to a Philadelphia hotel in 1775."

"It's like a detective story. What did you do?"

"I went pit bull learning about that hotel. It was a fairly posh place, with a dozen rooms. Apparently, in 1775, the hotel's owners ordered a new table for every room. I had a lot of confidence that my table was, at one time, in one of those rooms." I smiled, remembering the exhilaration I'd felt when I got a look at the hotel's records. "Thomas Jefferson stayed in that hotel for nearly two years, including the period during which he wrote the Declaration of Independence. Can you imagine?"

His eyes widened. "The table must be worth hundreds of thousands of dollars."

I sighed, exaggerating it for effect. "Sadly, it was all for naught." I caught the waitress's eye and raised my mug, requesting more coffee. She nodded and headed for the kitchen. "In any appraisal, there are two parts — authentication and valuation. I made an amateur mistake. I was so hot on the valuation trail, I didn't pay enough attention to authentication, to the table itself. Under the pegs and dowels were screws. Manufactured screws. Can you believe it? I nearly fell for one of the oldest tricks in the book."

"Screws in the eighteenth century would have been handmade."

"If they were used at all. I learned my lesson. We authenticate first. Only then do we move on to valuation."

"Complicated," Ian said, as the waitress refilled our mugs.

"Everything of any substance is complicated. Creating software for the trucking industry can't be simple."

"Do you think that's true? That everything is complicated?"

I sipped some coffee and thought about his question. "Yes, but that doesn't make it bad. It's popular nowadays to say that simplicity is a virtue, but I don't believe it. At least, it's not a virtue in my life." I smiled. "Between you and me and this two-hundred-year-old brick wall, I relish complexity. Simplicity bores me."

"You have real depth, Josie."

"I don't know about that, and I don't mean to imply that people who prefer a simple life lack depth." I smiled again. "It's why they make both chocolate and vanilla ice cream, right? People have different tastes."

"I agree on all accounts. When I retired I thought I'd relish a simple life. Instead, I got bored. That's why I began dabbling in genealogy."

"Gee," I said, "maybe we're related." We grinned at one another for a few seconds. "Ty said he thought we'd have a lot in common."

Ian reached across the table and patted my hand. "He was right."

"So do you agree that everything of substance is complicated?"

Ian gazed out the window, past the gazebo where local bands played familiar tunes on warm summer nights, into the far distance. This time of year, the gazebo housed Rocky Point's Christmas tree, a ten-footer all decked out in multicolored lights, icicle-shaped ornaments, and shimmering silver garlands. A huge gold-toned menorah shared the space. One electric candle flickered, marking last evening's start of Hanukkah. After several seconds, he turned back to face me.

"No, I can't say I do. I think many things are simple, but it is our nature to perceive them as complex. Sometimes we do it to delude ourselves that our lives have importance. Other times we do it because we can't handle something, so we conclude it must be complicated — to do otherwise implies we're stupid or inept."

"Or ill prepared. Or inexperienced."

"Exactly. Don't you agree?"

"I see your point, but I stand my ground. A baker thinks baking a cake is simple, but that's only because she knows how. Life used to be simpler, and I think people crave that simplicity. I just don't think it's available, not today, not unless you want to go off the grid. I think people who want to live a simple life often romanticize the good old days, forgetting the inconveniences they'd endure if they could go back and undervaluing the advantages we enjoy today."

"And now we know something else," Ian said. "In addition to having a lot in common, we're able to agree to disagree respectfully."

The waitress placed the vinyl folder containing the check on the table with a thank-you, and Ian whisked it away.

"You're on my turf," I protested, reaching for it.

"It's my pleasure, Josie."

"But I invited you!"

"Next time."

"How about lunch tomorrow before you head to Boston?"

"Sold."

"Good, but I don't trust you . . . I'll prepay."

He laughed. "Deal!"

We sat there through one more coffee until Ian said he needed to leave, to take a nap so he would be in top form for his date with Lia.

I often walked the quarter mile from Prescott's to the Congregational church, taking the meandering pathway that runs through the woods. The walk provided a perfect mind-clearing break during a hectic day. Sunday evening, though, Ty parked his government-issued SUV at the church.

"My boss left a message," Ty said as we walked across the lot. "I may need to go to D.C. tomorrow for a meeting first thing Tuesday morning. New training protocols for unmonitored coastal areas. He wants me on the committee."

I tucked my hand into the crook of his elbow. "That sounds impressive."

"You think? Maybe. Anyway, even if it

happens, I'll be home in time for dinner Tuesday. He'll let me know in the morning if the meeting is on."

The temperature had dropped into the low twenties.

"Do you think it's going to snow?" I asked.

"Yes."

I sniffed. "It doesn't smell like snow."

"Sure it does. Your sniffer is out of order."

I sniffed again. "You're teasing me. My sniffer's fine."

"Mark my words."

I squeezed his arm playfully as we climbed the steps to the entryway.

Ted, the pastor, greeted us as friends, which we were. He was one of my best buddies, a gardening enthusiast, and I'd often find him planting or weeding in the lush gardens surrounding the church. We stepped into the candlelit nave.

Inside, we walked down the center aisle, past pews decorated with sweeping boughs of evergreens and big red velvet bows. The dark wood seemed to glow. Tall white tapers, tucked into hanging metal holders, flickered throughout the church.

For most of the concert, I watched the choir, mostly keeping my eyes on Fred. He brought his laserlike focus to everything he did, singing included. It was inspiring to watch his performance. Occasionally, I let my eyes wander to the night-dark, backlit stained-glass windows and soaring cathedral ceiling, trying to follow glints of candlelight.

It was during the choir's rendition of one of my most-loved songs, "Carol of the Bells," that I glanced behind me, curious as to whether there were empty seats, and spotted Lia standing alone in a corner, half hidden by a thick arching beam. She seemed to be looking for someone, craning her neck, her eyes on the move. I gently pushed up Ty's sleeve to get a peek at his watch. It said 8:15. When I looked back a second time, she was gone.

Chapter Five

I normally get into work around eight, and Monday morning was no exception. My sniffer proved to be in working order after all — it hadn't snowed overnight, and now it smelled like snow. The weatherman concurred, stating that a light snow would be starting within the hour, with a few inches accumulating before the snow ended mid-afternoon.

Ty and I had listened to the weather forecast on the six-thirty news this morning, and I giggled, recalling our silliness.

I'd said, teasing, "See? I told you it didn't smell like snow last night. You maligned my nose."

Ty should have been abashed, but he wasn't. He said that all it proved was that his sniffer was more finely tuned than mine.

I was still smiling at the memory as I pulled into Prescott's parking lot.

Lia was waiting for me, sitting in her silver

Lexus with the engine running. She was on the stoop before I parked, her face framed by the oversized wreath, a twisty confection of bluish green cypress branches and ice blue juniper berries. I'd had Gretchen order a dozen of them, one for every door and window. Lia's cobalt wool coat fell below her knees. The dark faux-fur collar and cuffs added flair. She wore a matching beret and dark brown, French-heeled, knee-high boots. Her eyes were narrowed. Her expression was severe.

"Are you all right?" I asked.

"Absolutely," she said with patently fake bonhomie. "I wanted to tell you what a great time I had at the party."

I unlocked the front door, setting the wind chimes Gretchen had hung years earlier jangling. As I punched in the code to shift the security system from night to day, I said, "Thanks! I had a terrific time myself, which I always think is a good sign."

Lia tossed her coat and hat onto a chair at the guest table and fluffed her hair. She'd lightened it since the party, adding delicate copper highlights. She was wearing a black wool pencil skirt with a raspberry cashmere sweater.

"Have a seat," I said. "I'll get coffee going."

"Thanks," she said, pulling out a chair. "I think you're right. If the host is happy, everyone is happy."

I measured out our house blend of coffee, two-thirds dark roast Colombian to one-third Costa Rican. I pushed the START button, and the machine sprang to life with a loud whoosh.

"How was dinner last night?" I asked, sitting across from her.

Lia shrugged and laughed, a hollow, brittle sound, intending, I conjectured, to communicate indifference but having the opposite effect. I inferred her date with Ian hadn't gone well, or hadn't gone as she'd hoped. Poor Lia, a quavering mass of needs all gussied up in a classy package. She lowered her eyes to her knees and smoothed an invisible wrinkle on her skirt.

"It didn't happen," she said. She waved it aside. "I can't remember the last time I got stood up."

"Ian?" I asked, incredulous. My mouth opened, but no words came. I stared at her, stunned. I tried again to talk. "I can't imagine him doing such a thing."

"Maybe he changed his mind."

"Without telling you?"

She shrugged. "I have no idea why he did what he did. I'm just reporting facts."

"Perhaps he overslept. I know he was struggling with jet lag."

She raised her eyes to the big wall clock. "It's more than thirteen hours since we were supposed to meet. You think he's still asleep?"

"When and where were you to meet?"

"At the Blue Dolphin at seven. He made a reservation. I waited until seven thirty before calling his hotel. He wasn't in. At eight, I gave up and drove to the Congregational church — you were there. Ian had mentioned that you'd invited him, so I thought maybe he'd decided to go. I know how stupid that sounds . . . he skipped dinner with me to go to listen to a church choir!" She paused for a moment. "He wasn't there. I called the hotel again this morning — he's still not there. Or at least, he's not answering his phone."

"This makes no sense, Lia! There has to be some explanation."

"You haven't heard from him?"

"No"

Lia stood and shrugged into her coat. "Anything is possible, right? Maybe it will be eighty degrees and sunny by noon. That's just as likely as Ian still being asleep. He's a man. He changed his mind and didn't want the hassle of telling me. Why should he care?

He's leaving for Boston today. Who knows if he'll ever be back in Rocky Point." She tugged on her blue leather gloves. "Sorry to bother you. I've got to go open the spa. No rest for the weary, right? See ya!"

The wind chimes' jingly music sounded, then waned. I stared at the door, listening to the homey hums and pops of coffee brewing, reached for a phone, and called Ian's hotel. The operator connected me to his room. The phone rang and rang and rang. No answer. The operator picked up and asked if I wanted to leave a message. I didn't like it. I'd counted eleven rings, enough to wake the dead.

"Yes, please," I said. "Ask him to call Josie."

I wasn't too worried. There were lots of reasons why he might not have answered. Maybe he was in the shower. Or out for a run. Or downstairs eating breakfast. Perhaps Lia was right, and he'd changed his mind about taking her to dinner. It was ungentlemanly not to call her to cancel, but it was certainly expedient. He might simply have wished to avoid Lia's angst. While I was certain I'd hear from Ian within an hour or two, I couldn't quite dismiss Lia's distress from my mind. I decided I needed a hug, and I knew where to find one.

I pushed open the heavy door to the warehouse.

"Hank!" I called. "Hank? Where are you, baby?"

He meowed from off to the left, his domain. I walked in that direction and found him in his basket, half asleep.

"There you are. Good boy!"

He yawned.

"Such a big yawn for such a little boy."

I changed his water and refreshed his food. He stood up and mewed again, arching his back, his way of asking for a cuddle.

"Are you ready for your morning cuddle, sweet boy?"

He mewed. *Yes, please,* he was saying.

"Good. I need one, too."

I picked him up and kissed his cheek, cradling him like a baby, rubbing his jowls, scratching under his chin, kissing him behind his ears and on his little forehead.

"I don't know, Hank. I wasn't worried about Ian, and now I am. Lia planted an uncomfortable seed. What do you think? Should I be anxious?"

He purred and nuzzled my cheek.

"I agree. Let's wait awhile and see whether he calls back."

I placed Hank on his carpet, told him he was a good boy, and hurried up the spiral stairs to my office.

My idea to wait for a few hours was sensible but unrealistic. Ian had given me his mobile number, and I stared at it. I didn't want to overreact. I'd already left him a message. I shrugged and punched in the numbers. My call went directly to voice mail — his phone was off.

I booted up my computer and began scrolling through the e-mails that had come in overnight. A Japanese client had a question about a Van Gogh he bought last year. I forwarded it to Sasha. A curator from a Los Angeles museum was hoping we had additional photos of a lute we'd sold at one of last year's auctions. That one went to Fred. I couldn't stop thinking about Ian. An e-mail from my accountant asking for clarification about our new carpet. Was it truly new, an asset to be depreciated, or a replacement, a repair to be expensed? I replied that it was a replacement. I continued on until I was caught up. When I was done, I called Ian's hotel back and explained to the woman who answered that I was a little worried about him. I asked her to knock on his door. She refused, saying he'd had the DO NOT DISTURB sign up since yesterday afternoon and they had a strict policy — if guests didn't want to be disturbed, they didn't disturb them. I thanked her and hung up. I couldn't think of what else I could or should do.

Surely, I thought, Ian would keep our lunch date.

Ian didn't show up for lunch. I'd made a reservation at a restaurant on Route 1. I waited fifteen minutes, apologized to the hostess, and drove through the gently falling snow to the Rocky Point Sea View Hotel.

I parked in the guest lot and walked along the snow-dusted fieldstone walkway to the porch. The wraparound porch provided an unobstructed view of the ocean. Ragged lines of wind-driven whitecaps danced across the surface. The sky was thick with leaden clouds, and waves crashed against the granite boulders that edged the shore, sending sprays of foamy froth twenty feet in the air.

The sprawling Victorian building was one of Rocky Point's finest hotels, a reputation it had enjoyed since it had first opened, and the current owners, a couple named Taylor and Jonah Carmona, were keeping the tradition of excellence alive. Taylor was a fan of our tag sale, often stopping by to see if we had any new vintage perfume bottles, her favorite collectible.

A carved wooden sign hanging on the front door below a wreath of birch twigs and clusters of plump red berries read COME ON IN!

As I stepped inside, a bell chimed. The lobby was huge, a former warren of small parlors and receiving rooms that had been renovated into one open-plan space about five years earlier. A large arrangement of bloodred roses and silvery fir branches sat on a round oak table in the center of the room. A pair of red and ivory plaid club chairs was angled toward the reception desk on the right. Two love seats covered with a nubby red fabric faced one another at ninety-degree angles to the fireplace. The fireplace featured a fieldstone surround and hearth. A fire was burning, orange and yellow flames curling over and around charred hardwood logs. Brass lamps sat on small oak tables. A wing chair stood alone in a corner under a standing reading lamp. The current issue of *Yankee* topped a stack of magazines; I recognized the *Coastal Living* masthead from the corner protruding under it. Red and white floral drapes were held back by red rope ties, the kind with tassels. Multicolored oval rag rugs were positioned here and there throughout the space. A brass chandelier hung over the flowers, and recessed lamps illuminated the room. Dome security cameras were mounted in each corner. An old-fashioned brass service bell rested on the reception counter. Before I could tap it, Taylor's head popped out from a swinging door behind the reception desk.

"Hi, Josie!" she said, smiling.

Taylor was short and stout, with chin-length curly brown hair and big brown eyes. She wore khakis and a red sweater. She approached the counter.

"Hi, Taylor! I have a favor to ask. Ian Bennington hasn't been seen since yesterday afternoon. He didn't keep a dinner date last night, and he missed lunch with me today. Will you go check on him?"

"Come again?"

"Just knock on his door."

Taylor tapped into a computer. She raised her eyes from the monitor to my face. "He doesn't want to be disturbed."

"He might be hurt."

"Or he might be taking a bath or listening to music through headphones. Do not disturb means do not disturb. You know that, Josie."

"I'm worried."

"I'm sorry."

I looked around, seeking inspiration. None came. "What should I do?"

"If you think the situation merits it, talk to the police. Until then, let him be. Grown-ups are allowed to hole up if they want."

I knew in my gut that Ian was in trouble, but I couldn't think of how to convince Taylor, so I thanked her and left.

Outside, I studied the parking lot. There was one silver Taurus, but I had no way to know if the super-popular rental model was Ian's.

Taylor said that if I thought the situation warranted it, I should talk to the police. She was right.

Ellis wasn't convinced, either.

I sat in his office under a print of *The Gossips,* one of his favorite Norman Rockwell illustrations, and tried to persuade him that Ian hadn't simply decided he wanted to be alone for a while.

"It's barely been twenty-four hours since you last saw him, Josie," he said. "Give the guy a break."

I walked across Ocean Avenue and climbed a sand dune. The snow was falling more thickly now, forming a white scrim through which the churning near-black ocean looked as deadly as it was. The snow was beginning to stick to the bottle green tangles of seaweed that quivered in the steady wind. No way was the storm passing by mid-afternoon.

As I walked back to my car, I dug my phone out from my tote bag and called Ty. He was at the airport, waiting for his flight to D.C. He told me to hold on while he moved to a quieter area. I got settled in the driver's seat and turned up the heat.

"Is your flight on time?" I asked when he was back on the line.

"So they say. Why?"

"Because up here the snow is picking up."

"It's all clear here."

"I don't know. I'm worried."

"Something besides the snow is bothering you."

"It's Ian. I'm fretting." I explained my concerns, adding, "I don't know what to do."

"He'll turn up," Ty said without hesitation.

"Why would you think so? You told me once that lots of guys just up and disappear."

"Disenfranchised guys, not men with a daughter to visit and plenty of money."

"Then where is he?"

"Maybe he found some female companionship."

"No," I said.

"Why are you so certain?"

"Because he's not a horny twenty-year-old. Because he had a hot date with a gorgeous woman. Because he was glad to have connected with me and he wouldn't have simply blown off our lunch."

"Your logic is sound, but people defy logic all the time. Sure, Lia's good-looking but . . . well . . . let me put it this way . . . if I were a betting man, I'd place all my chips on an eighteen-year-old hottie he ran into at the mall over an almost forty-year-old glamour-puss with a ton of baggage and a PhD in sarcasm."

"Really?"

"I know men. It's easier to apologize after the fact than explain yourself before you do whatever it is you're going to do."

"You're not like that."

"True, but lots of guys are."

I knew men, too, and I simply couldn't believe that Ian wouldn't have called, texted, or e-mailed if he'd changed his mind about seeing us.

"You're just trying to reassure me."

"Well, yes. But that doesn't mean it isn't true."

I sighed. "I appreciate it, Ty, I really do, but I just can't imagine Ian picking up a teenager. Maybe Lia did something that turned him off and he left town in a funk." I shook my head. "Except he didn't check out of his hotel. They would have told me."

"He's rich. If he left, either with the teenager or in that funk, he wouldn't have worried about checking out. He'll be back in a day or two, get his stuff, and settle his bill."

When I didn't reply, he added, "I really think he'll resurface in a few hours or a few days, Josie, depending on how hot she is, but why don't you call the hospital, just in case?"

I closed my eyes for a moment. "You're very smart, you know that?"

"I'm a cop," he said.

"Not anymore. Now you're a Homeland Security bigwig."

"You think I'm a bigwig?"

"Yes. Do you really think Ian is okay?"

He didn't answer right away. "I did such a good job with my hottie scenario, I almost convinced myself."

"I love you."

"I love you, too."

After I hung up, I clutched the phone to my chest for a moment, keeping Ty close, then called the Rocky Point Hospital. I punched through their interactive menu until I reached Patient Information. They had no record of a patient named Ian Bennington. No unidentified male patients had been admitted to the hospital.

I'd tried everything I could think of to find Ian, without success, so I did what I always do when I reach a dead end — I called Wes.

"Whatcha got?" he asked, skipping hello, as always.

"A request. I'm worried about my cousin. This isn't news, Wes. It's personal. I'm asking a favor."

"Shoot."

"I don't want to see it on the front page of tomorrow's paper."

"No problem, Josie. You asked for a favor. You've got it."

"Wow, Wes. I wasn't expecting that."

"Jeez, Josie. Why not? We're friends."

An unexpected wave of emotion washed over me, and I choked and coughed, finally managing a croaking "Sorry." I pawed around in my tote bag for a bottle of water. "One sec." I drank some water and tried talking again. "That means a lot to me, Wes. Thanks." I explained the situation. "I'm hoping you might be able to get more information from the hotel, or whether his credit cards had been used, or something. I'm so worried."

"Give me an hour."

I was in my office struggling to read my accountant's latest good-news report, unable to concentrate. I swiveled to stare out my window. An inch or so of snow covered each tiny twig, a brown and white kaleidoscope of winter. I squinted my eyes and tilted my head and watched as reality mutated into abstract art. Finally, right on schedule, Wes called.

"I have some info," Wes said, "but no shockeroonies."

I was used to Wes's colorful vocabulary. "I'm ready," I said.

"Ian's in room two-eighteen. His keycard was last swiped at one thirty-eight Sunday afternoon."

I didn't ask him how he'd learned that. From past experience, I knew Wes's web of contacts was both broad and deep — and confidential. He might have sweet-talked a hotel employee into revealing Ian's keycard swipes, but it was just as likely he had an in at the security company that monitored the activity.

"We left the restaurant at ten after one," I said, "so Ian must have gone directly back to his room. Did he leave the hotel after that?"

"The system doesn't record when people leave their rooms, only keycard swipes, so there is no way of knowing when, or if, he left."

"What about security cameras? I saw a bunch in the lobby."

"There are none on the guest floors, only where you were, in the lobby, and in the back office. Plus, he could have gone out a side entrance."

"Can you get his rental car's license plate number? I don't know which company he used, but he was driving a silver Taurus."

"Got it," he said, and rattled off a Massachusetts plate number. "It looks like the hotel was right and he's in his room. At least, he hasn't used his charge cards."

"Thanks, Wes."

"Anything for a pal," he said, and hung up.

I rushed downstairs, told Cara I didn't know when I'd be back, and retraced my route to the Rocky Point Sea View Hotel, certain the car I'd seen in the parking would prove to be Ian's.

I found the Taurus parked in the same spot. From the snow cover, I could tell that it hadn't been disturbed since my earlier visit. I drove around the vehicle so I could see the rear plate. The tags were from

Vermont. It wasn't Ian's rental.

My eyes filled. I'd felt so hopeful. I brushed the wetness aside with the side of my hand.

I cruised the property and checked the overflow parking lot, which was empty, no surprise in January. There were six cars in the staff lot, none of them a Taurus.

I drove back to the guest lot and parked. Stairs led to the side of the wraparound porch and a door. A laminated sign penned in elegant calligraphy hung from a gold hook near the top of the door. It read:

After ten p.m.,
please use the front entrance.

I stepped inside.

In front of me was a long corridor leading to the ground-floor guest rooms. To my right was a back staircase leading up. Wes said there were no security cameras in the hallways.

I climbed the steps. Room 218 faced the ocean. I knocked, then knocked again. I tore a sheet from my notebook, found a pen, and wrote: *Dear Ian.* I couldn't think of what else to write. I had nothing to add to my request to call me. I stuffed the paper back in my bag, tossed the pen in after it, and knocked one more time. I pressed my ear against the door and held my breath. All I heard was silence.

As I retraced my steps to the staircase, I counted doors. Ian's room was third from the end. Outside again, I counted balconies, found the third one from the end, and tried to see in the windows. The drapes were open, but the room was dark. I saw no movement, no telltale shadows, no glimmer of light from the television, nothing that suggested someone was in the room. An image of Ian's body lying on the carpet came to me unbeckoned and unwanted. He could be ill. He could be injured. *Except,* I reminded myself, my optimism soaring, *his car isn't here.*

Not knowing what else to do, I drove to Ellie's and the Blue Dolphin, looking for his car. I even drove around every level of the central parking garage. I cruised the streets, going every which way, looking everywhere and anywhere. A few minutes into my seemingly aimless trek, Ty called to tell me his plane had landed. I pulled to the side of the road and set my flashers.

"How are you holding up?" he asked.

"I've become philosophical." I filled him in about what I'd learned from Wes and what I'd done to try to see into Ian's room and locate his car. "Ian is either fine or he's not, and if he's not, there's nothing I can do about it that I haven't already done. I'm driving around to satisfy myself I've done all I can, not because I expect to find him or his car."

Ty told me he thought my attitude was sensible, and we agreed to talk later, just before bed. As dusk descended and the snow picked up, I called it a day and drove home.

Chapter Six

Tuesday morning. I woke up just after six, as breathless and befuddled as if I'd run a marathon. I struggled onto one elbow, fighting the haze of sleep, inexplicably twizzled between the top sheet and a blanket like a braid. I tried to recall whether I'd had a bad dream, and if so, what it had been about, but I couldn't. I untwirled myself and sat up.

Ian.

It wasn't a dream.

I grabbed my iPhone and checked for messages. Ty had sent an "I love you" text around midnight, after I'd fallen asleep, but there was nothing from Ian. I texted Ty that I loved him, too, ratcheted up my willpower, shook off the residual mist, and rolled out of bed.

Downstairs, I poured myself a cup of coffee and called Ian's mobile phone and his hotel room, and as expected, he didn't answer either. I didn't leave messages. Instead, I put on my happy face, telling myself that Ty was right, that Ian had hooked up with a super-hot date and would resurface soon. Optimism was my default position in most things, and until Ellis would accept a missing persons report, my best strategy was to wait as patiently as I could. Trying to get media attention and calling Becca and asking her if she'd heard from her dad, the only two proactive options that had occurred to me overnight, were fraught with problems. If Ian strutted in with a cutie on his arm only to find an outraged daughter and a bank of cameras, he'd probably never speak to me again. I got Ellis's point. Grown-ups have every right to do exactly what they want.

Around eleven that morning, Cara called me on the intercom. She had an antiques dealer on the phone she thought I should talk to. He had a piece of Civil War ephemera that sounded good to her.

We were planning an antique auction for next fall called Southern Life. So far, we had two remarkable examples of Southern-crafted furniture, a seventeenth-century pie cabinet and an 1823 hand-hewn rocking cradle, as well as three Alabama-made ornate brass escutcheons dating from the 1730s and an 1859 blue pottery hooded candle holder. Given the enduring popularity of Civil War collectibles and the scarcity of Confederate objects, I was determined to add in as many Civil War–era Southern pieces as I could. To that end we were calling antiques dealers throughout the South. Normally Sasha or Fred would make the calls, but today Sasha was at an appraisal in Rye and Fred was meeting with a Boston museum curator about a Cambodian artifact we were trying to authenticate, so I had Cara calling around, knowing I was on-site and able to jump in as needed.

"I know how silly that must sound," Cara said, laughing a little. "I don't know enough about antiques to tell you it's good . . . but, well . . . you'll understand when you talk to him. His name is Mitchell Glascowl, and he's from Oxford, Mississippi. His company is Glascowl's Junque." She spelled out "Junque" for me. "He said he has a Civil War recruiting poster."

"Get out of town. Confederate?"

"Yes. From Tennessee."

"Thanks, Cara." I clicked through to the call. "Mr. Glascowl, this is Josie Prescott. I understand you're going to make my day."

"I don't know about that, young lady.

You're in a buying mood, are you?"

"I am if what Cara tells me is true. I understand you have a Civil War recruiting poster. I'd love to hear about it."

"It's plenty valuable."

"Only to someone who wants to buy it."

He made a noise like a train in a tunnel, a low rumble, not loud — a laugh, I guessed.

"I guess that's you," he said.

"Maybe, if it's real-deal good stuff."

"That's what I got."

"May I call you Mitch?"

"Mitchie Rich, if we're gonna be friends."

"I get a sense we're going to be good buddies, Mitchie Rich. I'm Josie."

"I never did understand why you Northerners only get one name."

"Me either. Any chance you can send me a photo or scan of that poster so I can get a look at it?"

"Sure. I'll do that now and e-mail you."

I sat by my computer, eagerly awaiting the poster's arrival. Most extant Civil War recruiting posters were from Northern states. Finding a Confederate one in good condition would be a real coup. It wasn't merely that it would sell for top dollar as part of an important auction of Southern objects; including a significant Confederate component would also help us generate national publicity for the show itself. Three minutes later, Mitchie Rich's e-mail arrived.

The poster was black on pale ocher, although the paper might have started out white. If so, it had faded fairly evenly, but there was no way to tell for sure until I had it in hand under strong white light. The text was a stirring call to arms. "The Yankee War is now being raged for 'beauty and booty,' " it read. "To excite their hired and ruffian soldiers, they promise them our lands, and tell them our women are beautiful — that beauty is the reward of the brave." It went on to ask, "Shall we wait until our homes are desolated; until sword and rape shall have visited them? Never!" It was chilling. It was war.

I called back. "Hey, Mitchie Rich, I got it. Thanks for sending it on. It looks to be in pretty good condition. How much are you looking for?"

"What's it worth to you?"

"Seller names the price."

He paused, and I could tell he was pricing the customer — me — not the poster. I hated that. I waited, a lesson learned long ago from my dad. Let the silence hang.

"Eight hundred," he said, almost making it a question.

Considering the impact of overhead,

research, and marketing costs, Prescott's policy was that we never paid more than a third of what we thought an object would sell for at retail. This poster would sell for more than $2,400, far more, if it was real. Prescott's had another policy, though. We tried our best to buy cheap and sell high. We never lied, but neither did we do the other guy's job for him.

"What can you tell me about provenance?" I asked, hoping Mitchie Rich would assume I was stunned by the high price and trying to justify it to myself.

"What do you want to know?" he countered.

His question got me wondering whether he was covering that he was unfamiliar with the word, and that got me wondering about his business. He might be a one-man operation, storing his inventory in his garage and attending flea markets on weekends. I tapped "Glascowl's Junque" into Google. Mitchie Rich rented a small space in a shared antiques barn, the kind of place where he paid rent or commission and maybe had to work a shift or two a week to boot.

"Where you got it," I said.

He gave another low rumble. "You know better than that, young lady. Sources are confidential."

I also Googled "TN Civil War recruiting poster antique buy" and saw there were none for sale. I checked two subscription antiques Web sites with the same inquiry. Nothing, which was both good and bad news. Mitchie Rich wouldn't know its value relative to its competition, but neither would I.

"I can't pay top dollar unless I know the poster is real."

"It's real all right. I got it out of an attic in Collierville, Tennessee, along with a lot of other old stuff. An estate sale."

"I'll need the family's name to see what role they played in the war."

"Well," he said, "since I bought the entire estate, there's no poaching I need to worry about. If you buy the poster, I'll tell you anything you want to know."

"What other antiques might I be interested in? I think Cara explained that I'm putting together a show on Southern life. We're open as to period, so long as the objects are at least a hundred years old and reflect some distinctive element of Southern living."

Mitchie Rich had lots of suggestions, none good. I was a stickler for maintaining our definition of an antique. If an object was less than a hundred years old, we called it vintage or a collectible. We sold plenty of collectibles in the tag sale, but none in our high-end auctions. The cookie jar he suggested had MADE IN OCCUPIED JAPAN stamped on the bottom, dating it between 1945 and 1952. The Orrefors vase was Scandinavian, and from his description — squared-off, black-and-white textured glass — I knew it had been produced in the 1960s. He also offered undated, routine pottery pieces, miscellaneous costume jewelry, used furniture, and a quilt, which, he said, was in perfect condition except for a small tear in a corner. I was also a stickler for condition. If it was chipped, ripped, burned, scarred, or otherwise marred, we wouldn't offer it at auction.

"It looks like this one poster is all I'll be buying," I said, "but that's all right. I'm glad to have it. Eight hundred is too rich for my blood, though. I'm thinking four hundred is fair."

"No can do. Seven hundred."

"Less a dealer's discount?"

He paused, thinking it over. "Ten percent."

"Twenty."

"You drive a hard bargain, young lady."

"Are you kidding me?" I said. "You're a shark. Can we settle on five hundred sixty, then?"

"Seven hundred is fair, but I'll give you ten percent. Call it six thirty, and you've got a deal."

When I said okay, he gave his trainlike rumbling laugh, and I knew he thought I was a sucker. That made our transaction the best of the best — I might not like someone taking me for a patsy, but at the end of the day, we both felt like winners.

At noon, I found myself sinking back into depression, gloomy thoughts about Ian stubbornly refusing to be vanquished. I reheated some roasted vegetable soup I'd prepared over the weekend, using the recipe my mother got from her good friend Linda Plastina, and the rich aroma soothed me a bit. It wasn't enough, though, to dispel my anxiety. I wasn't good at waiting. I needed to act.

The photographer who'd worked my holiday party had sent us all the photos he'd taken. It was Gretchen's job to sort through them and select an appropriate mix for our archives. She also culled any beauties that might appeal to individuals; those were framed as special gifts from Prescott's. I remembered that I'd been cc'd on an e-mail from the photographer giving Gretchen the access codes to the photo storage site.

I found the link and password and opened the folder. I ran through the photos quickly looking for a clear full-face shot of Ian, noting that we never did get a photo of the two of us. Ian must have left before Gretchen could organize it. There weren't many options, but in between a fun photo of me and Zoë toasting the camera with our glasses of Prescott's Punch and a crowd scene where everyone was near the stage listening to Timothy, I found the perfect image. Ian was focused on Lia, unaware of the camera aimed his way. I copied the photo onto my desktop, cropped it to eliminate all extraneous material, including Lia, and printed two copies.

Lia's Spa was located four doors down from Ellie's in a prime location across from the village green. It also occupied an old manufacturer, although not a chocolate factory, and it, too, had been renovated to preserve the original character. A wall of mellowed brick meshed perfectly with the eggplant and turquoise color scheme. Old wooden cross beams accentuated the high ceilings. For the holidays, dark purple and teal plaid bows adorned the windows and walls, Pinecone- and peppermint-scented candles stood on tall wooden stands that ringed the room, their flames twinkling. More of the ribbon twirled around the stands from base to holder. A silvery pink aluminum Christmas tree stood on the reception desk next to an olive-wood menorah. Silver, seafoam green, and purple teardrop-shaped ornaments dangled from the tree's metal branches. Seashell pink crocheted angels suspended on clear filament from the wooden beams drifted in the ambient breeze and appeared to be flying. The overall look was as unexpected and elegant as Lia.

I pushed open the oak door just as Lia was shaking hands with a middle-aged man in jeans and a blue parka.

"Thanks for taking the time to come and take a look at it," she said. "Maybe I'll be able to swing it later in the year."

"Anytime," the man said, and left.

Lia smiled at me. "Look what the breeze blew in! How you doing, Josie?"

"Pretty good. Do you have a minute to talk?"

"Sure," she said, her eyes growing wary.

She didn't look defensive, exactly, but there was something in her demeanor that made me feel as if I were walking on eggshells, or ought to be.

"Hi, Missy," I said, smiling at the receptionist.

I'd known Missy for as long as I'd been coming to Lia's spa, which was the whole time I'd been living in Rocky Point. Last spring, Missy had asked my opinion about whether it was safe for her daughter to move to New York City. As if she could stop an aspiring actress who'd landed a full-ride scholarship to NYU from moving.

"How's your daughter liking the big city?"

She looked a little wistful. "She loves it."

"I knew she would."

"Allen and I are going down for Christmas. My first visit."

"New York is very special during the holidays."

Lia held open the nondescript white door marked PRIVATE, and with a "see ya!" wave to Missy, I followed Lia down a long corridor. Lia's office was, I knew, at the rear. The austere stark white walls and muted gray industrial carpeting contrasted sharply with the opulence of the client areas. Her office was equally plain, a place to work, not relax. I couldn't help but notice that the paint was chipped and scratched and the carpet near the threshold was threadbare.

"I hope I'm not disturbing you," I said. "I'll only keep you a minute."

"Not at all," she said. "Have a seat. Tell me what I can do to help."

"It's Ian. I haven't heard from him, so I thought I'd stop by and ask if you have."

Lia raised her chin. "No."

"I'm so worried," I said. "I try not to be, but I am."

"I'd be worried, too, Josie. It's worrying. I barely know him and I'm upset. Do you have thoughts about what might be going on?"

"No," I said, stopping myself just in time from sharing Ty's opinion that Ian might be off with another woman.

As Lia walked me out, we agreed to let one another know the minute we heard anything. I waved good-bye, got in my car, and for the second time in two days drove straight to the Rocky Point police station.

Chapter Seven

As I walked through the densely falling snow toward the weathered, cottage-looking building that housed the Rocky Point Police Department, a bitter wind tore off the water. I flipped my hood up, glad I'd parked close to the door. Inside, I approached the chest-high counter that divided the lobby from the working area and waited for someone to look up. Two uniformed police officers were huddled together in the back talking. Ellis was leaning over someone's desk reading from the monitor. Cathy, the civilian admin who served as office manager, was pouring a cup of coffee from a Mr. Coffee machine that lived on a two-drawer file cabinet near her desk.

Cathy saw me out of the corner of her eye and smiled. She was plus-sized, with blond hair teased high and ice blue eyes, and she knew more about the inner workings of the police station than anyone else.

"Hi, Josie," she said.

Ellis looked up.

"Hi, Cathy." I met Ellis's gaze, pumping mine full of gravitas. "We need to talk."

"Sure," he said.

He unlatched the swinging partition, stepped through into the lobby, and headed to his private office. I trailed along. He swung the door closed, and it latched with a sharp snap.

"Is this about Ian Bennington?" he asked once I was inside. "Nothing's changed, Josie."

"Sure it has. It's now forty-eight hours, give or take, since anyone has seen him. He's a foreigner, Ellis, a stranger to Rocky Point. Do you need me to raise hell with the British Embassy, or will you act as if I'm a rational person making a reasonable request?"

His lips pressed together. "What exactly are you asking me to do?"

"See if he's in his hotel room. He may be sick. Maybe he slipped in the bathtub and hurt his head. Trace his car. What if he lost control on black ice and plummeted into a ravine? He told me he was struggling with driving on the opposite side of the road from what he was used to, and I doubt he's ever driven in the kind of winter conditions we have around here. Find him."

Ellis sat behind his desk and pointed at one of the two guest chairs. I perched on the edge, impatient and annoyed. I didn't understand his hesitation.

"I have a photo," I said. I handed over one copy of the photograph I'd printed earlier.

Ellis stared at it. "I'd need a court order to enter his room, and at this point, I don't have enough evidence to ask for one. While I know you well enough to trust your judgment, I know of no facts that suggest a crime has been committed. I'm sorry, Josie. My hands are tied."

"I thought you had to accept a missing persons report and act on it after a certain number of days."

"The law changed. Unless the person who's gone missing has a physical or mental disability that puts him or her at risk, there's nothing I can do. The actual wording of the statute is that the person has to have a 'proven physical or mental disability or is senile,' which Ian doesn't and isn't. If something about his disappearance indicated that he was in danger, if people reported that they saw him being tossed into the back of a van, for instance, I could act. But no one has reported a kidnapping. The only other way I could accept your report was if I have reason to believe that his disappearance wasn't voluntary, and I'm afraid your gut instinct isn't sufficient."

"Can you give me some examples of what it would take to convince you?"

"If we found Ian's burned-out car under a bridge or even deserted behind a warehouse. If the maid reported that his hotel room had been ransacked. I need actual evidence that indicates he's in trouble." He flipped his palms up. "What if he decided on a whim to take a side trip to Montreal or New York City? He wouldn't appreciate your making a hoot-and-holler about his vacation." He shook his head. "I'm sorry, Josie."

"Thank you for explaining the situation to me," I said, and stomped out.

Back at my office, I considered my next-step options. I was going to try to avoid making Ian's apparent disappearance public, but I had to do something. I decided to start with his daughter. I was convinced that the only reason Ian would have left Rocky Point ahead of schedule voluntarily was to connect with Becca. I didn't for a minute believe that was what had happened, but it was a possibility that needed to be eliminated.

I consulted the genealogical chart Ian had e-mailed. Becca's legal name was Rebecca Anne Bennington.

I searched online for her phone number, with no luck. I called directory assistance; they had no record of her. I Googled her name and found a score of scholarly references, articles she'd authored or co-authored, papers she'd presented at conferences, and grants she'd received. However, I could find no indication that she lived in Boston.

Ian had mentioned that Becca was working on a marine biology research project involving clams. For all I knew, she could have been retained by a commercial supplier to help it improve its clam-shipping methods, but if she was a visiting scholar, no matter what she was working on or who was funding it, she was probably affiliated with a college or university. Since Reynard University had one of the best marine biology programs in the world, I decided to start there.

I brought up the university's Web site and went to the Marine Biology Department faculty page. Becca wasn't listed.

I looked up the main number for the department and got a woman's voice mail. I didn't leave a message. I called the registrar's office. Whoever answered the phone, a student worker, I guessed, interrupted me before I finished posing my question.

"Sorry," she said. "We never release student information."

"This isn't a student. This is a visiting scholar."

"Sorry. I wouldn't know anything about that."

Since most organizations follow a set policy in structuring e-mail addresses, I suspected that if I could discover anyone's e-mail address, I could follow the pattern to reach Becca, assuming she had some kind of affiliation with the university. I asked the woman to transfer me to IT.

"We never give out e-mail addresses," the young man who answered said.

"Can you tell me the format of e-mails? First name, dot, last name, for instance? Or last name, first initial?"

"No. Sorry."

I randomly clicked on a professor's e-mail link. Instead of an auto-filled e-mail opening up, though, a contact form popped up instead.

"Grrrr," I said aloud. Using my pen, I rat-a-tat-tatted a frustrated drumbeat on my desk. "There has to be a way."

I IM'd Sasha and Fred and asked if either

of them knew anyone at Reynard. Sasha reminded me that she'd spoken briefly to a professor in the university's Film Studies Department when we'd been trying to authenticate a series of silent movie posters.*

She gave me Dr. Marcus Achen's cell phone number, and I got him.

"Let me check," he said, in heavily accented English, once I'd explained who I was and what I was after. After a brief pause, he murmured, *"Da ist sie."*

There she is, I translated, pleased I recalled even that amount of my mostly forgotten middle school German.

"Her e-mail address is rabennington@reynard.uk.edu," he said. "She's based at our Plymouth campus."

"Plymouth, Massachusetts?" I asked. "No, of course not — 'uk,' got it. England."

"Exactly. But she's obviously here, since her phone number is for this campus."

He read it off. The number listed for her was the same as the department's number, not an unusual occurrence, Dr. Achen explained, when a researcher spends most of her time in the field.

I thanked him, but my sense of accom-

* Please see *Lethal Treasure.*

plishment was short-lived. I didn't want to e-mail Becca. I wanted to talk to her, face-to-face, to be there for her if Ian wasn't with her, if I was the bearer of bad news.

Hank mewed as he walked up to my chair. He stretched, first his top half, then his bottom half; then he jumped into my lap and licked my chin.

"Do I have a dirty spot?" I asked him, stroking his back. "What would you do, Hank, if you were me?" I scratched behind his ears, one of his favorite spots. "She has to live somewhere. She has to have a phone. How can I find her?"

He mewed again, louder this time.

"You know, you're right. What a smart fellow you are. When in doubt, call Wes."

"Becca Bennington lives in Boston," I told Wes, "and I need to find her. Her full name is Rebecca Anne Bennington."

"Ian is still missing," Wes said.

"Don't sound so happy about it."

"I'm not happy. I'm intrigued."

"Don't sound so intrigued."

"You're the one who called me, remember? Is he missing or not, Josie?"

"Yes."

"What do you think she knows?"

"Nothing."

"Then why do you want to reach her?"

"Because I don't know what else to do," I said, my throat tightening as I spoke, causing me to stumble over the last words. "I don't want to raise a ruckus, but I need to do something. I'm upset."

"I'll check it out."

"Thanks, Wes."

It took Wes five minutes to find Becca. His contact at the electric company gave him her address, an apartment on Park Drive, across from the Fens, not far from the Museum of Fine Arts, and only a ten-minute walk to Reynard University. I was out the door and in my car two minutes after we hung up.

Chapter Eight

Becca Bennington lived in a real beauty of an 1850-ish three-story brick town house. Built originally as a single-family home, it had been converted, along with scores of similar homes, into apartments sometime during the mid-twentieth century. Inside the vestibule, I counted buzzers. There were six apartments, two to a floor. The sign next to the 1R buzzer, which I assumed referenced the rear apartment on the first floor, read FERGUSON/BENNINGTON. I pushed the button.

When the click came, I opened the heavy wooden door and stepped into a square entryway. The walls were covered with white and gold striped wallpaper. A small crystal chandelier sparkled overhead. Elegantly framed nineteenth-century floral prints lined the long corridor. This was not a budget rental.

Fifty feet down the corridor, a tall, lean,

handsome man about my age wearing jeans and a dark blue collared short-sleeved T-shirt stood in the doorway of the rear apartment. He was barefoot. He had long blond hair, strong patrician features, and a welcoming smile.

"This way!" he called.

"Hi," I said as I walked toward him. "I'm Josie Prescott. Is Becca around?"

"Sorry . . . no."

"Darn! I really need to talk to her. Any idea how I can get in touch?"

A door near the front opened, and a middle-aged woman leaning on a silver cane asked, "Is everything all right?"

"You bet, Mrs. Damori." He winked at me. "Come on in." As soon as he shut the door, he added, "Mrs. Damori's a love . . . but . . ."

"Inquiring minds want to know," I quipped. "So . . . about Becca."

"I'm sorry, she's in the field. What was your name again?"

"Josie Prescott. I'm an antiques dealer." Diving gear laid out across the hardwood floor caught my eye. Clothes, bathing suits, shorts, and T-shirts were piled on the butterscotch leather sofa. "You're a diver."

"How'd you guess?"

I smiled, as much in response to his cute

crooked grin as his playful words. "I'm smart. Your last name is Ferguson."

"You got that from the doorbell label." He tapped his temple with his index finger. "I'm smart, too." He extended a hand for a shake. "Ethan Ferguson. I just made a pot of coffee — I'm on break. Want to join me for a cup?"

"Thanks. I'd love to."

I followed Ethan into the kitchen, which was located at one end of the expansive open-plan room. En route, we passed three eight-foot-high windows that overlooked what must have been a glorious garden back in the building's heyday but was now an unkempt wilderness. The kitchen was huge and recently renovated, definitely a step or eight up from typical student housing. Becca could afford it, I knew, and maybe Ethan could, too. The granite that covered the counter and oversized island was black with silver specks. All the appliances were chef-kitchen quality and fashioned of stainless steel. An oak plank farm table was large enough to seat ten. I took a stool at the island.

Three photographs hung near the front door, all underwater shots. The one closest to the door showed a welter of colorful coral, sponges, and anemones. I recognized golden elkhorn, purple fan, orange-tipped fire, and brain corals; yellow and pink sponges; and countless orange and yellow anemones, waving like beach grass in a gentle breeze.

I pointed to it. "That's unbelievably gorgeous. Are you the photographer?"

"Thanks. I took that one last winter on the Great Barrier Reef."

"I've snorkeled there."

"You don't dive?"

"No. I prefer staying on the surface." I pointed to the next photo. "That's an oyster."

"You're just showing off."

I laughed at his super-dry delivery. I focused on the third image. "And that's a clam."

"Can't get anything past you."

"Becca's into clams."

"I'm not sure she'd like it put exactly that way, but yes, she studies bivalve mollusks, specifically clams."

"Are you a marine biologist, like Becca?" I asked.

"Sort of like Becca." He poured coffee into matching blue pottery mugs. "I'm an oyster man."

I tried to stop myself from laughing but failed. "I'm sorry," I said, once I regained my composure. "You must know how funny that sounds."

"No," he said, his eyes dancing. "Tell me."

I shook my head, embarrassed. "Do you work at Reynard, too?"

"Like a dog." He carried the mugs to the table. "Milk? Sugar?"

"Milk is good, thanks."

He took a green floral jug from the fridge and slid it across to me, peeling away the plastic film covering the opening.

"Room with a Brit," he said, "and you serve milk in a jug. Becca can't stand plastic containers set out on the table."

"I'm with her. I latch on to any excuse to use my nice china."

"Do you know Becca well?" he asked.

"We've never met. I heard about her from her dad. Have you ever met him?"

"No." He sat two stools down from me. "Tell me about being an antiques dealer."

"I love it. I get to spend most of my time researching beautiful objects."

"Research is my chief passion, too. Don't even talk to me about writing."

"Is research also Becca's favorite part?" I asked, hoping my dragging Becca back into our conversation wasn't too obvious.

"Becca excels at everything. She's only about three years out of grad school, but she already has a world-class reputation in the bivalve mollusk community."

"Does your work ever overlap?"

"All the time." He held up crossed fingers. "Becca is considering letting me piggyback on one of her grant applications, which would be a gift and a half since poor little me has had three grant applications rejected in the last year, and for a tenure-track assistant professor, the only thing that would be worse is if he hadn't had any publications accepted, either. Oh, wait! I haven't!"

His self-deprecating humor was infectious.

"Why were your grant applications rejected? Do you know?"

He stretched out his long legs and crossed his ankles. "Same old, same old. Shrinking funding. Increased competition. Similar projects. It's criminal and it's stupid. My work revolves around helping communities like Florida's Gulf Coast and the New England shoreline restore their nearly extinct oyster populations — a certain way to boost the economy and feed the people. You'd think they'd be lining up to put their name on a project guaranteed to win awards and acclaim, but they're not."

"Frustrating," I said.

He waved it away. "I cope well. I get out of town as often as I can to go diving."

I smiled, attracted to his cheerful, breezy attitude toward life. "Where are you going?"

"I'm just back, actually. From Florida. A friend is tracking lionfish, among the most aggressively invasive species on earth. Just right for my current mood. I figured I could learn something I could apply to academia."

"It sounds like you're having a tough go of it."

"Ah! But it's a marathon, not a sprint, right? I'll finish the race triumphant, just you wait and see."

"I believe you," I said, smiling, hoping it was true. I finished my coffee. "I need to go. Do you have any idea when Becca will be back?"

"Sorry."

"Is she still in Nova Scotia?" I asked as I placed my mug in the sink and gathered up my tote bag.

"No. She's in New Hampshire."

"New Hampshire! That's where I'm from."

"Do you know Rocky Point Oceanographic Institute? Reynard partners with them. She often bunks up there."

I laughed, buoyed. "I live and work in Rocky Point." Maybe Becca and Ian had connected on Sunday and he simply forgot his other plans in the excitement of seeing his daughter.

He laughed, too. "And you drove down here to see her?"

"And the paintings. She has two seventeenth-century miniatures." I glanced around. "I don't see them."

"Becca showed them to me once," he said, walking me to the door. "They're remarkable. Do you have a card? I work at the institute sometimes, too. Maybe we can get together for a coffee again."

"Sounds good." I extracted a business card from the sterling silver holder Ty gave me for my birthday and handed it to him. "Do you happen to have Becca's cell phone number?"

"Sure."

He walked to a triangular cherry table tucked in a corner. A portable phone cradle sat next to a small apple-shaped pad of paper and an old-style answering machine. He wrote on the top piece for a minute, ripped it from the pad, and handed it over.

"There's mine, too. In case you need me."

I thanked him and told him it was a pleasure to meet him, meaning it, and left.

The sky was overcast, and it was bone-numbingly cold. Ethan was like any of a gazillion divers I'd met over the years during snorkeling vacations. He was fit, curious, confident, athletic, friendly, technically oriented, and a quintessential risk-lover. I couldn't recall how many nights I'd spent listening to their stories about cave dives and night dives and how they saw eight sharks circling and dove deeper to gain a better view. Divers were a breed apart. Ethan was as chatty as any of them, exuding the same devil-may-care insouciance that always seemed at odds with their technical expertise. I couldn't really explain it, but I had always loved to be around them, and nothing had changed. I sure had warmed to Ethan.

As I got settled behind the wheel, I wondered if Ethan and Becca were an item. If so, it must be hard for both of them to be on such different career trajectories. Sort of like Lia and her ex. I recalled something Oliver Stone, the filmmaker, once said: *Never underestimate the power of jealousy to destroy. Never forget that.*

While my car was warming up, I called Becca. She answered on the third ring. Her voice was soft, and she sounded young, younger than she was.

I introduced myself, adding how much I was looking forward to meeting her, then asked, "I was wondering if you've heard from your dad."

"What?" she said, her voice strident.

I paused momentarily, trying to understand her unexpected reaction. "Your dad. Have you heard from him?"

"Is this some kind of sick joke?" she asked, sounding appalled, her British accent more pronounced than Ian's.

"No, of course not," I replied, mystified.

"What do you want from me?" she asked, her voice heavy with emotion.

I hesitated, uncertain of my ground. "Truly, I was calling about your dad. I was hoping you were with him."

"This is just cruel!" She hung up.

My mouth agape, I stared at the phone. A moment later, I called back, but she didn't pick up. "Becca," I said after the beep, keeping my voice calm, "I'm so sorry I upset you. Please call me." I left my work, home, and cell phone numbers. I sat awhile longer, trying to understand what had just happened, but couldn't. I looked up the Rocky Point Oceanographic Institute's main phone number and dialed.

"RPOI," a young man with a Downeast accent said. "This is Nate. How can I help you?"

"Is Becca Bennington there?"

"Let me check."

I heard tapping and papers rustling.

"Yup. Want me to ring her room?"

"Yes, please."

"Hold on."

I held on for a good minute before Nate came back on the line.

"Sorry, no answer in her room or at her desk."

"And you don't know where she is?"

"Sorry, no."

"When did she arrive?"

"What did you say your name was?" he asked, suddenly cautious.

"Josie Prescott. I'm a friend of her dad's. It's important that I talk to her."

"All I can do is take a message."

"Sure," I said, and left my contact information, knowing she wouldn't call back.

I headed back to Rocky Point. The snow started up again around Burlington, big flakes swirling in a wild wind.

No matter what I listened to on the radio or what I tried to think about, my mind kept swinging back to Ian. Ellis's instructions echoed in my brain. I tried on different scenarios until I found one that fit. By the time I passed the Amesbury exit, I knew what I needed to do to get Ellis to help find Ian.

Chapter Nine

I pulled onto the shoulder just before the New Hampshire border and punched the button to activate my blinkers. I wanted to look for holes in my idea about how to get Ellis to accept my missing person report. I didn't find any, but I still only gave myself a fifty-fifty chance. I didn't have the hard evidence Ellis wanted, but I was certain I could make one heckuva case nonetheless. Success rested squarely on my ability to communicate persuasively. I rehearsed what I would say for the next ten miles, and when I felt ready, I pulled off onto the shoulder again.

Ellis didn't answer his office line, his cell phone went directly to voice mail, and when I called the station's main number, Cathy told me he wasn't available. I didn't leave a message. I decided it was just as well. Since all I had in my arsenal was my subjective interpretation of events and inductive reasoning, it would be preferable to pitch it in person, rather than on the phone.

Just because I couldn't rouse him by phone, I couldn't conclude that he wasn't at work, so I drove to the police station. Ellis's SUV wasn't there. I swung west to his apartment, a modern condo overlooking Mill Pond, but his vehicle wasn't in that lot, either. I called Zoë, thinking she might know where he was, but as I listened to the droning rings, I glanced at the dashboard time display, and realized why she wasn't picking up. It was 5:22. Zoë was on chauffeur duty. Her daughter, Emma, took ballet at a dance school in a strip mall on Route 1. Her son, Jake, studied karate at a studio three doors down, and she was probably hanging out in one or the other of the parents' observation areas.

Out of ideas, I drove home.

Ellis's SUV was parked in Zoë's driveway, the double-wide one we shared. I pulled in beside him. My house, the one I rented from Zoë, was a miniature of hers, an in-law home built during a more stately time.

I stepped out of my car and looked toward my second-floor bedroom, comforted to see the soft golden glow from the window. I always left a light on, a private welcome home. I climbed Zoë's porch steps and rang the bell.

Ellis opened the door wearing a lobster apron, the red claws circling his neck.

"It's lobster night."

"It's the first apron I found. I'm baking brownies, a surprise for the kids."

"What a guy."

"Come on in. Want a drink?"

"No. I need you to find a judge."

"You have evidence?"

"Yes."

He stepped back so I could enter.

"Tell me about it."

I followed him into Zoë's cheery red and white kitchen. Her red mixer was in use. The oven was preheating. I pushed aside a momentary flash of guilt for interrupting him.

"From what you told me about the law, I understand that you can't accept a missing persons report of a nondisabled adult, unless the person is in danger — right?"

"Right."

"Ian is."

"Convince me and I'll convince a judge."

"Ian's daughter hasn't heard from him. She freaked out at the question. Something is wrong."

"Maybe he lied to you about her. If there was a serious breach that he's hoping to repair, it's possible he didn't tell her he was coming — he just planned to show up."

I shook my head. "You can come up with plausible alternatives forever, Ellis, but why would you? Look at the evidence." I held up my index finger. "One: Ian stood Lia up for a dinner date that he told me he was looking forward to." I raised another finger. "Two: Ian stood me up for a lunch date he told me he was looking forward to." A third finger went up. "Three: No one at the hotel has seen him, yet he hasn't checked out." I lifted my pinkie. "Four: His daughter hasn't heard from him, and she went bananas at my innocent question. She hung up on me, Ellis." I lowered my hand. "I'm not an alarmist. You know I'm not. Taken together, these events lead to only one conclusion — Ian is missing. Add in that he's a foreign national and I can't imagine that you wouldn't want to reassure yourself that he's okay."

Ellis kept his eyes on mine while he ran my points through some kind of filter in his brain. "How do you know no one at the hotel has seen him and that he hasn't checked out?"

"My information isn't to-the-minute current, but the last time I asked, Taylor, the owner, talked about their policy of honoring guests' requests to be left alone when they hang out a Do Not Disturb sign. If he'd checked out I think she would have told me so. If she'd seen him, it would have come up in conversation."

"Okay," he said, stripping off his apron and hanging it on a hook by the pantry door. "Let me find out which judge is on duty and I'll get the paperwork started."

"How long will that take?" I asked, my impatience flaring.

"Half an hour, more or less. I'll call the hotel first and confirm he still hasn't checked out."

"I'll finish mixing the batter and put it in the fridge."

He patted my shoulder and left the room.

I turned off the oven, finished with the batter, and loaded the dishwasher. I glanced at the wall clock. Only eight minutes had passed. I sat at Zoë's kitchen table, the place where I'd played tiddlywinks with Emma and Jake, shared countless meals, enjoyed more than a few martinis, confided my fears and anxieties to Zoë, and listened to hers. It was fully dark and still snowing. I watched fluffy flakes whirl and flutter as they passed into the light cast by the yellow bulb mounted over the back door. I hoped traffic from the airport wasn't snarled by the legion of drivers who seemed unable to handle a little snow. I wanted to see Ty. He hadn't told me how his meeting went, which usually meant something was complicated.

I leaned back and stretched. Where, I asked myself, was Ian?

"Let's go," Ellis said, startling me. "Judge Alexander is at home, and I need you to come with me. She may want to talk to you."

"Of course."

Ellis unlocked the passenger door and held it for me while I hoisted myself up. As we drove, I said a private prayer that Judge Alexander would sign the order.

Judge Hazel Alexander came to the front door with a Wii remote in her hand. She wore gray sweatpants and a red hoodie over a gray T-shirt. She was curvy and fit, older than me — about Ellis's age, I guessed — with brown shoulder-length hair and blue eyes. Ellis and I stood under an overhang, protected from the steady snow.

"You're going to screw up my timing, Ellis. I've just figured out how to get some English on my bowling ball."

Cackles and raspberries exploded from a room on the left. "English!" a man called, laughing. "More like Latin!"

"My husband," she said, "the academic.

When he plays games, he makes a hammerhead look like a cozy companion." She glanced at me. "And you are?"

"Josie Prescott," Ellis replied. "My witness. I brought her in case you want to question her directly."

"Your Honor," I said by way of greeting.

"Ms. Prescott." She turned back to Ellis. "So, what can I do for you?"

"Sign this petition." He handed her a blue-jacketed sheaf of papers.

The judge flipped through, reading with expert eyes. "You feeling all right, Ellis? A grown man isn't where you thought he'd be and you want me to authorize a look-see of his hotel room? You have a fever? A touch of sun? You been on the toodle?"

Ellis didn't flinch. "No, ma'am. Based on solid evidence, I've concluded that it's appropriate for us to locate this missing foreign national."

"Where's he from?"

"England."

"When did he arrive in this country?"

While the judge peppered Ellis with questions, I peeked through the crack left by the semiclosed door into her house. French doors dressed with pale white sheer curtains separated the room on the left from the rest of the house. I couldn't see in, but I could sure hear the fun squeals. One child at least, a boy.

Judge Alexander raised her eyes to meet mine. Her expression wasn't humorless. It was grave.

"Before I take away one of Mr. Bennington's most sacred rights, his right to privacy, I want to hear why you're so convinced that he intended to keep the date with Ms. Lia Jones. Don't give me the summary. Tell me exactly what he said and what you said. Word for word, or as close as you can get. Don't lie. Don't embellish. Don't leave anything out."

I bristled at the implication I would do any of those things, but I didn't let my resentment show. Instead, I did as I was told.

"I had a party last Saturday night. Midway through, I asked, 'How about dinner tomorrow?' He said he'd love to, but he couldn't. Lia just agreed to have dinner with him. I also invited him to a Christmas concert, Sunday evening, after dinner. I thought he might want to bring Lia. That got a lukewarm 'maybe.' I think he had other ideas about what they might do after dinner."

The judge was not amused. "Your thoughts aren't evidence."

I regrouped on the fly. "Ian was excited about the plans he was making." I recounted how he playfully deputized me to convince Lia to agree to dinner by bragging on our connection to Churchill. "We had brunch the next day, on Sunday. Just the two of us. He was happy. He talked about seeing Lia and about his plans to drive to Boston to see his daughter the next day. We set a time to have lunch the next day before he left for Boston. Just about the last thing he told me was that he was going back to his hotel to take a nap because he wanted to rest up before his big date with Lia." I paused, wanting the judge to feel the gravitas I hoped I was conveying. "He came all the way from England to see his daughter — and me. We're related, and we'd just found one another. No way would he vanish without a word."

"Have you spoken to Ms. Jones to confirm this story?" the judge asked Ellis.

"Yes, ma'am."

After a few seconds, she nodded and said, "Give me the form."

She signed it, Ellis thanked her, and we left. As the door closed, sounds of fun still rippled from that room on the left. We slogged through calf-high drifts of snow to his SUV.

"When did you speak to Lia?" I asked once we were en route.

"While you were finishing mixing up my brownies. I called both the hotel and Lia."

"What do you know about Judge Alexander?"

"She's tough, but fair. And she recently learned to put some English on her bowling balls."

"It sounded like they were having fun, didn't it?" I asked. "Do you bowl?"

"No. But if you want to try a line or two, I'd be up for placing a small wager. As you know, I'm pretty athletic, so I'm sure I'll get up to speed quickly."

"You are a prevaricator, my friend."

"Does that mean you don't believe me?"

"You forget I've played miniature golf with you. You're a snake in the grass, coiled and ready to strike."

"Where do you think Ian is?" Ellis asked, changing the mood, bringing home the trouble I was certain we'd find.

I stared out the window, seeing nothing. I couldn't express my worst fears aloud. I wouldn't. I didn't have to. I knew Ellis shared them.

"I don't know," I said.

We rode the rest of the way to the hotel in silence.

Chapter Ten

Jonah Carmona, the co-owner of the Rocky Point Sea View Hotel, stood at the front desk chatting with a middle-aged couple. An older man sat on one of the love seats near the fireplace, reading the sports section from today's *Boston Globe.* A teenage girl sat across from him, her chin resting on her hand, watching the flames lick the edges of the already blackened wood. She looked dreamy, a million miles away. From the sweet aroma, I could tell they were burning applewood.

The woman standing at the counter was thumbing through a binder of menus, pausing at the plastic sleeve containing the one from the Blue Dolphin. I recognized it from the restaurant's distinctive diving-dolphin logo. She said something to Jonah that I couldn't hear.

"The roads should be clear," Jonah said to the couple. "It takes more than a few inches of snow to slow us down around here."

The man looked at his companion. She nodded.

"All right then," he said. "The Blue Dolphin it is. Would you make us a reservation? For eight?"

"You bet," Jonah said. "I'll leave a message on your room voice mail once it's confirmed."

They thanked him, and Jonah left them still scanning the binder and approached us, giving me a wide smile, but looking askance at Ellis.

Jonah was about five-nine and built like a wrestler, wiry and tough. His wavy black hair was cut short. His red and black flannel shirt and black jeans were his winter uniform; in the summer he wore collared T-shirts and khaki shorts. Jonah had a go-with-the-flow attitude toward most things, unlike his wife, Taylor, who was more of a by-the-book sort of gal.

"Is there somewhere private we can talk?" Ellis asked.

"Of course," Jonah said, no longer smiling. "Give me a minute."

He disappeared through a door marked PRIVATE. Two minutes later a thin young woman with curly blond hair appeared behind the front desk. Jonah stuck his head out from the private area and waggled his fingers, inviting us in.

"We don't need to sit," Ellis said in the hallway to Jonah's back, stopping him from leading us into an office. "I didn't want to disturb your guests." He handed over the signed order. "When I spoke to you earlier, you said Ian Bennington had not checked out, is that correct?"

"Right."

"When was he supposed to leave?"

"Monday morning."

"What's your policy about people who stay beyond their scheduled departure?" Ellis asked.

"It depends how full we are. In the summer, when we're booked solid, we'll follow up within a few minutes of checkout, which is eleven, and we keep at it until they leave. This time of year, there's no urgency, but of course, we tried to contact him. We've left two voice mails a day apart, and we left them on both his cell phone and his room messaging system saying that we assume he wants to extend his stay. I called the first time myself. That was on Monday, around noon. Taylor called up to his room on Tuesday about the same time. We e-mailed him, too, so we'd have the communication in writing. We told him that we'll run his credit card on a day-by-day basis for the room charge, and that's what we've done."

"When was the last time you saw him?"

"Sunday, early afternoon. He said hello on his way in. When Josie asked about him the last time, telling me he'd missed some appointments, I checked his keycard usage and our security photos. He left the hotel through the lobby around three. A couple of minutes later, he drove out of the lot. He hasn't entered his room since I saw him on Sunday. No one has."

"That's very helpful," Ellis said. "We may need to take that testimony as a formal statement, but for now, let's go look at his room."

A red and blue laminated DO NOT DISTURB sign hung from room 218's brass doorknob. Jonah knocked on the door with a shave-and-a-haircut beat three times, waiting a few seconds between sequences.

"Mr. Bennington?" he called, his mouth close to the door. "Mr. Bennington? We're coming in." He slid his master keycard through the slot and opened the door.

Ellis stepped in first, then Jonah, then me. We sidestepped to avoid two small pieces of paper lying just over the threshold. They were preprinted notes from housekeeping inviting him to call if he wanted anything, explaining that because he'd hung the DO NOT DISTURB sign on his door, they weren't coming in to make up the room. My eyes flew around the room. I'd hoped to find Ian wearing headphones, deep in writing or painting or something, and I'd dreaded that I'd discover his corpse, that I'd learn he'd suffered a heart attack or had a stroke and was dead. From my vantage point, I could see the entire room, even into the bathroom and out over the small balcony into the blackness beyond. Ian wasn't in sight.

Jonah and I stood against the back wall watching Ellis work. He opened the double closet doors and got onto his knees to peer under the bed, which from all appearances hadn't been slept in.

"So the maid was in here Sunday?" Ellis asked.

"Right. Late morning."

A brown leather shaving kit hung from a towel bar in the bathroom. A large black hard-sided suitcase rested on a luggage rack. A pair of cordovan slip-on shoes stood neatly aligned under it. A laptop computer, with the lid closed, sat on the desk next to a stack of papers, including one I could identify from afar: the kind of paper sleeve car rental companies issue. The contract would be folded up inside.

"I don't see his wallet," I said. "Or his cell phone."

"His car keys seem to be missing, too," Ellis said.

Ellis walked to the sliding glass doors that opened onto the balcony. He stood with his back to us while he made a phone call.

The call lasted longer than I expected. Ellis was checking something, not merely reporting or issuing orders.

"Two officers will be arriving shortly," Ellis told Jonah as he swung around to face us. He surveyed the room as if he thought he might have missed something. "I've asked them to go through everything." He shifted his eyes to my face. "Ian's car hasn't been returned to the rental company."

"Which means Ian left his room on Sunday," I said, "under his own steam, drove off the property, and hasn't been seen or heard from since."

"That about sums it up."

"Isn't the car outfitted with GPS?"

"So they say. But they need permission from higher-ups to track it. Once I get back to the station, I'll fax them a copy of the court order, which has to be reviewed by their legal team." He brushed it aside. "If we get lucky, it'll be days, not weeks, before they respond."

My shoulders tensed. I understood the rental car company's position. It was the same as the hotel's. Privacy. I got it, but that didn't mean I liked it.

Jonah closed the door behind us, leaving the DO NOT DISTURB sign in place.

Ellis thanked him, and we left.

As we walked down the freshly shoveled pathway to the parking lot, I asked, "What do we do now?"

Ellis double-clicked his remote, and the SUV's lights flicked on and off.

"We find him."

Ty's flight landed at Boston's Logan Airport on time at six, and he got home just before eight thirty. After a late dinner, Ty and I went over to Zoë's for dessert, Ellis's brownies, warm from the oven. I sat on the floor by the fire, leaning against a pillow, braced against a club chair. Ty sat in the chair. If I leaned my head to the right, I could nuzzle his knee with my cheek.

"There's more than ninety-five thousand miles of shoreline in the country," Ty said, "the overwhelming majority of it unmonitored. We want to set up trip wires, figuratively speaking. That's why my boss formed this committee — to identify and implement tactics to spot breaches sooner, rather than later."

Ellis took a poker from the black metal hanging tool stand and flipped the top log in the smoldering pile. Orange and red flames flared for a few seconds. He balanced another log on top and the fire burst to life.

"What's an example of a trip wire?" Zoë asked.

"A webcam configured to recognize heat or motion."

"Out in the middle of nowhere?" she asked, incredulous. "Can that really be done?"

"Sure."

"We're going to install security cameras along stretches of deserted shoreline?" I asked.

"We might. Some communities already have. You sound surprised. How come?"

"Because there aren't any cameras installed in the corridor outside Ian's room. We're not even able to protect people where they sleep, let alone on tens of thousands of miles of unguarded coastline. It's hopeless."

"It's not hopeless," Ty said. "It's just deciding to do it. Like going to the moon. Once we put our collective mind on the problem, we solved it."

"I guess," I said, my eyes on the fire.

"We're doing everything we can to find Ian, Josie," Ellis said quietly. "We've sent out BOLOs for him and his car. We've got alerts on his credit cards. I have calls in to his daughter."

I watched flames touch the smoldering logs. I knew Ellis was doing his best. I also knew it wasn't good enough.

Later, when Ty and I were on my porch, Ty paused with the key in the lock.

"I still think there's a good chance Ian will resurface with one heck of a good story."

I rubbed his cheek, knowing he was only saying it to bolster me, and I was grateful. It allowed me to hold on to a glimmer of hope, and sometimes a glimmer is enough to be able to navigate your way out of despair.

Upstairs, I switched off my lamp and closed my eyes and surrendered myself to the dark.

Chapter Eleven

Just before ten next morning, Wednesday, I sat in my office, staring out the window, trying to talk myself out of my funk. There was no news of Ian, and Becca hadn't called back.

"Get to work," I said aloud.

I didn't move. The snow had stopped overnight, and the temperature had warmed to heat wave status, forty-five degrees. Mica embedded in the granite boulders that dotted the woods twinkled like faraway stars. A small bird, black with white tips on some of its feathers, caught my eye as it fluttered through the thick green branches of a pine tree. I wondered why, speculating that it might have built a nest on a protected branch.

A buzz from the intercom startled me. It was Cara calling to tell me Lia was on line one. I grabbed the phone.

"Lia!" I said. "Tell me you have news."

"No. But I need to talk. Can you have lunch?"

"Of course," I said.

We arranged to meet at twelve thirty at the Portsmouth Diner. I stared at the receiver for a moment before placing it in the cradle. She sounded both morose and agitated. Something was up.

Lia was in a booth toward the back when I arrived at the diner.

"Thank you for coming on such short notice," she said.

I slid onto the bench across from her. "You seem upset."

"I am." She shook her head and sighed. "I'm a mess."

The waitress appeared. I ordered a grilled cheese sandwich, a random decision. Lia ordered a Caesar salad, no meat.

As soon as the waitress stepped away, Lia said, "I'm not on such solid ground as I thought I was. I'm so ashamed of myself."

"I don't understand. Why?"

She looked down and began twirling a gold bangle. On the one hand, she looked the same as always, her hair perfectly coiffed, her makeup subtle and elegant, her cherry red silk blouse fitted by an expert. On the other hand, I could see the tension along her jaw and neck, and when she raised her eyes again to mine, there was a sorrowfulness in them that I couldn't miss. I recognized it. I'd felt it. It was the look of grief.

"I know how I sound most of the time — at least lately. Cynical. Jaded. Bitter. I'm sorry."

"You have nothing to apologize for, Lia. Anyone in your situation would feel horrible, and many of us would act way worse than you have."

She straightened her knife, moving it a micro-smidge, then lined up the spoon. "He's moved a girl into his condo — the condo I'm paying for."

"Your ex?"

"The jerk."

"Awful. How do you know?"

"Missy told me this morning."

"Missy?" I asked in disbelief.

Lia snorted. "Everyone wants to be the first to deliver bad news. That way they get to watch."

"That doesn't sound like Missy."

The waitress appeared with food. We didn't speak until she left.

"She's eighteen," Lia said, stabbing a lettuce leaf with a fork. "Her name is Tiffany. He'll live with her, but they'll never marry because that would end my obligation to pay spousal support."

I nibbled at my sandwich, not tasting it. I didn't know what to say.

Lia's story was up there with most women's worst nightmares. Twenty years after her jock-hunky high school boyfriend ditched her for a girl he met on a field trip to the United Nations, he friended her on Facebook. A whirlwind romance ensued, with all her friends singing, "Fairy tales do come true . . . it can happen to you . . ." A month later, she married him, and learned the truth. He was a helluva good talker who couldn't hold a job and had a disastrously wandering eye. I wished I could do more to help Lia recover from the wounds her pride and pocketbook had endured.

She kept talking, expanding on her ex-husband's flaws, her comments becoming more personal and snarkier. When she started in about his bald spot, I stopped listening. I kept my eyes on her face, watching her expression harden, feeling disloyal and guilty in wishing I were anywhere but listening to her repetitive and acerbic rant.

She didn't pause to eat.

I lowered my sandwich onto my plate, my appetite gone. I hoped venting was good for her, suspecting, though, that it would only serve to stir up all the spiteful negativity that surged around her like a maelstrom.

Finally, after ten minutes or more, she stopped. She dropped her fork and it clinked against the bowl. She slid toward the booth opening.

"Oh, God. I'm sorry, Josie. I don't know why I asked you to meet me. I thought I needed to talk. I don't. There's nothing to say and nothing to do, and the more I talk the worse I feel. Forgive me." She stood up. "I'll settle the bill on the way out."

She walked out, her chin up, her back straight. I felt battered.

The waitress hurried over, thinking she was dissatisfied with something. "Is something wrong?"

"Not a bit," I said, forcing a smile. "Could I have some more water, please?"

I pecked away at my sandwich for a few minutes before giving up. I pushed it aside, left a big tip, and fled.

Wes called just as I reached my car.

"You were in Ian's hotel room and you didn't call me afterward," he said.

"Hi, Wes. I'm fine. How are you?"

"Good, good, so did you get any photos?"

"Of course not!"

He sighed, letting me know he was disappointed in me. "I have an info-bomb, but I'm all give and you're all take."

"You know I tell you everything I can, Wes. What's your news?"

"The police have cordoned off Cable Road."

"Why?"

"A couple walking their dog found a man's body."

My heart stopped. I knew the street. Cable Road dead-ended at the ocean. It wasn't the kind of place anyone went in December.

"Tell me," I whispered.

His tone softened, more kid brother than tough-nosed reporter. "I'm sorry, Josie. It's all I know. I'm en route now."

While I waited for the engine to warm up, I called Ty. I got his voice mail.

"They found a man's body, Ty." I paused, thinking of what else to add, but there was nothing. "I'll talk to you later. I love you."

I couldn't think where to go or what to do. I felt muddled, as if I'd just awakened from a drug-induced sleep. I needed more information, but I couldn't think of how to get it. Ellis never opened up. Wes had already told me the little that he knew.

I turned on the radio to the local station, thinking maybe they'd have early details.

They didn't. I listened to the host of a local politically themed talk show discuss the need to expand library hours. The host's name was Al Thornton. His guest, Cherie Hubbard, was a member of the school board.

I decided to drive to my office. I knew myself: Working always helped me cope with life's worst disappointments and losses.

I wasn't even out of the diner parking lot when Al interrupted Cherie, announcing that Wes Smith was on the phone with breaking news. I pulled into a parking spot and set the emergency brake.

Listening to Wes announce that a body had been found, I understood that in all probability Ian was dead, but somehow I couldn't process the information. I was shocked, but at the same time, I wasn't surprised. I'd been braced for bad news for days.

"Who discovered the body, Wes?" Al asked, following up on Wes's announcement with an off-the-cuff interview.

"A local couple — John and Wendy Anderson. They took their dog on a long walk because of the warm weather. If it hadn't been such a nice day, they wouldn't have turned onto Cable Road to look at the water, and who knows when the body would have been found."

"How did he die, Wes?"

"It looks like he was hit by a car."

"I always think hit-and-run accidents are among the most cowardly of acts. It's bad enough to hit someone — but to leave the scene. Come on."

"I agree," Wes said, "but to be fair, we need to stress that the police haven't yet revealed the cause of death."

"Do we have a time of death?"

"Not yet. There are so many variables in making that determination — outside temperature, the fact that it snowed yesterday, what the person was wearing, to name a few."

"Do you know who it is?"

I held my breath, waiting for Wes's reply. Every muscle tensed. I clutched the steering wheel as if I hoped to break it, bracing myself.

"No," Wes said. "Not yet. A British tourist named Ian Bennington was reported missing yesterday, though."

His reply wasn't the least bit reassuring.

"Do we know what Ian Bennington was doing in Rocky Point?"

"He was here to meet Josie Prescott, the owner of Prescott's Antiques and Auctions, who, it turns out, is a distant cousin."

"So sad," Al said. "If it's him and let's repeat for our listeners who might just be turning in — we have no reason to think the corpse found today on Cable Road is Ian Bennington, the missing British tourist, but if it is, it's a real blow. He comes to connect with family and ends up dead."

After Wes's report was finished, I sat in my car for a long time, not crying, exactly, but with tears streaming down my cheeks.

CHAPTER TWELVE

"I can't let you in," Officer F. Meade said. "It's an active crime scene."

I'd run into Officer Meade for years, and I'd always wondered what the *F* stood for, but I'd never asked. She didn't encourage chitchat. She was a tall ice blond, with a no-nonsense demeanor and unexpressive eyes. Her hair was pulled back into a tight bun. She was thin, more scrawny than willowy. I had nothing against her, but I didn't know anything in her favor either.

"I just want to take a quick look," I said, knowing she'd refuse.

"I'm sorry, Josie."

We stood on the Ocean Avenue side of the yellow crime scene tape that stretched across the entry to Cable Road. Ellis's SUV was parked three cars back from the intersection of Cable and Ocean, on Ocean, behind a patrol car and a CSI van. A vehicle that could be Ian's Taurus was parked at the ocean end of Cable. I couldn't see the tags. A man wearing an orange CSI safety vest over a heavy blue parka was on his hands and knees, video-recording the street where it abutted the curb, his camera barely moving. Branches from a scraggly bush hung low, nearly touching the asphalt where he was working. A white van with ROCKY POINT MEDICAL EXAMINER'S OFFICE stenciled on the side was parked sideways across the street, blocking most of the ocean view. I squatted to look under it and saw a mélange of legs and feet. I stood up.

"Is that where the body was found?" I asked, my eyes on the technician.

"Yes."

I glanced around. "I don't see Chief Hunter."

"He's here."

"Was he able to make an identification?"

"You'll need to ask him."

My eyes on the technician, I asked, "What's he recording?"

"I don't know."

"I heard on the news," I said, "that the body was found by a couple walking their dog."

She shot a sidewise glance at me. "What else did you hear?"

"That it was Ian Bennington."

"That's what I heard, too," she said.

My throat closed unexpectedly; I swallowed hard to quell my spiking emotion. My chest heaved, and I shut my eyes for a moment.

"Did you know him?" she asked, her tone softer, kinder.

"Yes."

"I'm sorry."

We both focused on the technician.

"Can't you tell me anything?" I asked. "Ian was my cousin."

She shook her head.

I pointed at the Taurus. "Is that Ian's car?"

"I don't know."

I spotted black tire marks near the technician's knees and traced them backward to where they started, near where I stood. I looked back at the technician. I could see Officer Meade's face out of the corner of my eye.

"Ian was murdered, wasn't he?" I asked, aiming for a neutral, casual tone.

She nodded, one nod, unaware that I saw her reaction.

"They're considering all possibilities," she said, revealing nothing, a trick she must have learned from Ellis.

"I ask because these tire tracks start here," I said, pointing, "and go all the way to where the technician is working. Someone spun off Ocean going fast. Do you see how they get darker and darker, then swerve to the right, then stop altogether? The car must have sped up along Cable, only stopping when it hit Ian."

"The technician will record everything," Officer Meade said.

"This wasn't an accident," I said. "This was murder."

I dug around in my tote bag for my phone and texted Ellis: *I'm here. Can I help w/ the ID?*

I kept my eyes on my phone, waiting for his reply, looking up every few seconds in case he responded in person. A minute after I hit the SEND button, Ellis's head appeared at the front of the van. He saw me and strode in my direction.

He was wearing an anorak open to show a navy bluc blazcr, gray slacks, and a pale blue shirt. His tie was blue with small gray dots. In the unforgiving daylight, his scar looked dark and glossy.

"Josie," Ellis said, when he reached me. His eyes and voice communicated sympathy and empathy and pathos, all in that one word, my name.

"Can I see him?"

He nodded, and Officer Meade lifted the

tape. I crouched to pass under it. Ellis and I walked to the rear of the van. A young man chomping gum like he wanted to kill it leaned against the doors. He wore a black parka with the medical examiner's logo embroidered on it in gold. His wispy blond hair matched his scruffy goatee. His wraparound sunglasses were so dark, I had no sense that there were eyes behind the lenses.

"Open it up," Ellis told him. "She's a relative and can give an official ID."

Another technician, this one older and shorter, joined him. Together, they drew out the gurney and unzipped enough of the body bag for me to see the corpse's face.

It was Ian. I stumbled on nothing and grasped Ellis's arm to steady myself. Ian's features were the same as I recalled, but his skin was blue-white.

"Do you know this man?" the older technician asked.

"Yes. That's my cousin, Ian Bennington."

"Thank you."

Ellis turned me around, keeping a hold on my arm.

"I'll give you her name and contact information in a minute," he told the technician. To me, he said, "I'll walk you out." A moment later, he asked, "Are you going to be okay to drive?"

"Yes. Thank you for letting me see him."
"I'll be in touch later."
"Was he murdered?"
"It's too early in the investigation to make that kind of determinations."
"I know he was."
Ellis didn't speak again until we reached Officer Meade. "Josie is going now."
I patted Ellis's arm, ducked under the tape, and walked slowly to my car. I sat for a few minutes letting the reality sink in. Ian was dead. I'd never get to know him. I'd never see him again. The worst part of someone dying is that they're gone. I texted Ty the bad news.
I set off, heading to Lia's spa to keep my promise, the one we'd exchanged, to let one another know as soon as we learned something. Glancing in my rearview mirror just before I turned onto Patchogue Street, I saw Wes's shiny red Ford Focus jerk to a halt not far from where I'd parked.

Lia said she only had a minute, so I led her by the elbow to a corner of the reception area. She had the same pinched look I'd grown to dread seeing over the last few months. The sunniness that had bubbled to the surface at my party was long gone.
"I have bad news," I said. "About Ian."

"He's married and decided to go back to his wife," she said.

"No. He's dead."

She covered her mouth with her hand. "I'm sorry. I didn't mean to sound so . . . What happened?"

"They've just begun the investigation. Some people found his body on Cable Road. I think he was hit by a car, but that's just conjecture."

"When?" she asked.

"I don't know."

"But maybe as long ago as Sunday?"

"I guess. Why?"

"That would mean he didn't stand me up."

I stared at her for several seconds, my stomach tightening, unable to think of how to respond. "That's one way of looking at it, I guess."

"Come on, Josie. I met the guy once. How do you expect me to react?"

"Differently from this." I walked out.

I drove to work. Cara stood up as I entered, her expression somber. Gretchen was on the phone, but her eyes communicated her concern. Neither Sasha nor Fred was in sight.

"You heard," I said.

Cara nodded. "Gretchen gets breaking news tweets from the *Seacoast Star.* I'm so sorry, Josie. So very, very sorry. Ian was a fine man."

I swallowed tears, thanked her, nodded a thank-you at Gretchen, and headed into the warehouse.

I went to Hank's area, thinking I could use a cuddle, but he was asleep in his basket, and I didn't want to disturb him. Gretchen had been busy. Hank was lying on his Christmas pillow, which had a red and green tartan plaid removable slipcover Cara had sewn for him. He had his own Christmas tree, too, a four-foot-tall artificial number adorned with whatever ornaments Gretchen thought might please him, but no tinsel to tempt him. There were several mice, a stuffed toy in the shape of a lobster, and a dozen or more birds. Closer to Christmas, she'd tuck his gifts under the tree: new felt mice, bags of his favorite kitty treats, and a catnip-infused burlap bag that he loved to roll around on. After our celebration lunch, I decided, we'd troop in here and watch Hank open his gifts.

"Sleep tight, little boy," I whispered, and headed upstairs.

Ty had left a message saying how sorry he was to hear the news. I texted Zoë, too.

Although she might already have heard from Ellis, I wanted her to know I was upset. She texted back, inviting us to dinner. I accepted, then called every number I had for Becca. She wasn't at Reynard. Her cell phone went to voice mail immediately, indicating she'd turned it off. The man who answered the phone at the Rocky Point Oceanographic Institute said Becca hadn't been in all day.

I called Ethan's cell phone and got him.

"That's really too bad," he said after I told him what was going on, and that I was hoping to reach Becca. "I haven't seen her, though. Or heard from her. If I do — who should I have her call?"

"Me," I said, thinking Ellis wouldn't approve.

"Will do," he said. "The poor kid."

We chatted for another minute about the shock of unexpected death, then ended the call.

I tried to think of something to do, but I couldn't. There was no point in contacting Ellis. At this early stage of the investigation, he wouldn't know much, and I was certain that he wouldn't tell me anything regardless. Time to get to work. I headed downstairs to resume going through the boxes we'd hauled away from the Arkin garage.

After Gail Arkin died peacefully at ninety-four, her niece, Sarah Arkin, asked us to buy everything in Aunt Gail's home. Since Sarah was herself in her sixties and had just retired to Scottsdale, she was focused on downsizing, not acquiring. Buying full households was fabulous for us. Inevitably we'd secure valuable stock for the tag sale, and sometimes we'd find a gem. So far, we'd found hundreds of salable items of low to medium value, but no treasures.

We'd cordoned off a section of the warehouse to hold everything. Chairs were stacked, side tables abutted one another, and boxes of china and flatware covered the dining room table. More boxes, these filled with kitchen miscellany and knickknacks, were off to one side next to the contents of the garage. I set up a video recorder on a tripod and opened a box we'd numbered 27.

"This is a brown speckled pottery bowl," I said to the camera, creating an annotated video recording documenting each piece, as per Prescott's protocol. I talked as I recorded all sides and angles of each object. "It's unmarked, but in perfect condition. Not worth appraising." I set it aside. "This is a cookie jar, red with white poppy-like flowers." I held it sideways so the bottom faced the camera. "No mark, but charming." I came to a set of Susan Winget "Le Rooster" canisters and set them aside. Zoë didn't have a canister set. These would match her kitchen perfectly. *Yay!* I thought. *A perfect Christmas gift for Zoë.* Next up was a Dedham Pottery rabbit soup tureen with cover, a fun retro piece. Because REGISTERED appeared with the rabbit mark on the bottom, I identified it as 1929–1943. It too was in perfect condition and would sell, I knew, for about $250. I continued on. Most of the objects were nothing-special vintage decorative items from the 1940s and 1950s, all of them perfect for the tag sale, certain to find loving homes. The redware vessel depicting an African American preacher with clasped hands and a brimmed hat that I extracted from box 28, however, was a different ball of wax altogether. It was crafted with superior artistry and detail, and if it was authentic, it was a rare and extraordinary example of early American folk art.

I turned off the recorder, notated where I was leaving off, and called to the front to ask Sasha to join me.

I held up the vessel as she approached and said, "Looky what I found."

Sasha didn't reach for it. Instead, she kept her eyes on my face. "I heard about Ian," she said, "that he was run over and that it might have been deliberate."

"I hadn't heard that last part."

"Wes tweets a lot. Anyway, it's just so awful . . . but I do understand how you're feeling."

"Thank you." Sasha was uncomfortable with emotion, so I knew what this expression of sympathy was costing her. I met her eyes. "It's kind of surrealistic, to tell you the truth. I had no family. Then I had Ian. Now he's dead."

She tucked her hair behind her ear. "I know people say they understand all the time, but I mean it. My best friend's mother was murdered. Katrina Wilson. You've met her."

My eyes rounded. "What?" I placed the vessel on the worktable. "When?"

She lowered her eyes. "We were ten. We lived next door to one another. We were at Katrina's house playing with our Barbie dolls when her dad shot her mother."

"Oh, my God, Sasha."

She nodded, acknowledging my reaction.

"We heard the shot, and talked about it. We figured it was a car backfiring. Jon Myerson was a hot-rod guy. He lived across the street and was always doing something with cars. Mr. Wilson came into Katrina's room and said good-bye, be a good girl. He walked out and we heard another shot. He killed himself. Katrina and I have always wondered why he didn't kill us, too. Katrina says she wasn't worth killing, that he didn't love her as much as he loved her mom."

"No, no. He must have loved her too much to kill."

She shrugged. "Maybe. I almost never talk about it. It doesn't matter. It's just . . . I remembered how much I hated it when people told me they understood how I was feeling. How could they? Had their best friend's father killed her mother while they were playing dolls?" She paused. "I wanted you to know that when I say I understand what it means that your family might have been killed, well, I do."

"I can't imagine what you've been through. I really can't."

"Please don't tell anyone."

"I won't." I smiled, a small one. "Thank you, Sasha." I turned and focused on the vessel. "So, changing the subject . . . I think this might have value. Will you check it out?"

"Of course," she said, her attention riveted. She ran her finger lightly over the hat brim. "It's remarkable, isn't it?"

"Yes." I glanced around. "I've found some nice things." I walked back to the staircase, paused with my hand on the banister, and turned back toward the workstation. Sasha was holding the vessel up to the light. "Sasha?" She looked up. "Thank you."

She nodded, her expression back to normal, detached, but not unfriendly.

Cara's voice crackled over the PA system. Ellis, she said, was on line one and needed to talk to me, urgently.

Chapter Thirteen

"I need you to come to Rebecca Bennington's room here at the institute," Ellis said. "Can you come now?"

"Of course. Why? What's going on?"

"I'll explain when you get here."

Five minutes later, as I turned onto Route 1, I slipped in my earpiece and called Wes. If anyone besides the police would know why I was being summoned, it was him.

For a change, I was the one delivering breaking news.

"Why the institute?" he demanded after I'd explained where I was driving and why I was calling.

"Becca works there sometimes," I said. "It must have something to do with her."

"She's missing," Wes said with relish.

"What?"

"Yup. The police canvass identified two people who live on Ocean near Cable who saw a couple — a man who matches Ian's description and a woman who could be Becca — standing at the end of Cable Street by the ocean on the day Ian died, talking. The woman, maybe Becca, ran away from him after some kind of altercation, and she hasn't been heard from since."

"One sec," I told Wes. I needed to focus. To think. I spun into a strip mall and parked. "I thought Becca wasn't returning my calls because I'd offended her — don't ask me how, because I don't know."

"Apparently not. It looks like she's involved somehow."

"Oh, my God, Wes! I can't believe this." Dread followed shock, and I felt the color drain from my cheeks. "Did the witnesses see Becca and Ian fighting?"

"Not exactly. There was an older guy outside getting his place done up for Christmas, you know, twirling garlands around the lamppost, that kind of thing. The female witness was inside her house, placing holiday candles in her living room windows. The old man thought it was weird that people would simply stand by the ocean in December, even though it was kind of a warm day, but that was all he noticed. He was more focused on getting his wreath attached securely than on a random couple sightseeing, which is what he assumed they were doing. The woman says she saw the couple talking. There were lots of gestures that, in her mind, looked angry. Then the man reached for the woman to grab her. The woman shook her head, no, no, no, and ran toward a car. The woman's baby started crying, and she didn't think about them anymore until the police asked her what she saw."

"This was Sunday afternoon?"

"Right. Sometime around three thirty or four. Neither one of them can get the timing closer than that."

"And neither of them saw Ian get run over?" I asked.

"So they say."

"Do you doubt them?"

"Nope. Just saying."

"What makes the police think Becca has vanished? Maybe she's just freaked out for some reason and is holed up in a cabin in the woods somewhere. Ian told me she's pretty private."

"If the police left you a voice mail and sent you an e-mail telling you your dad was dead, wouldn't you respond?"

"Yes."

"Plus, she hasn't used her cell phone, a credit or debit card, or her E-ZPass since Sunday. But on Sunday at two minutes after six, she withdrew seven hundred dollars from an ATM near her Boston apartment. That's her bank's daily limit. The police have put out a BOLO for her and her vehicle, a silver Prius." He lowered his voiced conspiratorially. "They think there's a chance she killed Ian and booked."

I was appalled. "No. No way."

"Way," Wes said ghoulishly.

"It can't be!"

"Why not?"

I had no answer. It was just too horrific to think of a daughter killing her father. I closed my eyes, hoping to chase away the nightmare vision of a girl killing her dad.

"So what does the Rocky Point Oceanographic Institute have to do with anything?" Wes asked.

I opened my eyes and stared at passing traffic, seeing nothing. "Becca roomed there sometimes."

"Take pictures."

"Of what?"

"Of whatever I can use. You owe me, Josie. It's time to pay up."

The Rocky Point Oceanographic Institute had just celebrated its seventy-fifth anniversary. Built in the years before World War II, it had been the brainchild of a

Reynard University alumnus, Christopher Foley. A marine biologist, Foley had shepherded the institute from inception to international acclaim bequeathing it to Reynard with an endowment designed to ensure it thrived.

The building itself was a sprawling one-story fieldstone structure built on a high cliff overlooking a hundred feet of rugged coastline. I turned off Ocean Avenue into the parking lot, parked near the front door, and followed the winding pathway to the entryway at the southernmost end.

A young man sat behind the reception desk, a low pine plank counter. As soon as he spoke, I recognized his Downeast twang. He was Nate, the man I'd spoken to when I'd called trying to find Becca. He was tall and thin, in his midtwenties. His hair was brown and crewcut-short.

I told him my name, and he nodded as if he were expecting me. He punched three digits on his phone. "Josie Prescott's here." He hung up and told me, "Someone will be right out."

"You're from Maine," I said.

He grinned. "Calais. Most beautiful place on earth."

"You embrace the dialect."

"What dialect?" he asked with assumed

innocence,

I half-smiled and turned to look out the window.

A minute later, Ellis pushed through from a heavy wooden inside door. "Thanks for coming," he said. He nodded at Nate and held the door open until I was through. "You've heard about Ian?"

"Yes."

"I'm sorry, Josie."

We were in a long, wide hallway. A wall of windows on the right looked out over a large open room. I saw cubicle-style workstations, long stainless-steel worktables, and chest-high round tanks, their diameters ranging from six to ten feet. Three men huddled by one of the tanks, staring at a meter mounted on the side. A woman stood next to a worktable, her concentration apparent.

"Was it murder?" I asked.

"The ME hasn't announced her findings yet."

"I know," I said. "But what do you think?"

Ellis stopped walking and turned toward me. "I think we need to wait for the report."

"Why am I here?" I asked, giving up.

"We're investigating what appears to be a break-in. You mentioned that Becca had some valuable art, but I don't see anything. I was hoping you might recognize something

I don't, or at least, that you'll be able to tell me more specifically what we're looking for."

Ellis turned to look through the glass panels. I followed his gaze, past the equipment and furnishings to the bank of windows on the other side and the forest beyond. A police officer in uniform stood by one of the workstations that faced the window. He was watching as a beautiful blonde tapped into a computer. The blonde's name was Katie. I'd met her years earlier in her role as the Rocky Point police tech expert.*

Ellis pointed. "That's Becca's workstation. After we're done with her room, I'll ask you to go through her desk, to see if you spot anything."

"Sure."

The corridor ended in a T, and we turned left. Fifty feet farther on, we turned right. Becca's room was sixth in. Officer Griffin, who'd been on the force for nearly thirty years, stood with his back to the door, his arms crossed.

"Thanks, Griff," Ellis said, and Griff stepped aside. Ellis swung open the door

* Please see *Lethal Treasure.*

and waited for me to enter before following me in.

"Oh, God, Ellis," I said.

A window that overlooked the ocean was broken, and an icy chill permeated the space. Clothes were strewn across the floor. The twin-sized mattress was upended and shredded. The plain vanilla white cotton sheets and pillowcases were ripped. The furniture was standard college dorm room. The shelves on the built-in bookcase were empty. Books lay in haphazard heaps on the hardwood floor, some open, their pages crumpled, others splayed, spine up. There were no rugs or pictures or decorative pillows. The room was Spartan, designed for short-term bunking, not for settling in.

"The techs are done. I'll give you gloves, so you can feel free to open anything, look anywhere, touch at will. Take your time. If you find anything, tell Griff."

"Any security cameras?" I asked.

"No. Not even in the labs or work areas."

I spun to face him. "How can that be?"

"Other than painting every decade or so and keeping up with whatever technology the scientists need, they see no reason to fuss. That's a quote from the director. This is their first break-in."

"It's comforting to know this kind of place

exists," I said, scanning the walls, looking for picture hooks, or holes where picture hooks might have been, seeing none. The walls were paneled in old-style knotty pine, and it would require a careful examination to spot thin nail holes amid the gnarly imperfections. If I assumed the paintings were hidden, and if I was in a hurry, the mess I was looking at would be exactly what I'd leave behind. "If the thief was after the paintings, he thought they were hidden."

"Tell me about them," Ellis said.

"I've never seen them, so everything I'm telling you is via Ian and Ethan." I described the two miniatures. "If they're real, they're worth several hundred thousand dollars each."

He soft-whistled as he looked around. "If you were Becca, where would you hide them?"

"In a safety-deposit box."

"There's no record of her having one."

"Ian said she was thinking of having them appraised. Maybe they're safe and sound in some reputable dealer's vault."

"We'll check." Ellis made a note. "If you were going to hide them here, where would you put them?"

I pointed to a thick book with an ordinary-looking dark red binding. "I'd get a fake book and place it on that shelf among all the others. You know what I mean, right? A hollowed-out book."

"These are real."

"Maybe I'd tuck the paintings in a corner of the mattress."

"We examined both the mattress and the box spring for a slit among the slashes. I figured that if Becca was going to hide something there, she'd use a sharp blade and create a single incision along a seam, maybe even stitching it up after she secreted the paintings. We didn't find anything."

"Did you move the furniture?" I asked. "Maybe she taped the paintings to the backside of the chest or desk."

He nodded. "Nothing."

"The paintings themselves are watercolor on vellum," I told Ellis, "probably encased behind protective glass, and most likely, they're in period-appropriate gilt frames. You won't find any trace of paint, but there may be flecks of gilt left behind."

He made a note. "Good. I'll ask the technicians to check their samples. What else?"

"They should test any residue they find. If the paintings are in silver frames, for example, they may find a bit of tarnish that rubbed off on fabric. If they're in wooden frames, perhaps some furniture polish or wax or oil left a mark on something."

"Got it."

I approached a wall, detached the mini-flashlight I kept latched to my belt, and began examining a swath running horizontally at eye level, where art would logically be hung, looking for holes.

Two men came into view through the missing window. They wore matching dark green maintenance outfits. One carried a roll of heavy plastic.

"Quick response," Ellis said, his eyes on them. "Looks like you won't freeze to death after all."

"A good thing."

I continued my inspection. I found scratches, mars, nicks, and nubs galore, but no evidence that anyone had ever hung a picture. Ellis's phone rang, and he stepped out into the hallway to take the call. When he was done, he stuck his head back into the room.

"I've got to go," he said. "Don't forget to have Griff take you to Becca's desk when you're done here. Call me when you leave, okay?"

I promised I would, doubting that I'd have any news to report.

As I worked, I took a few snapshots. I

didn't know whether or when I might give them to Wes, but there was no harm in taking them.

I was right about not uncovering any of Becca's secrets. An hour after I started, as I took one last look at the mess in her room, I was as certain as I could be that either the thief had found the paintings or they'd never been here in the first place.

Chapter Fourteen

I told Griff the bad news, that I had no news, that as far as I could tell, Becca's room contained no secrets, and he brought me to her workstation. He paused by one of the glass doors built into the wall, his hand on the knob, and I could see why — he didn't want to interrupt Katie and the police officer. Their conversation didn't look like an altercation exactly, but it sure looked like something.

Katie was annoyed. She pointed at the computer and shook her head no. The police officer said something, and Katie shook her head again, more furiously this time. The officer shrugged and said something to which Katie didn't reply. She tapped some keys, sat at the desk, and began disconnecting cables. Evidently, Katie wasn't mad at the officer; she was irritated at the situation. I gathered she couldn't access something and was therefore taking the machine away.

Griff opened the door.

The room smelled of the ocean, briny. I could almost taste the salt. It was cooler than the rest of the place, and more humid, maybe from the open tanks of ocean water. We walked across the concrete floor to Becca's workstation.

"This is Josie Prescott," Griff told the officer.

His badge said his name was Officer Pete Rivera. He was young, in his early twenties, with black hair combed back off his forehead and skin the color of honey.

"She's here to look through Becca's desk. You got gloves for her?"

"Yup," Officer Rivera said. He reached into a side pocket and handed me a pair of blue plastic gloves.

I put them on.

Griff nodded at me but spoke to his colleague. "I've got to get back to the room. Use a separate evidence bag for each thing she finds. Mark them properly. Walk her out when she's done, then come find me."

"Will do," Officer Rivera said.

Griff left.

Katie was coiling cords and cables. "I'll be out of here in a minute."

Officer Rivera and I watched Katie finish

up. She lifted the computer and all its accessories onto a wheeled cart and pushed it to the door.

I sat on the desk chair. There was nothing on the top of the desk, not even a pen.

"This was just a temporary office," I said. "I doubt she kept much here."

At first glance, it seemed I was right. The top left drawer held miscellaneous office supplies, a pad of yellow Post-it notes, a stapler, a plastic Scotch tape dispenser, and a stapler. The next drawer down held sundry food-related items: takeout-sized paper-wrapped salt and pepper containers, napkins, paper-wrapped straws, and plastic-encased portions of mayonnaise, ketchup, mustard, and soy sauce. The bottom drawer held personal items, including a lipstick, which I hadn't expected Becca would wear. It was an expensive brand in a dusky pink color called Victorian Rose. I wondered if it was a gift. There was also a ChapStick, a small tube of drugstore brand moisturizer, three purse-sized bottles of hand sanitizer, and a box of Yorkshire Gold tea bags. The center drawer contained paper clips, two no-name ballpoint pens, three disposable mechanical pencils, a No. 2 yellow pencil, and an eraser. The right drawers contained even less. The top one was empty. The middle one contained a wooden box, nicely constructed of ash and rosewood, about 8″ × 12″ × 6″.

I lifted the lid. Inside was a three-inch-deep empty space lined in green felt. I took the box out and turned it over. Nothing. I righted the box and lifted the lid again. Three inches of depth was unaccounted for. I ran my finger along the bottom edge, my heart pounding an extra beat when I felt an indentation. I pushed, and a drawer opened on the left. I eased my index finger in and pulled it all the way out. There were no miniature paintings, but there was a book. I lifted it out. A small oval with the letters *MV* inside had been burned into the wood like a brand, a maker's mark. I placed the box on the desk and turned to the book.

I touched the supple red leather, so soft you could sleep on it, and examined the stitching. It was beautifully bound. Gilt lettering on the cover and spine read "*Poems for My Daughter.* Edited by Ian Bennington." The title page repeated those words, also in gilt, adding in small print at the bottom: "Privately Published. 2007."

The dedication page read "To Becca, with your father's love. You are the finest daughter a man could ever have."

"Look at this," I said.

"What?" Officer Rivera asked.

I held the book open so he could read it.

He read the dedication and said, "Nice."

The first poem was an excerpt from Lord Byron's "Childe Harold's Pilgrimage." It read:

She looks a sea Cybele, fresh from ocean,
Rising with her tiara of proud towers
At airy distance, with majestic motion,
A ruler of the waters and their powers.

I was reaching to turn the page when Officer Rivera cleared his throat and I looked up.

He held up two clear plastic evidence bags, one larger than the other. "Probably you shouldn't touch the box or the book any more than you already have."

"Right. Sure. Sorry."

I slipped them into the bags as he held them open and watched as he sealed and labeled them.

I opened the right-hand bottom drawer, a double-deep one, and came upon two cut-crystal Waterford rocks glasses, a bottle of Pimm's, and another of Royal Lochnager, a single malt Scotch. I stared, my mouth open. That Scotch had been my father's drink.

I touched the label, and I was transported back in time. A memory came to me. We were in our living room. I had a martini. My dad had his Scotch, two fingers, one ice cube, and a splash of water. It was the last time I saw him alive. He asked me what I liked best about living in New York.

"The energy," I said, not having to think about my answer. "I always have the sense that anything is possible."

He laughed. "That's not New York, Josie. That's you."

I sighed and the picture was gone, replaced by an image of Becca, sitting with her dad. She was drinking her Pimm's and lemonade. Her dad sipped his Scotch. *What,* I wondered, *did they talk about?*

I closed the drawer and stood up. Officer Rivera took a step forward.

"That's it," I said.

"Okay, then."

He walked me to the corridor. I felt his eyes on me as I walked to the reception area, but when I glanced back just before the door closed behind me, he wasn't anywhere in sight.

Nate was reading from a thick book called *The Biology and Conservation of Horseshoe Crabs.* He looked to be about halfway through.

"Nate, right?" I asked.

Nate looked up, blinking the horseshoe crabs out of his head.

"Sorry to disturb you," I added.

"No problem," Nate said, smiling. He stuck a thumb in his book to hold his place. "Sorry. I was deep into sperm attachment."

"Who could resist?"

Nate stood, balancing the book on its spine.

"How can I help you?" he asked.

"I don't know if you caught my name . . . I'm Josie Prescott. I knew Becca's dad. We're cousins, actually. As you might imagine, I'm pretty upset about the whole situation."

His grin evaporated. He placed the book on the counter, replacing his thumb with a pad of old-fashioned pink WHILE YOU WERE OUT message notes. "We all are."

"Was she particularly close to anyone here?"

Nate shook his head. "Not that I know of. She'd come in, say hi, and go to work. That's what most of us do."

"When did you see her last?"

"Maybe Monday. The police asked me that, too, and I just don't remember. She signed in on Sunday and she hasn't signed out. I know I haven't seen her today."

"You don't maintain any kind of records about who's on the property at any given time? No time logs or anything?"

"No. We're pretty old-school, pretty informal. We just keep a list of rooms, so we know what's available if someone wants to bunk down."

While I tried to think of something else to ask, I nodded toward his book. "You're into horseshoe crabs."

"Not really." His eyes twinkled. "They just come along for the ride."

I laughed.

"Bad pun, right?" he asked.

"Pretty good, if you ask me," I said.

"My field is lobsters." He patted the book. "This is just light reading."

"Tell me you're joking."

"Sadly, I'm not."

I laughed again. "Who would you say knows Becca best?"

He paused, thinking. "Maybe Ethan Ferguson. They room together in Boston. They seem kind of tight."

"I know he comes up here sometimes. Is he here now, by any chance?"

Nate shuffled through some papers, found a room listing, and shook his head. "Nope. Not since Monday."

"So it's not unusual that no one would see Becca for a day or two or more?"

"Unless you're working with someone on some specific aspect of a project, you have no particular reason to interact with them. As a principal investigator, Becca supervises a bunch of people, grad assistants and so on, but all the fieldwork is conducted autonomously."

"Might some of her grad assistants know where she is?"

"I doubt it. Up here, Becca's all about being in the field."

I handed Nate a card. "If you hear from her, will you call me? It's about some paintings. I really need to talk to her."

"Sure," Nate said.

He slipped the card into his shirt pocket. I glanced back as I closed the outside door. He had already returned to his light reading. I smiled, but I was also resigned to never hearing from him. I knew that when he took my card out of his pocket probably he wouldn't remember who I was or why he had it.

After a quiet dinner at Zoë's featuring her famous beef stew, Ty suggested we watch some TV, hoping it would help me relax.

"You get the impression I'm not relaxed?"

"I get the impression you're going to bust a gut."

"Bust a gut?"

"In a ladylike way, of course."

"Of course."

"I wish Ellis had been home."

"He'll be working late for days on this one."

We settled on a cooking competition reality show, and as I watched, I found myself becoming involved in their stories, rooting for my favorite, enjoying watching their creative choices end up on the plate.

When the show was over, I said, "That really helped take my mind off things."

"You're still anxious."

"I don't know about anxious, but I'm clearly wound up like a spring."

"Take a bubble bath. That always relaxes you."

"I will, but it won't."

"Wake me if you need me."

"There's nothing you can do."

"True, but sometimes having someone who loves you keep you company while doing nothing is just what the doctor ordered."

"You're a wonderful man, Ty."

"You're a wonderful woman, Josie."

After Ty headed up for the night, I sat for a long time thinking about fathers and daughters. For some girls, their relationship with their father was fraught with difficulties or worse. Becca and I, it seemed, were among the lucky ones. Our fathers adored us, supported our dreams, encouraged us, were proud of us, and enjoyed our company. What a gift to give a girl.

I walked slowly upstairs to take a hot bath and then, I hoped, to sleep.

Chapter Fifteen

Thursday morning, I awoke in a swelter of restive apprehension after a night filled with tumultuous dreams where I found myself in empty, dark, labyrinthine alleys running from I didn't know what. It was exhausting, and I got out of bed more tired than when I'd lain down.

Ty had made coffee, a good thing, since I didn't know if I'd have the strength to do so. He'd also left a note. *I might have time for lunch today if you do. XO.*

I poured myself a cup of coffee, sat at my kitchen table, and texted him: *Thanks. I don't know about lunch. I'm all befuddled. XO.*

Moving slowly, I made my way into work. Hank was asleep in his basket, and he didn't wiggle as I moved around changing his water and pouring fresh crunchy bits into his food bowl.

"I'm glad one of us is able to sleep soundly," I told him, but he didn't hear me.

I sat at my desk staring out over bare trees watching an occasional snowflake drift past my window. The meteorologist said a minor squall would be passing through from now until midafternoon, with no accumulation to speak of.

Questions popped into my mind, but no answers followed. I had no idea why Ian had been killed, if it was indeed murder. I didn't know where Becca was or why she'd disappeared. I didn't understand Lia's crass indifference. I didn't know whether Ethan's jocund sprightliness was genuine, or whether his jealousy of Becca's success ran deeper than he was willing to publicly acknowledge. Sarcasm was amusing, but sometimes the speaker's efforts to camouflage a vulnerability only served to highlight it. I didn't understand why Becca's room at the institute had been burglarized. From the damage, the attack seemed personal. Ian came into my mind again, and I replayed our conversations, seeking out incongruities or clues. All I got out of it was a whole lot of nothing.

I watched a few fine flakes dance around my window some more. I read some catalogue copy. I scanned through e-mails. I brought up the *Seacoast Star*'s Web site to see if anything was new. It wasn't. Finally, around eleven, frustrated with the situation and myself, I went downstairs and cuddled Hank.

"How are you, sweet boy?" I asked as I scooped him up.

He opened sleepy eyes and mewed.

"Good. I'm glad to hear it."

I heard the patter of Gretchen's high heels. She appeared around the corner of a storage unit and smiled.

"Aren't you lucky," she said, "to be getting some kitty love."

"So lucky." I make a smacking sound against Hank's cheek. "And he's so delicious."

Her smile broadened. "I know. He really is." She glanced over her shoulder and lowered her voice. "I wanted to let you know that I've booked the Blue Dolphin and Academy Brass for our luncheon two weeks from today, the twenty-second. Suzanne was ecstatic that you wanted to use their services and swears she won't say a word to Fred. I've blocked out noon to two on everyone's calendar. I labeled it a mandatory staff meeting — an end-of-the-year review and planning session." She giggled. "I put down that you'll be providing pizza."

"Very clever! I'll actually be holding a meeting like that the week after, so they'll be ahead of the game in preparing. I thought after we eat we could come in here and watch Hank open his gifts."

She tickled under his chin. "He's been such a good boy this year, Santa was very good to him!"

"Josie, line one, please," Cara said, her voice crackling over the loudspeaker. "It's about a possible appraisal. Celeste Gastron."

"He has," I said, kissing him again. I placed Hank in his basket. He mewed in protest, wanting another hug. "Maybe later, baby."

Gretchen waved good-bye and headed back to the office.

I picked up the closest phone. "This is Josie."

"Hi. I'm Celeste Gastron. I have a collection of Amberina glass I want to sell. As a first step, I need a formal appraisal, so I'm asking a few dealers to submit proposals. Would you be interested?"

"You bet! I love Amberina glass."

Celeste Gastron was as eager to get the process rolling as I was to get out of my office, so we made an immediate appointment. After telling Cara where I was going, I headed east, toward the coast.

"Call me Celeste," she said, welcoming

me into her beachfront condo with a big smile.

She looked like a latter-day hippie. I put her at about fifty. Her waist-long braid was fastened at the bottom with a seashell clip. Her hair was medium brown, flecked with gray. She wore faded low-cut jeans, a white turtleneck, and lots of orange and blue beads. Her complexion was olive. As far as I could tell, she wore no makeup.

"My mother collected the Amberina," she explained, leading the way to a glass-fronted display cabinet. "I'm taking early retirement — I'm an art teacher — and moving to St. Thomas, so it's time for it to go."

"St. Thomas! What fun."

"Thanks," she replied as if I'd complimented her on something, which I guess I had, her choice in retirement locales.

"It's beautiful," I said, my eyes on the golden-orange pieces.

Amberina glass was patented in the late nineteenth century by Joseph Locke. The techniques he used — integrating real gold into the molten mix and reheating certain parts of the glass — created coloration patterns that faded from pale amber to ruby red, like a sunset. Most of the pieces featured the darker, richer colors on top. When the object was reheated at the base, the red tones appeared at the bottom. This coloration pattern was known as a reverse.

Celeste's collection, which included what looked to be a spooner — an extremely rare and scarce example of the American-made art glass — was, from my initial glance, in perfect condition. Spooners, also called spoon holders, were a status symbol of the late nineteenth century. Designed to keep sterling silver spoons readily available, spooners demonstrated more than easy hospitality; they allowed members of the burgeoning middle class to show off their newfound affluence — they could afford the spoons to put in them. By 1930 or so, when the middle class was well established, interest in fragile glass spooners had all but vanished. It was only in the last few years that they'd emerged as a collectible. American-made art glass spooners ticked all the boxes: They were old, rare, scarce, beautiful, and popular.

"There are eight pieces," Celeste said, "all different."

I took out my video camera and asked her to bring out each piece, one at a time, so I could create an annotated recording of the lot. In addition to the spooner, the collection included a ruffled vase; a lily vase with an etched manufacturer's mark reading LIB-

BEY; a whisky tumbler; a bulbous water pitcher; a cruet with an amber stopper; a reverse-colored small water jug; and a diamond-cut egg-shaped bowl with three feet.

"Do you have any receipts?" I asked.

"Three." She handed me a sheet of paper. All three receipts, which had been issued from small New Hampshire shops in the mid-1980s, had been photocopied onto one page. "The others were bought at tag sales or flea markets for cash."

"We'll do some preliminary research to figure out how long we think a full appraisal will take and prepare a proposal for your review within a few days."

"Perfect," she said, shaking hands.

I thanked her again for giving us the opportunity, then left.

Sitting in my idling car, listening to the waves thunder in to shore, I realized I was still in no frame of mind to work. I had very little memory of my interaction with Celeste. I'd been on autopilot, half my brain in the room with her, the other half gone, lost in a tangle of half-formed thoughts and roiling emotions. I uploaded the video, e-mailed it to Sasha, and asked her to prepare the proposal. I turned off the engine and got out of my car.

I walked a ways along the shoreline, kicking snow-pocked ribbons of slick seaweed, clambered through brittle grass and twisted vines to the top of a dune, and watched the tide charge in. Gazing west, I could see the sun trying to peek through the clouds. To the east, though, the cloud cover was thick, a yellowish gray, and the ocean's surface was still turbid, a cauldron of bubbling dark danger. I felt myself relax, just a little. Whether the tide was gently rolling in or attacking the shore with the devil's own fury, the water's rhythmic ebb and flow always calmed me. When enough cold had leached through my boots to make standing on the frozen sand a punishment, I headed back to work.

As I turned off I-95 toward Prescott's, Ellis called. I slipped in my earpiece.

"I'm in Boston at Becca's apartment," he said, "and I hate to ask, but I could really use your help."

"Of course. What's going on?"

"Becca is now officially a person of interest in Ian Bennington's death."

"No!" I exclaimed, horrified. Ian was her father. It wasn't possible.

"Note I'm not specifying how Ian died, because the ME hasn't issued her final report. Based on her preliminary findings, however, it looks like Ian was hit by a car, receiving life-threatening wounds from the impact."

My eyes welled up. "Did he die instantly?"

"There's no way to know. I'm sorry, Josie. The ME is working to determine whether the car hit him accidentally or purposefully, whether it's manslaughter or murder."

"I saw the skid marks. The car sped up as it approached him, then veered right."

"I know. Why we're here . . . I have two witnesses who place Becca at the scene, which makes her a material witness, at least. She has, apparently, disappeared. Put all that together with the break-in at the institute and I was able to get a court order allowing me to search for information as to her whereabouts. Airline tickets, charge card records, letters indicating a friend she might contact, and so on. I haven't found anything. Katie is looking at her work computer to see if she did electronic banking. However, I think there's a chance there are things here I can't see. There's a drawer that was obviously built into her desk as a hidden compartment. It wasn't fully closed, the kind of hair-thin gap you might leave if you grabbed something from a drawer and shoved it closed it in a hurry. The drawer was empty, but it got me wondering if there might be other secret cubbyholes in the furniture. A lot of the pieces seem to match, and if there's a secret compartment in one, it seems logical there might be others. Especially since you found that box that had a hidden drawer in it. I couldn't find anything, but I don't really know what I'm looking for. I'm hoping you'll take a look and tell me what's what. Maybe you'll see something that helps us find her, that helps find Ian's killer."

"Of course. Now?"

"If you can."

I glanced at my phone. It was just after one. "I should be there by three."

"Thanks, Josie." He cleared his throat. "One thing . . . don't tell Wes until you're done, okay?"

"Wes?" I asked, wondering what Ellis had up his sleeve.

"I was thinking that if Wes writes about Becca's new status as a person of interest, it might spur the community on to help us find her."

"That makes sense," I said, waiting for more information. None came. The silence stretched on for several seconds. Finally, I asked the obvious question. "Why don't you tell him yourself? He'd love to quote a police chief."

"If you're his source, you build up a little credit. You might hear something from him that I never would. And if you hear something that's pertinent, you might just tell me. I'm just trying to cover all the angles."

"You're a very clever man, Ellis."

"I'm not feeling very clever. I'm feeling a dollar short and a day late."

"I'll do my best to help."

"Thanks. Don't worry about parking. There is none around here. I don't know how people cope. The Boston police are cooperating — they've left a man out front. He'll watch your car. I'll let him know you're coming."

I called Cara to tell her I wouldn't be back and Ty to tell him I would be late, grabbed a fast-food lunch to eat en route, and got back on the interstate, this time heading south.

Chapter Sixteen

The uniformed police officer standing on the stoop of Becca and Ethan's apartment building looked about fourteen. He had dark brown hair gelled to a center peak and walked with a teenager's strut. His gold-toned nameplate read OFFICER E. O'KEEFE. As soon as I double-parked, he took the steps two at a time, reaching me before I'd turned off the engine.

"Ms. Prescott? Chief Hunter asked me to send you right in. If you'll set your flashers and leave the key, I'll take care of your car."

I swung my tote bag over my shoulder, thanked him as I tossed him my key ring, and hurried up the steps.

I tugged on the entryway door, expecting it to be locked, but it opened freely. Masking tape covered the locking mechanism. Becca's apartment door stood open. I stuck my head in and peeked around the corner.

Ellis stood in front of Ethan's photo of

the neon coral and sponges, his head tilted to the left, his hands on his hips, concentrating.

I knocked twice and walked in.

He looked up and smiled. "You made good time."

"No traffic." I nodded at the photo. "What do you think?"

"Do you really see that when you snorkel?"

"Not often. This is what you see in deeper water. How come you've never tried it?"

"It's never come my way." He stared at the photo. "It must be something to spend time in this world. Maybe this is why Becca is a marine biologist."

"Ethan, too. He's the photographer."

He turned his back to the photo. "Thanks for coming, Josie."

"You're welcome."

"You look upset," he said.

"I feel upset."

"About what?"

"I liked Ian so much."

"Me, too. Okay, then . . . the apartment is comprised of one large open-plan room, two bedrooms, each with its own private bathroom, and a powder room. Our court order allows us to search Becca's known property and any other place we have a reasonable expectation she might have stored or hidden things. We've defined that as anything in her room and bath or the public areas of the apartment. Don't go into Ethan's room or his bathroom. The half bath is fair game."

He walked to an open door on the left, Becca's bedroom, and stood aside so I could enter first. I took a long look around. Evidently, she was a fan of fine midcentury and Shaker-style furniture. The bed and matching desk and tallboy were constructed of maple. The rug, 12' × 15' or so, was of high-quality wool, in a mod beige and cream color-block pattern. Oak hardwood flooring showed around the perimeter of the room. Bone-colored Roman shades were lowered halfway.

I got down on my hands and knees and used my flashlight to examine the underside of a triangular-shaped side table. With its urbane feel and distinctive crossed legs, I wasn't surprised to learn it was a David Hicks original.

"This was crafted by a top designer, probably in the 1960s. Assuming it's genuine, it's worth thousands of dollars."

"But not tens of thousands."

"Probably not." I stood up, brushing a few stray dusty bits from my knees.

"Nice art, huh?" Ellis asked. Three paintings, a Renoir, a Cézanne, and a Matisse, all presumably copies, hung on the walls. No empty picture hooks were visible.

I approached one to study the brush strokes.

"I bet they're modern replicas," I said. "If I can take them back to my office, we can confirm it."

"Sure."

He lifted the Renoir down so I could examine the back.

"See," I said, pointing to a glue-on label. "It's from an outfit called Masterpiece Replicas."

I confirmed there wasn't a false backing. The other two were also from Masterpiece Replicas.

"They probably sell for a few hundred dollars," I said.

"They look pretty good for knock-offs."

I agreed. A silver-framed photograph caught my eye. Becca was standing next to an older man. The man was tall and slim, with thinning gray hair combed to cover a bald patch. He wore thick black glasses and looked to be in his late fifties or early sixties. They seemed happy being together.

"Who is he?"

"No one knows. We asked Ethan and sent a scan to Becca's departments at both

Reynard and the institute. So far, no one recognizes him."

I put the photo down and turned toward Ellis. "Does Ethan know I'm here?"

"Yes. I tracked him down at Reynard after you and I spoke. I explained that you consult for the department." Ellis glanced at his watch. "He'll be back sometime after five — he's in an all-day Assessment Committee meeting until then."

"Does he know where Becca is?"

"He says he hasn't seen her since before she left for Canada. Ditto everyone at the university." Ellis scanned the room with a professional eye. "Where will you start?"

"The desk. I want to see the hidden compartment you found."

"We dusted it for fingerprints and found several latents. They're probably Becca's. We're checking if she's in any database."

"What about Immigration?"

"That's on the list. There's certain paperwork that needs to be completed."

His tone communicated his unspoken words: ". . . and it will take days, not hours."

The three main pieces of furniture were all interpretations of a traditional Shaker style, minimalist and functional, without adornment. The desk legs were squared off and tapered. A raised attached cupboard that ran the length of the desk provided easy-to-access storage. There were no drawers.

I slid my tote bag under the desk and extracted my video recorder and the metal measuring tape I always carried. Ellis handed me a pair of plastic gloves. I snapped them on and began the process of recording everything I saw. I wrote down the dimensions in a spiral-bound notebook I carried for the purpose.

The desk measured 60″ × 30″ × 30″. The raised panel was two feet tall and one foot deep. Three sets of asymmetrically arranged doors took up all the space except for a narrow panel between the door on the right and the two doors on the left.

"That's where the drawer is," I said, pointing.

Ellis nodded. "Right."

I pushed against the panel, and the drawer glided out effortlessly. It was empty.

"A spring-loaded latch, smooth as silk." I noted a logo burned into the bottom of the drawer, a small oval with the letters *MV* inside, similar to the one burned into the box I found in Becca's desk drawer at the institute.

"It's beautifully made," I said. "Someone knew what he was doing. What do you figure was in here?"

"The missing miniatures."

"A kind of cash equivalent. Like gold or diamonds."

"Can she sell them easily?" he asked.

"Sure. According to Ian, she owns them."

I opened the three cupboard doors. Each cabinet held a white square plate filled with clamshells. I recognized steamers and Manilas and razors and big dark purple ones I'd seen on Nantasket Beach when I was a kid, quahogs, I thought they were called.

"Now what?" Ellis asked.

I did a slow survey, considering the options. Ellis was right: Since the furniture matched, it was a good bet that whoever built it added secret cubbyholes to each piece.

"The tallboy."

I began taking measurements. The tallboy wasn't, actually, all that tall, only five and a half feet. The body stood on the same tapered legs as the desk and bed. There were five large drawers topped by a pair of small drawers, all featuring round wooden pulls. Side braces added a bit of visual interest to the otherwise plain design.

"The bottom drawer is filled with papers," Ellis said, pointing at it. "Receipts and so on. We didn't see anything relating to the paintings."

"Ian said there was an old appraisal."

"We didn't find it."

"Maybe she took the paperwork with her. Being able to confirm provenance would help her get top dollar. Having an appraisal, no matter how old, gives you a starting place to negotiate price."

I pulled it open. It was, as Ellis had said, stuffed with receipts and letters.

"I would have expected her to be more organized," Ellis said, his eyes on the papers.

"I suspect she's super-organized about clams but not about much else."

"That's funny."

"I know."

The other drawers contained clothing: jeans and khakis, sweaters and T-shirts, workout gear, socks, all-white cotton underwear, standard-issue floral-patterned nightgowns, and pajamas. Becca was not a clotheshorse.

"Would you like us to issue a call for sightings on the miniatures? If I ask people to contact me, they'll think I have a buyer, not that it's a police matter."

"Good idea. Let's do it right away in case selling them tops Becca's to-do list."

I called work, asked Cara to put me on with Sasha, and explained what I wanted her to do.

"Got it," she said.

"Thanks, Sasha." I ended the call and turned toward Ellis. "We subscribe to proprietary Web sites and forums, where we'll post the notice. We'll also send out a general alert to all antiques dealers in the country."

"Good deal." Ellis looked around. "Now what?"

"Now I continue working."

I turned back to the tallboy and began pushing on things, seeking out another spring lock.

After a minute, Ellis said, "Nothing personal, Joz, but watching you work is like watching tomatoes ripen. Can I do anything to help?"

I laughed. "Watch many tomatoes ripen, do you? No, there's nothing you can do. It's a process."

"Then I'll leave you to it." He handed me a small zip-close bag containing some plastic gloves. "In case you need a spare pair or three. Call me if you find the paintings, or need me, and when you're done."

I promised I would. He left, and I heard the door latch catch behind him.

I continued my meticulous examination, moving methodically across each surface, seeking out anomalies or latches that would reveal another hidden cubbyhole. I pushed a spot toward the bottom of the rear left brace, and a narrow drawer popped open.

Inside was a pair of dazzlingly beautiful diamond drop earrings resting on a miniature black velvet pillow. If I moved my head slightly to the left, I could get the overhead light to spark a prism, sending cascades of radiating rainbows out and over the small pillow. It was a miracle of light and color.

I lifted the pillow out, and saw the same oval-shaped logo burned into the bottom. It also read *MV.* I took photos of the logo, replaced the pillow and diamonds, and took more photos before closing the drawer. I notated where to push to pop the latch and continued my examination. Just because I found one secret drawer didn't mean there weren't others. I pushed and prodded every inch of wood, front, back, bottom, and sides, without finding a second cubbyhole.

I turned my attention to the bed. I tapped and jabbed along the bed's headboard. Nothing. I moved to the sideboards. Nothing. Given that the desk, tallboy, and bed matched, and that I found cubbyholes in two of them, I felt a high degree of confidence that there must be a hidden compartment in the bed as well. Lying on the rug, flashlight in hand, I performed an inch-by-inch inspection without success. I stood up and stretched.

"It's here," I said aloud. "I just can't find it."

I moved my search to the moldings, an unlikely option in a rental apartment, but not impossible. I found a stepstool in the kitchen pantry and used it to check every seam in the crown molding. Nothing. I tapped every inch, without luck. The hardwood flooring reaped no reward either, nor did the closet. Becca had two dresses, both black, four pairs of nice wool slacks, four blazers in various colors, and eight silk blouses. To my surprise, she also had a pair of black leather pants and a color-coordinated zip-up leather jacket. She had only one pair of high heels, and they were red and very high — four-inch stilettos. If she wore those with the leather, she'd be making quite a statement. I tapped the walls and tried prying up drawer bottoms.

The phone rang. I went into the great room, thinking maybe Becca would leave a message for Ethan, perhaps revealing her location. Five rings in, the answering machine clicked on, and the caller hung up. I was five paces short of Becca's room when the phone rang again. I stood where I was, watching the machine. The red light meant it was ready to record, but again, as soon as the message clicked on, the caller hung up. A wrong number, perhaps, or a sales call, or someone who simply didn't want to leave a message. I went back to work.

I opened the bottom drawer in the tallboy, the one filled with paperwork. I sat cross-legged on the floor and began going through things. Ten minutes after I started, I found what I was looking for: a receipt for all three pieces of furniture and the box, from a company in Franklin, New Hampshire, called Meadow's Village. The logo on the top of the receipt matched the ones I'd found in the secret drawers. I wrote the name down in my notebook and took a photo of the receipt.

Wanting a change of scenery, I took Ethan's photographs down in the great room and examined the walls where they'd hung. No hidden safe. I repeated the process I'd used in the bedroom, tapping walls, prodding and prying, to see if I could find a hidden compartment. I examined the ice cube container in the freezer and checked whether anything, from a pint of frozen yogurt to a can of free-range chicken soup, had a false bottom. I didn't find anything, but I learned a lot about Becca and Ethan.

They stocked mostly organic products, used Spode bone china as their everyday dishes, and kept a store of four different kinds of loose tea in airtight containers. I checked, but there was nothing in the containers except tea.

I examined the powder room carefully. I looked in the toilet tank, medicine cabinet, and vanity, but if Becca had fabricated a hidden compartment behind the tiles, the police would have to find it.

Back in Becca's bathroom, I looked in all the same places, then pushed aside the burgundy and forest green tartan shower curtain. The tub looked like a tub, except jetted. I scanned the burgundy walls, examined the pewter light fixture, and lifted the shaggy cotton dark green rugs. Nothing.

I heard a knock, then another, soft taps. I started for the door, thinking it might be Officer O'Keefe. I paused midstep and gently lowered my foot to the floor. Those taps weren't knocks. Another tap sounded, a sharp rap, the kind of noise a glazier makes when he's removing glass from a windowpane. Another tap, much louder, reverberated through the bathroom, followed immediately by tinkling glass. Someone was breaking in.

I gasped and covered my mouth with my

hands to stop myself from making any noise. I stood in petrified rigor, unable to move, barely able to breathe. I could picture the glass piling up under the window. It went on and on and on, ending with a final cataclysmic crash. My mouth went dry and I fought the urge to cough. Standing with my mouth agape, my heart pounding, and my pulse throbbing, I stared at the bathroom door. It was mostly closed. I risked a gentle push and the door swung closer to the jamb, leaving only a sliver of clearance. Footsteps grew louder, moving closer, and my heart jumped into my throat before plunging to my knees. I felt dizzy. I thought I might be ill. I exhaled slowly, breathed in consciously, purposefully. *Get a grip,* I told myself.

It didn't work.

Panic-fueled blood raced through my veins. Terror made my skin crawl, as if spiders were running up and down my arms and legs. I looked up and over and around. There was nowhere to go. I was trapped.

Oh, no, I mouthed. *My tote bag.*

I'd left it under the desk. It wasn't out in the open, but to someone searching, it would be apparent.

Thrashing and cracking sounds thundered outside the door. Remembering what I'd seen at the institute, I could easily imagine what was happening here. The attacker was dumping Becca's clothing, hurling drawers against walls or smashing them against the floor, and shredding the mattress. No one spoke. Either it was a well-organized team or one person was working alone.

With my eyes fixed on the narrow crack, I gingerly stepped into the tub. The rupturing and tearing noises continued, one act of destruction followed by another. I lay flat, scrunching my way up toward the faucet, out of sight, I hoped, from someone who might enter looking not for a person hiding but for booty to steal. Grasping the shower curtain hem, I eased it toward the back until I was cocooned. I rolled onto my side, raised my knees toward my chest, and curled my shoulders inward, tucking my head down, trying to make myself as small as possible.

A big piece of furniture, maybe the tallboy, went down with an earthshaking boom. I winced and closed my eyes. Smaller thumps followed. Fabric tore.

The silence, when it came, was as stunning as the previous cacophony had been. I held my breath waiting for the next round of destruction to begin. It didn't come. I felt like a mouse knowing there's a cat right outside the door. I waited more. A door opened, then closed.

"Ms. Prescott?" a man called.

I didn't recognize the voice and was terrified it was a setup designed to draw me out.

"Ms. Prescott?" the same voice called again.

After two more calls, I heard footsteps drawing closer.

"What the —" A pause. A change in tone, from casual to worried. "Ms. Prescott, this is Officer O'Keefe. Are you all right?"

I sat up and leaned my head against the cold tiles. "I'm —" I broke off, coughing, and tried again. "I'm in the bathroom." My eyes filled with tears of relief.

"Are you okay?" Officer O'Keefe asked again. His eyes were round with concern. He squatted beside me. "Do you need medical attention?"

"No." I extended a hand and he helped me up. "Thanks."

With his hand on my elbow, he walked me out of the bathroom and into the vortex.

Chapter Seventeen

I stood in the center of Becca's room while Officer O'Keefe called in the burglary. I couldn't stop shivering, maybe from the cold. The wind whistled through the shattered window. My tote bag had been emptied upside down and tossed aside. He told me not to touch anything. I saw my wallet, my phone, my notebook, and my silver card case. Hard as it was to believe, it looked as if nothing had been stolen.

From what I could see, no inch of the room had been left unscathed. All the furniture was toppled over; the mattress lay askew from the frame, slashed and torn; clothes were heaped on the bed; papers were strewn across the floor.

"The detectives are on their way," Officer O'Keefe told me.

"Can I borrow your phone?" I asked. "I want to call Chief Hunter."

"Sure." He handed it over. Ellis answered

on the first ring.

"We have a kind of situation down here," I said. "I think you're going to want to be on-site for the investigation."

As soon as I explained what had happened, he said he'd see me in an hour.

Officer O'Keefe and I picked our way across the floor and walked into the kitchen. Ethan opened the front door and frowned when he saw us.

"This is getting to be quite a habit," he said, his eyes on me. He turned his gaze on Officer O'Keefe. "Not for nothing, but I'd like a little privacy."

"Sorry, sir," O'Keefe said. "This is a crime scene."

"What's going on?"

"Sir, I'm going to have to ask you not to touch anything and to join us here in the kitchen."

"Who are you?"

"Officer O'Keefe. And you are?"

Ethan held up his key. "A tenant."

"There's been a break-in. The detectives will be here shortly."

"Josie?" Ethan asked, turning my name into a question.

"Let's wait for the detectives," O'Keefe interjected before I could reply.

Ethan closed the door, tossed his keys

onto the telephone table, and swung his backpack off, wedging it against the wall.

"It's cold in here," he said.

A rat-a-tat sounded, and two men in suits strode in.

I was stuck in Becca and Ethan's apartment for an hour recounting what happened, then at the precinct house for two more giving a formal statement. Ellis listened in on my last rendition, the one I delivered to a video camera. His first act was to convince his contact to start the technicians on my tote bag and its contents, so everything could be released to me before I left.

"Thank you," I said as he walked me to my car. "Any fingerprints on my stuff?"

"No. It looks like whoever broke in wore gloves, no surprise."

"I figure he found my tote bag, realized I was probably somewhere in the apartment, and tore out of there."

"That's what I think, too. How long did you stay in the bathroom after it got quiet?"

"I don't know. A while. I was scared. Why did Officer O'Keefe come in?"

"Shift change. He was going off duty and wanted to introduce you to his replacement," he said. "He's a good cop."

"I'll pass that along."

"Do you think the phone calls were to verify that no one was at home?" I asked.

"Probably. Or they were from a robo-call telemarketer."

"Can you check?"

"We already have. They came from a disposable phone that was purchased at a small electronics store in New York City five months ago. Someone bought six of them."

"That's fast work!" I said.

"One of the detectives has a contact at the phone company. No one on staff remembers the buyer."

"Any security cameras?"

"Yup. They only keep the digital recordings for ninety days, though."

I looked up but couldn't see any stars. I wondered if it was cloud cover shrouding the sky or city lights that made the sky look ink black. I was exhausted, the kind of to-your-bones fatigue that weighs you down after a crisis. And, oddly, I was ravenous.

"Ty texted that he's waiting dinner for me. By the time I get home, it'll be ten."

Ellis glanced at his watch. "Nine thirty, probably. Call him before you leave, so he'll have it ready."

"Yeah. I will." I raised my shoulders and lowered them, and turned my head to the left, then to the right. All my muscles were tight. "How about you? When will you eat?"

"I'll be fine." He touched my upper arm. "Are you okay? For real?"

"Yeah." I clicked open my driver's door. As I reached for the handle, I added, "I should have tried to get a look at him. I could have hidden behind the door and peeked out."

"Don't, Josie. Don't beat yourself up. You did exactly the right thing. You focused on staying safe."

"I feel all wussy."

"That's silly," he said.

Anger flared. Telling me not to feel what I was feeling was like telling someone with a headache to shake it off.

"It's how I feel," I said.

"Fair enough. Just know I don't think you're wussy."

"Thanks." I stood up straight and stretched, arching my back, working the kinks out.

"Are you okay to drive? I can get someone to take you home."

"I'm fine." I looked Ellis in the eyes as I opened the car door. "Whoever did this killed Ian."

"We don't know that."

I slid behind the wheel and started the engine. Ellis closed the door. I lowered the window.

"You're a good friend, Ellis," I said.

"You are, too, Josie."

I raised the window, put the car in gear, and drove home.

After a hot bath, a cold Prescott's Punch, and a bowl of leftover pot roast, I leaned back against the pillows at the short end of the L-shaped bench framing my kitchen table and sighed, an exhalation of pleasure.

"Yum," I said.

"I reheat a mean pot roast," Ty said.

I smiled and took his hand.

"I got so scared lying in the tub," I said. "I felt so powerless. So vulnerable."

"Makes sense. You were."

We sat for another hour as I recounted what I'd heard and seen and felt. Ty was unwaveringly calm and reassuring, and as I slid off the bench, I thought how lucky I was to have him in my life. Even though I knew it was nothing more than an illusion that things actually got better through talking, I felt better, and that was something.

I hadn't returned any of Wes's texts or calls, but when the phone rang at seven thirty Friday morning, I recognized his number and took the call.

"I can't believe you didn't call me back," he said by way of greeting.

"I had a hard day."

"That's no excuse, Josie, and you know it."

"Give me a break, Wes."

"You can make it up to me. Tell me exactly what happened at Becca's. Let's meet for breakfast."

"I've already eaten," I told him to give myself time to decide whether I felt like dealing with him or not. I adored Wes like a kid brother, but boy oh boy, was he work.

"Come on, Joz," he whined. "Meet me for coffee."

Wes might think I owed him, and maybe I did, but that didn't mean I had to pay up now. I wasn't going to share the photos I took; that was certain. Not when so much was unclear. The last thing I wanted to do was complicate the police investigation. I decided to go, not to give, but to take. I was willing to bet Wes had information he would share. I would even up the tally later. Plus, Ellis wanted me to talk to Wes, to get him to rally the troops.

"Okay," I said. I glanced at the clock mounted high on the wall over the refrigerator, a mahogany beauty, a Chessman original. "Half an hour. The Portsmouth Diner."

I got there first and ordered coffee.

Since Wes had hooked up with his Maggie, he'd cleaned up his act. No longer did he breakfast on a double order of bacon and a Coke; instead, he ordered a fruit salad, coffee, and an English muffin, no butter.

"So . . . talk," he said to me, after the waitress had delivered our coffees.

I did. I told him about the break-in and my paralyzing terror. I described the sounds the glass made as it tumbled to the ground, hiding in the tub curled in the fetal position, and the shambles the burglar left behind.

I sighed, remembering the anxiety, the fear, the helplessness. "What about Becca? Is there any word on her whereabouts?"

"Nope. Same old, same old. No sightings. No credit or debit card usage. No E-ZPass records at the tollbooths. Her car is old; it doesn't have GPS built in."

"What about planes?"

Wes shook his head. "She's not on any passenger manifest. She could have bought a train ticket for cash. They're checking security cameras."

"How could they? There must be thousands of train riders each day."

"They use facial recognition software."

"Really? That's amazing."

The waitress delivered Wes's food and refilled our cups.

"Do you think Becca has the paintings with her?"

I thought of the secret drawer in the desk, empty, not quite closed. "Maybe. Any word from the medical examiner?"

"Based on the points of impact, she's determined that Ian was struck by a small sedan, and that there is likely to have been significant damage to the vehicle."

My eyes opened wide. "Becca drives a small car."

"I know," he said, with relish. "The ME estimates that the car was moving at thirty-five to forty miles per hour at the moment of impact."

"On a short dead-end street?"

"There's more. From the tire tracks, there's no way the body could have ended up where it was found, facedown, under a bush, without human intervention. She's ruled the death a homicide."

"Oh, Wes," I whispered. "How awful."

"Yeah," he agreed, sounding bloodthirsty.

"You should write an article asking people to call the police if they see her, saying that maybe she's in trouble and needs help."

"Do you think she's in trouble?" Wes asked, intrigued.

"I don't know."

"So you don't think Becca killed her dad?"

"I can't bear to think about it, Wes. I just can't."

I couldn't stop the image of Ian and Lia laughing and flirting at my party from coming into my mind, either. Lia's first moment of hope after a year of misery, as dead as Ian. As unseemly and off-putting as Lia's initial reaction to Ian's death had been, I understood how she could feel that way. Poor Lia. She seemed unable to yank herself out of the quagmire that was sucking her into a morass of wretched despair.

"I looked it up," Wes said. "When a daughter kills her father, it's called patricide. It's rare. Only about a hundred occurrences a year."

"But it happens."

Wes grinned. "Oh, yeah."

When I got to my office around nine, Gretchen showed me Wes's tweets. Within minutes of leaving the diner, he tweeted: *Becca Bennington, call the Rocky Point police at 603.555.1919. Your help is needed. #FindBecca.* The second one read *Have you seen Becca Bennington? She may be injured or sick. If you've seen her, call 603.555.1919. #FindBecca.*

I didn't know how to react to Wes's tweets. He was doing as I asked, but it seemed so out there, I couldn't imagine anyone responding.

"What's the early reaction?" I asked.

"Good. Lots of retweeting, expressing concern, encouraging people to call in if they've seen her. Community support."

"I hope it works."

I turned to Sasha and asked if there'd been any hits in response to our call for sightings regarding the miniatures.

"No," she said, "but I got a call from a dealer in San Francisco wanting to sell one."

"Not of Arabella or the king?"

"No, but it is a Cooper."

I smiled. "And of course you got a full description, including price information, for future reference."

She smiled back, pleased. "Already filed away."

"You're so good!"

Her eyes brightened with pleasure. "I have news about the Amberina glass, too. Ms. Gastron accepted our proposal."

"That's terrific! What do you think of the collection?"

"It's lovely. The most valuable piece is probably the spooner. It might go for as much as six thousand dollars."

"Great news."

Upstairs, I tapped through the photos on my phone until I came to the Meadow's receipt. I e-mailed it to Ellis with a note that I was following up, then called the company.

"Meadow's," a pleasant-sounding woman said. "This is Belle."

I introduced myself. "I'm trying to find a secret compartment in a Meadow's bed, and I'm hoping you can tell me how to locate the latch."

"A secret compartment?"

"Yes. It's a match piece to a tallboy and a desk. I found those hidden compartments, but I can't find the one in the bed."

"I wouldn't know anything about that," she said.

"Who would?"

"I don't know."

"Is there a furniture designer there I could talk to, Belle?"

"What did you say your name was?" she asked, sounding harried.

"Never mind," I said. "I'll stop by. What are your hours?"

She rattled them off, relieved to answer a normal question, and eagerly got off the phone.

I was halfway down the steps when Cara's

voice came on the PA system.

"Pick up, Josie," she said.

I grabbed a wall phone.

"A woman named Marney Alred to see you," Cara said. "About some miniature paintings."

"Bring her up!" I told Cara, and dashed back to my office.

I was standing by my desk when an attractive woman in her forties stepped into the room. Her light brown hair fell to her shoulders. She had long bangs. She wore a red waffle-knit Henley over sensible black wool pants. She wore no makeup, but she didn't need any. She looked as if she'd walked off a billboard touting the benefits of wholesome country living.

"Thank you, Cara," I said.

"Would you like something to drink?" Cara asked her. "Coffee? Tea? Lemonade?"

"No, thank you," the woman said.

"Have a seat," I invited as Cara left, pointing to one of the guest chairs. I sat behind my desk. "I'm Josie Prescott."

"Thank you for seeing me without an appointment," she said. "I'm Marney Alred. I stopped in because a friend of mine, Rebecca Bennington, told me she planned to sell two paintings, and I want to buy them." She raised a fluttering hand. "At such a time, with her dad dead, and in such a way, well, I don't want to push. But I don't want to miss out, either. I thought I ought to come to you directly."

"I understand . . . It's terrible about Ian. I'd love to facilitate the sale, but I don't have any of Ms. Bennington's paintings." Realizing I shouldn't reveal that I knew anything about a pair of miniatures, I asked, "Which ones are you interested in?"

"The watercolor miniatures." She smiled. "I saw them once — and fell in love with them. You don't have them?"

"No."

"Rebecca said she was calling you."

"When was that?"

She thought for a moment. "Monday, I think."

"Where did you see her?"

Her brow wrinkled. "Why?"

I grinned. "Occupational hazard for a researcher. I ask whatever occurs to me. I never know what's important until after the process is over."

"Amusing," she said, with a hint of a smile. "So Rebecca didn't call?"

"No. I wish she had. Do you have her contact information? I'll be glad to reach out to her and let her know you're interested in buying the miniatures. Sometimes knowing there's a willing buyer is all it takes to motivate a seller."

She rattled off Becca's number, and I jotted it down on a small sheet of notepaper. I was disappointed to see that it was the same one Ethan gave me. She provided her own contact information, too.

"You must know her well to have her number in your head," I said

"Well enough."

I slipped the paper under the glass paperweight Zoë gave me for Christmas last year. It was the kind that had a sleeve built in for a photo. The photo Zoë chose was one of her and me on a sled, tearing down the hill in back of her house on Christmas Day, a year earlier. Ty took it from the flat at the bottom of the hill. We were a blur of legs and arms and open mouths shouting in joyous exhilaration. I wiggled one of my business cards from the leather holder I kept on my desk.

"Here's mine. The number on the bottom is my cell. You can reach me anytime."

She dropped it into her handbag and stood up. "I'll hope to hear from you soon."

I walked out from behind my desk, swinging my tote bag up onto my shoulder.

"Thanks for coming in," I said. "I'll walk out with you."

As we crossed the warehouse, she chatted easily about how lovely Rebecca was, how shocking and upsetting it was to learn that her father had been murdered, and how impressed she was with Becca's accomplishments. I murmured appropriate nothing-sayings. Marney smiled politely around the office and left.

I watched her make her way to her silver Lexus, grabbed my coat from the rack, and told Cara, "I'm heading out. I'll be back in a few hours."

Someone at Meadow's knew something. I was sure of it.

Chapter Eighteen

It took almost an hour and a half to reach Franklin, the birthplace of the renowned statesman Daniel Webster. Nineteenth-century stone buildings sat amid rolling farmland, now covered in snow. I followed the AREA ATTRACTION signs to Meadow's Village.

Before turning in, I pulled over to the side of the road and Googled "Meadow's Village." The community had been formed as a Shaker village in 1787; it closed in 1973. The current owners, two brothers named Will and Buddy Bisset, had converted the thirty-five-acre property into a multiuse destination site. One factory on the property produced wooden gift products like candlesticks and baskets; another crafted fine furniture. The village also housed a country restaurant, a small museum featuring exhibits from the area's Shaker heritage, a pick-your-own herb garden, cross-country ski runs, and a gift shop.

I turned in, passing fifteen-foot-high granite columns connected by a wrought-iron arch. The gilded MV logo was in the center. Gilt letters read WELCOME TO on the left and MEADOW'S VILLAGE on the right. The drive was long, a quarter mile or so. I parked next to the Welcome Center and went in.

The small octagonal freestanding building was modern in design and construction. Sun streamed in through the skylights and double-paned windows, rhomboids of golden light crisscrossed the hardwood flooring. A sixty-inch flat-screen TV stood on a tall pedestal in the center of the room. The show, a documentary, or a promotional video, perhaps, was muted. I watched for a moment as a middle-aged woman in a mob cap and long gray gown churned butter.

Racks and display cases scattered throughout the room showcased the various attractions available at Meadow's Village. Two women and one man sat behind a blond wood, S-shaped counter. All three wore headsets. The man, older than me by a lot, was typing on his computer. One of the women was young, barely out of high school, I suspected. She was talking to someone, giving directions. I wondered if

Cara would like headphones. The other woman, about my age, smiled, welcoming me in.

"Hi," I said, smiling back. "I have a question about a hidden compartment in one of your beds."

Her smile dissolved into nervousness. "We spoke on the phone."

"You're Belle. Hi! May I talk to someone in the furniture department?"

"Did you want to go to the showroom?"

"Good idea."

Belle gave me directions, and I left through the back door. I walked along a winding pathway, past the now-dormant herb garden, next to the snow-shoeing pavilion, and through the brightly lit gift shop. *Clever merchandising,* I thought, *to take me on a tour.*

I reached the wood-framed structure Belle had described. It looked more like a ski lodge than a cabinetmaker's shop or showroom. The sign over the double-wide doors featured the now-familiar logo and read "MEADOW'S VILLAGE FURNITURE."

Inside, the showroom was warm and gently lit. Sample rooms ranged around the perimeter: bedrooms on the right; living-dining room combos against the back wall; dens, game rooms, and media rooms on the left. In the center were additional samples arranged in seating areas, as well as displays of wood finishes and, directly in front of me, samples of hidden cabinets. A wooden sign embellished with gilt letters read MEADOW'S FURNITURE: THE WORLD'S LEADER IN PRIVACY COMPARTMENTS.

A woman in a burgundy and pink plaid pleated skirt, burgundy turtleneck sweater, and black knee-high boots approached from the left. She was about my age, with chin-length blond hair and dark blue eyes.

"Hi," she said. "I'm Monica. Can I show you anything in particular or did you just want to look around for a while?"

I nodded toward the privacy compartments. "I'm interested in seeing one of these in action. On a bed."

"Sure. Follow me!"

Monica led the way to a display table in the center of the room.

"All our privacy compartments are custom designed and fitted, so what I'm showing you are samples that reflect the kinds of work we can do."

She reached for a block of golden oak, about 12″ × 7″ × 6″, and held it chest high so I could see it clearly. She tapped a slender piece of molding that ran along the top.

"Do you see this molding? If you push it here, look what happens."

She pushed a spot about halfway across lightly, and a narrow rectangular drawer, only about 4″ wide and 3″ deep, slid outward.

"Isn't that precious?" Monica asked.

"Precious," I agreed. "What would someone use it for?"

"We call it a ring drawer — most often this one's in a makeup table. Don't you love it?"

"I do, but I'm looking for compartments in a bed."

"The ring drawer could be in a bed."

I didn't want to interrupt her well-rehearsed and well-staged demonstration, but seeing examples of what might be created wasn't helpful to either one of us. I wasn't a customer and didn't want to waste her time, or my own.

"It might be easier," I said, "if I explain why I'm asking." I pulled out Becca's receipt. "I need to locate the hidden compartment built into this particular bed."

Monica frowned, her eyes on the receipt. "I don't understand. You bought the bed and now you can't find the privacy compartment?"

"I'm an antiques appraiser." I dug out a

business card and handed it over. “I need to find the secret cubbyhole — the privacy compartment,” I said, correcting myself, knowing that using the same words as the other guy was one of the ways you build rapport, “as part of an appraisal.”

“How interesting!” Monica’s brow smoothed out. “I don’t know if I can help you, though. Since every piece is customized, it could be anywhere. Or nowhere if the buyer chose not to put one in.” She opened her arms, palms up. “Sorry.”

“Who would know?”

Monica bit the side of her bottom lip, thinking.

After several seconds, I added, “The receipt shows an account number. Surely you can look it up.”

“I think I’d better take you to the shop foreman.”

“Thanks!”

She wove a circuitous path through the displays. Every piece of furniture featured well-oiled matched-grain wood. Between the graceful lines and unadorned style, the designs were modern, yet evocative of Shaker simplicity.

“Who designs the furniture?”

“Buddy Bisset, one of the owners. He doesn’t like to be called an owner, though.

Or a designer. If you ask him, he'll tell you he's a cabinetmaker."

"My grandfather was a cabinetmaker."

"Mr. Bisset will be glad to know that." She lowered her voice. "He's also the shop foreman."

She pushed open an unmarked door in the middle of the rear wall and we were on the factory floor, facing a desk and the security guard seated behind it. The guard, who looked Scandinavian, like a Viking, stood up. He was six-five, at least.

"Hi, Walt," Monica said. "Ms. Prescott is an antiques appraiser. She needs to talk to Mr. Bisset."

"I'll let him know."

Walt set off toward the back.

"You can wait here," Monica said, pointing to a nearby bench. She extended her hand for a shake. "It was a pleasure meeting you. If I can do anything else, let me know!"

I thanked her, impressed with her polished professionalism. I sat down.

The workroom was larger than a football field, with eighteen-foot-high ceilings, and while I saw lots of high-end saws and lathes and dies, there were no assembly lines, no automation of any kind. A boy wearing old-fashioned blue jean coveralls pushed a broom down an open aisle, brushing sawdust along the cement floor. All the workers were men. I counted thirty-seven of them. Light came from fluorescent and incandescent lights high overhead and the transoms on all three outside walls just below the ceiling.

I followed Walt's progress as he wended his way to the back. He towered over everyone. He spoke to an older man, glancing at me periodically.

The other man shook his head. He was only about six feet, taller than average, but dwarfed by the guard. He looked over seventy, possibly over eighty. His hair was gray with a white streak cutting diagonally from right temple to crown. He looked grumpy and impatient. The guard said something else, and the old man looked at me, hitched up his jeans, and headed my way.

"I'm the shop foreman," he said when he reached me. "Walt says you need to see me."

"I'm helping the Rocky Point police in an investigation," I said, matching his no-nonsense manner. "I found two of your hidden compartments, one in a desk, the other in a tallboy, but I can't find the third. It's in a bed." I showed him my phone display. "Tell me how to access it and I'll be out of your hair."

His eyes dropped to the phone, then raised up again.

"There's no set place. Each one is different."

"Surely you keep records."

"Confidential records. People build in privacy compartments because they want, you know, privacy."

"This is an official request," I said, hedging a little.

"It doesn't sound official to me. I don't know you from Adam."

"You're Mr. Bisset, right? One of the owners?"

"What's it to you?"

"Because it seems to me you're looking at my request like a shop foreman, not an owner. You don't have a privileged relationship with your customers. You're not a lawyer or a preacher. If you won't help me now, I'll have to ask Rocky Point's police chief, Chief Hunter, to get a court order requiring your cooperation. Do you really want it on the public record that you refused to help the police?"

"Sounds like good publicity to me." He turned toward Walt, the guard. "This little lady's leaving." He walked away.

"Wait!" I called.

Bissct pauscd.

"It's urgent," I said. "Please don't force us to delay. If you help me now, I'll make certain your company gets glowing mentions in every report I give to the police and the press. I work with a reporter from the *Seacoast Star.* I guarantee you'll get fabulous coverage. I'll be sure and talk about your furniture's clever designs."

I could see the wheels turning in his head.

"You're a smooth operator, aren't you?" he asked.

"No, sir. Just a woman on a mission."

He reached out a hand. "Give me that phone."

I handed it over.

"Walt, take this number down." He read off the account number.

"Got it," Walt said.

Mr. Bisset handed back my phone. "Go wait in the front, in the reception lobby. I'll get the information you want." He tramped off. Before I'd done more than turn around, he called, "I'll be checking for that story!"

"You have my word."

"Guess we'll know what's it worth soon enough."

I watched him disappear through a door on the right, nodded at Walt, and retraced my steps to the reception area.

I sat on another wooden bench to wait.

Five minutes later, a young man with a clipped goatee walked into the reception area. He wore jeans and a blue and green plaid flannel shirt He didn't look my way but headed straight for Belle. She nodded in my direction.

He handed me a photocopy of a schematic. The hidden compartment was accessed by sliding open a hinged faux dowel positioned where the headboard joined the frame and pushing a spring latch. *Clever,* I thought. The triangular opening was larger than the other two. As I walked slowly to my car, I stared at the drawing trying to figure out why it was shaped as it was.

I was on the interstate heading back to Boston before I answered my question. The privacy cubbyhole was shaped to hold a gun.

Chapter Nineteen

The police officer on guard at Becca's apartment wasn't inclined to let me in. His name badge read L. LAWSON. He was somewhere in his twenties. His cheeks were red and chapped, windburned. His collar was turned up and his earflaps were pulled down. He looked cold.

"Sorry," he said. "I can't watch your car."

"I'll get Chief Hunter on the phone," I said. "He's the police chief in Rocky Point, New Hampshire." I smiled, colleague to colleague. "He'll tell you I'm okay."

"Nothing personal," Officer Lawson said, shaking his head, "but I don't work for him."

I stopped smiling. "Good point. Chief Hunter can give us the name of his contact in the Boston Police Department, though."

"Even if he did, I don't have the keys. I can't let you in."

I shifted my gaze from Officer Lawson's face to the Fenway. The snow along the curb was streaked with soot. The sky was dull pewter. The temperature hovered around freezing. I scanned the street in both directions. Cars were parked bumper to bumper.

I turned back to the police officer. "I'll only be a few minutes. No matter what, I promise it won't be on you."

He shook his head. "Sorry."

I dug around in my tote bag for my phone and dialed Ellis's cell phone.

"Hi," I said, when he answered. "It's Josie. I have the answer about the bed. I'm at Becca's apartment. There's a new police officer on duty, and he's a cautious man. He doesn't feel comfortable watching my car while I knock on the door to see if Ethan will let me in. Who can blame him? No one told him about me, or about you, for that matter. There's nowhere to park, so I'm kind of up the creek."

"Let me talk to him for a moment."

"Sure." I handed Officer Lawson my phone. "Here. Chief Hunter wants to talk to you."

I listened to a series of grunts, then, "Yes, sir."

Officer Lawson pushed the END CALL button and handed back my phone.

"I'll be getting instructions shortly," the officer said.

"Good."

"Chief Hunter told me I was doing the right thing, that he wished more of his officers followed the rules."

"Chief Hunter recognized one of his own," I said, "a good cop."

Officer Lawson's red cheeks flushed a warmer pink. "Thanks."

I waited in my idling car for word to come down from on high. I kept peeking at Officer Lawson, so I saw him slide his iPhone from an inside pocket, talk, listen, and nod. He leaned over and caught my eye. He nodded and waggled his fingers, signaling that he had his official authorization to help.

"We have to stop meeting this way," Ethan said, as he stepped back to let me in.

A green duffel bag sat next to a tan leather backpack.

"You're going somewhere," I said.

"You're still sharp as a tack."

I laughed. "Sorry. I don't mean to be inquisitive. I need to check something in Becca's room. I'll only be a minute."

"Help yourself. You know the way."

Becca's door was closed. I paused with my hand on the knob and looked back. "Still no word from her?"

"Not as far as I know. But I'm not sure

I'd be her first phone call."

I turned to face him. "Why is that?"

"We're roommates, not lovers, you know?"

I recalled my college roommate, a pleasant young woman named Robyn something. I hadn't thought about her in years, despite our having roomed together for three of my four years on campus.

"You're acquaintances," I said, "not friends."

"Friendly colleagues," he said, "not buddies."

"Who's her best bud?"

"I don't know."

"I'm worried about her."

"Me, too."

I glanced at his luggage. "Do you need to leave? I can let myself out, if you want. I'll make certain the door is locked."

"What does it matter? People who want in come through the window."

"It's awful. Terrifying."

"Disconcerting, at the least. That's why I'm leaving. I've got to work, and to work I need quiet. I'm heading up to the institute for a few days. Maybe you'll take pity on a stranger to those parts and share a meal with me while I'm there."

I couldn't tell if he was hoping I'd be a friendly acquaintance like Becca or whether he was interested in a romantic relationship. Either my radar was on the fritz or he was sending mixed signals. I was tempted to invite him to join Ty and me for dinner as a way of letting him know that I wasn't available romantically, but I wasn't so sure I wanted him in my life at all, even as a friendly acquaintance. His jocosity was amusing, but I knew from past experience that keeping up with constant repartee was exhausting.

"Maybe," I said, wanting to avoid committing myself.

"I'll let you know when I leave," he said in a colder tone, taking my response as a brush-off, which I guess it was.

Someone had nailed plywood over the broken window, so standing in the room was no longer like being inside an ice cube. I closed the door.

The fake dowel worked exactly as the drawing indicated, swinging aside soundlessly. I sprang the latch, and the privacy compartment fanned out. I aimed my flashlight into the aperture. A good-sized black velvet pouch looked small in the large space. There was no gun. I worked my hands into a pair of the plastic gloves Ellis had given me and eased the pouch out. I loosened the ribbed tie strings and gently shook an inner piece of velvet into my hand, unfurling it carefully.

My throat closed, as it always did in the presence of inordinate beauty. Moments like this were why I'd gone into the antiques appraisal business. The watercolor miniatures were exactly as described, oval shaped and tiny, yet so meticulously rendered that even the subtlest details shone through. The gilt frames were fitted with flourishes and curls.

I sat back on my haunches and stared at my ancestor. Arabella Churchill was classically beautiful, with soulful eyes and a knowing smile. Her skin was nearly pure white, not pallid; rather, the color of fine vanilla ice cream. Her hair was golden blond and fell in loose ringlets to her shoulders. Her eyes were cerulean. She wore a celery green low-cut dress with short bouffant sleeves, trimmed in ornate white lace, a sign of opulence, then and now. Her lover, King James II, had a long narrow face, with features to match. He wasn't exactly handsome, but he exuded masculinity. He wore a rich burgundy coat and stood at a slight angle, with his chest pushed out. I wondered if Arabella had enjoyed her time with him, or whether she'd endured it.

A double-knock rat-a-tat-tat sounded on

the door, and I jumped, startled.

"Coming!" I called.

I quickly rolled the paintings into the velvet, slipped them into the pouch, slid the pouch into my tote bag, closed the secret cubbyhole, and ran to the door.

Ethan looked over my shoulder, his eyes pausing for a moment on the wood-blocked window.

"Find what you're looking for?" he asked.

"It's a process," I said, avoiding answering. "Are you off?"

"Like a prom dress," he said, surprising another laugh out of me.

"I'll be a few more minutes. Do I need a key to lock up?"

"No. The door locks automatically when you shut it. I ought to know. I've locked myself out often enough." He glanced around again. "What are you doing, anyway?"

"Searching for secret compartments in the furniture."

"Get out of town. Did you find any?"

"If so, it's Becca's secret to tell, not mine."

One corner of his mouth shot up. "You're cute as a bug, smart as paint, über successful, and to top it all off, you're discreet. Want to marry me?"

I laughed again. "I'll have to introduce

you to my boyfriend some time."

"Does he travel a lot? I'm discreet, too."

I shook my head, embarrassed at the direction our conversation was taking. "I've got to get back to work, Ethan. And you need to hit the road."

"Story of my life." He gave a cheery wave and left.

I closed the door again, just in case Ethan decided he'd forgotten something and came back in. With Wes in mind, I took a series of photographs: the pouch inside the compartment, the paintings side by side on the black velvet, and close-ups of each painting. I redid the packaging and placed the miniatures at the bottom of my tote bag, closed the hidden compartment, texted Ellis the good news, e-mailed the photos to myself and him, and took one last look around to ensure I hadn't forgotten something. Words to live by, my dad once told me: Always look back.

I closed the apartment door, testing it to confirm the lock caught, and joined Officer Lawson on the stoop.

"You look happy," he said, handing me my keys.

"Oh, baby," I said, giving a cocky grin, "you have no idea."

"Good."

"How long do you have to stay here?" I asked, looking out over the barren Fens.

"Another hour or so."

"What's the point? The break-in was at the back."

"Perception, I guess. Seeing a police presence reassures people that they're safe."

Perception, I thought, *trumps reality every day of the week.*

"Thanks for your help," I said.

He touched his hat brim, an old-world gesture of respect. "Just doing my job, miss."

I smiled and walked to my car, aware as I moved that there was a jaunty bounce to my step. I opened the car door and allowed myself the pleasure of doing a fist pump to celebrate my find. I was just doing my job, too.

"Yes!" I said aloud, punctuating the word with a second fist pump.

Chapter Twenty

I pulled into a service area off I-95 just north of Peabody to grab a late lunch, glad I'd worn my heavy coat. The temperature was sinking fast and had already fallen into the low teens.

My phone sounded, alerting me that a text had arrived. It was from Ellis. *Call me,* it read. I dialed his number.

"I love good news," he said.

"Isn't it fab? I found the miniatures. They're gorgeous, Ellis, even more spectacular than the photos. As good as described, maybe better. They're definitely worth biggo-buckos."

"Worth killing for."

"Anything is worth killing for if you want it or fear it enough."

"True. Where are you now?"

I told him, then said, "My plan is to take the paintings back to my place. We can keep them in the vault and have them handy for an appraisal. I'm thinking my first step should be to verify provenance, kind of a backward treasure hunt."

"What will that tell you?"

"That Becca has the right to own them."

"Excellent. We need to make your possession of them official — it's a chain of evidence thing. Why don't you call me when you're close to your office? I'll meet you there."

"Sounds good," I said. "I'll keep you posted."

I surveyed the food options — same old, same old. I finally made my choice, a slice of pizza, and settled into a table by the window.

While I ate the better-than-expected pizza, I called Ty.

"I was just about to call you," he said. "Rudy's in the hospital — he broke his arm."

Rudy was Ty's boss, a career security pro, and an all-around good egg.

"What happened? Is he okay?"

"Yeah. He was in his backyard sawing off a dead tree limb, and he fell off the ladder."

"Ouch."

"Double ouch. He knocked himself unconscious, too. It sounds worse than it is. They're keeping him overnight for observation, but I spoke to him and he sounds fine."

"How's Rosie? Out of her mind, right?" Rudy was Mr. Calm. His wife, Rosie, was Ms. Drama Queen. I'd witnessed her cry over a hangnail.

"I suspect she's in her element. Rudy was chuckling when he told me two of her sisters and three of her nieces had taken over the waiting room, petting her, and reassuring her, and you know."

"I do indeed. Good for her. She knows what she needs and she makes it happen."

"The thing is, Rudy's boss, the deputy director, asked me to cover for him."

My eyes rounded. "Ty! Out of eight of you at your level, he asked you? You must be thrilled."

"Except that I'm in Boston, on the shuttle bus from the long-term parking lot to the terminal. I fly out in ninety minutes."

"Long-term parking? That sounds, I don't know, long-term."

"A week. Maybe ten days."

"Starting on a Friday?"

"I get to be on call, which means I can't be more than fifteen minutes from headquarters. Rudy says the doctor told him he'll be good as new in two months. And cleared to go back to work in a week or so, depending on how he's feeling. Knowing

Rudy, he'll show up in a suit and tie next Wednesday."

"I'm really proud of you, Ty, but I miss you already."

"I miss you, too, Joz."

"Maybe I'll come visit."

"We can go to that restaurant you like."

"And visit the National Gallery."

"And do some Christmas shopping."

"I love you, Ty."

"I love you, too, Josie."

We promised to talk before bed.

I bought a coffee, returned to my place by the window, and called Sasha. Cara told me she was out on an appraisal inquiry. A recent widow was updating her will and needed to know the value of her antiques so she could divvy them up fairly, finance-wise, among her children.

"How about Fred? Is he there?"

He was, and while Cara transferred me, I e-mailed him the photographs of the miniatures.

"Have some photos arrived?" I asked him after we exchanged hellos.

"Hold on . . . yup. Got 'em! Very cool. You found them!"

I grinned like a cat confident the mouse didn't have a chance. "I did indeed. It was a fine moment, I must say. So . . . as far as I know, Ian Bennington bought them as a pair in the last several years and gave them to his daughter, Rebecca Bennington, as a housewarming gift. There's supposed to be an old appraisal, but I didn't find it among her possessions. The police don't have it, either. It may turn up — maybe she scanned it in and they'll find it on her computer. In any event, the police have asked us to help verify provenance. I'm on my way back with the miniatures now, but in the meantime, I'm hoping you can do some preliminary research to get me started."

"Do you know where Ian bought them?" Fred asked.

"No, he didn't say."

"I'll check auction records."

"You have to start somewhere. Thanks, Fred!"

As soon as I was off the phone with Fred, I called Wes.

"Whatcha got?" he asked.

"A lot, but you can't use most of it, at least not now."

"Josie," he griped.

"Here's one you can write about right away. Most of Becca's furniture was made by a custom company called Meadow's Village Furniture. They're known for cleverly designing and installing what they call privacy compartments, which you and I would refer to as hidden cubbyholes. The company, which is a family attraction, is located in Franklin, New Hampshire, and for a little color, you can write about how it's on the site of a former Shaker community. The designers have maintained the Shaker style, which as I'm sure you know is identifiable from its simple lines, lack of nonfunctional embellishments, and superb craftsmanship."

"You want to tell me why you're suggesting that I write a lifestyle fluff piece?"

"Because I promised the owner you would. He wouldn't talk to me otherwise."

"You got some chutzpah, Josie, I'll give you that."

"I want to fill you in, but you have to promise that you won't publish a word or a picture unless I tell you it's okay to do so."

"What pictures?"

"The ones I'm going to e-mail you showing a hidden compartment I found in Becca's bed."

"What? Talk to me."

"Promise?"

"Josie!" he sputtered. "I need facts I *can* use."

"Not now. Not from me."

He sighed to his toenails, Wes-speak for

how disappointed he was in me. I waited.

"Okay," he said begrudgingly, "I promise."

"Good. I'll send you the photos in a minute. The information I needed related to the placement of hidden cubbyholes. You can write about the company in general, but you can't say I found one in Becca's bed. Here's the thing . . . I found the missing paintings, Wes! I don't know how the police plan on playing it, so mum's the word. I have photos for you of the cubbyhole and the paintings."

"You're the bomb, Joz. The complete bomb."

"Thanks. What about Becca? Any news?"

"Not a word or a sign. You think she's been killed, too?"

"Oh, God, Wes, I hope not."

After we were done, I e-mailed Wes the photos of the miniatures and the hiding place. I finished my coffee and walked back to my car.

Where, I asked myself as I merged back onto the highway, *is Becca*? The more I thought about the situation, the more confused I became.

I spoke to Becca on Tuesday, and by any standard, her reaction to my innocent question was odd — or was it? If Becca had killed her father, the question might have touched her on the raw.

And what about Lia? Did she see Ian with Becca on Sunday, misunderstand their relationship, and flip out? Ashamed of myself for suspecting Lia, my friend, I nonetheless couldn't stop myself from wondering whether she'd been home alone the whole afternoon as she said or whether she'd gone out for some reason, for new makeup or a different color of stockings, for instance.

Lia could have driven into town to do her shopping, taking the scenic route home. I did it all the time. If she'd driven down Ocean Avenue, she might have passed just as Ian and Becca were standing out in the open at the end of Cable Road. She sees Ian deep in conversation with Becca and loses it.

Becca, now a witness to a crime, flees, panicked.

While I'd seen Lia enraged, beyond furious, I'd never seen her violent. Still, I couldn't shake a niggling feeling that seeing Ian with a young woman might have been the straw that broke the camel's back.

Ian was rich, handsome, available, and attracted to her. The idea of losing a man this appealing to a younger woman, especially after losing a husband because of his obsession with, as Lia put it, jailbait-aged girls, might have tipped her over the edge.

Though I felt like a Judas, my incriminating thoughts continued unabated. Lia needs money. She makes no secret of it. Hearing that Becca had vanished, she might have risked breaking into Becca's housing in the hopes of snaring a treasure, the miniatures. She'd heard me talk about how hard it is to sell stolen art — or rather, how hard it is to sell stolen art for top dollar. It's easy to sell if you're willing to work with a sleazy dealer and take pennies on the dollar. It might only be pennies, but pennies on more than one and a quarter million dollars, my quick and dirty estimate of the retail value of the two paintings, wasn't hay. Realistically, she could expect to sell them, no questions asked, for 20 percent of retail, about $250,000. Tax free. Money her ex would never know about, would never be able to claim.

My cell phone rang. I glanced at the display but didn't recognize the number, a 917 area code. New York City. I pulled off to the shoulder, set my flashers, and took the call.

A woman with the husky voice of a smoker said, "A woman I work with said you can tell me if I have an antique that's worth anything."

"We do our best! What's the object?"

"A pair of wrought-iron chairs. They've got claw feet and gargoyle heads at the ends of the arms and lots of flowers and things woven into the design."

"They sound beautiful. I'd love to get a look at them."

"I'm not far from your company. Can you stop by now?"

I was about to ask her to schedule an appointment for tomorrow or Monday when I realized Ty was in D.C., so I had no reason to hurry home. I could connect with Ellis, get the paintings in the vault, then head to her place.

"Definitely!"

She gave me her name, Pat Weston, and her address, 14 Rochand Road. I knew the street. It was the second right after my place, heading to the coast. I calculated the time. I was about ten minutes from my exit. Another ten minutes would get me to Prescott's. It would only take a minute or two to sign off on the evidence with Ellis and store the paintings. Five minutes to her place. I told Ms. Weston I'd be there in forty-five minutes, give or take. I called Ellis, and we agreed to meet at my place in half an hour.

Twenty minutes later, along a dark stretch

of road about a quarter mile before the turn-in to my parking lot, my headlights illuminated a gray or silver sedan parked diagonally across the road, as if it had died while the driver was attempting a U-turn, or perhaps something had happened to incapacitate him. I rolled to a stop fifty feet from the vehicle and turned on my brights. No one was visible behind the wheel.

I found my phone and called 911. I told the emergency operator that either the car had broken down and the driver had set off for help or the driver had fallen ill, but regardless, the road was blocked. She said she'd send the police right away. I wondered who'd arrive first, the officers assigned to respond to the emergency call or Ellis.

I pulled off to the side of the road, parking on frozen dirt and low-growing brush, and got out. The woods on either side were impenetrable, thick and near-black. The road in either direction was empty. I jogged to the car to see if the driver had collapsed. I knew CPR, and if I could help, I wanted to. I switched on my flashlight and sent the light around the inside of the car, peering into the back floor. The vehicle was empty. The key wasn't in the ignition. The driver had gone to find assistance.

I had started back to my car when a soft

rustling caught my attention. *A rabbit, maybe,* I thought, *or a deer.* Just as I approached the driver's-side door, I heard a whoosh. I spun toward the noise. In the faint light from my headlights, I saw what looked like tree bark, a sturdy limb, aimed at my head. I screeched and cantered right, and the blow landed with a thud on my left shoulder.

Shock waves of pain shot up my neck and down my back to my legs, and I stumbled forward. I screamed in shock and fear and pain, my yells echoing in the cold, dry, dark night. I tried to run, but I could only totter. My legs had gone tingly-numb. I heard another whoosh and knew a second blow was coming. I sank to the ground, the air swirling around me as the tree limb whizzed by my head, thunking on the hood of my car.

I tried to push myself upright, but I didn't have the strength. I lay in a dazed heap, mired in terror. *Roll,* I told myself, knowing that unless I moved, I was a sitting duck, certain to be killed. I raised myself up a few inches, grunting when my shoulder muscles flexed. I sank back to the ground and gyrated sideways, away from my car, and the third strike glanced off my left arm. I scooted away as best I could, scraping my hands on the pebble-laden asphalt. My screams trailed off into whimpers. The pain was dazzling. Gold flecks danced before my eyes. I quit moving, knowing it was hopeless. I rolled over, trying to see something I could use to identify my attacker, but before I could focus, both my headlights and blinkers went out and I was left in the middle of the road in total darkness. I closed my eyes and prepared to die.

Chapter Twenty-One

I heard footsteps, followed by a slamming door. An engine turned over and a car sped off. Silence settled in like a London fog, punctuated only by occasional forest sounds, a swish of something pushing through dense growth, followed by crunching steps, small paws on brittle leaves. The road to my office wasn't a major thoroughfare, but neither was it deserted. If I didn't get off the road, someone would run over me before the police arrived.

I took stock. The sharp pain of impact had eased, but I felt disoriented and a little woozy, as if I had just awakened from a troubled sleep. I could arch my back and roll my head and lift my arms. I clenched, then spread, my fingers. The heels of my hands were bloodied. Nothing was broken. Lucky for me I'd worn my heavy, puffy coat and my attacker had lousy aim, the blows landing on my shoulder and arm, missing my head and back.

Using my fingertips, I pushed myself to my knees. I took in a deep breath, got myself upright, and stumbled toward my car. I slid behind the wheel and reached for the key — it was missing. I turned on the map light. In the eerie glow cast by the overhead dome, I saw that the passenger seat was empty. My tote bag was gone.

"Oh, no," I whispered. "God, no."

I leaned my head against the frozen steering wheel. The police were en route. I could wait and they would help me. I was cold. Too cold to sit. I was wearing a super-warm coat. I got out and started walking. During my slow, painful trek, I realized what must have transpired, and why.

Fred, a night owl who often worked late, was there to let me in.

"I need you to do something for me," I said, leaning heavily against one of the guest chairs. "Call Ellis, Chief Hunter, and tell him to come here right away, then go to my office and get my spare keys from my desk drawer."

Fred pushed up his square-framed glasses, his brow furrowed. "Are you all right?"

I sat down. "No." He made a movement, as if he were going to walk toward me. When

I shook my head, he stopped. "Please. Make the call. Get the keys."

"Okay," he said.

Fred looked up the police station number and dialed. When he told whoever answered that he was calling on my behalf and that he had an urgent message, they patched the call through. I listened in.

"I don't know," he said after he explained why he was calling. "No . . . Okay." He covered the mouthpiece with his hand. "He wants to talk to you."

I shook my head. "Tell him to come quickly."

He did so, glancing at me. "Maybe an accident. I don't know."

He listened for a moment. "I don't think so, but I'm not sure. I'll ask." He covered the mouthpiece again. "He wants to know if he should send an ambulance."

"No."

Fred repeated my answer, listened for a moment, said, "Okay," and hung up. "He said he was close by. He'll be here in two minutes."

"Thanks."

Fred pushed open the heavy door that led to the warehouse, and Hank scooted out.

He mewed. *Hello,* he was saying. *I'm glad you're back.* He pranced toward me and rubbed his jowl against my calf. After a few seconds, he leapt into my lap, allowing me to pet him. My hands throbbed. Scrapes are the worst. Using the tips of my fingers, I stroked his chin and breastbone.

"You're such a good boy, Hank," I murmured. "Such a good friend."

He mewled and curled up, resting his head against my tummy.

"The appointment to look at that wrought-iron furniture was a ruse," I told him, "to lure me, to ensure I would come down this road."

Hank raised his chin, offering me access to his neck, asking for a nice pettie.

"Good boy, baby."

He flopped over, wanting a tummy rub.

"Someone knew I found the miniatures," I said. "Neither Wes nor Ellis would tell anyone, which means someone was watching me. He saw me all happy and proud when I left the apartment and knew what it meant. He followed me to the interstate, so he figured I was heading back to Rocky Point. When I stopped for lunch, he continued on and got his plan organized."

Hank licked my fingers, a thank-you.

"Oh, Hank . . . you're such a precious boy."

He rearranged himself, his thick front

paws hanging over my knees. I gently dragged my fingernails along his spine, and his purring machine whirred onto high.

"He had to know that as soon as I reached my office, the paintings would be beyond his reach."

Fred returned with the key ring in hand. I heard a car engine rev up, then idle, then shut down.

"Is that Ellis?" I asked him. "Chief Hunter?"

Fred leaned over to look out the window. "Yes."

"Good. A quarter mile from here, toward the interstate, you'll find my car parked on the shoulder. Ellis can drive you there."

"I can walk it, Josie, no problem — but what's going on?"

Ellis opened the door, setting Gretchen's wind chimes jingling.

"Hey," Ellis said, his eyes narrowing when he saw me, his gaze lingering on my face. "What's wrong?"

I raised a hand to my cheek and felt grit. My fingers came away dirty. "It's nothing, only dirt."

"Your hands are bleeding."

I looked at them. "It's dried now. I scraped them."

"Talk to me, Josie. I just asked two police

officers why they were standing by your car. They explained they were responding to your call that a car was blocking the road. What gives?"

"I'll explain, but first, will you drive Fred to get my car? It'll only take you a minute."

"Were you in an accident?"

"No." The two men stood and waited. "It wasn't an accident — it was an ambush." I closed my eyes. "I was a complete sucker. It never even occurred to me that it was a trap. Whoever did it stole my tote bag. Oh, Ellis. I'm so upset! The miniatures were in it. So were my keys. My phone. Everything." Tears escaped and ran down my cheeks. "Everything is gone."

"Are you hurt besides your hands?" Ellis asked, his tone soft and empathetic, as calm as always.

"A little. Not much." I opened my eyes and brushed aside the wetness. "I was a patsy. The more I think about it, the angrier I'm getting."

"Tell me — the short version."

With Fred listening in, his eyes growing wider as the story went on, I recounted what had transpired.

"My phone has the Find My iPhone app on it."

"Good," Ellis said.

"I'm on it," Fred said, typing at his computer. He asked for my user information. I called it out. Fred tapped it into his computer and rotated his monitor so Ellis and I could see, zooming in on the green dot.

"That's I-95," Ellis said.

"Near the liquor store, heading south," Fred said. "It's not moving, though."

"The thief turned it off," I said, my eyes on the monitor. "That's the last spot the phone was on. He grabbed my tote bag and headed for the interstate. Once he was under way, he turned off my phone in case I had this app." I raised my eyes to Fred's face. "Erase the data. I just synched my phone, so I have everything I need."

"Are you sure?"

"Yes."

He tapped the codes. "Done."

"I'm going to get a team to go over your car," Ellis said. "I doubt we'll find anything, but you never know. When we're done, we'll drive it back to the police garage for further examination. You'll need to get the dealer to change the locks." He paused, thinking. "You said you saw the weapon, a tree limb. Probably it just got tossed into the woods."

"You won't find it," I said, discouraged. "You won't find the attacker, either. I didn't see much. Just a hint of a tree branch aiming at my head."

"From what angle?"

My brow scrunched. "What do you mean?"

"Was the person swinging the branch like a baseball bat? Or was it more straight down, as if he were splitting a log?"

"More like a bat, I think. It seemed disorganized to me. The swings were wild, kind of uncontrolled."

"How about the car? What do you remember about it?"

"It was gray or silver," I said. "Normal-looking." I shrugged. "A sedan."

"How about the caller? Did her voice sound familiar?"

"Not at all."

"You said she had a husky voice, like a smoker. How certain are you it was a woman? The name Pat can go either way."

"At the time, I didn't question it. Now, I don't know. I suppose it could have been a man trying to sound like a woman."

"Or a woman you know trying to disguise her voice?"

"Like who?" I asked.

"Like anyone. Could it have been?"

"Yes. Maybe. I don't know."

"That about covers it," Ellis said, half-smiling.

I turned to Fred. "Will you call the security company here and tell them my bag was stolen? And wait for them to get here to change the locks?"

"Of course." He headed to his desk to make the call.

"Zoë is home," Ellis told me. "She can take care of the locks at your house."

"I need to get Ty's changed, too." I leaned down to kiss Hank, and my muscles let me know they existed. "Ow!" The pain was more a spikey throbbing than a sharp stabbing, but the overall effect was intense. Fred took a step toward me. "I'm okay." I tried to smile but doubted it looked like much. "My shoulder hurts a little, that's all." I shook my head, frustrated. "This is such a monumental hassle."

"In spades," Ellis said. "You're the victim and you end up being the one who has to deal with the fallout."

I knew Ellis well enough to know his empathy was genuine, but it didn't make me feel any better. I was annoyed at the hassle I knew I had to face, irritated that I couldn't simply blink and make it go away, angry as all get-out that I'd been caught in such a simple snare, and beyond furious that valuable antiques under my control had been stolen.

"Will you call Ty for me?" I asked. "Tell him I'm okay, just mad enough to spit."

"Sure."

Hank didn't like it that I'd slowed down on petting him. He gave a stern kitty-harrumph, jumped off my lap, and sauntered away. At the warehouse door, he mewed imperiously, and Fred, still talking to the security company, opened it for him. Hank had us well trained.

"Do you want us to add alerts that the paintings have been stolen to our call for sightings?" I asked. "If the thief is smart, he'll sell them pronto, before the word is out that they've been stolen."

"Is there any benefit in keeping the theft under our hat?"

"I can't think," I said, "so I can't help you decide."

"You think just fine," Ellis said. "You've just been battered is all." He stared into space for several seconds before adding, "I think the more publicity we have on this, the better. Let's make it as hard as possible for the thief to dispose of the paintings."

"Wes can publish an article about the theft and tweet about it and so on," I said. "I sent him the photos, too."

"You sent Wes photos?" Ellis asked, his tone suddenly icy.

"With the promise he wouldn't use them until I said it was okay."

He gave me a long disapproving look. I didn't flinch. Instead, I said, "Will you explain our ideas to Wes or do you want me to?"

"I will," he said, and from his tone, I got the impression that Wes was in for it.

I wasn't concerned; Wes could take care of himself. I looked at Fred, just off the phone.

"They'll be here in ten minutes," Fred said.

Ellis laughed, a quick ha. "Ten minutes? That's pretty incredible service."

"I buy the Platinum Plan for just that reason." I turned toward Fred. "I need you to work with the police to get the stolen art protocols going."

"Sure," he said.

I thanked him, then sat quietly while the two men worked, each on the phone, issuing instructions, setting various protocols in motion.

Three conversations later, Ellis handed me his phone. "Ty wants to talk to you."

"Hey," I said.

"Ellis says you're pretty banged up."

"Not really. A few bruised muscles,

scraped hands, and seriously wounded pride."

"There's a late flight I can make, which means I could be home by midnight."

"Thanks, but there's no point. The way I feel, I'll be long asleep by midnight."

"Ellis told me your keys were stolen. You shouldn't be in the house alone, even after they change the lock, not until we know what's going on."

"The thief has what he was after, so I don't think there's any risk . . . but I was thinking of staying in Zoë's guest room anyway. She'll make me tea and soup and martinis, not necessarily in that order."

"That'll work." He paused. "You know if you want me to come home, all you have to do is say the word."

"Thank you. Yes, I know. You're wonderful. At this point, there's nothing you can do and nothing I need, so while you know I'd love to have you with me, there's no reason to mess up your schedule and find an emergency replacement and all."

He said he understood but was glad to mess up his schedule any time I said the word. We agreed to talk later, once I was in for the night, and I handed the phone back to Ellis.

"Ty is so great," I said.

"So are you. He's a lucky man."

"Wow. Thanks."

I heard a car and shifted my position enough to glance out the window. Ellis walked closer so he could look, too.

A black SUV, a match for the one Ellis drove, rolled to a stop close to the front. When the driver's door opened and the overhead light came on, I saw Detective Claire Brownley.

"Once I get Claire up to speed," he said, "I'm taking you to the hospital for a once-over."

"I'm fine. All I want is a hot bath, some Tylenol, a martini, food, and a bed. And maybe tea."

He paused, his hand on the doorknob. "I don't think that's smart."

"I just can't face the prospect of an examination right now." I pressed my fingers against my temples. "I'm getting a headache. I need to lie down."

"Did you lose consciousness at all, even for a second or two?"

"No."

"Still. It's better to be safe than sorry. Think about it for a minute."

"Okay," I said, to appease him. I didn't want to think about it, but neither did I want to argue.

The two men from the security company, our regular account manager, Russ, and a helper named Terry, arrived eight minutes after they were called.

"Any chance one of the cameras is aimed at the road?" Ellis asked them.

"No," Russ said. "The range stops at the perimeter of the parking lot."

I listened in as Ellis described our publicity plan to Wes. I was relieved that my having sent Wes the photos didn't come up.

Half an hour later, the two men from the security company had finished changing the door locks, Fred was uploading the photos to the last of the stolen-art Web sites we subscribed to, Detective Brownley was working the crime scene, and Ellis had agreed to drive me to Zoë's.

"There is no number fourteen Rochand Road," Ellis told me once we were under way. "There's no forty-one, either. I checked in case Pat Weston transposed the numbers by mistake."

"And I bet there's no Pat Weston, either."

"Not that we can find. We have officers canvassing door to door."

"You won't find her because she doesn't exist." I slapped my thigh. "I feel like such a fool."

"I don't know why. You couldn't possibly have anticipated this, Josie."

I turned to watch the night. It was so dark, I couldn't discern anything, not even the shape of a tree. I looked up. The sky was solid black; not a glimmer of moonlight shone through the cloud cover. "Is it supposed to snow?"

"I don't think so. Why?"

"The night is so black."

"On cloudy nights, it's darker up here than anywhere I've ever lived before."

We drove in silence for several minutes. As Ellis turned off the interstate, I asked, "Is there any word about Becca?"

"No."

"We need to talk to the chair of the Marine Biology Department."

"Dr. Bennett? I met him when I was at Reynard. What about?"

"Becca."

He shot me a glance. "That's pretty broad."

"She drives a silver car."

"A 2008 Prius," he said. "Not much of a car for a rich girl."

"But perfect for a girl who cares about the environment and isn't materialistic."

"True," he said. "What do you think Dr. Bennett knows?"

"How Becca and Ethan get along."

"You think there's some kind of conspiracy going on?" he asked.

"No. It's just, the more we know, the more we know, if you know what I mean."

"And we don't know about their relationship."

"I know Ethan told me they were not romantically involved."

"You don't believe him?"

"I don't disbelieve him. I also wonder if he and Becca are fiercely competitive or friendly competitive. My dad had a friend who was the chair of the History Department at Hitchens years ago. He said his department was filled with well-wishers, colleagues determined to help one another succeed, whereas the Philosophy Department operated like scorpions in a bottle."

"Are you kidding me?"

"No."

"Jesus. I'll set up a meeting tomorrow." He glanced at me again. "In the afternoon, so you can sleep late."

"I'm okay," I said. "Just a little stiff."

Ellis didn't comment, and I knew why. He thought that by morning I wouldn't be able to move.

Chapter Twenty-Two

Ellis ran into Zoë's place to get my new keys and kept me company as I gathered what I needed for the night. We walked across the icy driveway to Zoë's house. She had hearty chicken noodle soup warming on the stove and a pot of black currant tea steeping on the counter. I swallowed two painkillers with my first swallow of tea.

Later, after I'd taken a long hot lavender-scented bath, I put on my pink chenille robe and fuzzy slippers. Sitting in her comfy kitchen, I drank a second cup of tea and polished off two bowls of soup. Ellis, she told me, was in her den, working. She sat beside me, not talking unless I did. It was perfect.

I called good night to Ellis, blew Zoë a kiss, and climbed the stairs to her guest room, one stiff and painful step at a time. The room was painted sky blue. The wall-to-wall carpet was a deep, rich shade of blue, almost navy, but not. I used the phone Zoë kept on the bedside table to call Ty. He sounded worried about me. We told each other we loved one another; then I lay down, sighing with relief. Zoë had converted the Double Wedding Ring quilt her great-grandmother had sewn during the Depression into a duvet cover, creating the softest, most cuddly comforter ever. I snuggled my chin over the soft cotton and fell asleep within seconds.

I didn't wake up until nine the next morning, Saturday, tag sale day, which meant I was super late. I reached for the phone, pausing with my arm in midair as knives pierced my shoulder. Ellis had been right. A night in bed was debilitating.

I sat up, ignoring the pain as best I could, and dialed my office. Cara answered with her usual cheery welcome.

"It's me," I said, and licked my lips. I was parched.

"Oh, Josie," she said. "Fred told us what happened. How are you?"

"Fine. A little stiff, that's all. I'm sorry I'm late."

"You don't need to worry about anything. Fred is covering for you."

We took turns working Saturdays, and today was Fred's day off. "Please thank him, and let him know I'll be in soon."

"I'll tell him," she said, her concern apparent, "but are you sure you should?"

"You know me — I hate coddling myself. Plus, there's nothing better for stiff muscles than moving around."

As soon as I was off the phone, I stood up and tottered, hunched over like an old woman, to the bathroom. Moving around might hurt in the short run, but it was the quickest way to healing. I found painkillers in the medicine cabinet and took two with water I slurped from my hand.

Getting ready took twice as long as usual. Bending was a penance. Stretching was a nightmare. I was proud that I got myself clean and downstairs without crying. I didn't so much as whimper.

Zoë was at the sink rinsing breakfast dishes before sliding them into slots in the dishwasher.

"You're alive!" she said, drying her hands on a Santa Claus tea towel.

"Not really," I said, easing myself into a chair. "I hurt."

"My blueberry pancakes will set you back up. Want a cup of coffee while I get the griddle going?"

"I can't. I'm late."

"A girl needs to eat."

"True. Okay. Thanks. Coffee would be welcome."

Zoë poured pineapple juice into a holly-decorated glass.

"Ouch," she said, her eyes on my hands.

"I know. Scrapes hurt."

"Can I take a peek at your bruises?"

"Why?"

"I want to see how badly you're hurt."

"Let's not know. There's nothing to be done but let nature run its healing course, so why make an issue of it?"

"No open wounds that need attention?"

"None."

"Okay, then pancakes are on their way."

I watched her add butter to the griddle and lay partially cooked strips of bacon in a roasting pan.

"Is Ellis gone?" I asked.

"Yes. He wanted me to let you know that Wes has reported your attack and that the theft is the lead story everywhere. Wes is writing a feature for *New York Today* on the brazen nature of the attack and another for *Antiques Insights* magazine on the ease of stealing small objects."

"Oh, joy. I'll be a laughingstock nation-wide."

"No one is laughing, Josie."

I knew what I was in for. The press would

be all over me hurling questions like bombs, hoping one would explode inside me, rattling me enough so they would get a juicy quote.

"What else did Ellis say?"

"No one has used your phone or credit cards."

"I can't believe I forgot to worry about that." I started to lift myself up and groaned. "I need to cancel them."

"Ty took care of it last night."

"Really?" I sank back down. "That's incredible."

"You're the one who was so organized you gave him a list of your account numbers."

"That's me. Little Miss Organized."

Zoë turned toward me, her concern apparent. "What's wrong, Josie?"

"Nothing you don't know about."

"I wish there was something I could do."

"There is," I said. "You're doing it."

Zoë adjusted the flame under the griddle and put the bacon in the oven. She took a bowl of batter from the refrigerator and scooped a half-cupful onto the sizzling surface.

"What else do I need to know?" I asked.

"You have an appointment at the police station at three. To talk to someone named Dr. Bennett. I'll drive you to work. Ellis will send a car to get you at two thirty."

"Thank you, Zoë."

"Dr. Bennett is Becca's boss. Do I have that right?"

"I don't think 'boss' is exactly the way to put it. He's the chair of the Marine Biology Department at the Boston campus of Reynard, but she's only here for a year on some kind of grant. She's based at their British campus."

"And you think he might know something about where Becca is?" she asked, flipping the pancake.

"No, but it wouldn't surprise me one bit if he knows something about Becca's relationship with Ethan."

"How does that figure into things?"

"I've wondered if Ethan was underplaying his relationship with Becca in the hopes that he might get over on me. He is pretty flirtatious." I started to shrug, stopping when my muscles protested. "If they have an actual boyfriend-girlfriend relationship, it's worth considering how Ethan might have reacted if Ian didn't approve."

"Why wouldn't he have approved?"

"I have no idea. It's all just speculation."

"It always comes back to the boy-girl thing, doesn't it?" she asked.

"Or fear. Or greed. Or revenge."

"Do you think Becca and Ethan are an item?"

"He's pretty charming."

She turned toward me for a moment. "You don't say that about many men."

"Not many men are charming."

"Ain't that the truth," she said, laughing.

She took the bacon from the oven, rolled it in a paper towel, and added it to my plate beside the pancake. I drizzled the warm maple syrup she'd poured into a jug over the pancake and took a bite. "Ummm. This is incredible. Are these the blueberries we picked last summer?"

"Yes." She leaned back against the counter. "Freezing them works like a charm."

"I'll say!" I finished my juice, weighing a new thought. "It doesn't have to be jealousy. It could be anger. What if Becca *doesn't* agree with me that Ethan is all that charming?"

"Lots of people don't take rejection well."

"Ethan jokes a lot about how much better than him Becca is, you know, teasing in a sardonic kind of way. It's not snide. He really is funny and sort of cute about it. I'm betting Dr. Bennett will know if his humility is artifice or real."

"I'll look forward to an update."

Zoë wouldn't let me clean up, so I sat and

kept her company while she did the work. I left Ty a voice mail, telling him I was stiff but fine.

Around ten thirty, Zoë dropped me at my office. "Call if you need me."

I promised I would and, with doddering steps, made it inside. Gretchen, manning the phones so Cara got a break, leapt up from her desk and ran toward me, her beautiful green eyes communicating anxiety alongside the caring.

"You shouldn't be here," she said, her hands extended.

"I'm okay. Thanks, Gretchen." I raised my palms. "I'm sure you'll understand if I skip a handshake, though."

"Of course."

She tried to hustle me into a chair.

"Really," I said sternly. "I'm fine." I smiled to rob my words of surliness. "I appreciate your concern, Gretchen, you know I do. Tell me what's going on with the tag sale."

"Things are good. People are three deep at the vintage ornament displays. Sasha told me the clip-on candle holders were all gone by ten."

"It's all about stocking up, right?"

"And you start buying in January!"

"What are you talking about? I start buying the day after Christmas!"

The wind chimes tinkled, and we both turned toward the door. Ethan walked in. He smiled when he saw me, but it didn't reach his eyes. He looked upset.

"Hey," he said. "It looks like I got lucky. Got a minute?"

"Sure."

I introduced them, watching for Gretchen's reaction. She had a good nose for bad men, having dated more than her share before finally meeting her prince, her husband, Jack. From what I could see as they chatted easily about how today's forty-degree warm-up after yesterday's below-freezing temperatures proved the old saw about New Hampshire — if you don't like the weather, wait five minutes — she thought he was a keeper.

"You go help out at the tag sale," I told her after a minute. "I'll cover the phones."

"Are you sure?" she asked.

I cringed at the picture climbing the spiral staircase conjured up in my mind's eye. Me clinging painfully to the banister as I lurched my way up one step at a time. No way.

"Yes," I said. "I'll call when we're done, and you or Cara can come back. Tell Cara, okay?"

Gretchen didn't want to leave me, offering coffee or tea, suggesting a footstool, fussing and fretting until finally I shooed her away.

When she opened the door, Hank popped through.

"She sure thinks you're a weak Nellie, doesn't she?" Ethan asked once the door was closed behind her.

"Weak Nellie!" I said, laughing. "Where did that expression come from?"

"My mother from her grandmother. It was most decidedly not a compliment."

"I can tell." I pointed to the chairs surrounding the guest table. I got myself settled at Cara's desk, and with an impatient mew, Hank leapt up into my lap. "Have a seat. I'll stay here by the phone."

"Are you all right?" he asked as he sat down near the window

"Just a little stiff." I petted Hank. "A minor accident."

"I read about it in the *Seacoast Star.* That's why I'm here. From what that reporter wrote, it wasn't an accident, and it wasn't minor."

"Don't believe everything you read." I smiled. "It's sweet of you to stop by, though."

Ethan frowned at the floor for a moment. He raised his eyes to mine. "The police asked me where I was when you were attacked."

"That would get my attention."

"It sure got mine."

"What did you tell them?"

"The truth. I was in my room at the institute, writing a paper on oysters and soil erosion."

"Alone."

He smiled, a crooked one, and I knew one of his trademark witty remarks was coming. "All night, I'm sorry to report. Want to hear about how oysters can save the world?"

"Another time, maybe."

He looked at Hank, or maybe at me petting Hank, I couldn't be sure. He began an unconscious pitter-patter fingertip drumbeat on the tabletop.

"I'm worried about Becca," he said after a few seconds. "I think she might be in danger."

"Why?"

"Because she's disappeared. No way is she a killer, so the only alternative is that something bad has happened to her. What else could be going on?"

"And both her rooms have been broken into."

"Exactly. Whatever is happening, she seems to be at the center of it."

I couldn't tell if Ethan had come to check

on me, like he said, or if he hoped that if I knew anything about Becca, I could be tricked into revealing it, as I feared. I stroked Hank's tummy, and his purrs grew louder.

"I've never met Becca," I said.

"She's fun."

"Really? I got the impression she was pretty serious."

"Yeah, she's not real fun. I just said that 'cause, you know . . ."

I wondered what else Ethan had said just 'cause, you know.

"So," he said, crossing his long legs at the ankles, leaning back comfortably, "what have the police discovered about your attack?"

"I don't know. I just got into work a few minutes before you arrived. I haven't heard a word."

"It's a helluva thing."

"What do you think might have happened?"

"What do I think?" he asked, taken aback at my question. "No clue." He glanced at the wall clock and stood up. "I'm glad you're okay."

"I appreciate it, Ethan."

"Is there anything I can do? Can I bring

you food or something? I do a mean take-out."

"Thanks, but I'm all set."

"Well, then," he said, "you take care." He left.

I sat where I was, fielding calls from customers asking for directions or for our hours of operation and thinking about Becca, a serious woman living with a humorous man, maybe as roommates, maybe as more than roommates.

Every Saturday, I provided pizza for all my staff, and when the delivery came just before noon, I relocated to the guest table and called Cara back in so she could organize everyone's lunch schedule.

I couldn't shake off a nebulous feeling that I was missing the significance of something I'd seen or heard. Finally, I gave up thinking about it and focused instead on mushroom pizza, my favorite.

Chapter Twenty-Three

Griff got me to the police station about ten to three. I thanked him for the ride and walked inside in time to hear Detective Brownley say, "Not along that stretch."

"So you can get from the interstate to the church without seeing a security camera," Ellis said.

"Right. If the car came from Main Street, there's a bank on the corner of Walnut that might capture an image, but there's no evidence that's the route the driver took."

"Another dead end." Ellis saw me, nodded thanks to the detective, and came out from behind the counter.

"Hey," I said.

"How you holding up?"

"About as you'd expect."

"I know you don't want me hovering over you or anything, but —"

"That's for sure," I said, interrupting. I smiled, meaning it, and touched his forearm. "If I need anything, I'll ask. Actually, I'd love a cup of tea."

He communicated my request to Cathy and led the way to his office. He pointed to the round guest table, and I took a seat near the window. A faint yellow glow radiated from behind the still-thick cloud cover. Sunlight was trying to nudge through. A thermometer Ellis had mounted outside the front window showed 41. A two-foot-tall pine tree in a red pot sat in the middle of the table. Little red and green shiny balls hung from the branches. A lacy angel perched on the top.

"This is new," I said.

"Zoë insisted I had to have a little holiday cheer in my office."

"It's cute."

"We'll plant it out back in the spring."

"That's a super idea. You can watch it grow."

"Dr. Bennett was already in Rocky Point," Ellis said, leaning back. "He's meeting with the Oceanographic Institute folks, developing a plan to carry on Becca's research — it seems someone needs to check on her clams and monitor her experiments or all her work to date will be lost. I told him you were helping us out with an antiques aspect to the case, so he won't be surprised to see you." He glanced at his watch. "He'll be here in a few minutes."

"I assume there's no news about the missing paintings or you would have told me."

"Nothing definitive yet."

"I'm still reeling at the loss."

"Don't give up hope. We've just launched our investigation."

"I know. I understand." I pointed to a red tin with a sleigh on top. "Did Zoë bake cookies?"

"No, I did." He smiled. "Not cookies. Brownies. You know me. I'm a brownie-making machine. Want one?"

"Heck, yes!"

Cathy came in with the tea, and while we waited for Dr. Bennett, I sat nibbling and sipping, as content as I could be under the circumstances. Ellis moved to his desk and began fussing with some papers.

"Can I use your phone to text Ty?" I asked.

"Sure," he said, handing it over.

I texted Ty that I was with Ellis, using his phone, that I was fine, and that I loved him. He texted back that he'd definitely be home next Thursday. *Yay!* I typed.

Ellis came back to the guest table and sat across from me. I slid his phone back to him.

Cathy knocked once, opened the door without waiting for an invitation, and escorted Dr. Bennett into the room.

"Thanks," Dr. Bennett told her, striding into the office with the confidence of a man used to being in charge.

Ellis stood, and the two men shook hands.

Josiah Bennett was a big man, taller than Ellis by several inches, and Ellis was a hair more than six feet tall. Bennett wore a tan corduroy sports coat, an ivory shirt with a blue and brown striped tie, dark blue jeans, and hiking boots. He was nice-looking, without any one feature standing out. His hair was brown and cut short. He had a small mole near his left ear. I guessed he was about sixty.

"Thanks for coming in," Ellis said. "This is Josie Prescott."

The professor reached across the table, and I raised my palms, showing him my wounds.

"Sorry," I said.

"My God, are you all right?"

"I'm fine. Just a few minor scrapes."

"Good, good," Dr. Bennett said with jovial enthusiasm. "It's a real pleasure to meet you. My wife is a huge fan of your tag sale. She collects old picture frames."

"Nice," I said. "What kinds?"

"All kinds, but the old gilt ones are her favorites. Entire walls in our house are covered with them."

"What does she display?"

"Family photos in the den," he said, settling in between Ellis and me. "Nothing in the dining room. She says the empty frames let the viewer step inside."

"I love that idea!" I said.

"Coffee?" Ellis asked him, ready to bring us back to business. "Tea?"

"Nothing, thanks."

"As I told you, we're investigating several crimes, all of which seem to involve Rebecca Bennington. I've asked Josie to help out because of an antiques angle, and that's probably as good a place to start as any."

Ellis nodded at me. Dr. Bennett cocked his head and looked at me, interested in what I might ask.

"Have you seen any small paintings Becca had?" I asked. "Miniatures, they're called. Oval-shaped portraits."

"No."

"Did she ever talk about them?"

"Not that I recall." He opened his palms and turned to face Ellis. "I don't know Becca all that well, except by her reputation, which is extraordinary. I met her for the first time last August when she joined our department for a year's work. Before then, our contact was solely via e-mail."

"I understand," Ellis said. "Nonetheless, we need to talk to everyone who knows her."

"What crimes are we talking about?"

"The break-ins at her apartment and her room at the institute, and her dad's murder. Also, not that it's a crime, per se, but she seems to be missing."

Professor Bennett leaned back, nodding slowly. "We're very concerned about that."

"Have you heard anything that might shed some light on the situation?"

"No Just a lot of silly gossip."

"Like what?"

Dr. Bennett shook his head. "I don't repeat rumors."

"Good policy in most circumstances," Ellis said. "This is different. Don't think of it as rumors or gossip. Think of it as potential leads. You know the old saying about how there's no smoke without fire. Sometimes, of course, what we perceive as smoke is really harmless steam. We need to look into everything so we can tell what we're dealing with, smoke or steam. We're discreet and circumspect and respectful, but we need to know."

The professor pushed out his bottom lip out and nodded slightly. "Intriguing spin.

It's all in how you position it. I study zooplankton, you know, diatoms, radiolarians, krill, and the like. They're weak swimmers, so people think they're weak. Hardly. The most prevalent rumor is that Becca has fled back to England."

"Based on what?" Ellis asked.

"She's missing."

"But why England?"

"It's her home."

"What else have you heard?"

"From what she confided in a colleague, she's recently out of a bad marriage. Some people speculate that she went back to her husband."

"Why?"

"Because women do that sort of thing."

"So do men," Ellis remarked, his tone dry.

"True."

"Who's her ex?"

"I never heard the name."

"Do different people hold different opinions or is there a consensus?"

"I try not to listen." He smiled. "I'm simply passing on the remarks I've heard."

"Understood. What else?"

"Nothing."

I glanced at Ellis. His eyes were fixed on Dr. Bennett's face. I suspected he didn't believe that Bennett had fully emptied the bag and he was looking for a way to shake the rest loose.

"Chief Hunter mentioned you were up here to figure out how to protect Becca's research," I said. "What have you come up with?"

"A colleague of hers has kindly stepped up. Ethan Ferguson. One of her large grants is from the Petro Group Foundation. We're meeting with them Monday. Everyone agrees that it's crucial her work continue uninterrupted."

"Does that mean Ethan will take over her grant?"

"No. We've simply asked the foundation to let Dr. Ferguson be listed as 'acting principal investigator.' They've told me they're receptive to the change — pending a meeting with him to hear his plans. It's pretty much pro forma. The foundation is excited about her findings to date. Her work focuses on breeding clams for harsher environments."

"Like oil spills," I said.

"Hopefully not that harsh, but certainly for surviving in less than pristine ocean waters."

"How do Ethan and Becca get along?"

"Very well, I should think. They room together."

"Are they romantically involved?" Ellis asked.

"Not that I know of, but I'm not sure I would."

Ellis asked a few more questions, trying to ferret out additional nuggets of gossip, without success. I got the sense that Dr. Bennett had given us all he had. Ellis thanked him, I told him I hoped to see him and his wife at the tag sale soon, and Ellis walked him out.

I'd just finished my tea when Ellis returned.

"What do you think?" he asked me.

"I think Becca's disappearance gives Ethan what he has yet to achieve on his own — the opportunity to spearhead a major grant."

"Let's talk to him about that." Ellis reached for his desk phone and punched three buttons, an internal call. "Ethan Ferguson . . . he's up here, right? . . . Send someone to pick him up . . . Tell him we have a few questions and could really use his help . . . Get him settled in an interview room and let me know he's here." He hung up and looked at me. "I'd like to ask you to sit in, Josie, in case the miniatures come up."

"That's fine. I've met him several times,

and we get along well."

Ellis thanked me. I said I'd like to rest while we waited for Ethan, and he left me in his office. I took more painkillers and lay down on his couch, under a Christmas green snowflake-patterned cotton throw. I didn't sleep. I rested my eyes and thought about Becca.

Ellis came and got me about an hour later.

Getting up was tricky, but with Ellis watching, I rolled myself upright, clenching my teeth to keep myself from crying out at the sharp jabs emanating from my left shoulder and arm.

"Are you certain you're up to this?" Ellis asked.

"Yes." When we walked into Interrogation Room One, Ethan was staring at the ceiling, his ladder-back chair tilted forty-five degrees, his heels perched on the tabletop.

The room was as I remembered it. A wall-long one-way mirror was on the right. The human-sized cage stood in the far left corner, ready to receive what Ty had called unruly guests. Tiny red lights told me the ceiling-mounted video cameras were recording. The ivory-colored drapes were drawn, covering the windows that overlooked the rear parking lot.

"Josie!" he said, swinging his feet off the table and leaning forward to bring his chair to level ground. "They drag you in, too?"

"Did the detective tell me wrong?" Ellis asked, his tone neutral. "I was under the impression you were here voluntarily."

"Is that what they're calling it these days? I was under the impression I'd been summoned."

"We certainly appreciate your cooperation. Are you okay with talking to me?"

"Sure." He jerked his head in my direction. "Do I get to talk to her, too?"

"I asked her to sit in in case any questions about the miniature portraits come up."

"I'm always glad to see Josie." He flashed a grin at me. "What do you say? Coffee after? A drink?"

"Maybe."

Ellis nodded at a chair to Ethan's right, and I sat down.

Ellis sat at the head of the table, directly opposite Ethan. "Tell me about this new job you're taking on, overseeing Becca's fieldwork in her absence."

"I have a better idea. Tell me why you're asking."

"I just spoke to Dr. Bennett."

"Okay, I'll bite."

"He said this was a pretty good gig for you."

"Is there a point here?"

"With Becca out of the picture, things are looking up for you."

He turned to me, patently unimpressed and unamused. "Did you put him up to this?"

"Me? No."

"I don't believe you. I'm betting you shared my jokes with the good police chief."

"I didn't think you were joking," I said.

"So I gather. I take back my offer of a drink."

"I'm sorry," I said.

"Me, too."

"Come on, Ethan," Ellis said, grinning. "What's the big deal? You're going to be named acting principal investigator, is that right?"

"Yes. And yes, it's good news for me, career-wise, but it's also good news for the program, the institute, the environment, the other scientists on the grant, the clams themselves, and all the businesses in Rocky Point we patronize while we're up here working on it. Losing a grant is good for no one."

"Understood," Ellis said. "Tell me about your relationship with Becca. Hot and heavy? Serious? Friends with benefits?"

"Roommates. Co-workers."

"That's it?" Ellis asked, his tone disbelieving.

"That's it."

Ellis jotted a note. "Were you in Rocky Point last Sunday?"

"Why?"

"Around four P.M. Where were you then?"

Ethan laughed. "Do I need an alibi for something?"

Ellis let the question hang for a moment. "Yes."

Ethan grinned and held out his arms, his wrists pressed together, ready for handcuffs. Evidently, he was amused that he was considered a suspect in some crime.

"I did it. You've got me."

"What did you do?"

"I killed him in the library with the candlestick."

"This isn't a joke, Mr. Ferguson."

"The hell it isn't. What happened Sunday at four?"

"Ian Bennington was murdered."

Ethan stopped laughing. He looked at me, then back at Ellis. "And you think I did it?" he asked, sounding incredulous.

"I'm following up on every lead. Where were you Sunday at four?"

"I was in Boston."

"Will anyone be able to attest to that?"

"No. I was alone."

"Thank you," Ellis said, jotting another note.

Ethan stood up and looked down at Ellis. "Someone in your department asked me about an alibi for yesterday, too, when Josie was attacked. I don't know what's going on, but I can assure you I'm not your man."

"Duly noted." Ellis stood up. "Let me walk you out."

Ethan didn't look at me on his way out. I sat there for a long time, staring at my lap thinking sad and lonely thoughts, until Ellis came back and told me my car was out front. He handed me the new key and the spare.

"Are you okay to drive?"

"A hundred percent. I can't believe it's done already."

"They rushed it," he said.

"Thank you, Ellis."

I left and patted my car hello, noting the small dent on the front hood where the tree limb had landed. As I turned onto Ocean, I smiled. I was glad to be behind the wheel, to be on my own, and to be away from the police station.

I spent Saturday night and all day Sunday

alone, never leaving my house. Zoë invited me for dinner, but I didn't want to go. Instead, I cooked. I made a week's worth of food, using recipes from my mom's handwritten cookbook, freezing everything in individual portions. I made lasagna, and orange chicken, and thyme-infused pork roast with a wine-apricot-mustard sauce, and chocolate bundles.

While my hands were busy, my mind was on Ian and what he'd told me about Becca, on Lia, and Ethan, and Pat Weston, and seventeenth-century miniature portraits. I reviewed every word and gesture, every call and hang-up, and every violent act. Mostly I thought about Becca, and the more I did, the more curious I became. I wondered what her relationship with her dad was like when she was a girl. I wondered what her mom had been like, and whether she had friends back home in England, or whether she was as self-contained and private there as she was here in a foreign land. I spoke to Ty twice, Zoë once, and when I finally feel asleep on Sunday, it was with the same nagging feeling I'd had before that I was missing something.

At 2:58 A.M., I woke up with a gasp and knew with utter clarity what had been bothering me.

Chapter Twenty-Four

By 3:10 A.M. Monday, I was sitting at my home computer, waiting for it to boot up. I stared at the gray screen, but what I saw was the photograph in Becca's Boston apartment. Becca standing next to an older man, leaning in toward him, just a little, their shoulders not quite touching. My dad and I used to stand like that.

I turned toward the silver-framed photo I kept on my desk, my dad and me at my college graduation. His eyes crinkled with pride. My smile was off the charts, half because I'd graduated and half because I'd pleased him. I touched the glass with my fingertip, stroking his arm.

I turned back to the monitor. Once the computer flashed to life, I Googled "Ian and Rebecca Bennington Christmas Common England," and when the search results appeared, I stared at the top link in stunned silence. The teaser copy was dated two weeks earlier and read IAN BENNINGTON DEAD.

I clicked through to an article in Christmas Common's local paper, the *Trumpet.* The article included a standard-issue head shot, the kind of photograph that was used in passports. Even though it was grainy, I could tell that this was the man in the photograph in Becca's room. Which meant the man I'd known as Ian was — I had no idea who.

I leaned back and stared into space, seeing nothing. It made no sense. Why would someone pretend to be Ian?

I continued reading. The real Ian Bennington had died of asphyxiation. He had, apparently, killed himself. His body had been found hanging from the rafters by his cleaning woman.

The article referred to his daughter as Rebecca Lewis. Apparently, she'd gone back to using her maiden name — or maybe she kept her maiden name for work purposes.

Ethan hadn't mentioned a husband or an ex-husband, though. Dr. Bennett had, repeating gossip that Becca had been in a bad marriage.

I Googled "Rebecca Bennington and Christmas Common" and learned more about Becca. She graduated at the top of her primary school class, was a nationally ranked swimmer at fourteen, had earned top marks in shooting competitions at fifteen, and by the time she went to university, her sole focus was on clams. She had married a man named Thomas Lewis in 2009. I scrolled down until I came to the wedding photo — and gasped, my eyes glued to the image. The blonde in the wedding photo was the same woman I'd seen standing alongside her dad in the photo in her room. Becca. Becca's husband was the man I'd known as Ian.

No wonder Ian — *Thomas,* I corrected myself — looked young. He'd said it was good genes, but the truth was he looked young because he *was* young. My instinct that anyone seeing Becca and the man I now knew to be Thomas might think they were a couple was on the mark — they looked like a couple because they *were* a couple. Or at least they used to be. Were they divorced? Separated? Why on earth had Thomas pretended to be Becca's father?

Completely befuddled, I continued my research.

According to an article about debutantes who worked instead of living a glittery social life, published in *London Society* magazine in 2012, Thomas Lewis was a real estate developer, specializing in resorts. Becca and Thomas met in 2008 when she worked for an environmental consulting firm assigned to study the impact of one of his proposed seaside resorts. Thomas's U.K.-based firm fell victim to the global recession, and in 2010, shortly after their June marriage, he sold it to a competitor at a fire-sale price.

An article in *New Hampshire Revealed* profiling New Hampshire start-ups discussed how Thomas Lewis moved to New Hampshire to open a new business with funding provided by his father-in-law, the real Ian. The couple moved to the resort town of North Conway so Thomas could form a real estate development consultancy with a sixty-one-year-old American named Rupert Morrishein. Thomas's consultancy's goal was to invest in projects up and down the East Coast.

Once she found herself in New Hampshire, Becca focused on finishing her dissertation. She connected with the Rocky Point Oceanographic Institute and used her preliminary research to win a grant to compare clam behavior at Reynard University's two oceanside research facilities, one in Plymouth, England, the other in Rocky Point.

I checked the North Conway Business

Licensing Bureau's Web site and discovered that the Lewis-Morrishein partnership did not go well. The firm filed for bankruptcy protection within ten months of opening its doors.

"Yikes," I said.

Both men lost everything they'd invested in the business. To Thomas, the loss was disastrous, and mortifying, I should think, given that it represented his second business failure in as many years. This one must have been especially humiliating — not only did it represent a personal failure, but he cost his father-in-law millions. The firm's collapse caught the attention of a reporter for *Real Estate Fortune.* "At least," Lewis was quoted as saying, "I'm young enough to start over yet again." In the accompanying photo, Becca beamed at him, a woman standing steadfastly by her man.

A follow-up article in the same magazine reported that Rupert Morrishein had filed a lawsuit accusing Thomas of fraud. Before the case was adjudicated, only three weeks after the firm went out of business, Morrishein died from a massive stroke. The lawsuit, now spearheaded by Morrishein's widow, Cheryl, was evidently still wending its way through the court system.

I kept digging around and found a Reynard University newsletter from 2011 announcing that Becca had accepted a lecturer position at the university's Plymouth campus in the United Kingdom. The reporter referred to Becca as Dr. Bennington.

I leaned back, trying to understand what might have happened. I knew financial troubles wrecked a lot of marriages; witness Lia, although her ex's wandering eye didn't help. Had Thomas pretended to be Ian because he'd been trying to reconnect with Becca? How could such a pretense possibly help that cause? I shook my head. No. That wasn't the answer to the mystery.

I recalled how often Thomas had mentioned Becca's miniatures. Thomas wasn't looking for Becca. He was looking for her possessions. He wasn't a romantic; he was a thief. A thief with a partner who killed him — and maybe Becca — then went on a one-man hunt for the paintings. Or one-woman. *The woman at the window.*

I logged on to my company's Web site and navigated my way to the security footage archives. Bringing up the shots of the woman peering in the window at my party, I studied the partial view. A woman in a dark cloche hat. A sliver of white skin. No sign of hair. Impossible to tell the color of her eyes. Her nose was hidden by her gloved hand. I didn't recognize her, but neither could I swear I'd never seen her before. If that was Thomas's partner, I had no clue as to her identity. I saved the image to my desktop and logged out.

What if Thomas and his mystery partner had a falling-out?

Had Thomas double-crossed him?

Had Becca found out what was going on and announced a plan to go to the police?

If so, how would Thomas's partner react to the threat? He'd kill her.

Oh, God.

If Thomas had tried to stop him, to protect Becca, whether motivated by chivalry or greed, his partner might have killed him first.

I shook my head. It was baffling.

What the witness perceived as Becca saying no, no, might have been Becca expressing dismay and disbelief at the news Thomas was delivering, that her life was in danger. She heard him out, then ran for it. The disgruntled partner witnessed the scene from his car around the corner and interpreted it accurately. He mowed down Thomas and headed out after Becca. She made it to her car before he could catch her and sped away.

No way the partner would give up anytime

soon. Becca was the only thing standing between him and a fortune.

"Oh, Becca," I said aloud. "I hope I'm wrong."

Stop it, I chastised myself.

Just because something was logical didn't make it true. Maybe the attempts to steal the miniatures were unrelated to Thomas's murder.

If Ethan and Becca were romantically involved, it was possible that he got a glimpse of Becca and Thomas talking and went ballistic. If Ethan exploded and ran Thomas down in a fit of passion-charged rage, Becca, witnessing the horror, might well have fled, hoping to escape his wrath.

Who knows? I e-mailed the photo of the mystery woman to Ellis. I explained what I'd discovered about Ian and where the photo came from.

I got up and stretched — or started to. My shoulder and arm were still tender to the touch, and my muscles shrieked if I tried raising my arm. I paced, ignoring the discomfort, walking from my small study through the living room to the front hall and back.

I returned to my computer and brought up Reynard University's Web site. According to his listing on the Marine Biology faculty page, Ethan used two middle initials, *K* and *Q*. He'd graduated from the University of California, Los Angeles, and done postdoc work at Tulane in New Orleans. I Googled his name, including his initials, and learned from his byline on an article about oyster propagation that he hailed from Andover, Massachusetts.

From what I could tell from my checks of public records in California, Louisiana, Massachusetts, and New Hampshire, he had no arrest record, he'd never been married, and he didn't own any property.

My fingers hovered over the keyboard, but I couldn't think of anything else to research.

I was out of ideas, so I e-mailed Wes.

Hi Wes,

I'm okay, and no, I didn't take any photos of my bruises.☺

Can you find out the skinny on Becca's roommate, Ethan Ferguson? His full name is

Ethan K. Q. Ferguson. He's from Andover, MA.

Thanks!

Josie

I was tired, but not sleepy. I paced some more. Finally, I went to the kitchen and made myself a cup of pomegranate tea. I settled on the living room couch and read a chapter of my current Nero Wolfe novel, Rex Stout's *Over My Dead Body,* ideas percolating on the back burner of my mind. By the time I finished the tea, I had a next-step idea.

I needed to know more about the real Ian Bennington. I rinsed my teacup and placed it in the dishwasher. Back at my desk, I brought up the listing of all the Oxfordshire government offices.

Using the time difference to my advantage, I decided to start with the police.

A constable named Brewer answered with businesslike precision.

"Hello," I said, aiming to match his tone. "This is Josie Prescott, calling from America. I have a question about the death of Ian Bennington. Who can I talk to about it?"

"Regarding what, ma'am?"

"The details. I'm a relative."

"I see. One moment, please."

I heard papers being shuffled and the distinctive tap-tap of a keyboard.

"Detective Higgins is assigned that case. Shall I ring him for you?"

"Yes, thank you. Before you do, though, what's his direct number, in case we're disconnected?"

He gave it to me, and I silently thanked my dad for the tip. A salesman always tries to gain direct access to the decision maker.

Detective Higgins was brusque, impatient, and uninterested in talking to a distant relative from a distant land about an unimportant (to him) case.

"Why haven't you closed the case?" I asked, ignoring his attitude. "The newspaper said it was a probable suicide."

"It's the coroner's job to determine the cause and manner of death."

"And he hasn't. Why not?"

"You'd have to ask him. Dr. Glaskin."

"What's the number, please?"

A sigh of exasperation rattled across the miles, but he gave me the number.

Dr. Glaskin wasn't available, but his assistant, an elderly-sounding woman named Polly Davidson-Fox, was, and she was glad to talk to me.

"I'm terribly sorry for your loss. We try to keep relatives in the loop as much as possible," she explained. "I don't see your name on our information sheet."

"Can we add me now?" I asked, avoiding the temptation to explain why I was coming late to the party. That was one can of worms I didn't want to open.

"Certainly."

I gave her my contact information. "Can you give me a status report?" I asked.

"While we can't release confidential information, of course, I can share what the detective assigned to the case has revealed to the media. Would that be helpful?"

"Yes, thank you."

"Mr. Bennington didn't leave a suicide note. Many poor souls don't, of course. But there was nothing to suggest the kind of despondency one expects to hear about with a suicide. He was in perfect heath, and Detective Higgins reports that he discussed his holiday plans with his neighbors the day before he died. He was looking forward to the trip, to meeting a relative he'd just located."

My throat tightened, and I couldn't speak.

"Would that be you, dear?"

I nodded, still unable to speak. I knew she was more than three thousand miles away and couldn't see my nod, but I did it anyway. I coughed, then tried again.

"Yes," I managed. My voice sounded odd, guttural and low.

"What a tragedy."

"Thank you. So the coroner is waiting for . . . what exactly?"

"More information."

"I know I'm probably sounding as dumb

as a doormat, but what information is the coroner waiting for?"

"You're not dumb! Hardly. It's a complicated situation. Dr. Glaskin hopes the detectives will provide some additional information, something that will shed light on whether Mr. Bennington killed himself. Until then, the case remains open."

"Thank you. That helps me understand what's going on. I wonder . . . do you have a contact number for anyone? His daughter, maybe?"

"Let me look." Two minutes passed before she said, "Mr. Bennington's solicitor, Marcia Earling, is the family representative."

She gave me her number, and I said, "I can't thank you enough."

"You call me anytime, dear. I know how hard it is not to have answers. If I have no news to report, I'll tell you so."

I thanked her again and hung up.

I sat for a while with my hand on the phone thinking that Polly Davidson-Fox was one of the kindest people I'd spoken to in a long time.

I dialed England again, this time reaching Ms. Earling's law clerk, a young man named Samuel Wellster.

"We're waiting on word from the coroner," he said when I asked where they were in the process of settling Ian Bennington's estate. "We filed for probate, of course, but the courts are leery to finalize things when the cause of death is up in the air."

"Who is his beneficiary?" I asked, understanding Mr. Wellster's unspoken message: A killer can't benefit from his crime.

"Give me a minute to look it up."

I sat listening to silence for several minutes until Mr. Wellster came back on the line.

"Mr. Bennington made some charitable donations. Everything else goes to his daughter, Rebecca."

"Is the estate substantial?"

He chuckled. "Yes."

"Are you Becca's solicitors, too?"

"I can't say. I can tell you about the will because that's part of the public record. Ms. Bennington's affairs are not."

"I understand," I said. "Are divorce records public?"

"Usually. In certain circumstances, they can be sealed."

"Can you tell me, then, if you handled Becca's divorce?"

"No, I'm afraid not."

"What charities did he donate to?"

He rattled off a list that included Reynard University, his local parish, a birdwatching club, and an organization that researched innovative treatment options for pediatric cancer. I tried to think of other questions to ask Mr. Wellster, but I couldn't. I thanked him and ended the call.

Learning the real Ian's preferences felt slightly voyeuristic. I hadn't ever met the man, yet here I was getting to know him after his death. From what I could see, Ian Bennington might be a semibillionaire, but essentially he was a simple man, loyal to the university that hired his daughter and fond of his community.

I brought up my work contact list and called a British lawyer I'd worked with in the past, Derek Carlson.

"In connection with a potential appraisal," I said, after we exchanged greetings, "I need information about a divorce. Would you please review the Bennington-Lewis divorce records and let me know its status?"

"Certainly."

He took down the specifics and told me that, unless there was something untoward in the case, he'd be able to report his findings within a few hours. I glanced at the time on my computer monitor — 4:37. I thanked him, and we chatted for a minute before hanging up.

I e-mailed Ellis a bulleted list detailing the additional facts I'd learned, then made my way on weary legs up the stairs to bed.

It felt as if I'd done a good day's work.

Chapter Twenty-Five

I awakened to a screech. I groaned and rolled over.

It didn't stop.

I slapped the pillow, and when that didn't quiet the noise either, I tossed the pillow across the room, I don't know why. By then I was awake enough to realize that the sound was coming from my old alarm clock, a relic from my childhood. I hoisted myself onto one elbow, moaning a little as my muscles objected to the move, and tapped the button to turn off the cacophony. I collapsed back onto the mattress.

It was nine thirty. Late for an early riser like me. I swung my legs over the side of the bed, preparing to get vertical. A memory came to me.

Midway through my senior year in college, I'd called home in a panic. I had three midterms to study for and two papers to complete and I couldn't figure out differential equations and I'd already met with my professor and understood the concepts when he explained them but couldn't apply them when working on my own, and I felt overwhelmed and upset and disgruntled, and I didn't know what to do.

"Go to the library," my dad told me, as assured and unruffled as always, "and look at different texts on the subject. Since different authors describe the same things differently, often one explanation gets through whereas others don't. Once you find a book that speaks to you, do the exercises."

"That all sounds logical," I said, snuffling, "but I can't. I just can't! I don't know what to do. I'm completely freaking out."

"Are you ready for my final words on the subject?"

I stopped snuffling. I didn't like the sound of that. "Final" sounded bad. "Yes."

"Don't think — do. Get through this week, then come home for the weekend, and I'll take you out for dinner."

I did as he recommended. I stopped thinking about how hard things were and started focusing on getting things done. It made all the difference. I aced everything, except for math, where I got a B. I'm pretty proud of that B.

Smiling at the memory, I stood up and

tested my range of motion. Not bad. I made my way to the shower.

"I'm doing. I'm doing," I said aloud.

I stumbled into the bathroom, ready to face the day.

My dad's keep-on-keeping-on approach saved me in college, and it saved me now.

I pulled Derek Carlson's fax regarding Thomas and Becca's marital status from the machine while Fred filled me in about Becca's watercolor miniatures.

We'd had no hits on our stolen-art postings, but he'd discovered that the two paintings had not been sold at auction since 1924. They had, however, been featured in a 1986 exhibition at the Midlands Art Museum in Newark-on-Trent, England, with the loan credited to "Anonymous." The exhibit had been called Love Lost.

"That's the most recent information I can find," Fred said.

"Almost thirty years. That's not recent by anybody's standard."

The phone rang. I paused as Cara answered it. She put the caller on hold.

"It's Wes," she said, her eyes clouded with worry. "He says it's urgent."

I wasn't concerned. To Wes, everything was urgent.

"Ask him to hold on for a minute." I turned back toward Fred. "Did you find the catalogue?"

"Just now. It was archived, with access limited to scholars only. Luckily, Sasha's PhD covers us." He grinned and pushed up his glasses. "I'm her research assistant."

I smiled. "You clever man, you. Well done! Send me the link, will you?"

"I'll e-mail you the document. I downloaded the PDF."

I gave him a thumbs-up and ran for the stairs, pleased that the stiffness and soreness on my left side had mellowed enough so that I could move with familiar ease.

"Ethan Ferguson is a fraud," Wes said, jumping in.

"What are you talking about?" I asked, dropping the fax on my desk and sliding into my comfy leather chair.

"He was born and reared by a single mother, a waitress, in the City Center section of East St. Louis, Illinois, which according to NeighborhoodScout is the most dangerous neighborhood in America. No joke. Not *one* of the most dangerous neighborhoods — the *most* dangerous. His mom died when he was sixteen. That same year, he graduated high school, won a scholarship to do an extra year at Phillips Academy, the hoity-toity prep school in Andover, Massachusetts, moved east the day after graduation, and never looked back. It was after he left that he acquired his middle names. Until then, he was just plain Ethan Ferguson. He wrote an article for the alumni blog explaining what happened. Two of his teachers helped him — I'm quoting here — 'understand that the past doesn't need to dictate the future.' That's good, right? Well put. Anyhow, Ethan named them: Ms. Klein and Mr. Quinn. He was so grateful, he went to court on his eighteenth birthday to take their names, so his legal name is now Ethan Klein Quinn Ferguson. Isn't that a hoot?"

"I think it's nice, Wes. He's not a fraud. He reinvented himself. Do you know how hard that is to do?"

"I guess."

"That's why he named Andover as his birthplace."

"Sounds like one heck of a school to have that much impact. I'm trying to get a photo of him when he was at Phillips."

"Why?"

"To go with the article. Following your lead, maybe I'll call it 'Fraud or Reinvention?' What do you think?"

"Oh, God, Wes — don't publish it!"

"What?" he asked, scandalized. "Why not?"

"Write about the man he is now, witty and hardworking, not the boy he used to be. Let the past stay past."

"I thought he was a suspect."

"Maybe he is," I said. A small brown bird landed on my maple tree and walked along the bare limb toward me. "That's unrelated to this discussion. Don't diminish his accomplishment by showing how the sausage was made."

"What's going on, Joz? It sounds like you've gone a little soft for him. You and Ty having trouble?"

"Of course not! My feelings for Ethan have nothing to do with my feelings for Ty."

"Really?" Wes asked, morphing from investigative reporter to kid brother. "If Maggie talked about another guy the way you're talking about Ethan, I'd be kind of, I don't know, jealous, I guess."

The little bird stared at me for a moment, then swooped toward the ground, veering left. I lost sight of it halfway across my parking lot. I swiveled back toward my computer.

"I can see that," I said. "If Ty talked about another woman that way, I'd be jealous, too."

"So what's the difference?"

"I know myself. I can enjoy a man's company without it meaning anything salacious. I don't flirt or mentally try on a relationship or anything."

"What does Ty think?"

"I don't know. Ethan hasn't come up."

"How about other guy friends?"

I thought of Ellis. "He's fine with it."

"Because he trusts you?"

"Because I'm trustworthy. Because I adore Ty and he knows it. I make him feel secure, not insecure."

"So doesn't learning this about Ethan make you suspect him more than before? I mean, now you know he's good at hiding secrets."

"I can't say he was hiding anything. His background never came up."

An IM window popped onto my screen. Cara wrote: *Chief Hunter on line 2.*

"I've got to go, Wes." I hit REPLY and typed: *OK. I'll take it.*

"Wait!" he called, back to his reporter self. "Talk to me. You've got to give me *something* I can print."

"I can't, Wes. Not now. I have another call."

"Josie! You owe me."

I thought about whether there was a

downside to telling him about Thomas Lewis. I'd discovered Ian's true identity through a simple Google search. My eyes took in Mr. Carlson's fax. Everything I knew was public information, including whatever it was Mr. Carlson had sent. I'd hired him as a time-saver, not to ferret out confidential information.

"Do an online search for 'Ian Bennington' and 'Christmas Common.' " I clicked over to Ellis. "Sorry to keep you waiting."

"No problem. I am a master of multi-tasking. I'm eating a ham sandwich, reading the *Seacoast Star,* and thinking about the real Ian Bennington, all at once."

"You are a master. I'm impressed."

"Thanks for letting me know what you learned. I had it on my radar to check Ian's background. Now I'll make it a priority."

"I have a fax I haven't read from England about Becca's marriage to Thomas. I'll e-mail you once I've read it. Any news for me?"

"No one's used your phone or credit cards. I set up alerts, so I'll know if and when."

"I hate this."

"I understand."

"I'm going to buy another phone today."

"Makes sense."

As soon as we hung up, I picked up the six-page document Mr. Carlson had faxed. In addition to the cover letter, he'd included a copy of the Lewises' separation agreement. Mr. Carlson wrote that he'd called Mr. Lewis's solicitor for an explanation as to why the divorce hadn't been finalized and learned that Mr. Lewis had filed a petition contending that his wife was hiding assets, specifying that two seventeenth-century miniature watercolors he knew were in her possession weren't listed in her declaration of assets. Ms. Rebecca Bennington's solicitor had countered that the paintings were her father's, not hers. While the court was considering Mr. Lewis's request, he filed an additional petition. This one, submitted a week after Ian Bennington's death, stated that since Rebecca was her father's sole heir, and since, by her own admission, the miniatures were owned by Mr. Bennington, and since he and Rebecca were still married, the paintings were now incontestably marital property. The petition included a demand that the paintings be produced for appraisal.

If I were Becca, I thought, I'd be beside myself with impotent fury, the rage of the righteous. Whether her dad had given her the paintings as a housewarming gift as Thomas said — which seemed credible, given they were in her possession — or whether they were merely on loan from her dad, once Ian died, they were unquestionably hers. If I were faced with the prospect of being ordered by a court to give half their value to a man I was divorcing, I'd be mad enough to kill. I wondered if Becca had been, too. I scanned in the document and e-mailed it to Ellis, then sat and stewed. My radar needed readjusting. Thomas Lewis was not a nice man. After a while, I turned my attention to the catalogue Fred had dug up.

The catalogue photographs appeared identical to the two oval-shaped paintings I'd removed from Becca's apartment. I called the Midlands Art Museum.

I spoke to a young woman with a clipped businesslike tone. Her name was Agnes Wollingford. She was the curatorial assistant, and all she had for me was bad news. She didn't know anything about the 1986 exhibit, Love Lost. She didn't know anything about Cooper miniatures. She didn't know who in the museum might know more. And what she did know didn't help me one bit. I read her the staff names from the exhibit catalogue, the curator and his two assistants.

"So sorry," she said. "They've all retired. I

heard Mr. Janson passed on last year."

"Do you have contact information for the others?"

"I don't. Perhaps the Human Resources people might, but I shouldn't think they'd give it out."

"True. What about the records, curatorial notes, and so on? You confirm provenance for every object, don't you?"

"Certainly, although if a loaned object comes with an appraisal from a reliable source, which they usually do, for insurance purposes, you know, then we might rely on that assessment."

"And the paperwork for this exhibit?"

"Gone, I'm afraid. We sent all records to a document conversion company in 2005, about time, right? Our goal was to go paperless, so we wanted all past documents scanned in. We hoped to create one mega- and searchable database. Before the company started the scanning, there was a fire. Everything was destroyed."

"That's an appalling loss," I said, horrified on the museum's behalf, on the art world's behalf.

"I know. We were all shattered. Just devastated. It happened during my first week on the job. Quite an introduction."

"I can't imagine. I'm so sorry." I stared at

the staff listing in the catalogue. "There's an intern listed, Florence Moore. Have you ever heard of her?"

"Certainly. Dr. Moore is a professor of art history at Baldine College in Manchester and the curator of its small but distinguished collection of Baroque art. She's quite well respected."

I thanked Agnes for her help, hung up, and Googled the college.

Thirty years is a long time. If Florence Moore had been in her twenties then, she'd be in her fifties now. I found the Web site, clicked through to the Art Department, and dialed the number.

"Dr. Moore, please," I said to the young woman who answered.

"I'm sorry. Dr. Moore is at a conference. Can someone else help you?"

"No, thank you. What's the conference?"

"Dr. Moore is keynoting," she said, pride rippling through the phone lines, "at the New England Museum of Contemporary Art conference on 'The New Baroque: Using Art to Fight Religious Oppression.' "

"That's here! I'm calling you from Rocky Point, New Hampshire. The museum is in Durham."

"Exactly! Do you know it?"

"Yes, indeed. It's only about half an hour

away. The topic sounds fascinating."

"We're all terribly excited. The speech title is the title of Dr. Moore's new book. She's getting interview requests from all sorts of media outlets. To bring the Baroque into a contemporary sociopolitical context — well, you can just imagine!"

I smiled. She reminded me of Sasha, passionate about art to her core and certain that her enthusiasm was universally shared. I found it endearing.

"When's Dr. Moore keynote?" I asked.

"Tomorrow at ten."

"What's going on tonight?"

"A cocktail party," she gushed, "at a restaurant called the Blue Dolphin. I've heard it's ever so smart."

"You heard right! It's a very special place." I thanked her again and hung up.

I typed in some keywords and navigated to the conference schedule. The cocktail party was due to start at six.

Chapter Twenty-Six

The Blue Dolphin was a world-class restaurant brought back to life after a crash-and-burn meltdown a few years back.* The company that bought it brought in a turnaround pro named Suzanne Dyre as general manager. Tall and elegant, Suzanne epitomized gracious hospitality, a perfect fit with the restaurant. She was a perfect fit for Fred, too, and they'd been a couple for a few years now.

The Blue Dolphin was housed on the ground floor of an eighteenth-century brick building wedged into the corner of Bow and Market Streets. A cobblestone alley separated the building from the tumultuous black Piscataqua River. A thick stand of hardwood trees, poplars, maples, birch, and oaks lined the riverbank. By early December, when the glittering gold, red, orange,

* Please see *Deadly Threads.*

and yellow leaves had fallen, you could see through the bare branches to Maine.

The restaurant's decor hadn't changed in the ten years I'd lived in Rocky Point. The wide plank oak floors were burnished to a rich golden patina. The drapes were blue and white toile. Crystal drops adorned the wall sconces, chandeliers, and table lamps. The linen was snowy white and crisply starched. Silver flatware gleamed. It was maybe the most beautiful place I'd ever seen. Now, decorated for the holidays with strands of tiny red lights running just below the crown molding, an eight-foot fir tree adorned with sequin-dotted red and gold balls, gold garlands, and red lights taking all of one corner of the entryway, and boughs of evergreen draped along every wall, it was exquisite, like a setting in a play, like a dream.

"Josie!" Frieda, the hostess, said.

Her welcoming smile always made walking into the Blue Dolphin feel like coming home.

"Hey, Frieda. I understand you're hosting a private party here tonight."

"That's right. It's sponsored by the New England Museum of Contemporary Art, part of a conference. They've taken over the lounge."

I turned that way. A gold-framed sign read THE LOUNGE IS CLOSED FOR A PRIVATE EVENT. SORRY FOR THE INCONVENIENCE.

"I came to the right place, then."

Frieda knew I dealt in antiques. She'd have no suspicion that I wasn't an invited guest. I thanked her and walked around the sign, stepping into the buzz of conversation, clinking glasses, and laughter.

Jimmy, my favorite bartender, was in his usual place behind the bar. Two other men worked alongside him.

The group, maybe seventy-five strong, appeared to be an eclectic mix. One woman wore a purple and gold sari, another a black chador. Two men wore dashikis, one blue and green, the other black and yellow. I spotted Dr. Elizabeth Grayman, the curator of decorative arts at the New England Museum of Contemporary Art in Durham and an expert on Victorian artifacts. I sidled through the crowd in her direction.

Dr. Grayman was close to seventy, one way or the other. She was about my height and stout, with curly gray hair cut short and light blue eyes. She wore her regular uniform, a tweed suit and sturdy shoes. Today's suit was dark orange with nubby brown flecks. Her shoes were brown oxfords.

"Dr. Grayman," I said, interrupting a

young man who had a full beard and was wearing a brown beret. I smiled at him. "Sorry to interrupt."

"Josie!" Dr. Grayman said. "What a surprise!" She glanced at her companion, then back at me. "Josie, this is Bertram Targus, from the University of Illinois. Bertram, please meet one of our local luminaries, Josie Prescott, an antiques appraiser."

Bertram and I exchanged hellos. "Congratulations on hosting the conference," I said to Dr. Grayman. "I'm impressed! I took the liberty of popping in because I want to meet Professor Moore, and I was hoping you'd introduce me."

"I'll catch up with you later," Bertram said.

"Please do," Dr. Grayman said. "I want to hear your views on Baroque versus contemporary identity."

He smiled and walked away.

"Sorry," I said again.

"No worries," she said, peering into the crowd, trying to find Dr. Moore. "We have three days to figure out identity."

I laughed. "When you do, I hope you'll fill me in."

She smiled. "Ah! There she is."

Dr. Grayman set off toward the window seats, with me following. A woman with sable black hair stood with her back to us, talking to a crowd that seemed to hang on her every word. She wore a black sweater and half a dozen gold bangles, a brown and black plaid pencil skirt, and high-heeled knee-high brown leather boots.

"You notice I'm not asking why you're crashing our party," Dr. Grayman said over her shoulder as we wended our way through the guests.

"It's nothing more mysterious than an appraisal I'm working on."

Dr. Grayman's sidewise glance indicated disbelief.

"Really. I know she's keynoting tomorrow. I didn't want to risk missing her."

"Something urgent, it seems."

I blushed and tried to avoid her penetrating gaze. "A little."

"Excuse us," Dr. Grayman said to the group surrounding Dr. Moore. "Flo, may I spirit your away for a few minutes?"

"Certainly," Dr. Moore said in a well-modulated British accent. To the group, she added, "More later!"

She turned to face us. Dr. Moore was classically beautiful with a hint of the exotic. Her cheekbones were high and prominent. Her almond-shaped eyes were amber, flecked with a darker brown and sparks of gold. I'd never seen eyes that color. Her lips were full. Dr. Grayman introduced us, and Dr. Moore smiled at me politely.

"Josie is a well-known antiques appraiser. She says she has an urgent question."

I thanked Dr. Grayman and turned to Florence Moore. "I'm sorry to crash in like this. May I pull you aside and ask you what I hope will be a quick question?"

"Certainly," she said. "I'm intrigued."

I led the way out of the lounge and turned right. "This way," I said, stepping into an alcove enclosed by burgundy velvet curtains.

Dr. Moore followed me into the narrow space that used to house three wall-mounted pay phones. Now it stored high chairs and booster seats.

"I'm trying to track a pair of Samuel Cooper miniatures. You were an intern at the Midlands Art Museum in the mid-1980s when an exhibit called Love Lost was mounted. I need to know about a pair of Cooper's watercolors, one of Arabella Churchill, the other of King James II."

"If you'd asked me to guess what your question was, never in a million years would I have lit on that exhibit. That was thirty years ago."

"It's not a random question, though. The loan of those miniatures was ascribed to

Anonymous. I need to know Anonymous's identity."

"You're appraising those paintings."

"Yes."

"I remember them. They were charming. But I'm not going to be able to help you, I'm afraid. As you correctly stated, I was but a lowly intern. I wasn't privy to donors' or contributors' names."

"Darn! I can't find anyone who can help me. The curators have retired or passed away. The paperwork was destroyed in a fire a decade ago. Can you think of anyone I could talk to who might be able to help? Shall I try to track down the retired staff?"

She pursed her beautiful, shapely lips and stared at the crown molding for a moment. "There was a consultant . . . What was his name?" She shook her head slightly, thinking. She remembered and looked at me full on, her luminous topaz eyes alive with delight. "Kirk Trevor. I haven't thought about him in years. I had a little crush on him."

"I don't suppose you know where he is now?"

"No, I'm afraid not. He's an American, though, so more than likely he's somewhere in your country."

"You've been very helpful."

We stepped out into the hall, and she started back toward the party. She gave me a good-bye smile and disappeared into the crowd.

I smiled at Frieda as I left, thinking about memory and love lost.

By ten Wednesday morning, I had all my data reloaded on my new iPhone and had configured my new tablet to my liking. The tablet was the newest model, an actual computer, equipped with all the latest bells and whistles. I hated change but had to admit that some changes were less onerous than others.

I reached Kirk Trevor in Chicago on my third try, at eleven Wednesday morning, ten his time.

"I got your name from Dr. Florence Moore, who was an intern when you consulted on the Love Lost exhibit for the Midlands Art Museum in 1986. I tracked you down through the Association of Art Historians."

"Love Lost. I remember it. It was an important show. What can I do for you?"

"I'm hoping you can help me confirm the provenance of some paintings." I explained who I was and what I wanted.

"Don't see why not. Who owns them now?"

"Rebecca Bennington. She recently inherited them from her father, Ian Bennington. Do you remember who the donor was?"

"Sure. The sellers didn't want their names made public, though."

"How come?"

"The usual. They don't want thieves to know what they own."

"Do you know if they sold the paintings?"

"I do. I co-brokered the sale to Mr. Bennington."

I smiled at Hank, ambling into my office. "Good. You must have told Mr. Bennington their names."

"Certainly. It was in the purchase agreement, and, of course, listing the names was necessary in providing proof of provenance. Mr. Bennington didn't want his name made public either. Since it was a private sale, there was no issue."

"And you can't give me the sellers' names? Even after all this time?"

"Sorry. No."

"You said you co-brokered the deal. Who was the other broker?"

"Are you trying an end-around?"

I laughed. "I guess I am."

"I'm not at liberty to reveal anything else,

I'm afraid."

"Let me just ask —"

"Sorry. Best of luck."

He ended the call just as Hank jumped into my lap. I put the phone down and scratched Hank behind his right ear. He began purring and dipped his head into the motion, signaling he wanted me to rub more, more, harder, please. I followed his instructions.

"What do you make of that, Hank?" I asked.

Hank licked my hand, a kitty kiss.

"I love you, too, sweetheart, but I was asking about Kirk Trevor. Was he being cagey or circumspect? What do you think?"

Hank purred louder.

"I think you're right. He was simply honoring a promise of confidentiality."

I reached across Hank's flank for the phone and called Ellis.

"Did you find anything on Becca's computer about the portraits?" I asked.

"No. Nothing personal at all. Why?"

"I need to know where her dad got them."

"If the paperwork wasn't in that drawer of receipts and things, and if it wasn't stored as a file on her computer, where would she keep it?"

"On a laptop or a tablet," I suggested. "Or

a flash drive."

"That she has with her. We didn't find anything like that."

"Presumably. Maybe her dad kept a copy. Could you call the police in Christmas Common and ask them?"

"Come here and we'll do it together. You can explain why we're asking."

"I'm on my way."

I nuzzled Hank for a moment, then placed him on the floor, ignoring his protesting mew.

"Sorry, baby. I've got to go."

He stretched, a half-stretch, lengthening his back paws in a dancer's extension, and strolled off.

Just before noon, 5:00 P.M. in Christmas Common, Ellis called the police superintendent, Gerald Shorling. When he came on the line, Ellis punched the SPEAKER button so I could listen in.

"What's your interest?" Mr. Shorling asked, his voice reverberating through the speaker, after Ellis introduced himself and me and explained he had questions relating to the Ian Bennington case.

"In the course of an investigation, the murder of a British citizen named Thomas Lewis, I need to know the details of Ian

Bennington's purchase of two antique miniature paintings. This might have relevance into your investigation of his death as well. My question to you is this: Did you find the purchase agreement among Ian Bennington's possessions or on his computer? We've been told that there was a list of past owners attached to it."

"Provenance, it's called," I added.

"That's a question for the detective on the case."

"That would be Detective Higgins," Ellis said. "I've left two messages about other issues. He hasn't called me back."

"Is that so?" Superintendent Shorling asked. "When was your last call?"

"Yesterday about ten, East Coast time, three in your part of the world."

"Twenty-one hours is long enough to get back to a fellow police official who is conducting a murder investigation."

"That's what I'd say to my staff, too."

"I'll be in touch shortly."

Ellis thanked him and pushed the END CALL button.

"What do you think?" he asked me.

"I think Detective Higgins is in trouble. Couldn't happen to a nicer guy."

Ellis smiled and shook his head. "Will Superintendent Shorling find what you're looking for?"

"Probably. Most dads would keep copies of the paperwork before giving the original to a young daughter."

"Becca's not that young."

"Midtwenties," I said. My shoulders went up half an inch, then down. "How old were you when you matured?"

"Nineteen. February 24, 1991. Desert Storm. Kuwait."

"You were in the army."

"The marines."

"What happened?" I asked.

"Nothing good. It was over in a few days."

"Not for you."

"True. I grew up quick and stayed grown up."

"That's not the same as maturity."

He grinned. "It was for me. War changes you. It worked out all right for me."

"I saw a billboard once, an ad for the marines. It showed a handsome, wholesome young man, wearing his dress uniform, staring out with such earnestness. The headline read 'The change lasts forever.' "

"That's about right," Ellis said.

Back at my office, I checked whether any sales of Cooper miniatures had been reported on the various proprietary Web sites we subscribed to since Fred's last posting. They hadn't. If Becca had sold them in the few weeks since telling Marney Alred that she intended to do so, the sale was private and unrecorded. If the thief had sold them, the sale was private. I called the number Marney gave me, her cell phone.

"Hi, Ms. Alred. This is Josie Prescott. You asked that I contact you if I had any information about Becca Bennington's watercolor miniatures."

"Yes, thank you. Do you have news?"

"Not exactly. I was hoping you did. Have you spoken to Becca?"

"I don't understand."

"I have reason to think a sale might be in the works. A private sale. Do you know anything about that?"

"No. Why would you think they're being sold privately?"

"There's no public record of the sale, so that's the only alternative. It's very common with high-value objects."

"You're calling me to find out if I've heard from Becca, aren't you?"

"I'm looking for information, yes, about Becca and about the paintings."

"Please call back when you have some to share," she said, her tone sharp. She hung up with a snap.

■ ■ ■ ■

By two o'clock, I was too antsy to work. Time to go Christmas shopping.

I drove to Lia's spa.

Missy, the receptionist, was as warm as ever.

"Hi, Josie! Are you here to book a massage? We have a winter special you're going to love. Paraffin for your hands and feet to counteract winter dryness!"

"That sounds incredible. Next time. Right now, I'm looking for a gift for Ty, a stocking stuffer. I'm thinking of some manly dry skin cream. What do you recommend?"

Lia appeared from the spa area, smiling warmly. "I think Ty would love our Your Skin product line for men. It's new, all organic, and very popular." She pointed to shelves filled with steel gray and ice blue tubes.

I picked up one called Wake Up Call. The label said it was a mixture of green tea, glycerin, and menthol, to refresh and moisturize men's skin.

"Perfect," I said. "Sold."

While Missy rang it up, Lia asked, "I read about the attack. You look fine, but are you? Really?"

"I am. I got very lucky."

"No word on the missing paintings?"

"No. Nor about Becca. She's still missing. How are you doing?"

"Same old, same old." She smiled, the kind that turned up her lips but didn't reach her eyes. "Bitter. Hopeless. Angry." She leaned in for a butterfly kiss. "See ya!"

She moved off to greet another customer. I took the tube from Missy, wishing I felt more, rather than less, connected to Lia.

Chapter Twenty-Seven

Ty called Wednesday evening as I was taping a big red bow on his gift-wrapped moisturizer. I finished and slipped it into his stocking.

"I'm sitting here brooding," I said. "I'm worried about Becca. I'm worried about the paintings. I want my tote bag back. I'm feeling feckless."

"You always say that when you have more questions than answers, find something to research."

"About what?"

"What don't you know?" he asked.

"Everything."

"Well, that's certainly comprehensive."

"I'll think about it," I said. "What are you getting me for Christmas?"

"I'm not telling."

I smiled. "Will I like it?"

"Yes."

"I miss you, Ty."

"One more day. I'll be home tomorrow. I'm taking Friday off."

"Oh, yeah? How come?"

"To sleep late. To finish my Christmas shopping. To split logs. I have that pile of logs out back from when they took down the old apple tree last spring. I've been cooped up in an office for too long. I want to do some physical work."

"I'll be the beneficiary," I said. "I love the way applewood smells when you burn it."

"Appley."

We chatted another few minutes, ending with "I love you."

I checked e-mail around ten, just before I went to bed. Ellis had forwarded me an e-mail he'd received at nine, two in the morning in Christmas Common. In Ellis's cover note, he explained that Superintendent Shorling had called him back, as promised, explaining that Detective Higgins would be in touch within the next several hours.

Apparently, Detective Higgins had had a fire lit under him, and he in turn had lit others. The e-mail came from a woman in Superintendent Shorling's office, saying he'd asked her to forward on this document. It was a PDF of the purchase agreement Kirk Trevor had mentioned, which they'd found in Ian's desk.

The seller of the miniatures was a couple named Jeffrey and Nancy Cheviot, owners of a textile mill in Leeds, England. Nancy, whose maiden name was Worth, had inherited the miniatures from her grandmother, Mary Knight Worth. As I read the report, following the trail from owner to owner, I was impressed. Kirk Trevor had done meticulous work, and so had I — but the paintings were still missing.

Thursday morning, I woke up with an idea. The only two people who acknowledged seeing the miniature portraits were Marney Alred and Ethan Ferguson. Marney was a dead end, but maybe Ethan knew something more, something that would help me understand what was going on. I had no sense that he was withholding information; rather, I wondered if he might know something without recognizing its significance. I hoped he'd see me.

Just after nine, I called Ethan and asked if he was in Rocky Point, and when he said he was, I invited him to lunch.

"You're the answer to a prayer," he said. "I'm buried under oyster and clam data, and you're offering me a way to burrow out."

"Do clams and oysters burrow?" I asked, relieved he seemed to have forgotten that he'd disinvited me for a drink during his police interview.

"Like champs."

I smiled, as drawn to him as ever. "Then I'm glad I can offer a way out."

"Do you know Frank's Tavern?" he asked.

"On Route 1?"

"That's the place."

"I've passed it a thousand times, but I've never been there."

"They have killer onion rings."

"I'm in."

I got there first, just before noon. The oak bar stretched the whole length of the room on the right. Three men, spaced apart, sat on stools. Two had mugs of beer in front of them. One had a highball. I took a booth midway down the row on the left. I slid across the maroon vinyl, avoiding hitting my head on the low-hanging faux-Tiffany glass chandelier. The table was old-style Formica, black with red and white specks. A silver metal napkin holder sat at the far end next to a bottle of ketchup with dried bits on the lip of the bottle, and standard-issue glass salt and pepper shakers. A bored-looking waitress wearing jeans and a long-sleeved gray collared jersey with FRANK'S silkscreened across the front in black approached me, menu in hand. Her black plastic name tag read TAWNY. I told her we'd be two for lunch and asked for an iced tea.

"Sure," Tawny said, pronouncing it like a good New Englander: *shoo-ah.*

She was delivering my drink when Ethan came in, saw me, and smiled.

"A coffee, darlin'," he said to Tawny as he slid onto the bench across from me.

"You got it," she said, giving him a sassy grin, no longer the least bit bored. When she walked away, her hips swayed.

"You're not a stranger here," I said.

"Once again, you prove your observation wizardry." He settled in and looked me over. "No lasting injuries, I see."

"True. I got lucky."

"Luck. The dependence on luck is the hobgoblin of little minds."

"Foolish consistency," I said, "not luck."

"True. Emerson. It's just I've been thinking a lot about luck lately. One man's misfortune is another man's gain. Who said that?"

"I think it's a proverb, the attribution lost across the centuries. Why have you been thinking about luck and other people's misfortune?"

"My work is going well, and it wouldn't be if Becca were still in the picture."

"That's bittersweet."

"Not really." He gave his hallmark half-grin. "When she gets back, we'll both be doing well. The misfortune I alluded to was a reference to whatever is going on with her now."

He paused as Tawny placed his coffee and a small bowl filled with single-portion tubs of half-and-half on the table. She asked if we were ready to order. I did a quick once-through of the menu, choosing a Cobb salad, honey mustard dressing on the side.

"No onion rings?" Ethan asked me.

"I was hoping I could mooch."

"For you, anything."

Ethan ordered the burger deluxe, which came with French fries, and a side of onion rings.

"I love onion rings," I said. "I've tried to make them, but I can't get it right."

"That's why God made Frank's."

I laughed. "Tell me more about what's going on that both you and Becca are doing well."

"The foundation is impressed enough with my ideas on how I can mesh my research with Becca's without impinging on her data or findings to okay my new role as acting principal investigator." He grinned. "They've invited me to submit my own proposal. Now that I understand the structure they're looking for, the abstract wrote itself, and they approved it within a day."

"Holy cow! That's wonderful, Ethan! Beyond wonderful! You must be thrilled. What was different this time around?"

Ethan leaned back and rubbed his nose, thinking about it. When he spoke, his tone was serious, even grave.

"Reading Becca's materials was like having a private tutor. I was unprepared for her process, her writing style, her use of seemingly unrelated research to make new, insightful points. I studied her notes like a freshman cramming for finals, adapted her approach to my material, and just like that" — Ethan snapped his fingers — "it worked. She ought to write a textbook." He rubbed his nose some more. "I lied to the police, and you, about my alibi for when you were attacked. Stupid of me. I told them I was in my room writing because I didn't want to admit I was here reading."

"I don't understand."

"I was ashamed at my ignorance, so I lied. It sounded better to say that I was writing an article, rather than hanging out in a bar cribbing Becca's notes."

"That's some prideful moment," I said. "You'd rather pretend you didn't have an alibi for a crime? If you didn't want to admit to using Becca's notes, why not simply say you were here writing?"

"Because I had a spasm of attitude. If I told the cops I was here, I could see them coming in and asking Tawny or checking the security cameras to see what I was doing, to confirm I was here the whole time I said I was. They'd find out that I didn't write a word, and I'd be caught."

"That doesn't make much sense."

"Never underestimate the depravity of ambition." He looked guilty in an unconvincing way, like the proverbial little boy caught with his hand in the cookie jar. "It's not like I planned it. Spasms of attitude aren't planned."

Tawny delivered our food. I nabbed an onion ring as soon as she left.

It was thick and not the least bit greasy. The crust was more orange than golden. It was delicious, moist and flavorful, perfectly cooked and perfectly seasoned.

"Yum," I said, licking my fingers.

"Told you!" He took a bite of his burger, and as he chewed, he kept his eyes on my face. When he swallowed, he asked, "Do you have any information about Becca?"

"No. I wish I did."

"I always respected her," he said, lowering his eyes to his plate, "but I never fully appreciated her. She's a force of nature. I sure hope she's okay."

"You remember that you told me that you saw the paintings — the miniatures."

"Sure, like I said."

"How come she didn't display them?"

"She said it was complicated, that she would at some point."

I ate for a while, thinking about that. "Complicated" was one of those words that covered a multitude of sins.

"What did she mean by 'complicated'?" I asked.

He shrugged. "I didn't ask. Why?"

"I'm just trying to understand what's going on. Did you know Becca was married? Now widowed?"

"Becca?" he asked, sounding incredulous.

"She was separated when her husband died. There was a financial dispute holding up the divorce."

He placed his half-eaten burger on his plate and stared at it as if he'd never seen such a thing before. He looked up and took in my face. "It's funny, isn't it? Sometimes you don't realize how much you care about someone until they're gone."

Our conversation flagged. Neither one of us seemed to be able to find a new topic of interest. When the bill came, I insisted on paying, telling Ethan I'd invited him.

"Only because you ask so sweetly."

He stood up and said he had to go. He patted Tawny on the upper arm, and she smiled like she wanted more. While I waited for her to bring my change, I watched Ethan leave. I wondered which of us got more out of our conversation. All in all, I suspected he did.

I sat in my car and texted Ellis about Ethan's change in alibi, saying I'd explain why he'd fibbed when we spoke.

Driving back to work, I wondered if Becca had confided in anyone or whether she was truly as reclusive as Thomas had implied and as I sensed. Certainly she hadn't confided in Ethan. To have no one to confide in would be so hard, I thought, knowing how much I depended on Zoë and Ty. I thought it was kind of creepy that everyone involved in that real estate venture was, it seemed, dead or missing. Ian. Thomas. Becca. Rupert. Where was Rupert's widow, Cheryl?

As soon as I got back to work, I did two things. First, I e-mailed Zoë and Ty. To Zoë, I wrote: *You're so dear to me.* To Ty, I typed: *You mean the world to me.* I didn't want either of them to think I took them for granted, not even for a minute. Second, I Googled "Cheryl Morrishein and North Conway" and got a boatload of hits, all old, all insignificant, mostly one-line mentions.

I called Wes. "I need current information about Cheryl Morrishein."

"Why?"

"Because I don't know enough about her."

"Josie," he said with faux patience, "that's a nonreason."

"It's all I have."

"Whatcha got for me?"

"The police superintendent in Christmas Common, Gerald Shorling, located the purchase agreement for the two missing watercolors."

"Tell me."

"Where can we meet?"

"At Blackmore's."

I laughed at the non sequitur. "Why there?"

"I don't know what to get Maggie for Christmas. Maybe you can help me figure it out."

We agreed to meet in an hour.

Chapter Twenty-Eight

Blackmore's Jewelers was the finest jewelry store on the seacoast, bar none. A third-generation family business, Blackmore's carried remarkable items, most of them unique. I pushed open the heavy wooden door and entered another world.

I stood on cushy forest green carpet. The walls were oak, with box molding. The lighting was soft, emanating from recessed lamps hidden behind soffits and elegant crystal chandeliers. Vivaldi played softly in the background. Boughs of holly were draped just under the crown molding. Big red velvet bows adorned the walls in back of the display cases. A Victorian London Christmas scene sat on a round table in the center of the large shop. There were ceramic row houses, each one decorated for the holiday and porcelain characters scattered about, like a woman shopping, her husband a step behind her, carrying her bags, and children skating on a glistening painted glass pond. I stood, transfixed. I loved discovering unexpected details that added to the illusion, like the kitten sleeping under a Christmas tree inside one of the houses.

Nate Blackmore, the thirty-something grandson of the founder, was our go-to jewelry expert. He saw me and smiled. He was waiting on an older man standing at the bracelet display. Two female sales associates were busy, too. One was showing a young woman diamond studs. The other was helping a middle-aged woman choose a watch fob. The founder, Morton Blackmore, who had to be close to eighty, came out from his private office in the back, spotted me, and smiled.

"Josie!" he said, approaching me with both hands extended.

I grasped his hands and squeezed. "Mr. Blackmore. It's so good to see you!"

"You, too. You're admiring our Christmas scene."

"It's spectacular. I love the details."

"Thank you. It was Nate's idea, a new tradition. So, what can I show you today?"

"I'm meeting Wes Smith here. He wants advice on a gift for his wife. I don't know whether you'll remember him. He bought her engagement ring here."

"The reporter?"

"That's right."

"I do recall the purchase. He was very thorough in deciding which diamond to buy and which setting to choose. A good researcher."

"That's Wes," I said.

Wes walked in and joined us.

It was an education to watch Mr. Blackmore work. All he did was ask questions and use the answers to help Wes narrow his options.

What kind of jewelry did Maggie wear? Necklaces and earrings almost every day. No other rings than her engagement ring and wedding band.

What kind of necklaces? Strands of things, Wes said, out of his depth. Mr. Blackmore pointed to a turquoise and silver torsade. Like this one? No, simpler. One strand, usually. She doesn't like fussy things.

How about earrings? Do they dangle? No. Maybe just a little.

What color clothing does she wear most frequently? Black, brown, green. Some yellow.

Does she have pearls? Yes, she loves them. The pearl earrings have little diamonds where they go through her earlobes; the pearls dangle. The pearl necklace has only one strand, but the pearls go all the way around. Her parents gave her the set when she graduated college. Mr. Blackmore smiled knowingly and led us over to a counter near the back wall.

"These are Tahitian pearls," he explained, extracting a pair of simple green-black earrings from the case. "The color is called pistachio. They're rare because the color occurs naturally. It's not dyed or chemically treated."

He took a necklace out as well and laid it on a black velvet cushion. A single iridescent dark green pearl hung from a diamond-encrusted setting.

"They're beautiful," Wes said solemnly. He turned to me. "What do you think?"

"I think they're spectacular." I looked up at Mr. Blackmore. "The term 'Tahiti pearl' refers to a black pearl, doesn't it?"

"That's right, but as you can see, it's not a literal term. Even the blackest pearls generally have undertones or overtones of other colors, pink, yellow, cream." He smiled at Wes. "Since your wife wears brown, yellow, and green, she'll get a lot of use out of these. Are most of her settings gold or white?"

"Gold."

"Like this pair. What do you think?"

Wes's shoulders stiffened. "How much are they?"

"The earrings are two hundred and ninety-nine dollars. The necklace is only one ninety-nine."

Wes looked at me. "What do you think?"

"Is the price higher than what you had in mind?" I asked. "Because they may have smaller pearls."

"I think three hundred is okay. If it's all right with you, Mr. Blackmore, I could buy the earrings now for Christmas, and make payments on the necklace between now and March. Maggie's birthday is in March."

"Certainly. We'd be pleased to put the necklace on layaway for you."

"Should I do it?" Wes asked me.

"Yes!" I said.

Wes turned to Mr. Blackmore. "I'll take them."

He handed over his credit card. Mr. Blackmore said he'd be back in a moment and left for a semienclosed workstation off to the side.

"I did what you said about Googling Ian Bennington and Christmas Common," Wes said while we waited. "Top-of-the-trees tip. What else have you found out?"

"Nothing yet, except the purchase agreement, which is useful to validate ownership, but doesn't help find who stole them, or who killed Thomas, or anything. How about you? Were you able to find out anything about Cheryl Morrishein?"

"I'm going to put you in touch with a friend of mine. Her name is Reggie Campbell. She's kind of a ski-bum whiz-kid who works part-time for the local North Conway paper, the *Town Bee.* She said she'll be glad to talk to you."

"That's great, Wes," I said. "Thanks."

"I vouched for you," he said in a warning tone.

I grinned. "I won't let you down."

He grinned back. "See you don't."

He e-mailed me Reggie's contact information as Mr. Blackmore reappeared with the elegantly wrapped box. It jangled. The box was covered in shiny red paper and gold stretchy ribbon. Tied on were three small silver bells.

"That's beautiful," I said.

"It's awesome!" Wes said. "Maggie's going to love it."

I left him filling out forms for the layaway. Outside, as I walked toward the Central Garage, I called Reggie Campbell.

Reggie Campbell's phone went to voice mail.

"Hi, Reggie," I said. "I'm Wes's friend, Josie Prescott. I look forward to talking to you about Cheryl Morrishein. I really appreciate your help." I left my phone number and e-mail address.

By the time I got back to work, both Zoë and Ty had replied to my e-mails. Zoë e-mailed me saying I was dear to her, too, and asking if I was okay. I replied that I was fine. Ty called and left an "I love you" message, saying he wasn't going to be able to get away as early as he'd hoped and would keep me posted.

Reggie had left a message, too. "We're now officially playing phone tag," she said, her words riding a riffle of laughter, "and I'm going to be tough to reach because the ski conditions are killer. Forty degrees and awesome snow, deep and packed." A chuckle. "Now you know my priorities. In between runs, I'll manage to squeeze in a little research. I'll put together a dossier for you. Why don't you come up here for the weekend? We can talk in person. Let me know if you want help booking a room. Give Wes my love. Ta-ta!"

I scanned the rest of my e-mails. Nothing was pressing. I considered the piles of work on my desk. Nothing that couldn't wait. Ty and I hadn't been away for a weekend in months. North Conway was a postcard-pretty resort town. Why not?

I texted Ty: *You can split logs tomorrow morning. At noon, I'm kidnapping you.*

Hank appeared with sleepy eyes and mewed, clearly wanting to know why I hadn't let him know I was back.

"I'm sorry, baby," I said. I held out my arm toward him and rubbed my thumb and fingers together. "Come here, little boy."

He walked toward me as if he might or might not be interested in a cuddle. He sniffed my hand with studied indifference, then deigned to leap into my lap. I kissed his head and thought about kidnapping Ty.

Ty texted: *What should I pack?*

I replied: *Winter wear. One sport coat/slacks outfit. Two nights. A bathing suit.*

He answered: *Done. Do you realize this is my first kidnapping?*

I wrote: *Me, too.*

I gave Hank a final pet-pet and picked up the phone. I reached Ellis on his cell phone.

"So was Ethan telling the truth about his revised alibi?"

"Yes. He got to Frank's at eleven, just as they were opening, took over a booth in the back, and didn't leave until after seven. The waitress said the table was covered with books and magazines and papers and she doesn't know what else. They didn't try to nudge him away because he kept ordering food and drinks and he tips big."

"I didn't think he was my attacker," I said. "As fit as he is, he would have crushed me."

"Eliminating someone as a suspect is progress."

"I understand. And just because he didn't ambush me doesn't mean he didn't kill Thomas. Have you made any progress on that front?"

"We have several viable leads," he said, saying nothing.

He might not, but I did.

Chapter Twenty-Nine

At four Friday afternoon, I twirled in front of the full-length mirror, trying to check my rear view. I was wearing a black sheath with a black sweater dotted with red sparkly bits and black knee-high boots.

"What do you think? I asked Ty. "Is this dress too fancy for these boots?"

Ty finished knotting his tie and looked at me. "You look gorgeous."

"What about the boots?"

His eyes lowered to my feet. "They look like nice boots."

I laughed. "Never mind."

Reggie had somehow gotten us in on an otherwise sold-out weekend. The White Birch Inn was a renovated mansion ten minutes out of town and fifteen minutes from the ski resort bar where we were scheduled to meet Reggie at five thirty. Our room had a king-sized bed, a gas fireplace, and a Jacuzzi tub. The hotel had a twenty-four-hour outdoor hot tub. I was a happy girl.

We left the inn at ten past four. I wanted to stop in the village to try to find a tote bag I liked. I hadn't given up hope on getting my other one back, but I needed to face the fact that for now, at least, it was gone. I found a black leather beauty in the first boutique we tried. It was big, with cubbyholes for my phone and tablet, two zippered compartments, and a built-in latch for my key ring.

We walked into Après Ski, the bar attached to the main chalet at the White Mountain Ridge Resort, at five twenty-five. The place was packed and loud. I stood in the entryway, uncertain where to go. There were no open seats.

"Now what?" I asked Ty.

"What does Reggie look like?"

"I have no idea. I forgot to ask."

"Maybe she'll recognize you. Look — there."

I followed his gaze. A woman with kinky red hair was standing near a club chair to the right of the fireplace, her eyes on my face, her arms high above her head, crisscrossing back and forth, like an aircraft marshaler signaling a pilot to make an emergency stop. Her grin was huge. The flames shooting off the six-foot logs leapt high and hot, and the gold and amber light glinted on her hair.

Ty and I hurried in her direction.

"Reggie?" I asked when we reached her.

"Josie! Welcome!"

I introduced Ty, and she turned to a college-age couple sitting on a love seat at right angles to her chair, their heads together, deep in conversation.

"Scoot," she said to them. "I told you I was holding it."

"Sure, Reggie," the man said.

The young woman gave her a hug, and they disappeared, swallowed up by the crowd surging toward the bar.

A waitress in jeans and a turtleneck sweater, wearing a white hash-slinger apron, appeared out of nowhere to take our order. I ordered champagne. Ty got his usual, Smuttynose. Reggie asked for another cognac.

"You must have some pull around here," Ty said as we got situated on the couch.

Reggie laughed but didn't respond to his unspoken question. Instead, she said, "It's so nice to meet you. Wes is such a cutie-pie, isn't he?"

I stopped myself laughing. Not once had I ever thought of Wes as a cutie-pie. "He is.

Totally adorable. I can't thank you enough for helping me."

"This is about an antiques appraisal?"

"Right. Some seventeenth-century paintings."

"Wicked cool." She stretched her hand behind her chair and brought out a black leather portfolio box. "Here you go!"

I took the box, raising and lowering it an inch or two several times, indicating its heft. "When you said a dossier, I expected you to hand me a manila envelope."

Reggie grinned again. "We do it up right around here."

"If you don't mind, I'd like to take a quick look through this."

She fluttered a hand. "Sure. I'll talk to the boyfriend." She smiled radiantly at Ty. "That's you, right?"

Ty smiled back at her and said, "That's me."

"So talk to me. What do you do?"

I opened the lid and found two inches' worth of documentation about Cheryl Morrishein and Thomas Lewis and anyone connected to them. There were bios of Cheryl and her husband, Rupert; his partner, Thomas Lewis; and Thomas's wife, Rebecca. One page was a list of magazines and blogs where Thomas Lewis had published articles and essays on cross-country skiing — according to his bio, he was a leading proponent of the sport. Newspaper clippings went back to 2010, shortly after Thomas and Becca moved to North Conway.

I tilted the first clipping I picked up toward the sconce, trying to find an angle where I could read it. The overall illumination was dim, appropriate for a bar but not helpful to a reader. The flickering fire didn't help.

As I perused the dossier, I half-listened to Reggie and Ty's conversation and wished I could participate. It sounded fun. Ty didn't like downhill skiing, and they were hot on the pros and cons of downhill versus cross-country as I got lost in scanning the contents of the box. One article discussed Thomas and Rupert's enthusiasm about their new venture; another looked at how their relationship degenerated while their partnership struggled to find traction; and several others analyzed the accusations and countercharges they'd flung at one another. Also in the box was the first announcement of Rupert's lawsuit; an update about Rebecca's work at the Rocky Point Oceanographic Institute; Rupert's obituary; and a follow-up article focusing on his widow's determination to pursue the case. I flipped through the remaining articles, impressed.

"I'll read these later. I can't thank you enough, Reggie. Any chance you have last known addresses for everyone?"

"Would a dossier be complete without them? Look at the bottom sheet."

I eased out the last sheet of paper and found a contact list.

"You're fabulous," I said. "Tell me about these places."

Reggie leaned forward. She pointed at Cheryl's address. "That's your neck of the woods."

"So it is," I said. "Those are yawner condos. Small, uninspired, builder grade."

She read the next name, Thomas, and address, local. "I bet Thomas decided to stay here in North Conway because of the cross-country skiing." She gave me a saucy look. "We're known for our adventurous trails. I've given you his London address, too. He owned a flat there. My preliminary research indicated it's mortgaged to the hilt." She tapped the paper again and handed it back to me. "Since you're not going to follow up on any of these addresses tonight, may I suggest that we retire to G's Steakhouse, a restaurant where they make killer steaks, natch, and to-die-for shrimp, flown in fresh from the Gulf, and where I took the liberty of making us a reservation."

Ty stood up. "You don't have to ask me twice."

"Food, baby," Reggie said.

I watched them fuss about who would pay the bill. Ty won. I followed them out of the lodge and half-listened to their banter as we waited for the valet to bring up our cars. I was with them, but I wasn't. It was the same through dinner.

I answered when I was asked a question, made such comments as occurred to me, and ate every bit of my meal, but my mind was in a whirl. I was more than distracted. I was deeply disturbed, and I wasn't liking the dark thoughts that loomed in front of me like an abyss.

Chapter Thirty

Ty and I sat in the hot tub under a canopy of twinkling stars. A single spotlight mounted near the roof at the far end of the deck facing the woods provided the only illumination, a faint golden glow, enough to discern objects but not enough to differentiate subtle variations in color or texture. I slouched down so the water came up to my chin. It was deliciously sultry. I pressed my back against the jet, allowing the pulsating water to massage my spine. The night was clear and silent and cold. We could have been the only two people on earth.

"Did you have a good time tonight?" Ty asked.

"Not really. I'm preoccupied."

"You missed some fun."

"I know. I liked Reggie."

"Me, too."

I leaned back and closed my eyes.

"Do you want to go cross-country skiing

tomorrow?" Ty asked.

"No. I want to track down Thomas and Becca's former neighbors."

"You sure know how to show a guy you kidnap a good time."

I opened my eyes. "I'm sorry."

"I was joking," Ty said.

"I know. Still, I'm sorry."

"You're tired."

"Very."

"Let's go to bed," he said.

"You go. I'll sleep here."

"You'll drown."

"You'll rescue me," I said.

"No, I won't, 'cause I'll drown, too."

"Then I guess we have to go upstairs. You go first and hold my robe for me."

"I thought you'd go first."

The jets timed out and shut off. "I guess we both have to go."

Ty climbed out and put on one of the terrycloth robes we'd found in the closet, then held mine up, ready for me. I followed suit and dashed inside, letting my feet drip on the sisal mat.

"That was sensational," I said, drying my feet and slipping on flip-flops for the trek back to the room.

"We like a hot tub."

"Why don't we put one in at home?"

"Good question."

"You should go cross-country skiing in the morning while I'm tracking down information about Becca. We can connect for lunch."

"You sure? I could keep you company while you search."

"No." I tucked my hand in the crook of his arm, and we walked side by side to the grand staircase. "You ski."

He leaned down and kissed the top of my head. "I love you."

I head-bumped his arm. "I love you, too."

I knocked on Thomas Lewis's front door in case his neighbor was watching, waited a few seconds, and knocked again. I spotted a doorbell and pushed it. The chimes sounded. I looked around as if I were uncertain what to do, then walked to the condo next door and rang the bell.

"I'm Josie Prescott," I said to the woman who answered. "I have a quick question."

"I'm Bitsy Mayeaux, who may or may not have a quick answer."

She was in her late twenties and a little heavy, what my mother used to call pleasingly plump. She had straight shoulder-length brown hair, hazel eyes, a lot of freckles, and an open, friendly expression. A toddler dressed in pink corduroy overalls, a white long-sleeved T-shirt, and white socks with pink bows on the ankles stood next to her, hiding behind her leg, curious but not wanting to engage. Her eyes were cornflower blue. Her hair was short, an adorable mass of platinum blond ringlets. She was sucking her thumb.

I smiled. "I was hoping you might know where your next-door neighbor, Thomas Lewis, is."

Her expression shifted from affable to reticent. "Do you know him?" she asked.

"No," I replied, thinking it was true. Just because you've met someone doesn't mean you know them.

"I'm afraid I have bad news. He's dead."

"Oh, my," I said, crossing my fingers behind my back to stave off the bad karma that came from fibbing. "I had no idea."

I shifted my gaze to the condo next door, scanning the forest beyond, as if I needed to gather my thoughts. Shards of yellow sunlight striped the deck and dappled the woods. Most of the condos were decorated for the holidays. Some had windows framed in lights; others sparkled with merry window art, like candy canes and Santa's sleigh; almost everyone had a wreath.

I turned back to Bitsy. "I'm an antiques

appraiser, and in connection with an important appraisal, I needed to talk to him or his wife — I guess I should say his widow — Rebecca. Do you know where she is?"

"Becca? She hasn't lived here in years."

"Oh! I didn't know. Are they divorced?"

"Probably. Not that it matters now that Thomas is dead."

"True. So they moved into the complex together?"

"That's right. They moved here from England. Becca left within a few months, six or eight months, maybe. I don't remember exactly. What's the appraisal you're working on?"

"A seventeenth-century antique," I said. "British, like them. Why did Becca leave?"

The little girl tugged on Bitsy's sweater, and Bitsy looked down, smoothing her daughter's curly blond hair with such devotion, I felt myself smile with vicarious pleasure. Bitsy looked back at me.

"All I know is they fought a lot, and apparently didn't care who heard them. Not that you can avoid hearing everything; the walls in this place are like paper. I actually called the cops once. Things were being thrown and breaking —" She paused and glanced at her daughter. When she spoke again, her eyes meeting mine, her tone was muted. "I was worried about Becca."

"What were they fighting about?" I asked in a gossipy tone.

Bitsy gave a little snort. "Money. What else do couples fight about?" She laughed, but not like she thought something was funny, and jerked her head toward the little girl. "G-rated answers only, please."

I nodded, acknowledging her unspoken request. "Money, honey. The love of which is the source of all evil. I thought they were very well off."

Bitsy lowered her voice as if she were sharing a secret. "I think it was Becca who had the money. Thomas wanted Becca to sell some paintings, and Becca said no way."

"Was that what the fight was about the day you called the police?"

Bitsy nodded. "It was about seven o'clock. I remember, because I'd just put Sophie here to bed. Becca shouted that she wasn't going to the lecture, that they were going to have it out here and now and settle it once and for all. It didn't take long before Becca's shouts became screams. Then I heard something shatter, like a vase. No joke. My husband was at work — he's the night manager at the North Conway Diner. I came out here on the porch. A woman was standing here, her mouth hanging open like she couldn't believe her ears. She told me she'd been about to knock on their door but got scared." She shook her head, remembering, almost wincing. "I hope I never hear anything like that again."

"Then what happened?" I asked, opening my eyes wide, communicating how absorbing I found her story.

"We whispered back and forth, agreeing that we ought to call the police. She was frightened to make the call, worried, she said, that her cell phone number would appear on the police report, and that Thomas would think she turned on him. I didn't care. Let him think what he wants, that was my attitude. Maybe it would make him think. I went into my place to make the call, and when I came out again, the woman was gone."

"Who was she?"

"I don't know. I never saw her before, and I haven't seen her since."

"How old was she?"

Bitsy made a "who knows?" face. "I'm not good guessing ages. Forties, maybe."

"Was she white?"

"Yes. White. Well dressed. Pretty." She shrugged. "It was a long time ago."

"What a situation! What happened when the police came?"

"They were only inside about ten or fifteen minutes; then out they come with Becca. She had two big suitcases. I never saw her again."

"Was Thomas arrested?"

"Not that I saw. The law up here is funky when it comes to domestic violence cases — it's up to each individual police officer's discretion." She smiled, a knowing one. "I'm from California. The police have a very different attitude there, I can tell you that. The North Conway cops probably figured that since Becca hadn't been hurt and was leaving, what was the point?"

"Sounds like Thomas got lucky."

"I'll say. And Becca got smart."

"Why do you say that?" I asked.

"Would you want to stay with a man who's only after your money, who threatens you if you won't sell some paintings?"

"No, I wouldn't."

"Me neither." She ruffled her daughter's hair. "And I want to make darn sure Sophie gets that message loud and clear."

I smiled down at Sophie. "She's beautiful."

Sophie disappeared behind her mother.

"Thanks."

"So Becca left, and Thomas stayed. When did you last see him?"

Bitsy pursed her lips. "A couple of weeks ago, I guess." Sophie reappeared and tugged Bitsy's sweater again. "I'm being summoned. It's snack time."

"Thank you." I waved. "Bye, Sophie."

Sophie ran into an inner room. Talk about shy.

I left, walking slowly, thinking about divorce. Not the emotional aspects to breaking a relationship apart, but the practical ones. Thomas had not left his marriage quietly. He seemed to have had no pride when it came to commandeering Becca's money — or trying to do so. I looked up at Thomas's condo and wondered just how low he'd sunk.

I sat in my car, extracted my phone from its made-to-fit slot, and called Wes.

"Wes," I said to his voice mail, "will you do me a favor? I hear Thomas Lewis had a flat in London that was heavily mortgaged. Can you confirm that? What was his financial situation in general? Also, did he travel to the U.K. in the last several months? Thanks."

I hung up. I stared into the woods for several seconds, then called Sasha. I got her just as she was finishing a turn at Prescott's Instant Appraisal booth.

"I need you to post a request for anyone

who has appraised the Cooper miniatures to contact me," I said. "Word it so it sounds urgent."

"On all the sites?"

"Yes, and all relevant social media. Get the word out."

I thanked her and called Ty.

"How was the skiing?" I asked.

"Top ten ever. No wind. Heat wave continuing. Decent snow. I feel invigorated. What's your ETA?"

"About twelve thirty, I should think. Should we meet somewhere for lunch?"

"Why don't you come back to the room? We'll pick a place and go from here."

I told him I was on my way.

I missed Wes's call because I was skiing alongside Ty on a level trail in back of the inn. I'm not a bad cross-country skier, especially on the flats. Hills kill me.

"You're good," Ty said, heading for the shower.

"I don't know whether I'm good, but I for sure know I'm hungry. That little frou-frou sandwich we had at that ever-so-cute tea shop is long gone. We need to order up food."

"Get a bottle of champagne, too."

"Really?"

He paused, resting against the doorjamb. "Hell, yes. We have things to celebrate."

"Like what?"

"Like our love. Like skiing. Like your TV show being renewed. Like my being tapped to fill in for Rudy. Like life is good for us right now and we ought to pay attention."

I walked over to where he stood, went up on tiptoe, and kissed him. He kissed me back and hit the shower.

As soon as I heard the water running, I placed the room service order, a bowl of French onion soup, two spoons, a cheese plate, and a bottle of Veuve Clicquot. My next call was to Wes.

"Thomas Lewis was broke," Wes said. "About ten years ago, he got a line of credit using his London apartment as collateral. He inherited the flat from his grandfather free and clear, by the way. He used the line of credit like a piggy bank, dipping his hand in whenever he needed money. From all accounts he was a good talker, but there was nothing behind the talk."

"Did he have any other sources of income?"

"Not as near as I can tell. It looks like he never actually earned a dime. Weird, huh?"

"Amazing. What about his travel?"

"He flew to England three weeks ago. He

returned, as scheduled, four days after his arrival. A long weekend. There was nothing unusual about it. He visited England once or twice a year ever since he moved to New Hampshire, sometimes for a week or so, often for a long weekend."

"Do you have the dates?"

"Yup. Got a pen?"

I told him I was ready and jotted the dates down on a notepad the inn had placed next to the phone.

"Ian Bennington died while Thomas was in England," I said.

"You think there's something there?"

"Maybe."

"What about Becca?" Wes asked. "Do you think she killed Thomas?"

"I don't know. I bet she wanted to, but I've never met her, so I don't know how well she's able to control herself. Most people wouldn't give in to the impulse. Some would."

"Why are you so sure she would have wanted to?"

I considered sharing what I'd just discovered from Bitsy, but I didn't. I didn't tell him about Thomas's petition to the divorce court, either. Another time, when I had more time, when my half-formed thoughts had crystallized. "My knowledge of human nature. Thanks for running the story about the paintings and tweeting about it and all."

"I could have used a quote."

Give Wes an inch and he expected a yard.

"Thanks for introducing me to Reggie, too."

"What did she tell you?"

"Nothing. She gave me a box of clippings, which I haven't read many of yet. I haven't even skimmed through them all."

"Reggie's pretty special, huh?" he asked, switching gears.

"Absolutely."

"Are you really telling me you have nothing for me?" he demanded, back in reporter mode.

"I gave you a hot story and leads to others! That's a huge credit on my side of the ledger. Have you heard whether the police got any hits from your articles and tweets?"

"So far nothing. Becca is in the wind. Your credit isn't all that big, by the way. Talk to me, Josie. Give me something."

I smiled, amused at his transparency. "Sorry," I said. "I have nothing to give."

Wes was so predictable.

Chapter Thirty-One

Monday morning I got into work about seven. By nine, I'd reviewed the tag sale financial and inventory reports, caught up with e-mails, and spent some time with Hank. At ten past, I called Lia and asked if she had time for a cup of coffee. She did, and we agreed to meet at ten thirty at Sweet Buns, a new tea shop not far from her spa.

I left at nine thirty and drove to Cheryl Morrishein's ho-hum condo complex. It backed a nice wooded chunk of land and faced the service road that paralleled the highway. Her unit was in the middle of the section closest to the street. I buzzed but got no answer. I tried knocking. A college-age young woman stepped out of the unit next door, slinging a backpack over her shoulder. She had chin-length black hair held off her face with orange barrettes.

"Hi," I said. "I'm Josie Prescott. You live next door to Cheryl Morrishein?"

"That's right." She extended a hand and we shook. "I'm Lucy Hillard."

"You don't happen to know where she is, do you?"

"Sorry. No. I haven't seen her in a few days."

"I need to see her about an antiques appraisal. It's pretty important that I speak to her. Any ideas?"

"She said she was going to Florida to escape the cold." She scanned the lot, pointing to a blue Lexus. "That's her car. Maybe she's left already."

"Wouldn't she have driven herself to the airport?"

"We talked about that. I'm at Hitchens studying physical therapy. I intern at Mass General twice a week, so I drive right by Logan. I offered to drop her if our schedules lined up, but she said it was just as easy to cab to Portsmouth Circle and take the bus."

"When did she plan on leaving?" I asked.

"I thought she said after New Year's, but what do I know? My head is full of ROMs." She made a silly face, crossing her eyes momentarily and scrunching up her mouth. "Range of motion — a little student humor. Sorry I can't be of more help."

I smiled, acknowledging her joke. "Is there anyone you can think of who might know more about Cheryl's schedule?"

She tilted her head for a moment, thinking. "She's pretty friendly with the cheese guy, Harry. Cornwall Cheese, do you know it? It's a dairy farm on Route 16. They sell their own cheese. They also have a little restaurant. She goes every morning for breakfast. I went with her once, and Harry made it pretty clear he thought she was hot, if you know what I mean."

"I do indeed," I said.

"They're cute together."

"Nice!"

I thanked her, watched her get into an old tan Honda, rang Cheryl's bell one more time, and drove to Cornwall Cheese.

I parked on gravel in front of Cornwall Cheese's long, low retail building. Inside, I took stock. Tables and chairs dotted the left side of the big, open room. The café offered walk-up service. A nice-looking middle-aged woman in a pink uniform stood behind a counter at the rear. In back of her were a coffeemaker and an iced-tea dispenser. Large chalkboard menus were mounted high above her head.

On the right side, self-service refrigerated cabinets and handcrafted shelving units allowed easy shopping. The refrigerated cases stocked cheese. The shelves were filled with boxes of crackers and jars of farm-made jams. Three women stood near one of the cheese cases discussing whether to try the hickory-smoked cheddar. A grandfather clock standing against the rear wall chimed the hour. It was just ten. Thick silver garlands were draped along the wall near the ceiling. Shimmering red balls were strung on silver wire in a crosshatch pattern above my head, creating a crown of glittery warmth.

"Howdy," a friendly-looking man said.

He wore a blue cotton shirt, the cuffs rolled up nearly to his elbows, and jeans. A white apron covered his clothes from neck to knees. He looked to be in his late fifties. From his receding hairline, I guessed he'd be completely bald in another year or two. He was about five-ten and thin, with an open, good-natured countenance.

"Are you Harry?" I asked.

"So my mother tells me," he said with a smile. "How can I help?"

"I'm Josie Prescott, and I hear that you know Cheryl Morrishein."

"I sure do. Glorious woman."

"I need her help with an antiques appraisal. By any chance, do you know where I can find her?"

"Home, maybe. She left about an hour ago."

"Oh, she had breakfast here?"

"Same as most days. Eight sharp."

"I'll try her there," I said.

"Tell her I told you she's beautiful, which she is." He winked. "Help me out some."

I smiled. "Harry, I have a feeling you don't need a bit of help when it comes to the ladies."

He puffed out his chest a little and chuckled.

I thanked him, then drove to Sweet Buns to meet Lia. I wondered why Cheryl hadn't answered her door, then recalled the list of reasons Taylor gave why Ian might not have answered his at the hotel. Maybe Cheryl was taking a bath or listening to music on headphones. Or maybe she just wasn't in the mood for company. I dismissed the question from my mind. That she drove a blue car was comforting.

Sweet Buns smelled of apples, cinnamon, and vanilla, the aroma of home. I ordered my new favorite flavor of tea, black currant, and a cinnamon roll-up. Lia had coffee. We paid at the counter and carried our trays to a small round table by the front window. A bright red poinsettia served as the centerpiece. An electric candle twinkled cheerfully on the windowsill. Across the street, the colorful lights twirled around the Christmas tree in the gazebo gleamed. Seven lights on the menorah were aglow. Wispy clouds sailed across a pale gray sky.

"Any news about your attacker?" Lia asked as we got ourselves situated.

"No, not that I've heard. I know they're talking to everyone they can think of."

"Me included," she said, shaking her head as if she couldn't believe the police considered her a suspect. "They called it an interview, but it felt more like the third degree. God only knows what they thought I could tell them. They even asked to see my car!"

"You drive a silver Lexus. The car that blocked the road was gray or silver — a sedan."

"Just about everyone drives a silver car."

"True. Did they satisfy themselves that your car was innocent?"

"It's in the shop for a tune-up. I told them they were welcome to go see it, or they could wait a few days until it was finished." Lia snorted, a soft huff that wasn't nearly as ladylike a sound as she probably thought it was. "I realized they seriously considered me a suspect when they asked where I took it." She waved it aside. "I told them that if I was going to kill anyone it would be my loser ex-husband, not my good friend Josie."

"What a mess," I said, not knowing what else to say. "Have you ever heard the name Thomas Lewis?"

Lia stared at me for a moment. She sipped her coffee. "No. Should I?"

"I think Wes might have reported it by now — that's the fake Ian's real name."

"Thomas Lewis," Lia repeated, as if she were trying recall why the name sounded familiar. She looked out the window. "Why do you figure he picked me to snooker?"

"I doubt it was a setup, Lia. I suspect he was sincere."

She half-laughed; her lips twisted into a semisneer. "Right."

I didn't know how to respond to her derision. Maybe she wanted reassurance. Maybe she wanted to indulge in some man bashing. I stayed quiet.

After a moment, she asked, "Was he British or was that a lie, too?"

"He was from England. London, I think. But he lived in North Conway."

"So close and yet so far away. I was there last year for that spa expo."

"I remember."

"This year it's in Pawtucket. Jeesh!"

"A long drive."

"And then you're somewhere you don't want to be," she said. "Pawtucket. Pa-leeze. So what are you and Ty doing for Christmas?"

"Nothing, I don't think. We like to keep holidays low-key. How about you?"

"Same old, same old. Nothing."

I couldn't think of what to say to that either. I finished my tea and the last bit of roll-up, licking the cinnamon sugar from my fingers. "I'm like a little kid with these roll-ups. If I weren't a mature adult, I'd lick the plate, too."

Lia laughed and stood, prepared to leave. "I love them, too, but I don't eat them anymore." She vamped a little. "I have to be careful to maintain my girlish figure."

"You look fabulous, Lia, so whatever you're doing is working."

"Too bad no men are noticing."

I stood up, loaded our dirty dishes onto a tray, and carried it to the receptacle.

"I'm sure I'll see you before the holiday," I said, putting on my coat.

"Thanks for calling," she said, and headed out.

I found her negativity exhausting, more so than I recalled. Either she was getting worse or I was becoming less tolerant.

■ ■ ■ ■

I'd only been back at my computer for ten minutes when my good buddy Shelley called from New York.

"Our paths keep crossing," she said.

"A good thing! I miss you, Shelley."

"I miss you, too, Josie. Are you ready to end your sweet little field trip up north and come back to New York?"

I glanced around my office, taking in the framed cover from the issue of *Antiques Insights* magazine where Prescott's was named a "small house to watch" in its annual roundup of the fastest-growing antiques auction houses in the nation, the plaque from the Chamber of Commerce commemorating Prescott's role as a business partner during Career Development Day at Rocky Point High School, and the nicely mounted certificate of appreciation from one of my favorite charities, New Hampshire Children First!, honoring my fund-raising skills. The charity offered innovative programs designed to help children with disabilities, like therapeutic horse rides and computer skills training.

"I think I'm here to stay, Shelley," I said. "You need to come up and visit. See what all the hoopla is about."

"Hoopla!" she repeated, chuckling. "So talk to me about your interest in the Cooper appraisal."

"Don't tell me you did it."

"All right. I won't. But our Boston location did. Jeremy Maran is the managing director there now. You remember Jeremy, don't you?"

"Suave. Saturnine. Sensible."

"You've got him pegged. He still dresses like an Italian count, talks about the impending end of the world, and runs the place like a well-oiled machine. He knows we're friends, so when he saw your posting, he called me. What gives?"

"When did he do the appraisal?"

"Clever, Josie. Instead of answering a question, ask one."

I smiled. I'd learned the information-gathering technique from Wes. It usually worked well.

"Just doing my due diligence. I'm getting ready to do an appraisal on what I'm guessing is the same pair of miniatures. The last appraisal I've seen is from a Chicago-based consultant in the mid-1980s as part of a purchase agreement, so yours is new to me. When did you do it?"

"These are the miniatures you listed as stolen."

"I'm confident they'll be found. When did Jeremy do the appraisal?"

"October 2014."

"Who was your client?"

"You know I can't reveal that information!"

"Sure you can. Just between us girls."

"And the next thing I hear is how you've poached a client. Jeremy will never forgive me."

"First of all, you know I'd never in a million years do such a thing. Second of all, there are complexities that make it a matter of some urgency. I need the name, Shelley."

"Oooh, you're scaring me."

"You scared." I laughed. "That's something I'd like to see."

"Have you ever seen me around a spider?"

"No, what happens?"

"I've been known to leap out of moving cars."

"Poor baby. So who's your client?"

"No can do."

I swiveled to face my window, assessing whether I had any leverage to pry the name loose. The still-fast-moving clouds had thickened and darkened, and the swirling sky looked bulbous, full of moisture and ready to burst.

"Was it Thomas Lewis?" I asked.

"Jeez, Joz, what are you, psychic?"

"He's dead. He was murdered. His wife's apartment in Boston was ransacked. Both the Rocky Point and Boston police think the crimes are connected and that the miniatures are involved somehow. Fill me in and I promise I'll never reveal my source. If you don't, I'll have to tell the local police and they'll have to tell the Boston police and court orders will be issued and the next thing you know —"

"— the next thing you know, Frisco's name will be splashed all over the media as a company that rigorously protects its clients' privacy," Shelley said, interrupting. "If any of those police officers are cute, remember I'm single."

"I can get you publicity. The good kind, how you're helping the police. I'll ensure your name is spelled right."

"What kind of press?"

"Local. The minor mention that gets retweeted and goes viral."

"Here's what I know from Jeremy: Thomas Lewis walked into the Boston office saying he wanted the paintings appraised for insurance purposes. The pair of miniatures was valued at $1.29 million. If sold separately,

Arabella would go for less than the king. Once the appraisal was complete, Mr. Lewis indicated he was interested in selling them. Jeremy e-mailed him the contract, and about a minute and a half later, Jeremy got an angry e-mail from a woman identifying herself as Thomas Lewis's wife, Rebecca Bennington. The paintings, she stated, were her property, not Thomas's, and she had no intention of selling them. She said she'd be there in an hour to pick them up. You can imagine the sticky wicket this put us in."

"I can indeed. What did you do? Besides call your lawyer."

"You better believe that was Jeremy's first call. The lawyer and Jeremy then double-teamed Mr. Lewis. He insisted the paintings were his, but when Ms. Bennington showed up to retrieve them, she had the documentation to prove her claim. Jeremy had confirmed provenance as part of the appraisal, of course, so he had already spoken to Ian Bennington, Rebecca's father. His notes read that Ian said he'd given the paintings to his daughter and that he was glad they were being appraised. Jeremy and the lawyer called him back, in England. His story changed, or maybe Jeremy misunderstood the nuances the first time around. Regardless, there was no misunderstanding this time. The lawyer taped the call. I've heard it with mine own ears. Ian said the paintings were his property, that he'd loaned them to his daughter, that he had no intention of selling them, and that Thomas Lewis had no right to do anything to or with them. Mr. Bennington instructed us to return them to Rebecca. We did so about twenty minutes before Thomas Lewis showed up, fit to kill."

"Will you e-mail me a copy of the appraisal?"

"Come on, Josie. That's over the top."

"The logo will really stand out in the news report."

"I'll send the cover letter, all right? Not the full report."

"Can the reporter reproduce it?"

"Sure. It's a form letter — thanks for letting us appraise your beautiful objects . . . the appraisal is attached . . . if you ever want to discuss selling your antiques, please contact us . . . blah, blah, blah."

"Perfect. Thanks, Shelley. The reporter's name is Wes Smith. He'll want to talk to you."

"Glad to. We don't like being taken advantage of."

"And you were."

"Water under the bridge. So, how much

snow do you have up there?"

Fluffy snowflakes were floating upward, then spiraling down. "Not that much, but it's snowing now. It's beautiful."

She laughed as if she thought I was a hoot and a holler. "Merry Christmas, Josie."

"Merry Christmas, Shelley."

I read the cover letter Shelley e-mailed, and it was exactly as described. I called Wes and filled him in. He was willing to acknowledge that we were now even up, and maybe I had nudged into the credit side of the balance sheet.

I texted Ellis to ask if he was at his office, and when he said he was, and that he was available if I needed him, I wrote that I'd be there in fifteen minutes.

By the time I arrived, the first of Wes's teaser headlines had been tweeted. *Read how Thomas Lewis's criminal impersonation at Frisco's might have led to murder. Frisco's turns over docs to cops. #ThomasLewismurder.* His second tweet came in as I was walking to the front door. He promised a comprehensive front-page exposé for the evening edition of the paper.

"There are two things I need to tell you about," I explained to Ellis once we were settled in his office.

I repeated what I'd learned from Shelley.

"Good deal, Josie. I'll contact Shelley directly. What's number two?"

I didn't answer right away. Instead, I looked across the parking lot, past Ocean Avenue to the dunes, now coated in white.

"Lia's my friend," I said, my eyes on the bucolic scene.

"She's troubled."

"Yes."

"What is it, Josie?"

I met his eyes. "I think she might be involved in my attack."

He nodded and stayed still, letting me find my own path.

"If I'd been hit by a man, I'd be dead."

"Why Lia?"

"Who else?"

"Becca."

"Becca wouldn't have to steal her own paintings."

"True." He raised an index finger to his nose and rubbed.

"Lia's car is in the shop," I said. "When did she bring it in?"

"The day after the attack. It was pretty banged up."

"How come?" I asked.

"She declines to say."

"Really? Is she allowed to do that?"

He smiled, a sour one. "We discourage it, but we're not really in a position to insist." His shoulders lifted a half inch, then sank the same amount. "It could be an innocent coincidence."

I lowered my gaze to my knees. "I hate this, Ellis. I feel awful."

"You're not responsible for my suspicions, Josie."

"I am if I put them in your head."

"Lia was already on my radar."

I raised my eyes. "She was?"

"Sure."

"Then I didn't need to say anything. Forget I did."

He tapped his temple. "Consider it forgotten."

"Thank you. I feel like such a rat. I hate tattletales."

He walked me to the front. "This isn't junior high. Reporting suspicions to the police chief isn't the same as snitching on a pal."

"Scruples. I've got a case of enlarged scruples."

He opened the heavy front door for me. A gust of snow blew at us, and I shivered.

"Your scruples are one of your many superlative qualities. Don't change."

I patted his shoulder, thanked him again, and ran for my car.

Chapter Thirty-Two

As soon as I stepped into the front office, Sasha asked me to come take a look at something. Her monitor showed a full-screen view of our African American folk pottery vessel.

"Look familiar?" she asked.

"You take a mean photo."

"It's not ours."

I looked at her, anticipation tingling my spine.

Her eyes on the computer, she said, "This photo is from a 1999 Christie's catalogue, *The John Gordon Collection of Folk Americana.*"

"You're kidding."

"Nope. I'm convinced this vessel is a twin to ours, or at least, one of only a handful. I've found two additional references to others that seem similar, but without examining those objects, I can't confirm the authenticity. Based on the appearance of the hat, the slip glaze, and the red highlights, which you'll note are on the lips, hat, and eyebrows, and which were almost certainly applied after firing, I'm as certain as I can be, without doing a direct object-to-object comparison, that our vessel was crafted by the same artisan as this one. He worked in what is known as the Alabama School. The vessels were produced between 1880 and 1890."

"What are the other two mentions?"

"Specific references in *American Folk Sculpture* by Robert Charles Bishop and *The African-American Tradition in Decorative Arts* by John Michael Vleck stating that very few preacher's-head vessels were made."

"And those that were are in important private collections like John Gordon's."

"Exactly. And museums." Sasha smiled, a big one. "It's rare, scarce, artistically and culturally important, and it's in perfect condition. And it's Southern."

"Give me a number."

"If we can find out what it was doing in that garage, fifty thousand plus."

I held up crossed fingers. "I'll call and ask."

I hurried upstairs and dialed Sarah Arkin's number. If we were as successful at confirming the vessel's provenance as Sasha had been in authenticating it, it was by far the rarest object we'd yet discovered for our Southern Living auction.

I greeted Ms. Arkin and said, "I have a question about an object we found in the garage."

"I won't take it back, no matter what," she said.

I laughed. "I don't want to give anything back. I want more. Actually, I'm calling for information. Did your aunt have any connection with the South?"

"My uncle Doug, her husband, did. Uncle Doug was from Birmingham. How come?"

"One of the decorative objects we bought might have a folk art history. I'm trying to validate it. How did your uncle end up here?"

"He went to Dartmouth. That's where he and Aunt Gail met. When he graduated, he got a job as an engineer at a company in Portsmouth. They got married and moved to Rocky Point. End of story. After his folks died, his sister cleaned out the house and sent up a couple of boxes of things. I remember hearing how Uncle Doug didn't want anything, but his sister insisted. He put the boxes in the garage, and there they've been ever since."

"Could I call his sister, the one who

cleaned out the house?"

"Marti? I'm afraid she's passed on."

"I'm sorry to hear that. Is there anyone who might be able to confirm that she selected a particular object and shipped it to him?"

"Marti's daughter, Amy, might know," she said. "She got married not long ago. She's Amy Greene now. I know she helped Marti clean out the house. This object you're talking about must be plenty valuable for you to be going to all this trouble. Should I have gotten an appraisal before I sold everything?"

A common question, with no clear answer. "I don't know. Sometimes folks pay the thousands of dollars that a proper appraisal costs, and never recoup the money. Other times, they do. You decided you didn't want the delay or the bother, that you just wanted to sell. If this particular object ends up having any value, I want you to know it will only be purchased by someone who will love it."

"It's like cocktails and coffee in a restaurant," she said. "That's where a restaurant makes its profit. You buy boxes of anything and hope to find a gem. Good for you!"

I thanked her again, wishing all clients were as wise and clear-headed as she was, got Amy Greene's contact information, and ended the call.

Amy Greene lived in Madison, Wisconsin, and our phone call lasted less than five minutes.

"Sure, I remember," Amy said. "My mother thought it was probably an important piece because her grandfather, Morris Patcher, had an eye for folk art. Mom remembered him saying he bought it at an antiques store back in the 1940s. He bought a Grandma Moses painting, too, from the same place, and since my mom decided to keep that for herself, she thought she ought to send the preacher head to her brother even though he said he didn't want it, just to be fair."

"You don't happen to recall the name of the store where he bought it, do you?"

"There's nothing to recall because I never knew it, and I doubt that Mom did, either. Her granddad never stepped foot outside Alabama, though, so it's a sure bet that it's from somewhere in the state. Probably Birmingham, which is where he lived all his life."

"A Grandma Moses," I said. "That's pretty special. Do you still own it?"

"You better believe it. It hangs in my living room. I love it."

I thanked her for her help and went downstairs to report.

"I suppose it's worth checking whether any antiques stores in Birmingham were in business in 1940," Sasha said, her skeptical tone making it clear she thought it was a long shot.

"I agree," I said. "It's probably a dead end, but we need to take the road to find out."

As I walked through the warehouse I wondered if Amy Greene knew she had a multimillion-dollar painting hanging on her living room wall.

Hank joined me as I started up the staircase. He dropped a purple felt mouse at my feet. It had a lime green feathery tail.

"Hi, baby," I said. "Do you want me to throw this for you?"

He mewed.

"Okay." I lobbed it toward the back, and he took off after it like a jaguar on the hunt.

Back upstairs in my office, I became aware that I was tired, the kind of fatigue that comes from fighting a losing emotional battle. I was struggling to keep an amorphous depression at bay, and losing. The trifecta of despair — what my mom used to call the "dreaded triple ad," mad, sad, and bad — had me in its grip. Entrenched feelings of futility outweighed any glimmers of hope that occasionally made their way through the miasma. Don't think, my dad had told me. Do.

I didn't want to be alone tonight. Ty was on one of his regular trips to check in with each of his region's state training directors. This time, he was meeting up with Maine's top trainers in Bangor. He'd be back tomorrow. I called Zoë.

"What are you doing for dinner?" I asked her.

"I'm coming to your house," she said. "What are we having?"

I smiled. "Yay! Spaghetti and meatballs with my mom's famous pomodoro sauce."

"Her meatballs are pretty famous, too."

"And the kids love them," I said.

"I made a Boston cream pie. I'll bring it for dessert."

"I've got a nice Chianti. And plenty of makings for Prescott's Punch. I can't wait!"

"See ya!"

And just like that, my depression lifted.

Zoë's son, Jake, was watching something on TV. Emma was asleep in her sleeping bag. Zoë and I were hanging out at the kitchen table talking about her online course. She'd decided to go back and finish her degree so when the kids were old enough, she could hit the employment ground running.

"Chemistry One is killing me," she said.

"Just wait for Chemistry Two," I said.

"I know."

"You're going to look back on your accomplishments and feel enormous pride, Zoë."

"If I pass."

"You'll pass. Are you kidding me? And nurse practitioner is a perfect choice. You'll be able to get a job anywhere."

"From your mouth to God's ears," she said, smiling, imagining the future.

The doorbell rang. Ellis stood under the porch light. His eyes were half closed, and his chin was almost on his chest, the stance of the weary.

"Come on in," I said. "We saved you some pasta."

"Thanks. I ate already, if you can call it that."

Ellis followed me into the kitchen. Zoë was on her feet and stepped into his embrace. He rested his chin on the top of her head for a moment, his eyes closed.

"I've changed my mind," he said. "It smells too good to resist. I'll have some."

"Good," I said as I turned the sauce up

from warm to medium-low. I turned on the toaster oven to preheat. "What do you want to drink? Chianti? Prescott's Punch? Beer?"

"Yes," he deadpanned.

I laughed and handed him a martini glass. "Start with a Prescott's Punch, the drink of choice for the downtrodden."

"I sure qualify."

"Hard day?" Zoë asked.

He sank onto one of the ladder-back chairs across from her. "They're all hard days. Today was just longer than usual."

I took a bowl of salad from the fridge, added the red wine vinaigrette I'd made earlier, and tossed.

"Bad news about the garlic bread," I told him. "We finished everything I baked."

"Gee, thanks."

"Good news about the garlic bread is that I set aside some for you! It'll take about fifteen minutes to heat up."

"You are a cruel and wicked woman to tease me in my weakened condition."

"Have some salad, oh weak one. Soon strength will flood your veins."

He began pecking at the salad, mostly moving it around the bowl.

I sat down and forked the last of my Boston cream pie.

Zoë was watching him with questioning

eyes, worried. I didn't blame her.

"You're not acting like yourself," she said. "Are you sure you're all right?"

He didn't answer right away. He ate some salad and drank some punch. "The truth?" he asked.

A panicky look flashed across her face. She raised her chin, braced for bad news. "Of course."

Ellis reached out a hand toward hers, and she took it and kissed his palm. "Talk to me," she whispered.

He looked at me, then at her hand, rubbing his.

"I'm out of leads. I'm out of ideas. From where I sit, it looks like someone is going to get away with murder."

Chapter Thirty-Three

I took one last look around the kitchen to be certain I hadn't missed a dirty glass or forgotten to wipe down a section of counter, then turned out the light, satisfied. The doorbell rang. I glanced at the digital time display on the range — 10:20. I smiled, wondering what Zoë and team forgot. When I reached the door and looked through the small window, my smile disappeared. Instead, I gawked. I staggered back, righted myself, and stepped forward for a closer look.

It was Becca.

She was wearing a brown knee-length puffy coat similar to mine, brown jeans, and scuffed hiking boots. Her boots had bits of snow stuck in the cleats. Her coat's hood was up and snapped snugly under her chin. Faux-fur trim encircled her pale face.

I looked beyond her to the driveway. The snow was falling steadily. Three inches, maybe four, lay on the ground.

I brought my eyes back to her face. She was plain, but not homely. She wore no makeup.

She stared directly into the glass, but since I was standing in the dark, I knew she couldn't see me. I didn't know what to do. If she'd shoved a gun under her waistband, I'd have no way of telling. She wasn't carrying a bag, but her coat was large and shapeless.

My Browning 9 mm was upstairs in my bedside table. I was a good shot, but that and a dime did me no good if the gun wasn't at hand. I toyed with running up to get it but dismissed the idea as paranoid. Becca would be a fool to come to my house and shoot me, and if one thing was certain, Becca was no fool. She was a brilliant scientist who'd fallen in love with the wrong man. My long-gone ex-boyfriend, Rick the Cretin, came to mind. We were all fools in our twenties. I opened the door the three inches the chain lock allowed.

"You're Becca," I said.

She tilted her head slightly so she could see me through the crack. "You're Josie."

"Where is your car?" I asked.

"Down the hill. I hiked up."

I looked out over the quiet night, then

back at her. "Why are you here?"

Her eyes dropped. "I didn't know where else to go," she whispered. "I've run out of cash. I'm afraid to use any of my credit cards or my debit card, even my E-ZPass." She raised her eyes and peered at me through the crack. "According to my dad, you're family."

I closed the door enough to remove the chain and opened it wide.

"Come in," I said.

I turned off the porch light and looked across the driveway at Zoë's house. Upstairs lights were on in Jake's room, Zoë's room, and the hall bathroom. I could only hope that Ellis hadn't chosen this moment to check out the snow. He would easily spot Becca's footprints and might even have seen her step onto my porch.

"I can take your coat," I said, closing and locking the door.

"Thanks," she said, pulling off her gloves and stuffing them in her coat pocket. She handed it over.

She wore an oversized lilac and green flannel shirt over a lilac cotton turtleneck, She ran her fingers through her hair, not fluffing it so much as scratching her scalp.

"In here," I said, leading the way into the living room. "I'll close the drapes before I turn on the lights."

I finished smoothing the last of the curtains, ensuring no crack appeared, and switched on the overhead light, a yellow globe with a fan attachment. I turned the fan on low, just to keep the air moving.

She stood by the couch and took her time looking around the living room and into my study, visible through the open French doors, pausing when she came to my father's favorite painting, *A River Crossing with a Ferry,* attributed to Jan Brueghel the Younger. Then she moved on to my mother's Georgian sterling silver candlesticks, the eighteenth-century Waterford cut-crystal bowl I'd purchased for myself to celebrate my first year in business, the rare books that lined the study shelves — reference books, mostly — the three framed antique maps, and the pair of antique blue floral-patterned Chinese vases.

"Your home is beautiful," she said.

"Thank you. Have a seat." I waited until she sat on the couch, then took one of the club chairs that faced it. "Are you hungry?"

"No, thanks." She smiled, a wan effort. "I used the last of my cash on a sandwich."

"Coffee? Tea? A drink?"

"Tea would be good. Thank you."

"There aren't any curtains in the kitchen,

so you should stay here while I prepare it." I pointed to the powder room door. "The bathroom is in there. I won't be long."

I set the kettle on to boil and took a teapot from the cabinet.

"Can you hear me?" I called over my shoulder.

"Yes."

"I have herbal tea or black. What would you like?"

"Black, please. With milk and sugar if you have it."

I heard her go into the bathroom, but by the time I brought the tray into the living room and slid it onto the coffee table, she was back on the couch. I poured her a cup and returned to my chair.

"What about Ethan?" I asked.

"What about him?" she asked, puzzled.

"You said you didn't know where to go . . . Aren't you two friends?"

"Sort of." She shrugged. "Roommate kind of friends. I wouldn't trust him with anything like this."

"Because you don't know him well? Or because he's not trustworthy?"

"Because I wouldn't want him to misunderstand a need for a desire."

"You were concerned he might think you were coming on to him."

"Many men would." She added a thimbleful of milk to her tea. "I owe you an apology. For hanging up on you. I didn't know then that Thomas was impersonating my father."

"I figured that was what was going on."

She stared into her teacup.

"It's horrible, isn't it," I added, "when relationships go bad?"

She raised her eyes to mine. "It didn't go bad. It was bad from the start. I was just too stupid to realize it."

"Not stupid," I said, hoping she would recognize the sincerity in my voice. "Human."

"I fell for the fairy tale," she said, and I thought of Lia. "Thomas was so much older than me. When he asked me out, I was flattered. Beyond flattered. Blinded. All the girls at the company where I worked were sweet on him. I couldn't believc hc picked little nerdy me."

On the face of it, Lia and Becca had nothing in common. They differed in age, experience, personality, style, and culture. Yet, on some level, they were sisters under the skin, each falling for a handsome gold digger with a good line. Lia's desperation to find a man made her vulnerable to a smooth talker. Becca hadn't been desperate. She'd been ignorant, and thus an easy mark.

"I bet you weren't real experienced with men," I said.

She made a noise, a soft chortle. "That's an understatement."

"Thomas took terrible advantage of your innocence."

"And look what's happened now — a murder, two break-ins, and an assault. I've been reading Wes Smith's postings. You were attacked."

"And they stole your miniature paintings. I'm sick about it."

"Me, too."

"They're insured, right?"

"Yes. My dad used Frisco's appraisal to increase the coverage."

"Thank goodness for small favors."

"Do you think they'll be found?" she asked.

"Yes."

"Why?"

"Because they haven't been sold."

"Lots of stolen art isn't sold on the open market."

"True," I said. "I don't think the thief is a professional, though, who would know how to go about selling stolen art on the black market. I think it's an amateur who's lying low, biding time. Professionals are better at it. Whoever is responsible for this is stumbling all over himself. Regardless, we've generated so much publicity, even illicit dealers would be leery about buying the paintings now." I watched her for a moment. "May I ask . . . will you tell me about Thomas?"

She stirred her tea far longer than necessary. "What is it you want to know?"

"What's going on? Was he holding up the divorce trying to get a better settlement?"

"Yes, but it wasn't only Thomas. Cheryl Morrishein was just as bad. Together, they were simply unrelenting in trying to get me to sell the miniatures. My telling them that they weren't mine to sell, and that I would never sell them in any event, had about as much effect as a . . . a puff of air in stopping a tornado."

"When did your dad give them to you?"

"When we moved to New Hampshire. I hung them in our living room when Thomas and I lived together, but since we broke up, well, I've kept them hidden. I was going to bring them back to my dad, actually, on my next visit."

"I saw your separation agreement, so I know that Thomas tried to get them included as marital property, and failed."

She nodded. "Thomas's latest effort is utterly galling, and it's not over yet." She sighed and leaned back against the cushions. "The court will probably allow it. His petition was correct. I do inherit the paintings, and we were still married. Thomas left everything to three cousins in England. I'm certain their solicitor will find the petition and try to get half the paintings' value included in his estate. Damn him! He made my life hell while he was alive, and he's making it hell now that he's dead."

"I understand Thomas's interest in the paintings, but where does Cheryl fit in?"

Her jaw tightened and her brow creased. "She's the most conniving woman I've ever met. I truly didn't know people like her existed. She manipulates the truth to suit her needs, acting as if her jury-rigged version is true. She blamed Thomas for the partnership tanking — which might be a fair assessment. I don't know enough about the business to say. Certainly Thomas made most of the decisions. Their first investment went south within weeks."

"What was it?"

"A luxury spa. The project involved getting government permission to build a new island off of Rocky Point. Can you imagine? They invested in the project before the government rendered an opinion, how crazy is that? Once the government said no, the banks pulled out, leaving Thomas and Rupert as the group's only investors. Thomas said their only hope of getting their money out was to put more in. To me it sounded like throwing good money after bad, but he wouldn't hear that."

"I don't understand. If the group couldn't build the island, wasn't the whole project dead?"

"No, they wanted to try again in Massachusetts. I thought it was insane, but Thomas thought it was a winner of an idea. When Rupert died, Cheryl demanded Rupert's investment back, accusing Thomas of fraud. I had and have no legal standing in Thomas's business dealings, but that hasn't stopped her. She'll probably egg on Thomas's cousins to try to get my inheritance included in the estate, then sue them to get her share before it's divvied up."

"If you have no ownership of Thomas's business, why would she think you'd pay her off?"

"She tried two tacks, one, a general 'do the right thing and make me whole' approach, the other that since Rupert died because of the business failure, which occurred because of Thomas's many misrepresentations — the basis of her claim that he committed fraud — Rupert's blood was on our hands."

"That's some stretch," I said, tucking a leg up under me.

"Cheryl's morality is as elastic as her pocketbook is empty. It's been a nightmare, an absolute nightmare."

"How do you cope?"

"I work."

I smiled at her. "That's how I cope in tough times, too."

She smiled back at me. "I guess we really are related."

"Why did you run?"

"I panicked. I'm still panicked. When I heard the news that Thomas had been murdered, I freaked out — I'd been on Cable Road what must have been mere minutes before he was struck and killed."

I waited for her to continue, and when she didn't I asked, "Were you afraid you'd be suspected of the murder?"

"Of course. I benefit most by his death." She pressed her fingertips against her cheeks for a moment. "But it's not only that. It's Cheryl, too. I'm powerless."

"I've got to ask, Becca. Please forgive me. Did you kill him?"

She didn't look at me or look away. She stared through me, unseeingly, into the past, or perhaps into the future. After several seconds, she scanned my face, maybe trying to suss out my intentions.

"No," she said, "but I'm glad he's dead."

"I don't blame you."

Her hands curled into fists and rested on her thighs. "I've been struggling with the rage. I can't control it."

"When you talk to the police," I said, "I wouldn't mention that part."

"I don't want to talk to the police."

"I don't know that you'll have much choice in the matter."

"Do you think I'll be arrested?"

"For what?"

"For killing Thomas. You asked me if I did it."

"And you told me you didn't."

She rubbed her forehead as if she were trying to ease a throbbing headache. "I've been driving aimlessly for days, neglecting my clams, trying to figure out what to do." She lowered her hands. "I didn't even try to make arrangements about my work."

"Ethan's been helping."

Her features froze for the three or four seconds it took for her to respond, but when she spoke, her voice sounded the same as it had before. "He is?"

"So Dr. Bennett says. I understand the

foundation has named him the acting principal investigator."

"That didn't take him long."

"Everyone was worried about your clams, about protecting your research."

"Of course." She paused for a moment, meeting my eyes. "I'm not surprised the police want to talk to me. I've been staying in cheap motels, dreadful places that made me feel as if I'm in a noir film about a woman on the run. I've been buying food from drive-through places, wearing sunglasses or hats so people won't recognize me, and skulking back to my miserable room to eat on the sly. I've been slinking into public libraries to read the news, too afraid that the police could trace me through my phone to even turn it on. To an outsider, I can only imagine how it looks — like I'm guilty."

"Have you ever been questioned by the police?"

"On the phone, briefly, after my father died. A detective called to ask if he had been suicidal."

"What did you say?"

Her chin went up an eighth of an inch. "I told him no, never, no way."

"When else?"

"That's the only time."

"It's going to be different this time around. The police here are going to ask you a thousand questions. I've been in that position, so you can believe me when I tell you that you're going to feel abused, betrayed, embarrassed, and outraged. It's horrific. What I'm saying is that you need a lawyer, a good one."

"I know."

"He'll tell you the same as me, but I'll start in case the police get to you before he has a chance. Don't say a word unless your lawyer says you should reply. Not one word. When you do talk, keep your answers responsive and short. Tell the truth, but don't volunteer any information. Don't let righteous indignation take hold. If your lawyer tells you to button it, button it."

"Thank you. This is very helpful."

"Do you have a lawyer in mind? I think you should call him now."

"At this hour?"

"Yes."

"I don't know any lawyers here. Just my father's solicitors in England. I suppose I could call and ask them to find someone appropriate."

"I can make a recommendation, Max Bixby. He's a rock. He's my lawyer. If you want, I can call him."

Her eyes brightened. "Thank you. Please do."

"Do you want to get on my computer and check him out? I don't want you to feel railroaded."

"I don't." She tried to smile. "You wouldn't mislead me. You're family."

I patted her shoulder as I passed by en route to the study. I got Max's home number from my contact list, snatched up the portable phone, and dialed. His wife answered on the second ring, sounding worried, a visceral reaction to a late-evening call.

"Hi, Babs, this is Josie. Josie Prescott. I'm sorry to call so late, but I need to talk to Max."

"Of course. Here he is. Merry Christmas, Josie."

"Merry Christmas to you, too, Babs."

"Josie?" Max said. "Is something wrong?"

"Kind of. Have you been following the Thomas Lewis murder case?"

"I read the paper, sure."

"Then you know the name Rebecca Bennington. She goes by Becca."

"Certainly. She's missing."

"Not anymore. She's in my living room. She thinks there's a chance she's going to be accused of murdering Thomas. They were legally separated at the time of his death, and there was a fair amount of acrimony between them. She asked me to call you on her behalf."

"Do you think she killed him?"

"She's here with me now."

"Give me a yes or no."

"No, tentatively."

"Can you say why no and why tentatively?"

I fixed my gaze on my kitchen counter, not wanting to see Becca's reaction to my reply. "Becca is whip-smart and would know that to run would make her look guilty. If she was guilty, she would have had the smarts to stay and tough it out."

"That's pretty convoluted."

"I know, but you asked."

"Why tentative?"

"Because that's pretty convoluted. Regardless, she needs a good lawyer, Max."

"Do the police know where she is?"

"No."

"Tell her not to talk to anyone about anything remotely related to the case. Including you. As your lawyer, I can tell you that the more you talk to her, the longer your own interview with the police will be."

"I didn't think of that."

"That's why you have a good lawyer."

I smiled. "Can you represent us both?"

"At this point, I don't see why not. Are you in any jeopardy?"

"No. I've been helping the police."

"Good. I'll be there in thirty minutes."

"Thank you, Max." I pushed the END CALL button. "He'll be here in half an hour. He said you're not to talk to anyone about the situation, including me."

"Thank you, Josie." Becca stood up. "I can't tell you how relieved I am, as if I've come out of the darkness into the light."

"Don't be too optimistic," I said. "You're going to be spending a lot of time with the police, and I've got to tell you, that can be pretty darn dark."

"After what I've been through," she said, picking up the tray, "being able to tell the truth will be a relief. I haven't done anything wrong." She smiled, a small one. "And now that I have a lawyer, I can walk into your kitchen without fear that someone will see me and report it to the police."

"You're right, but the need to make your presence known is a bit more urgent than you realize," I said, following her into the kitchen. I pointed through the big window toward Zoë's house. "Do you see that house? That's where my friend Zoë lives.

She dates Police Chief Hunter. He's there now."

She placed the tray on the counter and turned toward me, her lips forming a big O.

"Don't worry," I said. "Max will take care of everything."

I placed the dirty dishes in the dishwasher and put the milk away, then. "There is something else I need to ask you, though."

Her eyes narrowed as a guarded expression took hold.

"Come back into the living room."

She followed me without comment.

"Where's your gun?" I asked.

She took a step back as if I'd threatened her. "What?"

"I found the hidden compartment in your bed. The *privacy* compartment. From its shape, I could tell it was built to hold a gun, but there was no gun in it. The company told me all their work was custom, which means you ordered a compartment to fit a gun. Where is it?"

She didn't reply. She didn't move. The only change occurred in her eyes. She was looking at me as if I were a hunter and she were prey.

"Don't be foolish," I said. "You're about to be invited to the police station, Becca. If they find you carrying a weapon you neglected to mention, a bad situation will get much, much worse. Let me keep it for you."

"You'll report this to the police?"

"Only if you don't turn it over."

"And — assuming I have a gun — if I do?"

"I wouldn't tell anyone. Thomas wasn't shot, so it's not relevant."

Becca walked into the hall, moved her coat around to get it oriented the way she wanted, and dug into a partially zipped outside pocket. She handed me a shiny silver gun, butt first.

The gun had curved edges and decorative grooves of varying lengths and depths stamped into the metal. I'd never seen anything like it.

"An art deco weapon?" I asked.

"Earlier. It's a Dreyse 1907. German made in the early twentieth century. My grandfather brought it back after World War I."

"How on earth did you get it into this country?"

"I took it apart and shipped the pieces in separate boxes."

I gaped. "And all the boxes arrived intact?"

"Yes."

"That is so not reassuring."

"I know."

"Why? What made you decide to ship a gun to Boston?"

She walked to the front window and fingered the drapes apart. She stood that way, with her back to me, for close to a minute. "The weather report said we'd be getting a foot of snow," she said. "When it snows heavily like this, Ethan says it's snowing like a bastard. I tried to discover the origin of the phrase, but I couldn't. It sure is snowing like a bastard tonight." She turned to face me, apprehension darkening her eyes, as if she sensed that trouble was close by. "I was nearly raped once. I was in college. In Iceland. That's why I carry a gun."

"Oh, Becca."

"I was diving the Silfra Cathedral. It was afterward, back at the hotel. We were all exhilarated. It's one of the best dive spots in the world. He was young. He thought I was interested in him, and when he found out I wasn't —" She closed her eyes for a moment, and when she opened them, she no longer looked afraid. She looked angry. "I had to run for it."

"I'm so sorry."

"Don't be. I made it out without a scratch. He didn't. I kicked him where it hurts, just like my dad taught me."

"Sounds like you don't need a gun."

"He was drunk. The next one might be sober." She plunked down in one of the club chairs. "I showed the gun to Ethan."

"Because he had the wrong idea?"

"The best defense is the threat of a strong offense."

I stared at the jazzy-looking weapon. "I'll put this away until everything is cleared up."

As I headed upstairs, it occurred to me that if a woman who was known to carry a gun wanted to kill someone, she'd use another weapon altogether, like a fast-moving car.

Chapter Thirty-Four

I didn't get to bed until after one Tuesday morning.

While Max and Becca met privately over freshly brewed coffee, I took a shower, sent Ty a long e-mail explaining what was going on, and got the guest room ready. Just before Max left, around twelve thirty, he texted Ellis that Becca was his client and that she would appear for questioning at ten thirty that morning. Becca told me that she needed to set an alarm, that she was to be at Max's office at nine.

I got up with Becca at seven thirty and made us breakfast, cinnamon cheesy scrambled eggs and ham, and an English muffin with some of the wild raspberry jam Zoë put up last summer. Becca was quiet, introspective.

"Are you all right?" I asked.

"Not really," she said.

The snow had stopped overnight. The day was crisp and sunny, a halcyon winter morning. Only about six inches of snow had accumulated, enough to add luster to the world but not enough to cause any inconvenience. The driveway was clear, and Ellis's SUV was gone. He'd shoveled me out before leaving; what a guy.

I drove Becca to her car, helped her dig it out, and headed to work.

Ellis called as I was parking in my freshly plowed lot.

"You may be aware that I have an appointment to talk to Becca at ten thirty. When did she show up at your house?"

"I don't think I should answer any questions about that, but I have another idea I'd like to run by you. Can I come in?"

"If you come now, we can talk before Becca gets here."

"I'm on my way."

I called my office and left Cara a voice mail. "I have an errand," I said. "I don't know how long I'll be, but I expect I'll be able to check e-mail, so feel free to be in touch."

Then I hot-tailed it for the police station.

"Your Christmas cactus is spectacular," I said to Cathy while I waited for Ellis. "It's the biggest one I've ever seen."

The plant took up a quarter of the counter, its flattened stems and cerise blossoms spreading wide and hanging low.

"It's twenty-three years old," she told me, beaming at it as if it were a child she was especially proud of. "My grandmother gave it to me when I took this job. I started the first week of December that year."

"What? When you were ten?"

"As if. I was eighteen, right out of high school."

"All I can say is that working here obviously agrees with you."

She thanked me again, and I wandered over to the bulletin board. A black-and-white grainy photo from a low-end security camera showed a person of interest in a series of Boston-area bank robberies. All I could tell was that the suspect was a man. The coach of the Rocky Point Little League team was looking for sponsors. I took a photo of the notice, e-mailed it to Gretchen, and asked her to sign us up. A book club was inviting the community to join. I was already a member of the group, which was organized by a librarian named Phoebe Caron. Phoebe listed two e-mail addresses, one a Hotmail account, the other from AOL. I wondered why she used two accounts for the same purpose. I used my Prescott e-mail address for business and had a Gmail address for personal communications. Maybe she was phasing one out, but some of her contacts still used the old address. That didn't make sense. Maybe she had problems accessing each of them periodically, and she was a belt-and-suspender sort of gal. *Ian,* I thought. I dug into my tote bag for my phone and opened up my work e-mail, where Ian had first contacted me. I went back a month or so and found that he'd written from a Yahoo account. I scrolled up until I came to the day he died, then continued scrolling until I came to another of his e-mails. He'd written me the day after he died, this time from a Gmail address.

"Josie," Ellis said, joining me at the bulletin board.

"Hey," I said.

He looked far more rested than I would have expected, almost enthused

"Come on in," he said.

I sat at the guest table. "You look busy."

"I am. Police Work 101. If you're out of leads, start over."

"Have different people interview the suspects," I said, following his logic.

"Not just suspects, everyone." He looked

at his wrist. "The service manager at the shop where Lia took her car will be here in about fifteen minutes."

"How come?"

"Turns out the body damage was to the front end. First time she used this shop, too."

"What did she say about that?"

"She thought she'd give them a try."

"That could be."

"It's farther away than her regular place, and she never complained about the other shop's service."

"Oh, God, Ellis."

He grinned. "I'm looking forward to asking her more about it. We'll get more details about the damage first, which is why we asked Ace to come in. Ace is the service manager. Very observant fellow." He shifted position. "Ethan is coming in, too. As I told you, his alibi holds up. He was at Frank's, but what he neglected to mention was that he was gone for a little more than an hour in the late afternoon. He says he forgot some papers, so he ran back to the institute to get them. He left Frank's about three thirty and was back before five. The waitress and the security tape confirm the time. Another issue — he rides a bike in Boston and rents cars when he's working up here.

He rented a silver Chevy during the period that includes your attack."

"Silver."

"Silver," he repeated, sounding satisfied.

"Was the car damaged?"

"There's no record of it."

"So he's excluded."

"Not necessarily. The techs tell me the amount of damage we could expect to see would vary by car model, the height of the bumper, the exact speed the car was traveling, and so on." He shifted in his chair, settling in. "The two folks who saw a woman running to her car the day Thomas died are coming in, too. We'll see if they can identify Becca."

"I don't think she'll deny being there."

"Especially if she knows she's been ID'd. What did you want to tell me?"

"Three things." I held up my cell phone. "Someone created a new e-mail account for Ian the day after he died." I explained what I'd discovered and, at his request, forwarded him an e-mail from each account.

"That's good, Josie. I'll let Shorling know so he can get his team on it. What else?"

"Why was Becca with Thomas on Cable Road? I didn't ask her. I mean, think about it. Thomas is hounding her. She doesn't want anything to do with him. She's not going to negotiate with him. Why on earth did she agree to meet him?"

Ellis jotted a note. "Good. Next?"

"I think it's all right for me to tell you this. Becca is certain that her father didn't commit suicide, that he wouldn't, no matter what. She wasn't defensive about it. She was simply positive. It got me thinking. If Ian Bennington didn't commit suicide, he was killed. That means someone had to render him unconscious somehow, climb a ladder or high stool, tie a rope around the rafters and hoist his body up — a hundred eighty or so pounds of deadweight — and wrangle him into the noose, tighten the knot, and drop him, all without falling himself."

"Not so easy to do."

"How was he rendered unconscious?"

Ellis made another note. "I'll ask."

"There's more. Picture Ian's house. The article I read said the cleaning lady found his body hanging from the rafters. There you are on the ladder, a man slung over your shoulder. You ease the noose over his neck and tighten it. You're only able to use one hand, right? You've got to brace yourself somehow. What do you hold on to or lean against?"

Ellis focused his eyes on my face, but he wasn't seeing me; he was visualizing hanging a man.

"The top of the ladder," he said. "The rafters."

"Have they checked for fingerprints?"

Ellis nodded. "I'll ask. Although that's not how I'd hang a man. I'd put the noose around his neck while he was on the floor, unconscious, then hoist him up. I'd have better leverage."

"You've got the rope around his neck, then what?"

"Then I'd climb the ladder, twist the rope around the rafters five or six times, and let him go."

"You're twisting the rope around the rafters with one hand, holding the man, a deadweight, with the other?"

"Right." He smiled. "I'm very strong."

"I'll say. I bet you still touch the rafters."

"I'm probably wearing gloves, not just to avoid leaving fingerprints, but also to avoid ripping up my hands. Doing a rope pull is hell on skin."

"Maybe. Maybe not."

He consulted his watch again. "Let me make the call now."

He turned pages in his notebook, found Superintendent Shorling's number in Christmas Common, and dialed. He reached him and posed his questions, but from the one side of the conversation I could hear, it was apparent that he was going to have to wait for answers.

"He'll call me back on both points, the new e-mail account and the fingerprints," Ellis said as soon as he ended the call. "You think Thomas killed Ian."

"Yes. If Ian died before Thomas's divorce was final, Ian's entire estate, inherited by Becca, becomes part of their marital assets."

"Why was Thomas trying to get his hands on the miniatures?"

"Probate takes time. Selling art for cash is quick."

"Maybe . . . Still, you've just given Becca one helluva motive for murder."

"Not really. I've just given Thomas's heirs a helluva motive, not Becca."

"There are other motives besides money."

"Like what?"

"Fury."

I didn't repeat what Becca told me about feeling so enraged she was, essentially, out of control. She was in enough trouble without me adding fuel to the fire.

Chapter Thirty-Five

I asked Ellis if I could wait for Superintendent Shorling's call back. I was white-hot curious about what he might discover. He said sure, but he needed his office, so I'd have to wait in the lobby. I told him that was fine and got busy catching up on e-mails. I sat on a hard bench across from the big bulletin board.

Sasha reported that there were no stores in Birmingham that fit Amy's description of where her great-grandfather Morris Patcher might have purchased the preacher's-head vessel. Based on the information available, she felt confident validating the object's authenticity. She attached a draft of catalogue copy, and it was, as always, clear, concise, and descriptive, without being flowery. She assigned an estimated value of $65,000, higher than expected because, she explained in her cover note, rare ethnic folk art was at an all-time high in popularity and the anecdotal history was credible. I congratulated her on a job well done and asked her to start building a list of museums and known collectors who might be interested in bidding on the vessel.

A man about my age looking like he'd stepped out of the 1950s walked in. He had black hair cut in a classic duck's ass. He wore a scarred brown leather bomber jacket, jeans, and black pointy-toed shoes. He gave me an Elvis smile, ran a hand over his hair, and swaggered his way to the counter.

"I'm Ace Arons, from Durham Motors."

"Certainly, sir," Cathy said, standing. She smiled appreciatively at him.

A police officer named Daryl led him to the corridor on the left. Interview Rooms One and Two were down that way.

As soon as he disappeared, Cathy caught my eye. "Isn't he cute?"

"Do you know him?"

"He's in a band called the RP Acers. They played at my sister's wedding last year. They're really good. Golden oldies and bebop."

"Amazing," I said.

Cathy smiled, remembering the band, remembering the good times. After a few seconds, she sat down again. Soon I heard the tap-tap of her typing.

Sasha had turned over the Gastron Amberlina glass appraisal to Fred, and he'd e-mailed me his report before sending it to the client. The spooner was the most valuable piece, topping Sasha's off-the-cuff estimate of $6,000. Based on recent sales records, he set the auction estimate at $6,500; he placed a $12,250 value on the entire collection. I suspected that Celeste was going to be a very happy woman. I sent him a "great job!" message.

Gretchen wrote that we were all confirmed for Thursday's luncheon, asking if there was anything else she could do. I replied that I thought we were all set. I'd write everyone's bonus check myself, an annual tradition that was among my most favorite activities.

The door opened again, bringing a blast of icy wind in its wake. Officer F. Meade held the door for a young woman and an older man. The woman's eyes were big with fear. Her teeth were clamped on her lower lip. The man tramped in, his hands curled into loose fists.

"Have a seat," Officer Meade said. "We'll be with you shortly."

Lia stepped in. There were purplish gray smudges below her eyes that made me think she wasn't sleeping well. Her shoulders were bowed.

"Lia!" I said.

"Josie!" Lia said. "My God, I can't believe they caught you in their net!"

"Ms. Jones?" Cathy called from the counter.

"Yes?" Lia replied.

"Thanks for coming in. You can have a seat. It won't be long."

"I certainly hope not. I have a business to run."

"We appreciate your cooperation."

Lia sat next to me, her coat draped over her shoulders. "They can call it cooperation if they want. A rose by any other name is still fascism."

"That's quite a statement."

"Well, I mean, really. I've told them everything I know, several times. Their persistence has passed the level of absurdity and moved into the realm of the ridiculous."

"I can hear Ellis now . . . it's a process. What do you think they want to ask you?"

"God only knows. Last time they focused on my car. Yes, I told them. You caught me getting a tune-up! Guilty as charged!"

"I heard your car had some front-end damage. You weren't in an accident, were you?"

"If you must know, I tried to run over Tiffany, the little slut. Not really, but it was fun watching her leap out of the way. I hope she got all scraped up when she fell, the bitch." She smiled a devil's grin. "I hit my ex's trash cans. Squished them like the bug he is. It was no big deal. No major damage."

"That's pretty scary stuff, Lia."

"I hope she was scared."

"I meant you — how angry you are."

Lia leaned back against the hard wooden bench and stared straight ahead at the empty wall in front of her.

Officer Meade came and took the frightened young woman away. Daryl came and asked the old man to follow him. I peeked at Lia out of the corner of my eye. Her expression was unchanged.

"Josie?" Ellis said from his office door. He waggled his fingers, inviting me in.

I glanced at Lia as I stood up, but she didn't notice that I was leaving.

Ellis shut the door.

"I just got off the phone with Superintendent Shorling. I'll skip the technical details and terms. Ian's Gmail account, the one used to contact you after his death, was set up on a computer in a London hotel's business center. They have top-quality security cameras. Shorling sent me an image." Ellis walked to his desk, reached over, and pivoted his monitor ninety degrees. Thomas Lewis was seated at a computer workstation. His face was easy to identify.

"As clear as day," I said, realizing that as certain as I'd been that Thomas had really, truly pretended to be Ian, seeing him at work creating the fake persona was like hearing a cell door close behind you. *Abandon all hope, ye who enter here.* There was no escape from reality, no spin you could put on it. He'd come up with a plan to trick me, and he'd executed it well. "I can't believe Superintendent Shorling got the information and the photo so quickly."

"Their laws allow for easier searches than ours do. As to the murder itself, Shorling speculates that Ian was slipped a Mickey — Scotch and chloral hydrate. Chloral hydrate isn't a controlled substance in the U.K., but you still need a prescription. Shorling is checking whether Thomas Lewis filled one when he was there. The rope they removed from the body was one of half a dozen coils they found in Ian's garage. According to Ian's neighbors, he did a fair amount of boating, which accounts for the rope. They can't get any meaningful information from it because it's been so many places and touched by so many hands. Thomas Lewis's fingerprints are all over the house, which might be explained away. He was, after all, his son-in-law."

"Ian had a housekeeper."

"The defense would argue she wasn't very good at her job. It doesn't matter, because his fingerprints were also found in two places no one would expect them to be — on a ladder they found in the garage and on the rafters."

"Thomas could say he was helping Ian with something, painting or patching, which would account for his prints on the ladder."

"And the rafters?"

I paused, letting the truth sink in. "I was right."

"You were right."

"I don't feel good about it. I just feel sad."

"I can understand that, but don't go getting maudlin on me. You just helped them close a case." He squeezed my shoulder. "Now help me close one."

Chapter Thirty-Six

Ellis and I crossed the now-empty lobby and walked down the hallway on the left. He opened the door between Interview Rooms Three and Four, and we entered an observation room, a long narrow space with one-way glass on both sides and a small window at the end overlooking the back parking lot. Counters ran under the observation windows. Audio-video listening, viewing, and recording equipment was built in. Ellis faced the window that overlooked Room Four.

The door to the room opened. Detective Brownley, Becca, and Max walked in. Detective Brownley said something and left, pulling the door shut behind her.

Max was tall and thin and always wore a bow tie. He held Becca's chair, smiling reassuringly at her. She sat with her back to the prisoner-ready cage. That was the same chair I had selected the first time I'd been interviewed by the police.

Max extracted a yellow legal pad from his briefcase and squared it up to the table edge.

Becca said something, but the audio feed wasn't on, so we couldn't hear it. Max nodded.

Ellis spun a dial, and a faint whirr sounded. He raised his smart phone. "If I get the phrasing wrong when I ask about the paintings or if I miss anything, text me."

"Okay," I said, and sat down.

Two minutes later, it began. I listened in as Ellis reviewed the logistics, turned on the two video recorders mounted near the ceiling in opposite corners of the room, got Becca to sign a form indicating she understood her rights, and asked if she had any questions. She didn't.

"Thanks for coming in," Ellis said. "I'd like to start with this: Why were you on Cable Road the day Thomas Lewis was killed?"

"I was hoping to finish it. Thomas called me and said Cheryl and he had agreed to a settlement that would cost me nothing, but that because we were still married, I had to sign off on it."

"On Cable Road?" Ellis asked, allowing his skepticism to show.

"Are you asking if that's where they arranged to meet?" Max asked.

"Yes."

Max nodded at Becca.

"Yes."

"Why not a lawyer's office?"

"If I'd thought of it at all," Becca said, her voice strong and confident, "I would have assumed they worked the deal out on their own. Lawyers cost money."

"What happened once you got there?"

"Thomas lied, as usual. The settlement they worked out was that I would sell the miniatures and give Thomas half the proceeds. He would pay Cheryl out of his half." She shook her head, her disgust evident. "Since Thomas felt entitled to the money, he positioned it as good news. I told him to forget it. Thomas told me that I had no choice, that since we were still married, the inheritance from my dad was fifty percent his. I told him I would fight him to the highest court. Then Thomas called Cheryl and said I was refusing to hold up my end of the bargain. I wanted her to hear me, so I yelled that I hadn't made a bargain, that there was nothing to uphold. I was worn to a nub at being the heavy in all this. When Thomas rang off from Cheryl, he told me she wouldn't give up — ever — that she was determined to get whole, and if she didn't she was determined to get even. If I wanted them out of my life, I should consider this a fair offer, get it done, and move on. I told him never to contact me again and ran away."

Ellis tap-tapped his pen against the wooden table for a moment, then placed it crosswise on top of his notebook. "Have you been in touch with the Christmas Common police?"

"Not since shortly after my dad died. Why?"

"I have news that's going to be hard to hear."

Becca glanced at Max.

"Go ahead," Max said.

"The medical examiner, the coroner, has ruled your father's death a homicide."

Her hand flew to her mouth. Max gripped her shoulder and gave a little squeeze.

"I'm sorry," Ellis said.

"It was Thomas, wasn't it?" she asked, tears beginning to well in her eyes and spill onto her cheeks.

"Yes."

"Why? My God. My father was nothing but good to Thomas."

"We think he did it so he could share in your father's fortune."

She angrily wiped the wetness from her face. "How could he?"

Ellis slid a box of Kleenex from one end of the table toward Becca. "Greed is a strong motivator," he said.

"Rapaciousness, not greed," Becca said, tears streaming down her cheeks. "He plundered my world like a pirate. Damn him. Damn him."

"I know you were concerned that Thomas's heirs would come after you for money," Max said. "Now you can rest easy. A person can't benefit from a crime."

"That won't stop them from trying."

"But it will stop them from succeeding," Max said.

"I loathe him," she said, her voice a thin whisper. "I will hate him until the day I die. If he were alive, I'd kill him."

"Hyperbole," Max told Ellis. "She's not confessing."

"Of course I'm not confessing! I didn't kill him." She pounded the table. "I never would have done so, no matter how angry I got."

I texted: *Does she know Marney Alred?*

Ellis's phone vibrated. He read my message. "Have you ever heard of a woman named Marney Alred?"

"What?" Becca said, struggling to shift

gears. "Who?"

"Marney Alred."

"No. I don't think so. What was the name again?"

"I'd like to let my client have some time to assimilate this shocking revelation," Max said. "Surely this can wait."

"Just a few more questions, assuming that Becca will be available at a later date to give a full statement."

"Certainly," Max said.

Becca pulled a tissue from the box and wiped her eyes.

"Marney Alred."

Becca clutched the tissue. "No. I've never heard the name."

"Tell me about your relationship with Cheryl Morrishein."

"I have none."

"Was she there on Cable Road?"

"No."

"When's the last time you saw her?"

She leaned in and whispered into Max's ear. He whispered back and nodded.

"I haven't seen her in years," Becca said, "but I spoke to her an hour after I left Cable Road. She called me. She told me she was tired of being lied to, and that I shouldn't doubt for a minute she'd get the money she was owed. It scared me."

"What did you say?" Ellis asked.

"Nothing. I hung up on her."

"All right then," Ellis said, standing up. "That's it for now. Thank you again for your cooperation." He turned to Max. "If we could get a formal statement in the next few days."

"I'll call you," Max said.

Ellis walked them out. A minute later, Officer Meade opened the door to the observation room.

"Chief Hunter had to take a phone call," she said to me. "He's asked that you wait for him in the lobby."

I followed her out and took my same place on the hard wooden bench. Becca and Max stood huddled together by the bulletin board, talking.

Ethan walked in, and a blustery gust of wintery air blew in behind him. He saw me and smiled, then spotted Becca and smiled even more broadly.

"Becca!" he called. "You're here! You're safe!"

Becca looked up as soon as she heard her name, and her features froze for an instant. "Ethan."

He walked quickly toward her, his arms open.

"This is my lawyer, Max Bixby," she told

him. "Ethan Ferguson, my roommate and my colleague."

He dropped his arms, smoothly changing motions from a hug to a shake.

Max greeted him with his usual pleasant manner.

"I understand you've been looking after my clams," Becca said.

"They're fine. Your data is looking good."

"Thank you. We need to talk about the grant."

"Nothing to talk about. I'll call the foundation as soon as they spring me loose and tell them the good news, that you're back."

"What about your work?"

He grinned with unabashed delight. "They asked me to submit my own proposal. I just got word — it's been green-lighted."

For the first time since she saw him walk in, Becca smiled warmly. "Oh, Ethan. That's fantastic news! Congratulations."

"If they didn't love you so much, it never would have happened."

She patted his arm. "We'll talk later. Right now, I need to finish up a conversation with Max."

"Sure, sure. Just tell me, can I do something to help?"

"No. Thank you, though."

Ethan gave her a final dashing grin and

joined me on the bench.

"How you doing?" he asked.

"I'm okay. A lot going on. You seem to be in good spirits."

"Always." He looked around, pausing when he got to Cathy. "Guess I better check in with the dragon at the gate."

Ethan got up and approached the counter. Cathy stood up to talk to him. They chatted for a few seconds.

He strolled back and sat down next to me. "Do they have new information? Is that why we're all here?"

"Everyone and his brother is being interviewed again," I said.

"I can't imagine what they want with me."

"Probably to talk to you about your alibi."

"The one they busted open?" he asked, his eyes dancing. He lowered his voice and added a Teutonic cadence. "Why did it take you ninety minutes to make a twenty-minute trip?" He resumed his natural voice. "You want the truth?" He leaned in toward my ear and whispered, "I got talking to Nate."

"The lobster fellow who reads about horseshoe crabs for pleasure."

"Ah! I see you've met him."

"That's it?"

"Why?" Ethan asked, amused. "What did

you expect?"

"Nothing in particular. I guess I thought it would be more complicated than that."

"I'm a simple man."

"Simple, huh? I think you're a pretty cool customer, if the truth be told."

"That's me. Mr. Cool."

A police officer whose name I didn't know appeared from behind the counter and said, "Mr. Ferguson? This way, please."

Ethan got up and, with happy-go-lucky waves for me and Becca, disappeared down the corridor that led to Rooms One and Two.

Max and Becca approached me, and I stood up.

"I'm off now," Max told me. "Call if you need anything."

"I will," I said. "Thank you, Max."

Max turned toward Becca. "You, too."

"Thank you," she said. Her eyes were rimmed in red.

We watched Max leave.

"I need to hang here for a while longer," I said. "I can give you a key, though, and the alarm code, if you want to go home."

"Thank you ever so much, Josie. I truly appreciate all you've done for me. Max tells me I'm free to be myself again, to use my credit cards and so on." She sniffled, holding back tears. "I think I need to be alone for a while. I hope you're not offended, but I'm going to go to a hotel."

"I'm not offended at all — are you sure, though? I wouldn't pester you. You'd have your own room."

"Thank you. I'm quite certain."

"Where will you stay?"

"The Austin Arms. Do you know it? I went to a lunch meeting there once. It's quite posh." She smiled. "I'm tired of roughing it. I need a few days of luxury."

"If you change your mind, don't hesitate to call."

"Thank you."

She leaned in for an awkward hug, tugged on her gloves, zipped up her coat, pulled a watch-cap-style hat over her hair, and pushed her way out.

I sat back down and checked e-mail again. Nothing urgent had come in. I sat and thought and thought and no brilliant ideas came to me. Some of the brush was cleared away, but not enough that I could see my way.

I called work to check in. Gretchen answered and immediately started giggling.

"I put out Hank's presents today," she said. "I Bubble-Wrapped his new catnip mouse so that he wouldn't know what it was, and guess what?"

"He knew what it was."

Her laughter grew louder. Her joy was contagious.

"The naughty boy! He didn't merely know what it was. He clawed his way through the wrapping paper *and* the Bubble Wrap, shook that little mouse silly, trotted up the stairs, and hid it under one of the wing chair cushions. I know because I spied on him."

"That's like a dog hiding a favorite bone!"

"Hank doesn't know he's a cat," she said.

"You know Maine Coons! We've always known they fetch. Now we know they stockpile. What else did you get him?"

"You're going to have to wait until after . . . well, you know . . . just like Hank is, aren't you, you bad boy?"

"Until after our luncheon?"

"Exactly."

"That will be fun! Is Hank there? Put the phone to his ear."

"Okay." Her voice grew fainter. "Hank . . . here's Josie . . ."

"Hi, Hank. It's me. I hear you've been a bad boy, but between you and me and the gatepost, I don't believe it. Not my little Hank. You're a good boy, aren't you, sweetheart? I miss you, baby. I'll see you soon, all right, darling? I love you, Hank."

He mewed. Gretchen came back on the line.

"His ear twitched," she said. "He was really listening."

"Good. So is anything else going on I should know about?"

"Nothing urgent. Wes called. No message, just a request to call him back as soon as you can. And a man named Mitchell Glascowl called."

"Mitchie Rich! What did he want?"

"Cara took the message. She wrote that 'he has another one.' Do you know what that means?"

"Yes, indeed. Let me have the number."

As I pressed the END CALL button, a wave of gratitude and appreciation washed over me. A mark of achievement, perhaps, was having people in your life who helped raise your spirits, people you could trust.

I called Mitchie Rich.

"Josie Q!" Mitchie Rich said with warm familiarity. "How you doing up there in Yankee town?"

"Good, good. 'Josie Q'? What's with the *Q*?"

"Like Susie Q. I just can't get over a nice gal like you missing a name."

"You're too funny, Mitchie Rich. I'll tell you something not many folks know. I have a middle name but I don't use it. No reason. I like it. It just is a little cumbersome. But I'll let you use it. Kay. *K-A-Y.* My full name is Josie Kay Prescott. So how about you call me Josie Kay?"

"I love it. And it suits you better than Q. So, Josie Kay, I've got me some Harriman Blue Southern Pacific china from the early days of the Houston–New Orleans run of the railroad. About 1905. I've got a set of a dozen corn cob holders, all stamped on the bottom with 'Southern Pacific Company.' I've taken the photos, and if you're interested, I can send them to you."

"Yes, please do. What kind of price are you looking for?"

He gave his low train-rumbly laugh. "From what I can see, these pieces are plenty rare. This pattern was exclusive to this rail line. It's passed your hundred-year marker. Corn cob plates are among the scarcest pieces. And every one of them is in perfect condition. No nicks, mars, scratches, chips, nothing. Okay, the e-mail is sent."

I eased my new tablet from my new tote bag. "Give me a sec to look at the photos," I said. I turned it on, and by the time I got to my account, Mitchie Rich's e-mail had arrived.

The pattern was lovely, the design timeless. The small oblong plates were edged with a delicate, French-inspired blue band embellished with flourishes and flowery swaths. The logo on the bottom was enclosed in a red circle.

"Let me do some research. I'll get back to you."

"I'll look for your call, Josie Kay!"

As I ended that call and prepared to dial Sasha, a woman walked in wrapped in a blond mink coat with matching pillbox hat. Her boots and gloves were of black leather. At first I didn't recognize her, but then I did. It was Marney Alred.

I stood up and put on my best customer service face. "Marney! Hello." I extended a hand. "Josie Prescott. You remember. You stopped by the other day about the Cooper miniatures."

She froze in sudden, sullen shock. She didn't reply. She didn't shake my hand. She raced to the counter and said something to Cathy I couldn't hear. I stood, stupefied, as Detective Brownley appeared from an inside door, smiled at her with professional disinterest, and led her down the corridor toward Interview Rooms Three and Four.

Ellis's office door opened, and he stood on the threshold. "Come on in, Josie."

He shut the door.

"I'm just off the phone with Superintendent Shorling. Thomas Lewis filled a prescription for chloral hydrate the day before Ian Bennington died. The doctor who issued it doesn't remember him. His notes are vague. Shorling says that if Thomas were alive he'd arrest him for murder. He was ready to close the case before. Now he's certain. He considers this evidence conclusive."

"It's so twisted, Ellis. I hardly have the words." I shook my head. "Becca was rocked sideways."

"It would be more surprising if she wasn't."

"I guess."

He opened the door for me.

"How come you're interviewing Marney Alred?" I asked as I stepped out.

"I know that name . . . You had me ask Becca about her. Who is she?"

I explained how I knew her: that she'd come into my office without an appointment and told me that Becca had given her my name, and that she wanted to buy the Cooper miniatures, adding, "Detective Brownley took her to an interview room. Three or Four."

He reached for a formatted listing on his desk.

"Follow me," he said.

He brought me into the observation room between Interview Rooms Three and Four. Marney sat alone in Room Four, reading something on her tablet.

"That's her," I said, nodding at Marney.

Ellis picked up the wall phone and tapped in three numbers.

"Who's in Room Four?" he asked whoever answered. "Thank you." He hung up.

"Oh, my God," I whispered. I sank into a chair as my blood simmered to a throbbing boil, pulsing against my temple. "That's Cheryl Morrishein," I said. My breathing sped up as time slowed down. I stared at the woman's face. "I didn't go through everything Reggie gave me. I bet there's a photo of her in the dossier." I shook my head, disgusted at myself. "Reggie gave me the material on Friday. I scanned enough to get the gist of the situation. I can't believe I didn't go through everything."

"Fill me in."

I explained, adding that the dossier was in my car. I handed over the keys, and he called for Daryl to retrieve it from my trunk.

"Put it in a plastic bag in case you drop it," I said. "It's important that it doesn't get snow on it."

Daryl was back in five minutes. The dossier was inside an unsealed evidence bag, dry.

I extracted the clippings one at a time. About two-thirds of the way through, I came to one from December of 2010, a brief mention in the *Trumpet*'s "About Town" column — Rupert and Cheryl Morrishein held a party at a country club celebrating their ten-year wedding anniversary. The column had published a photograph of the couple. I tapped the photograph with my index finger, barely able to talk, I was so mad. Red flecks swam in front of my eyes. I spoke through gritted teeth.

"I've been played again." I pointed. "This is the woman who introduced herself as Marney Alred and expressed her eagerness to purchase Becca's two miniatures. When she showed up at my place, she was driving a silver Lexus."

Ellis picked up the phone again. "Go into Room Four," he said. "Ask her what kind of car she's driving. If she asks why, you can say a car's lights are on."

A minute later, Daryl stepped into the room and asked the question.

"A blue Lexus," she said.

"Thanks," he said.

"She had body work done and had it

painted," I said to Ellis.

Ellis dialed another three-digit code. "Cathy, get someone to get the tags of a blue Lexus in our lot. Call me here with the owner and date of registration. ASAP."

I couldn't drag my eyes from Cheryl's face. Her neighbor, Lucy, and Harry, the cheese guy, liked her. They were friends. How could such a hateful woman have friends? Ellis and I stood side by side without speaking until the phone rang.

Ellis listened, grunted, and listened some more. He hung the receiver on its wall mount and said, "This is a new-to-her car, purchased the day after you were attacked."

"Because I saw that it was silver."

"The silver one was totaled. She ran into a tree."

"I don't believe it," I said.

"It occurred in Portsmouth. She filed a police report."

"That's a pretty clever way of covering up front-end damage."

Ellis picked up the phone, punched a three-button code, and said, "Cathy, get Daryl on tracking Cheryl Moorshein's old car. Get the police report from Portsmouth. Have him talk to the responding officer. Find out if she was injured. Find the car."

With my eyes scorching Cheryl's skin

through the glass, I said, "My tote bag is in her trunk."

"Come again?"

"That's where I'd keep it. Maybe it's in her condo, but I'm betting it's in her trunk. In case I had to run for it, I'd have it with me."

"That's a stretch."

"Let's look," I said.

"There's a thing called probable cause."

"I hate that."

"I'll have to get her to incriminate herself."

"She never will."

"Then I'll go to Plan B."

Chapter Thirty-Seven

Ellis told me to go to work, to shoo and let him do his job. He promised to call me the minute he knew something but said there was no point in my hanging around.

"It's a process," he said, using his familiar phrase. "Let the process work."

I told him I'd hang around for a while. He shrugged and disappeared into his office. Half an hour later, I decided I was being silly, asked Cathy to let Ellis know I was going to work, and got myself bundled up.

Detective Brownley and I left the police station at the same time. She got into a waiting, warm patrol car. I leaned into the wind, my hood up and my eyes down, and trudged my way to my frozen car. Inside, waiting for the seat to warm up, I checked my voice mail and looked around. A two-foot-high ridge of snow ringed the parking lot. A plow was clearing Ocean Avenue. The snow was pristine. Everything looked fresh, untouched, innocent.

Wes had called twice. Ty had called from Maine. He was on his way home and he'd stop at the butcher shop en route. He was in a steak mood. I stared at Cheryl's blue Lexus. I pictured myself getting a crowbar out of my trunk and breaking into hers. I sat and stewed.

I called Wes back to learn what he'd discovered.

"You've been latched down all day," Wes said as soon as he heard my voice. "What do they have on you?"

"Hi, Wes," I said, resigned to his inflammatory style. "I've been here helping the police."

"How?"

"I had a thought about Thomas. You know how he said he'd give you an interview about his success as an amateur genealogist? He agreed because it was easier than saying no and making himself conspicuous by refusing. I went through the party photos, too. It's amazing how adroit he was at avoiding the camera. He simply never would have gotten back to you. He couldn't risk having his photo published in the paper under the name Ian Bennington."

"You sure ate your Wheaties on this one, huh, Joz?"

"It's all so ghastly, Wes. I'm just sick about it." I looked up at the sky. Streaks of puckered clouds swept across a pale blue sky. A buttermilk sky, Hoagy Carmichael called it. "Lia was here."

"A-a-a-nd?" he said, stretching out the word.

"She's really upset."

"No news. Old news."

"She took her car to a different place for service."

"Trying to fly under the radar. Good one, Josie!"

"I don't think so. I think she owed her regular place so much money she had to find a new place. Isn't that awful?"

"Yeah, but her appeal is under consideration."

"What appeal?" I asked.

"Having to pay her ex maintenance. Apparently she doesn't talk about it. I found out because I searched court records."

"Why wouldn't she have told me? I'm her friend."

"When I asked her, she said she didn't want to jinx the case by talking about it."

"I don't think she has a chance to get the ruling overturned. It's a fact-based decision — he's entitled to the money."

"The judge has some discretion. I didn't

look into the details, but it has to do with how short a time they were married."

"What a relief that would be to her," I said. "When is the decision supposed to be handed down?"

"Within the week."

"I'll keep my fingers crossed for her."

Ace Arons, the car repairman, and Ethan walked out. They walked with similar confident strides, yet it would be hard to find two such different men, one a rocker, the other a scientist. That Ethan was leaving was, I conjectured, good news. Only the innocent walk free. He saw me looking in my rearview mirror and waved. I waved back.

A patrol car pulled into the parking lot, crunching over the packed snow. I followed its progress through my rearview mirror. It rolled to a stop by the front door. Detective Brownley jumped out of the passenger door and hurried inside. I glanced at my dash clock. She'd been gone twenty-two minutes. Something was up.

"I've got to go, Wes."

"Why? What's going on?"

"I'll call you later."

I turned off the engine, grabbed my tote bag, and ran for the door.

The lobby was empty.

Cathy stood up as I entered. "Did you

forget something?" she asked.

"No. I was hoping to see Ellis."

"I'm pretty sure he's tied up. I'll check."

"I'll wait."

A minute later, Cathy said, "He'll be with you in a few minutes."

"Thanks," I said, and resumed my regular seat on the bench.

I e-mailed Ty that steaks sounded ideal and asked him to stop at a grocery store. I typed in a shopping list: potatoes and salad makings and mushrooms and a green vegetable of his choice and wine, a Cabernet, please.

Let's go to your house, I wrote. *I need a change of scene and a big fire.*

I also e-mailed Sasha, forwarding the photos of Mitchie Rich's corn cob plates, asking her to decide if they should be included in our Southern Living auction and to e-mail him with a request for provenance information.

"Josie?" Ellis said, coming from his office. He was buttoning up his coat. "Your timing is good. "We're about to look through Cheryl's car. We got a search warrant."

Daryl and Officer Meade appeared from the corridor that ran to Rooms One and Two.

"Really?" I said to Ellis. "I thought you

said you need a confession."

"I cobbled together a series of facts, helped along by the car dealer who accepted her silver Lexus in trade. There was significant damage to the front end, no surprise, since she ran into a tree, but it was concentrated on the right side. She had no explanation for the damage on the left side. He took photos, per the dealership's policy when buying damaged cars — a protection against future charges of insurance fraud. Add that to Becca's statement that Thomas told her he and Cheryl had reached a settlement that she needed to sign off on, and Thomas's phone logs, and we had enough to pull it off."

"You had his phone logs because he was murdered?"

"Exactly. Tracking the victim's recent contacts is routine in any murder investigation. We got Thomas's phone logs a few days ago. We were able to verify several calls between him and Cheryl, including one the morning he died. Thirty seconds after that call ended, he called Becca. A plus B equals C. As we speak, Detective Brownley is asking Cheryl whether she wants to give us the keys to her car or whether she wants us to break in."

"That's a heck of a choice."

Ellis smiled.

Detective Brownley and Cheryl entered the lobby from the corridor that led to Interview Room Four. The detective's hand was positioned behind Cheryl's elbow. Detective Brownley seemed the same as always, calm and aloof.

Cheryl's eyes shot poisoned darts at Ellis. She didn't notice me, but I wasn't surprised. Cheryl wasn't the sort of woman who noticed many people; she was more used to them noticing her. Her eyes were lined in dark brown with a hint of blue. Her lipstick was brick red. Her mink was open enough for me to see that she wore a Chanel tweed suit with a gold dragonfly brooch. Her hair was short and wavy. I suspected she'd paid someone a lot of money for those waves. I wondered if the hairdo she'd sported when she came to my office — longer, with bangs — had been a wig. She looked astonishingly different. It showed you what a little makeup, fancy clothes, and a supercilious attitude could do.

Her lips were compressed into one thin line. Officer Meade took a place on Cheryl's other side.

"Are you responsible for this outrage?" Cheryl asked Ellis in an educated, nasally tone.

"If you're referring to the search warrant, I'm the officer who signed the petition, yes. It's Judge Torley who signed the order. This way, please."

He held the door while we trooped out.

"Did she give you the key?" Ellis asked the detective.

"Yes."

"Good. You and I will examine the inside of the vehicle first, then the trunk." He turned to Daryl. "Please begin taping."

Daryl aimed a small video recorder at Ellis.

"Pursuant to the search warrant issued today," Ellis said, "we are searching the vehicle named in that order, which is owned by and registered to Cheryl Morrishein."

He clicked open the doors. The trunk lid lifted slightly. I approached the trunk, while Ellis and the detective went through the inside. Detective Brownley slipped the contents of the glove box into a clear plastic evidence bag.

"I'll be reporting this to my lawyer," Cheryl said, her tone threatening.

No one looked at her. No one replied. Officer Meade stood close behind her, ready to subdue her if necessary. I doubted Cheryl knew she was there.

As Ellis walked to the trunk and raised

the lid, Daryl stepped back, still holding the camera at eye level. I stepped closer. The bottom of the trunk was covered with a gray speckled mat. Off to the right was an opaque tub. Ellis removed the lid. Inside was a winter survival kit, similar to the one I kept in my trunk: kitty litter for traction on ice, flares, a thermo-blanket, and a folding shovel. My tote bag wasn't visible. Ellis lifted out the tub and raised the mat. A spare tire and jack lay nestled in a carved-out gully. He swung out the tire to reveal a black plastic trash bag. Ellis reached in and pulled out my tote bag.

I used my iPhone and took a photo of Ellis holding it up and one of Cheryl, her face sagging. Ellis didn't tell me to stop.

"I found the bag on the side of the road," Cheryl said. "I intended to bring it in to the police, but forgot."

"Open it," I requested. "Do you see a black velvet pouch?"

Ellis peered inside, gently shifting things so he could see to the bottom. He extracted the pouch and dangled it in front of the camera.

"This one?" he asked me.

I snapped a photo.

"Yes. May I look?"

"Let's do it inside." He turned to the

detective. "Please secure the vehicle." To Officer Meade, he added, "Bring Ms. Morrishein back to Room Four."

"Am I under arrest?" she demanded, her chin up.

"You're being detained," Ellis told her. He looked at Officer Meade. "Go."

Daryl continued recording until Detective Brownley had tugged on every door and the trunk lid to demonstrate that they were locked. The four of us made our way inside.

Still wearing gloves, Ellis unfurled the black velvet, revealing the two watercolor miniatures.

"Arabella," I said. "She's my ancestor."

"She's beautiful."

"Winsome."

"I'll have someone call Max and Becca with the good news."

"May I call Becca?"

Ellis paused for a few seconds. "We'll call Max. I can't stop you from calling whomever you'd like."

I took a quick photo of the two paintings and e-mailed it to Becca, then called her.

She answered with a "hello" that sounded more like a question than a greeting.

"This is Josie. I just e-mailed you a good-news photo. The paintings have been found safe and sound."

"Oh, Josie. Where?"

"In Cheryl's car."

"I knew it."

"The police will be calling Max to let him know in a formal way."

"Thank you, Josie, for calling me yourself."

"How are you doing?"

"Rallying a bit, I guess. Knowing is always better than not knowing."

"Even when the truth is hard to hear."

"Yes," she said. "Even then."

"I agree. Talk to you soon."

"Bye."

"Is she okay?" Ellis asked.

"More or less."

Ellis asked me to listen in to his interrogation so I could help him pose questions about how and where Cheryl intended to sell the paintings, if it came up. While we waited for her lawyer to arrive, he ordered us a sandwich lunch.

Between bites, I suggested he call Bitsy, Becca and Thomas's North Conway neighbor. "If you can e-mail her Cheryl's photo, she might be able to identify her as the woman who heard Becca and Thomas fighting about the paintings. That would show that Cheryl knew they existed, and that they were valuable."

He asked Detective Brownley to create a photo lineup and make the call.

Half an hour later, he asked, "Ready? Let's go see what story Cheryl has up her sleeve."

Chapter Thirty-Eight

Two hours later, I sat in the observation room watching Ellis question Cheryl about her role in Thomas's murder and my attack. She denied everything. Ellis wound his way back to the start — her husband's partnership and her lawsuit. Her lawyer was a stranger to me, an older man with a folksy manner named Grover Getty.

"Now let's not get ahead of ourselves," Getty said with a friendly smile. "This little lady has made an accusation, that part's right enough, but all you have to do is look at court documents to see how she handles her grievances — she files a lawsuit. She's no killer. She's no hooligan. She's a lady."

"That sounds like a good opening statement, counselor," Ellis said dryly. He focused on an unrepentant Cheryl. "The morning Thomas died you had a fifteen-minute conversation with him. What did you discuss?"

"I have no recollection of talking to him."

"An hour after he was killed, you called Becca. Why?"

"I have no memory of calling Becca."

"I have her phone logs."

She raised a fluttering hand. "Computers make mistakes."

Ellis shook his head slowly, half-smiling, as if to say she was some piece of work. "That's not going to fly in front of a jury."

"Now, now," Getty chastised. "Don't you be threatening her."

Ellis didn't even glance at him. He kept his eyes fixed on Cheryl. "Why did you go to Josie Prescott's office pretending to be Marney Alred?"

"I didn't."

"There are many photos of you. Her security cameras cover the entire property, inside and out."

"It wasn't me."

"One of those photos shows you sneaking a peek through a window the night of Josie Prescott's holiday party. What were you doing there?"

"I'm not a peeping Tom."

"Facial recognition software has confirmed it's you."

I doubted that was true.

Cheryl smiled, gaining confidence with

each denial. "Evidently, the software is not infallible. It can't be me. I wasn't there."

Her lawyer nodded in approval. I wondered if he believed her. If I didn't know better, I'd have been tempted to believe her myself.

"Do you think a jury will believe all these denials simply because you're an attractive woman?" Ellis asked.

"Chief Hunter," Getty admonished him, "please. There's no point in personal comments. If you have another relevant question, ask it. If not, we'll be on our way."

Ellis looked at Getty and shook his head. "It seems there's a little bit of shared delusion going on. Your client isn't going anywhere."

"Is she under arrest?"

"She will be. Right now, she's cooperating with our investigation, or so I thought." He turned toward Cheryl. "I get the impression you loved your husband very much."

Her eyes fell to the table. "Yes."

"Am I correct that you blamed Thomas Lewis for your husband's death?"

The defiance was back. "Without question. Thomas Lewis killed Rupert as surely as if he'd pulled the trigger of a gun. Thomas's death wasn't murder. It was justice."

"The word is 'retribution,' not 'justice.' "

"That sounds remarkably like an accusation," Getty said.

"Now that Thomas is dead," Ellis said to Cheryl, wholly disregarding Getty's interpolation, "you'll never get a payout. He was broke when he died."

She smirked. "He and Becca were still married when her father died. She's the sole heir. Grover tells me that once probate is granted, my lawsuit can move forward and I'll get my share."

"Then you didn't hear. . . . The British authorities have ruled Ian's murder a homicide and declared his killer to be Thomas. Ask your lawyer — a killer can't benefit from his crime."

Cheryl's mouth opened, then shut. She leaned back in her chair, whip-turned toward Getty, and spoke softly into his ear, her hands flying up and open and in and down. Getty replied, touching her arm, trying to calm her. He said something, patting the air — *relax,* the gesture communicated. They turned back to face Ellis.

Getty spoke. "Miss Cheryl is upset at the news. She had no idea Thomas Lewis was capable of such a heinous crime. The fact remains, however, that she was wronged and Thomas was married when he died. His widow, whom we believe to be an honorable woman, will no doubt do the right thing. If not, the lawsuit, which has named her as a co-conspirator from the start, will go forward."

"It will be dismissed," Ellis said. "Becca was not involved. She had no fiduciary interest in her husband's business ventures."

"If you're right," Cheryl said, her confidence reinvigorated after Getty's little speech, "it's obvious I have no motive for killing Thomas."

A knock sounded on the interview room door, and Detective Brownley entered.

"Excuse me," she said. She handed Ellis a folded sheet of paper and left.

Ellis read it and slipped it under his notebook. He pulled his earlobe and smiled.

"Let me tell you what I think happened," he said.

"Please do," Getty said. "Edify us."

"Becca and Thomas's breakup was ugly," Ellis said. "Thomas had done everything he could to get Becca to sell the paintings and share the proceeds, including lying to Frisco's that he had the right to sell them. When Becca caught on — perhaps because she discovered they were missing and confronted him, or possibly because she borrowed his smart phone to make a call and saw the e-mail from Frisco's — Thomas flew to England to kill Ian. Thomas staged Ian's death to look like suicide. If he'd thought of it, he would have left a note."

"All very interesting," Getty said, "but what does this have to do with my client?"

"Everything. He did it because Cheryl was relentless in her demands. She drove him to it. The DA is looking into whether we can charge her with Ian's murder under the racketeering laws."

"Absurd."

"Maybe. Maybe not. The Christmas Common police told me they found an e-mail in Ian's SENT folder to Becca saying he'd researched Prescott's, that the firm had a stellar reputation, and since it was convenient to where Becca was working, she should have the miniatures appraised there, that Frisco's, while a reputable firm, had been Thomas's choice, that she should have an independent assessment. Thomas must have read the e-mail when he was in Ian's house after killing him, and immediately crafted a plan to get his hands on the miniatures so he could either sell them under the table, or get them included in the divorce settlement. His lawyer probably told him that probate would take months, longer if Becca disputed his claim, as she was certain to do. Thomas didn't have time to wait — because of you."

"This is fantasy," Cheryl said. "Pure fantasy!"

" 'Speculation' is the legal term," Getty added.

"You want some things we can prove for sure? No problem. You first learned about the miniatures' existence during the knock-down, drag-out fight when Thomas and Becca still lived together in North Conway. We have a witness." Ellis fingered out the slip of paper Detective Brownley had delivered earlier and waved it. "She just picked you out of a photo lineup. My detective called Becca, too, to ask about that night. That's the evening she left Thomas. She'd planned on attending a lecture at Hitchens University on underwater drones. She remembered it very specifically. You had expected Becca to be out and were coming to spend time with *your* co-conspirator — Thomas." He turned to Getty. "They'd joined forces to try to get Becca to hand over cash — or the paintings." He resumed his focus on Cheryl. "Thomas told you he was going to England to take care of it. And he did. He killed Ian. When he got back, he told you all you had to do was be patient. You balked. You refused to wait for probate and the inevitable litany of lawsuits, probably because you were just about out of money. You knew Thomas had mortgaged his London flat and demanded that he give you some of the proceeds. You didn't believe him when he said he was tapped out. The bottom line is that when Thomas refused your final demand, you started following him, reiterating your ultimatum at every turn. One evening, you found yourself at the Prescott party. When you saw how friendly Thomas was with Josie, you assumed he'd lied to you, that he had the miniatures in his possession, that he'd hired Prescott's to handle the sale and was planning to cut you out. That's when ice filled your veins and you decided the time had come to act."

"I never did anything like that."

"I know you'd like to think so, but the reality is that phone and e-mail records don't lie. We have a trail of calls between you and Thomas going back years. You're done, Cheryl. Tell the truth. Get it off your chest."

"I have."

Ellis shook his head, his expression communicating that he thought she was pathetic.

"Grover," Cheryl said, "do something."

"Let him hang himself, Miss Cheryl. Let

him stretch that rope out all the way."

Ellis held Cheryl's eyes, tightening the vise. "You called Thomas, and he somehow managed to convince you that he didn't have the paintings — yet. Together you planned the trick that got Becca to meet you on Cable Road, thinking that since she'd just inherited her father's millions, she'd decide to pay you off rather than continue to put up with the harassment. When Thomas reported that Becca once again said no way, you lost control. You jumped in your car and mowed Thomas down, rolling his body to the curb and covering it as best you could with the bush, aiming to delay the discovery of the corpse."

"Everything you just said is fabrication," she said, her voice pulsating with barely contained anger. "You're trying to twist the facts. I'm the victim here. Me! Don't you get that?"

"You drove into a tree," Ellis continued, ignoring her question and evident despair, "hoping to disguise the front-end damage. It didn't. We have the videotape from the auto dealer. Desperation led to recklessness. You broke into Becca's room at the institute and her apartment. After you read the article in the *Seacoast Star* saying that Josie was helping us search for the miniatures, you followed her to Boston, to the furniture maker, and back to Boston. One glance at Josie's upbeat attitude when she left Becca's apartment made it clear she'd found the missing paintings. You called her, pretending to be Pat Weston, and arranged the meeting. You zipped ahead on the interstate and got in position. That showed real moxie, quick thinking, and clever planning. I'm impressed. If someone had come along before Josie, all you would have had to do is pretend your car stalled, and drive away. After whacking her, you grabbed her tote bag and headed for the interstate. Probably you pulled over a mile down the road, confirmed the miniatures were there, and tossed the tree limb into the forest."

Cheryl's face was growing redder by the second. "You can't prove any of this."

"Sure we can." Ellis smiled and held up a finger. "One: Motive. Locked." Another finger shot up. "Two: Means. The tech folks are already at work lining up photos of Thomas's wounds with the photos of your car's damage and checking Josie's phone for fingerprints. You turned it off somewhere near the liquor store." Up came the middle finger. "Three: Opportunity. Ask your lawyer. Honey, you're cooked. Both cases are about to be closed. Whether or not you'll also be charged in Ian's death, that's someone else's lookout, not mine."

Detective Brownley knocked, entered, and handed Ellis another folded piece of paper.

Ellis smiled broadly. "It took a little while to get this report because it comes from another jurisdiction, Portsmouth. They have a series of red-light cameras to catch speeders and people who run the lights." He waved the paper. "Guess what else they caught? You. Coming and going on the road by Prescott's at the appropriate times."

"This is all circumstantial," Getty argued.

"Look at her. She's ready to pop."

Cheryl was rigid with fury.

"What are you going to do next?" Ellis asked, baiting her. "Kill me?"

"I could. Easily."

"That's enough, now," Getty said, his hand on her arm.

She shook him off and stood up. "I've had enough. I'm glad Thomas is dead, do you hear me? I'm glad. I may not get the money he owed me, but at least I got revenge."

"Is that why you did it?"

She clutched the back of her chair. "He lorded over me how he didn't need Becca's help anymore, how he could live off the expectations from his share of Becca's inheritance, how he could wait for probate.

He told me to go find another sucker."

"I'll take that as a confession." He stood up. "Cheryl Morrishein, you're under arrest for the murder of Thomas Lewis and the attempted murder of Josie Prescott."

I listened as he recited the Miranda warning, and watched as he led her out in handcuffs, Grover Getty trailing along behind. She looked simultaneously righteous and astonished. I felt ill. I sat for a while longer. The blazing anger that had had me in its grasp for days was gone, and in its wake, all I felt was empty.

Chapter Thirty-Nine

Ty and I were sitting in front of the fire, Prescott's Punch in hand. Potatoes were baking, the sweet aroma comforting and rich.

"Ellis didn't need me," I said. "Cheryl's attempts to sell the paintings never came up."

"You were his ace in the hole."

"I guess."

"How are you feeling about everything?"

"Sad. Concerned for Becca."

"Did she decide if she wants to come for Christmas dinner?"

"Yes. She does."

"Good."

"I'm looking forward to getting to know her," I said.

He slid his arm around my shoulder and drew me closer, and we sat like that for a long, long time.

Thursday morning, I drove to the local card and gift store and bought festive bags and Santa Claus–themed tissue paper and twirly satin bows, then stood at the counter chatting to Sandy, the owner, while I packaged up my staff's bonus checks. Sandy helped arrange them in a cardboard box for easy transport.

Sunshine glistened off the icicles hanging off the gazebo, shooting sparks of gleaming yellow light across the village green. With Cheryl charged with Thomas's murder, the circumstances of Ian's death resolved, and the miniatures recovered, I felt the familiar thrill of festive anticipation. The lights circling the tall Christmas tree sparkled merrily. The electric candles on the menorah flickered with holiday cheer. Everywhere I looked, people filled the streets, smiling, laughing, carrying bags filled with carefully chosen gifts. A car pulled out from in front of Lia's spa, and on impulse, I grabbed the spot.

Lia agreed to see me, but she had a helper walk me back, and she didn't stand when I entered her office.

"I wanted to apologize," I said, "for ever suspecting you. I couldn't believe it, not really."

"You didn't seem ambivalent," Lia said,

her tone cold. "You seemed certain I was involved."

"I know. I was scared and confused."

Lia exhaled. "If we're on a truth-telling spree, I'll admit that I can see why you might have thought what you did." She raised her arm and flipped her hand backward, dismissing the issue. She smiled. "I'm feeling too good to hold a grudge. Don't get me wrong. It hurts — a lot — to think you might have perceived me as a killer, but I do understand how the facts might have looked."

"Thank you. Why are you feeling good?"

"I never told you — I never told anyone — I petitioned the judge to reconsider the maintenance order. And he did! He ruled that due to the brevity of our marriage and my ex's ability to earn a living, I owe him nothing more. It's over."

"Oh, Lia! What a relief!"

"The mooch is toast."

"That's been a long time coming."

"And I have a second date with a nice fellow. He just moved here from Chicago. He's never been married — he hasn't found the right girl, he says."

"I can tell from your eyes that you like him."

"He's different from other men I've been

attracted to. He's serious, a technical guy, kind of quiet. He's a financial analyst for one of the big firms. I met him on Rocky Point Singles. He contacted me."

"That sounds like a perfect fit for you."

"It does, doesn't it?"

We agreed to meet at Ellie's for lunch next Tuesday. I couldn't wait to hear about her second date.

The luncheon was as good as I'd expected. Perfect food, including Ana's Christmas-themed Fabergé egg cakes.* Perfect music from Academy Brass. Excitement and thanks from my staff on seeing their bonus checks, higher than in the past, a reflection of our better-than-expected year. Sasha announced that we'd bought Mitchie Rich's corn cob plates for $2,000, and that he was thrilled. She was estimating an auction sale in the $6,000 to $7,500 range. Gretchen told us we were now an official sponsor of the Rocky Point Little League. But it was Hank who was the star of the show, rolling over and over on his catnip-infused burlap, running after his new catnip mice, climbing into his condo, demanding cuddles.

I sat with him long after everyone else had

* Please see *Blood Rubies.*

gone back to work, petting him and kissing him and thanking him for his love.

"You're a perfect little cat, Hank."

He curled up on my lap, his head resting on his paws, ready to stay for hours.

I carried him back to his basket.

"Merry Christmas, baby."

I walked into the front office. Ethan was perched against the guest table chatting with Sasha. She was laughing. I couldn't remember ever hearing Sasha laugh.

"What's so funny?"

"Nothing," she said, a rosy flush coloring her cheeks.

"Hey, Josie," Ethan said. "I was telling Sasha how much she'd like helping me check my oysters. I think it was the hip boots that sold her on the idea."

Sasha laughed again, and I smiled, thinking how often opposites attract. An outgoing guy like Ethan might be a perfect match for a bashful gal like Sasha.

I called Becca to ask whether she'd given more thought to my appraising the miniature paintings. She said by all means, adding that she'd love for me to feature them on my TV show. I texted Timothy then and there, and he texted back that he'd be up with his team in early January to film the promo.

Sometimes Ty and I spent Christmas at his place so we could have a fire. This year, though, I felt like sticking close to home, especially since Becca was coming for dinner.

At three thirty Christmas afternoon, I stood in the archway between the kitchen and dining room, surveying the table. It was perfect, set with the elegant formality of my childhood. The linen tablecloth and napkins were snowy white. The Minton china was delicate and fine. The Lunt sterling silver flatware shone. The Waterford glassware gleamed. The stout white candles nestled in the driftwood centerpiece flickered gaily.

The bell rang. I felt an unexpected thrill of excitement. Becca was here!

She handed me a small Christmas cactus with orange blossoms. As I placed it on the ledge above my kitchen sink where it would get northern light and I'd see it every day, I thought of Cathy's decades-old Christmas cactus. Today marked the beginning of a new chapter, one that included family, and the plant would track its progress.

"How is it at the hotel?" I asked as we got settled in the living room.

Becca sat on the sofa across from the five-foot Scotch pine, the same place she'd sat before. I curled up in the same club chair across from her. "Take the A Train," from Duke Ellington's Christmas album, played softly in the background. The multicolored, star-shaped lights strung around the windows twinkled in the gathering dusk.

"Just what the doctor ordered," Becca said. "I needed the respite. I ended up staying far longer than I'd planned. I checked out just now, though. Too much time to think isn't good for me. I'm heading back to Boston tonight. I need to get back to work."

"I understand."

Ty served us Prescott's Punch in crystal glasses. Becca swirled hers, watching the glimmering light as it flitted across the cranberry concoction.

I turned toward toward the light source, tea-light candles floating in low bowls. The flickering flames made everything glow and shimmer. The silvery tinsel dangling from the tree branches glinted. The ornaments from my childhood, a set of a dozen opalescent glass teardrops; a porcelain pinecone; a Victorian dirigible; and, my favorite, a yellow bird perched on a metal nest. They hung next to the ones Ty and I had bought together, sterling silver hanging picture frames, each containing a picture of us, one for every year we'd been a couple, an annual tradition I cherished. Flecks of light sparked from the silver frames.

"Ethan's been an enormous help," she said, looking up.

"That's great to hear."

"To your continued success," Ty said, gently clinking her glass.

"Thank you," she said. She smiled as she touched her glass to mine. "I can't tell you how much it means to me to have connected with you, Josie. To have a new cousin! A wonderful new cousin."

"I feel the same," I said, meeting her eyes, smiling back.

We chatted easily until the kitchen timer sounded, letting me know that my turkey had finished resting. I left them comparing Christmas Common and Rocky Point, then called them into the dining room after I'd carved the bird.

As she sat down, Becca pointed at the driftwood centerpiece. "That's beautiful. I've never seen anything like it. Did you make it?"

"Yes." As I began passing dishes, holiday favorites like creamed pearl onions and herbed stuffing and new creations like my cranberry-orange relish, I added, "When I was a kid, every November my mom and I would go to the beach and walk until we found the perfect piece of driftwood. It had to be smooth and silvery gray and long enough, but not too long, and thick enough, but not too thick. Add a little holly, some pinecones, a few winter berries, tie it up with a big red bow, wedge in some candles, and boom — you have a great-looking, custom-made Christmas centerpiece. I restarted the tradition a few years ago."

"My mother and I used to do something similar. We'd go into the woods and collect pretty twigs and leaves and berries and so on, and weave our own wreaths. I haven't done it since she died. Maybe I will next year."

"Maybe we can do it together."

"I'd like that," she said shyly.

"Starting our own traditions," I said.

After dinner, Becca offered to help, but I could tell that she wanted to leave, so I declined the offer. Ty got started washing up, and I walked her to the door. I opened the center drawer in the hall table and extracted a yellow padded envelope.

"Here," I said, handing it to her. "Your Dreyse."

She accepted it, nodding, and peeked inside the envelope. "I'm glad to have it back. Thank you for taking care of it for me."

"You should ask Max about getting it licensed."

She smiled. "I will."

As she zipped her coat, she invited Ty and me for brunch on New Year's Day, and I eagerly accepted. She hugged me like she meant it and headed off to Boston. I stood at the window for a minute after she was gone. Her sadness was palpable, but so was her grit.

"I'm stuffed," I said, as I walked back to the kitchen and picked up a linen dish towel.

"Me, too," Ty said, handing me a glass to dry. "You're one heck of a cook."

"I just follow my mother's recipes."

"How about your cranberry-orange relish?"

"Don't you mean my *famous* cranberry-orange relish?"

"I stand corrected. That's exactly what I meant."

"You're right. I invented that one."

"Your mother would be proud."

I leaned my head against Ty's shoulder for a moment, a love-touch. "I think you're right. She would be."

When we were nearly done, Ty asked, "You know what time it is, right?"

"Present time!"

We made our way back to the living room. Our big red Christmas stockings dangled from brass holders I'd positioned on a side table. Presents were piled on the floor nearby. We like to give one another several little things and one big thing. My big present to Ty was a weekend gift certificate at his favorite ski resort, a place known for its cross-country trails. He gave me a diamond eternity circle pendant. Eternity. A perfect gift. Becca had snuck a gift bag into the pile. Wrapped in sheets of Christmas-tree-shaped tissue paper was a charming sterling silver filigreed glass jam pot with matching silver spoon. I hoped she'd like the 1937 Sheaffer Lifetime Balance mottled tortoiseshell and mother-of-pearl fountain pen I'd tucked into her purse. *Great minds,* I thought. Neither of us wanted to call attention to her gift.

Later, as Ty and I settled in for the evening, I said, "You know, I've been thinking . . . this whole series of horrible events was Shakespearean — like Hamlet avenging his father's murder."

"Shakespeare didn't make it up. He wrote about emotions that really exist, that really drive actions."

"Cheryl felt no remorse, not one iota."

"She was out for revenge."

"I remember something I learned in a Chinese philosophy course. Confucius said, 'Before you embark on a journey of revenge, dig two graves.' "

"You're very smart, Josie."

"I love you, Ty."

"I love you, too."

We sat like that, close to one another, thinking our separate thoughts.

After several minutes, I said, "Best Christmas ever."

"How come?"

"I have all the things I've loved about Christmas since you and I first got together, plus Becca. Family."

He kissed the top of my head and I tucked my hand in his, and we sat awhile longer.

ACKNOWLEDGMENTS

Thanks to G. D. Peters and Steve Shulman for their assistance with this novel.

Special thanks go to my literary agent, Cristina Concepcion of Don Congdon Associates, Inc. Thanks also go to Michael Congdon, Katie Kotchman, and Katie Grimm. I'd also like to thank Annie Nichol and Cara Bellucci.

The Minotaur Books team also gets special thanks, especially those I work with most closely, including executive editor Hope Dellon; associate editor Silissa Kenney; publicist Sarah Melnyk; director of library marketing and national accounts manager (Macmillan) Talia Ross; copy editor India Cooper; and cover designer David Baldeosingh Rotstein.

ABOUT THE AUTHOR

Jane K. Cleland once owned a New Hampshire-based antiques and rare books business. She is the author of nine previous Josie Prescott Antiques mysteries and has been a finalist for the Macavity, Anthony, and Agatha awards and has twice won the David Award for Best Novel. Jane is the former president of the New York chapter of the Mystery Writers of America and chairs the Wolfe Pack's Black Orchid Novella Award. She is part of the English faculty at Lehman College and lives in New York City.

The employees of Thorndike Press hope you have enjoyed this Large Print book. All our Thorndike, Wheeler, and Kennebec Large Print titles are designed for easy reading, and all our books are made to last. Other Thorndike Press Large Print books are available at your library, through selected bookstores, or directly from us.

For information about titles, please call:
(800) 223-1244

or visit our Web site at:
http://gale.cengage.com/thorndike

To share your comments, please write:
Publisher
Thorndike Press
10 Water St., Suite 310
Waterville, ME 04901